K gWn

Praise for Lois Ri

"Richer portrays the struggles
of her flawed but redeemable characters
realistically in this sweet story."
—*RT Book Reviews* on *A Doctor's Vow*

"These two warm stories depict love,
life and how not only nature can have
new growth in the spring."
—*RT Book Reviews* on *Easter Promises*

"This installment is a wonderful, emotionally
heartwarming story about loss and love."
—*RT Book Reviews* on *Twice Upon a Time*

"Richer's warm, strongly spiritual story has a
hero and heroine both struggling to hear from
God and discover His path for their future."
—*RT Book Reviews* on *Rocky Mountain Legacy*

LOIS RICHER
His Winter Rose
❦
Apple Blossom Bride

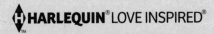
HARLEQUIN® LOVE INSPIRED®

Recycling programs
for this product may
not exist in your area.

LOVE INSPIRED BOOKS

ISBN-13: 978-0-373-65160-3

HIS WINTER ROSE AND APPLE BLOSSOM BRIDE
Copyright © 2013 by Harlequin Books S.A.

The publisher acknowledges the copyright holder
of the individual works as follows:

HIS WINTER ROSE
Copyright © 2007 by Lois M. Richer

APPLE BLOSSOM BRIDE
Copyright © 2007 by Lois M. Richer

www.LoveInspiredBooks.com

Printed in U.S.A.

CONTENTS

Books by Lois Richer

Love Inspired

This Child of Mine
*Mother's Day Miracle
*His Answered Prayer
*Blessed Baby
†Blessings
†Heaven's Kiss
†A Time to Remember
Past Secrets, Present Love
††His Winter Rose
††Apple Blossom Bride
††Spring Flowers,
   Summer Love
§Healing Tides
§Heart's Haven
§A Cowboy's Honor
§§Rocky Mountain Legacy
§§Twice Upon a Time
§§A Ring and a Promise
Easter Promises
   "Desert Rose"
‡The Holiday Nanny

‡A Baby by Easter
‡A Family for Summer
‡‡A Doctor's Vow
‡‡Yuletide Proposal
‡‡Perfectly Matched

Love Inspired Suspense

A Time to Protect
**Secrets of the Rose
**Silent Enemy
**Identity: Undercover

*If Wishes Were Weddings
†Blessings in Disguise
**Finders Inc.
††Serenity Bay
§Pennies from Heaven
§§Weddings by Woodwards
‡Love for All Seasons
‡‡Healing Hearts

LOIS RICHER

began her travels the day she read her first book and realized that fiction provided an extraordinary adventure. Creating that adventure for others became her obsession. With millions of books in print, Lois continues to enjoy creating stories of joy and hope. She and her husband love to travel, which makes it easy to find the perfect setting for her next story. Lois would love to hear from you via www.loisricher.com, loisricher@yahoo.com or on Facebook.

HIS WINTER ROSE

So whenever you speak, or whatever you do, remember that you will be judged by the law of love, the law that set you free. For there will be no mercy for you if you have not been merciful to others. But if you have been merciful, then God's mercy toward you will win out over his judgment against you.

—*James* 2:12–13

This book is for Judy, Ken and the kids.
Thanks for introducing me to cottage country.

Prologue

"Ms. Langley? Piper Langley?"

"Yes."

Maybe it was the suit that took his breath away—a tailored red power suit that fit her like a glove. But he didn't think of power when he looked at her. He thought of long-stemmed red roses—the kind a man chooses to give his love.

Maybe it was the way she so regally rose from the chair in Serenity Bay's town office and stepped forward to grasp his hand firmly. Or it could have been her hair—a curling, glossy mane that cascaded down her back like a river of dark chocolate.

His sudden lack of oxygen wasn't helped by the mega-watt smile that tilted her lips, lit up her chocolate-brown eyes and begged him to trust her.

From somewhere inside him a warning voice reminded, "Trust has to be earned." Immediately he recalled a verse he'd read this morning: Commit everything you do to the Lord. Trust Him to help you and He will.

"I'm Piper." Her words, firm, businesslike, drew him back to reality.

"Jason Franklin," he stated. "Would you like to come through to the boardroom?"

"Certainly." She followed him, her high heels clicking on the tile floor in a rhythmic pattern that bespoke her confidence.

Inside, Jason introduced the town's councillors, and waited till she was seated. Only then did he take his place at the table and pick up her résumé. It was good. Too good.

"Your credentials speak very well for you, Ms. Langley."

"Thank you."

He hadn't been paying her a compliment, simply telling the truth. She was overqualified for a little town like Serenity Bay, a place in Ontario's northern cottage country.

"I don't think we have any questions about your skills or your ability to achieve results." He glanced at the other board members for confirmation and realized all eyes were focused on the small, delicate woman seated at the end of the table.

Piper Langley had done nothing and yet they all seemed captivated by her. Himself included.

Careful! his brain warned.

"I'm happy to answer anything you wish to ask, Mr. Franklin." She picked an invisible bit of lint from her skirt, folded her hands in her lap and waited. When no one spoke, she chuckled, breaking the silence. "I'm sure you didn't ask me here just to look at me."

So she knew she drew attention. Was that good or bad?

"No, we didn't." He closed the folder filled with her accomplishments, set it aside. "It's obvious you have what we're looking for, but I can't help wondering–why do you want to leave Calgary? Especially now, after you've worked so hard to build your reputation, finally achieved the success you've earned? Why leave all that to work in Serenity Bay?"

She didn't move a muscle. Her smile didn't flicker. But something changed. If he had to put a name to it, Jason would have said Piper-the-rose grew prickly thorns.

"Several reasons, actually. As you noted, I've been working in the corporate world for some time now. I'm interested in a change."

That he understood. He'd come here to seek his own change.

"I was intrigued when I heard about your plans for Serenity Bay. The town has always been a tourist spot for summer vacationers."

"Lately the year-round population has been in decline," he admitted.

"Yes." Her gaze narrowed a fraction. "If I understood your ad correctly, you're hoping to change that." She glanced around the table, meeting every interested stare. "I'd like very much to be a part of that process."

Nice, but not really an answer to his question.

Why here? Why now?

Jason leaned back in his chair and began to dig for what he really wanted to know.

"How do you view this town, Ms. Langley?"

"Please call me Piper." She, too, leaned back, but her stare never wavered from his. "I don't want to hurt anyone's feelings, but to me Serenity Bay looks like a tired old lady much in need of a makeover. The assets are certainly here, but they're covered by years of wear and tear. I'd like to see her restored to a vibrant woman embracing life with open arms. I have some ideas as to how we might go about that."

Piper elaborated with confidence. Clearly she'd done her research, weighed every option and planned an all-out assault on the problems besieging the Bay. But she didn't stop there. She offered a plethora of possibilities Jason hadn't even considered. Two minutes into her speech she had the board eating out of her perfectly manicured hand. None of the other candidates had been so generous in sharing their ideas.

Jason was left to find a hole in her carefully prepared responses.

"You're used to large budgets, Ms. Langley. You won't have that here."

Her brown eyes sparked, her perfectly tinted lips pinched together as she leaned forward. So Miss Perfect had a temper. He found that oddly reassuring.

"Money isn't always the answer, Mr. Franklin." Her fingers splayed across the shiny tabletop, her voice deepened into a firmness that emphasized the sense of power that red suit radiated. "Yes, it will take some cash to initiate change. It will also require hard work, forward thinking, a vision that reaches beyond the usual means to something new, untried. There will be failures, but there will also be successes."

"I agree."

She stared at him hard, her focus unrelenting, searching. Then she nodded, just once.

"It will also take commitment. By you, your board, the community. No town gains a reputation for great tourism through one person's actions. It takes everyone committing to a common goal and pushing toward it—no matter what. It takes teamwork."

Jason hoped his face remained an expressionless mask, but his heart beat a hundred miles an hour. Of everything she'd said, that one word had made up his mind.

Teamwork.

It was what he'd been cheated of before.

It was the one thing he'd demand from the town's newest employee.

"Unless anyone has another question, or you have something more to say, Ms. Langley, I believe we're finished. Thank you for making the trip." He rose, surprised to see more than an hour had passed. "We will notify you of our decision by next week."

"It's been my pleasure." She worked her way around the table, shaking hands, flashing that movie-star smile. "Regardless of whom you chose as your new economic development officer, I wish you much success in your endeavor. I look forward to coming back in the summer to see the changes you've wrought."

Jason ushered her out of the room, back into the reception area.

"Thank you again," he said, holding out his hand toward her. "You've obviously put a lot of thought into how you'd do the job, Ms. Langley. We appreciate your interest."

"It's Piper," she murmured, shaking his hand. "And the pleasure was all mine. It's been good to see the town again." She picked up a long, white cashmere coat and before he could help she'd wrapped it around herself, fastened the two pearl buttons in front.

A winter rose.

He got stuck on that thought, gazing at her ivory face rising out of the petal-soft cashmere.

"Mr. Franklin."

"It's Jason," he told her automatically.

"Very well, Jason." She inclined her head, flicked the sheath of sable-toned hair over one shoulder, shook his hand in finality. "Thank you for the opportunity. Goodbye." Then she turned toward the door.

Jason kept watch as she strode to her car, a grey import

rental. He waited until she'd climbed inside, until the quiet motor glided away from the town office.

She was wrong about one thing.

It wasn't goodbye. He knew that for sure.

Chapter One

"A toast to each of us for thirty great years."

Piper pushed her sunglasses to the top of her head, protection not only against the March sun's watery rays, but against the reflected glare of those highest peaks surrounding the bay where traces of winter snow still clung to the crags and dips.

She held her steaming mug of tea aloft, waiting to clink it against those of her two friends in a tradition they'd kept alive since ninth grade.

"Happy birthday, ladies. May we each find the dreams of our heart before the next thirty years pass."

Rowena Davis drank to the toast, but her patrician nose wiggled with distaste at the mint tea. Rowena was a coffee girl, the stronger the better. She quickly set down her mug before studying the other two.

"We'll hardly find any dreams here in the Bay," she complained with a motion toward the thick evergreen forest. Her dubious tone mirrored the sour look marring her lovely face.

"Don't be a grump, Row." After a grin at Piper, Ashley Adams sipped her tea, savoring the flavor thoughtfully. Ash always took her time.

"A grump? Wake up, woman." Rowena shook her head. "I can't imagine why on earth you've moved back here, Piper. Serenity Bay isn't exactly a hot spot for someone with your qualifications."

In unison they scanned the untouched forest beyond the deck, its verdant lushness broken only by jutting granite monoliths dotted here and there across the landscape. Beyond that, the bay rippled, intensely blue in the sunshine with white bands of uninhabited beach banding its coastline.

"Maybe Serenity Bay's not a hot spot, but it is calm and peaceful. And she can sail whenever she wants." Ash turned over to lie on her tummy on the lounger and peered between the deck rails, down and out across the water.

"True." Rowena laid back, closed her eyes.

"Peace and quiet are big pluses in my books these days. I may just come and visit you this summer, Pip."

The old nickname had never died despite years of protest. Strangely enough, Piper liked it now; it reminded her that they cared about her, that she wasn't all alone.

"You'd leave the big city, Ash?" Piper struggled to hide her smile. It was impossible for her to imagine her friend ignoring the lure of the galleries and new artists' showings she adored for more than a weekend.

"Yep. For a while, anyway." Ashley's golden hair swung about her shoulders as she absorbed the panoramic view. "I'd forgotten how lovely it is here. No haze of pollution, no traffic snarls. Just God's glorious creation. This invitation to join you and Row for our annual weekend birthday bash has reminded me of all the things I give up to live in my condo in Vancouver. Especially after soaking in your posh hot tub last night! The stars were spectacular."

"Total privacy is a change, too." Rowena sighed as the

sun draped her with its warmth. "You know, Pip, Cathcart House could bring in millions if you turned it into a spa."

"It already is one," Ashley joked. "Welcome to Piper's own private chichi retreat. Which I'll happily share whenever she asks."

"Anytime." Piper chuckled. "I recall you were always partial to my grandparents' home, Ash."

"No kidding." Rowena snorted. "I think she spent more time on their dock than in her own backyard those summers on the Bay."

"My grandparents never minded. They loved to see you both." The pain of their deaths still squeezed Piper's heart, though time was easing the sting of loss. It helped to recall happier times. "Remember the year Papa bought the sailboat?"

"Yes. I also remember how many times we got dunked before we figured out how to sail it." Rowena's face puckered up. "The bay never gets warm."

"But didn't it feel good to whiz past the beach and know the summer kids were envying us? We wowed 'em that year." Ashley leaned over, laid a hand on Rowena's shoulder. "In retrospect, they weren't all bad times, Row."

"No, they weren't." After a long silence, Rowena managed to summon what, for her, passed as a smile. "I had you two to go with me to school. That meant a lot."

Rowena tossed back her auburn hair as if shaking off the bad memories, then took another tentative sip of tea.

"Now tell us, Pip. What exactly are you doing back here? Besides hosting our birthday bash, I mean."

Piper leaned back, her gaze on the bay below.

"I've accepted a position as economic development officer to organize Serenity Bay's tourism authority," she told them.

Stark silence greeted her announcement.

"Economic development?"

"Did she actually say that?"

Rowena looked at Ashley and both burst into giggles.

"What development? The place looks smaller now than when we used to live here. A few cottagers, some artists, a defunct lumber mill. What's to develop?"

Just as she had when she was fourteen and frustrated by their inability to see what was so clear to her, Piper clenched her jaw and grumbled, "You have no vision, Philistines."

"Oh, boy, that takes me back." Ashley laughed out loud. "Okay, David. Tell us how you're going to conquer your next Goliath."

Piper took her time, gathering her black hair into a knot and pinning it to the top of her head while making them wait. It was an old trick and it always worked. Their interest had been piqued.

"Spill it, Pip." Ashley wasn't kidding now.

She took a deep breath and began.

"It may interest you to know that Serenity Bay has a new, very forward-thinking mayor."

"Oh?"

Now they were curious. Good.

"He has plans that include making our lovely bay into a tourist mecca. And why not? We're sitting smack-dab in the middle of the most gorgeous country God ever created. All we have to do is tell the rest of the world about it."

Utter shock greeted her words. Piper knew the silence wouldn't last long. She leaned back, closed her eyes, and waited.

"You're kidding. Aren't you?" Uncertainty laced Ashley's whisper.

"She's not." The unflappable Rowena was less surprised. "Our Pip has always had a soft spot for this place. Except—"

Piper didn't like the sound of that. She opened her eyes. Sure enough, Rowena's intense scrutiny was centered on her. Faking a bland smile, Piper watched her hazel eyes change shades as quickly as her friend's thoughts. It wouldn't take Row long to home in on what she *hadn't* said.

"This new mayor you're going to be working for—"

"Aha." Ash leaned forward like a cat waiting to pounce.

"Tell us, Pip. What *exactly* is he like?" Rowena tapped one perfectly manicured fingertip against her cheek, eyes narrowed, intense.

Piper couldn't stop her blush as a picture of Jason Franklin, tousled and exceedingly handsome, swam into her brain. A most intriguing man.

To hide her thoughts she slipped on her sunglasses.

"What's he like?"

"Don't repeat the question. Answer it."

"I'm trying." Piper swallowed. "I don't know—like a mayor, I guess. He owns the marina."

"Short, fat, balding fellow, happily married with six kids?"

"Grease under his fingertips?" Ashley added.

"N-no. Not exactly."

"How 'not exactly,' Pip?" The old Row was back in form, and she was enjoying herself. She held up her fingers and began ticking them off. "No grease?"

"Uh-uh."

"Not short?"

"No."

"Not fat?"

Piper shook her head. That definitely didn't apply. Jason was lean, muscular and more toned than the men she knew who regularly worked out in expensive gyms.

"Balding? Six kids? Married?"

Flustered by the incessant questions about a man she hadn't been able to get out of her thoughts, Piper decided to spare herself the onslaught of questions and explain.

"He's—I don't know! Our age, I suppose. A little older, maybe. Tall. Sandy blond hair. Blue eyes. Good-looking."

Ashley and Rowena exchanged a look.

"Ah. So he's a beach boy."

"Beach boy? No. He owns the marina." Piper decided to change tactics. "I didn't really notice that much about him. He's just the mayor."

"Didn't notice much. Uh-huh." Rowena sniffed, checked with Ashley. "Thoughts?"

"'The lady doth protest too much, methinks,'" the blonde quoted.

"Methinks that, too."

"Look," Piper sputtered, regretting her choice of words. "It's not—"

"Maybe he's why she came back." Ashley frowned. "Either that or—" Her forehead pleated in a delicate frown. She focused on Piper. "Or there's another reason you're here."

They knew her too well.

"Is it your father? Is that why you left Calgary?"

Might as well admit it.

"Indirectly."

Both women sighed, their glances conveying their sympathy before Rowena deliberately shut down all expression. She had good reason to remember the past and even more to forget it.

"I knew it wouldn't be a young, eligible male that brought you back here." Ashley's eyes flashed with anger. "It has to be your old man at the bottom of this sudden change. How typical."

"What has the great Baron D. Wainwright done now?"

Piper didn't blame Rowena for the spite in her tone. Row and Ash had been there for her ever since that first summer when her angry father had repeatedly ordered her back to the house where her mother had died. When she'd refused to return to a world she hated, a world where he'd become so demanding, so strict, so unlike the loving mother who'd shielded her, these two had consoled her.

Her father's angry denunciation of her still stung today, even after so many years. And then of course there was the other.

Piper pushed that away.

"Pip? Please tell us what's wrong."

They'd always listened. She could trust them.

"It's not what he's done, it's what I think he's *going* to do. The company's conducted some research on the Bay's waterfront. Past experience tells me he intends to build one of his mega hotels right on the shores of Serenity Bay."

"Oh, no." Ashley couldn't hide her dismay. "Pavement, parking lots, bars open all night? It'll ruin the place."

"Like Baron cares about the ambience of Serenity Bay." Rowena sniffed. "I'd guess he's well aware of your mayor's plans and is trying to one-up him before you can get this tourism thing organized."

Piper nodded. "My thoughts exactly."

"So your mayor isn't the only one who's seen the potential of the area." Rowena's brows drew together. "I wonder who else is involved?"

"Jason's not *my* anything," Piper insisted as heat, which had nothing to do with the sun's rays, scorched her cheeks. "I don't think either he or the other council members know about the hotel. Not yet. That's not the way Wainwright Inc. works." She paused, then copied her father's brusque tones. "First buy up the land, then dazzle the locals with lots of promises. If that doesn't get you what you want, initiate a lawsuit."

Piper pushed her chair back into the upright position, picked up the plate with her slice of birthday cake on it and took a bite. "But that's not the only reason I decided to move back."

Ash and Row stared at her.

"Dare we ask?"

"I needed to come home. The house, these cliffs, the meadow—I spent some of my happiest times here."

They nodded, each transported back to carefree summer days when life's decisions were so much simpler. Ash, Row and Piper had walked every inch of this land many times, consoling each other through puppy love, acne and a host of other trials. No matter where they went, they always came back.

"I'm tired of the nonstop meetings, of cutthroat marketers trying to outdo each other to get another star on their A-list. I guess I'm tired of the rat race. None of it seems to matter much anymore."

"And this will?"

"I think so." Piper saw the concern in their eyes and knew they were only pushing because they cared. "I have such precious memories of this place, of my grandparents and you guys, of coming home at Christmas, watching fireworks displays from Lookout Point. I want other kids to have that."

"The past always looks rosy in hindsight," Rowena muttered. "Except for mine, that is."

Ashley patted her shoulder but kept her focus on Piper. "Serenity Bay may have changed," she warned.

"Trust me, it has." Piper turned her chair so she could look across the water toward the town. "I did a little research. There's barely anyone left that we know. After the lumber mill shut down I guess folks had to move away to find work. There are more than a hundred cottages for sale."

"A hundred?"

Both wore the same stunned expression she'd had the day she'd driven around the town.

"More than. I'm sure lots of people come back in the summer but the number of permanent residents is sinking fast. I'm guessing that's why the mayor thinks the town has to act now, before it's too late."

"Back to the mayor." Row and Ash exchanged looks, then watched her, waiting.

"Why are you looking at me like that?"

"Are you sure this mayor didn't have anything to do with your decision to move back?"

"No." Piper sighed, recognizing the futility of trying to withhold anything. "I've actually been considering it for a while. After Vance died I poured myself into work. I didn't want to think about God taking my husband—or anything else."

"And work hasn't been enough?" Ashley asked softly.

"For a while I thought it was. But this birthday has me thinking, I'm not getting any younger."

"Neither are we. But we're not closing up shop and moving back here." Rowena's voice sounded harsh, but her eyes brimmed with pity. "Have you been so unhappy?"

"That's not the right word, Row. I've been rudderless, without any real goal. Serenity Bay is offering me a chance to stretch, to think outside the box. I need that challenge."

"Need?"

Piper nodded.

"Need. I want the Bay to prosper, to grow, to provide years of fun and joy for other kids, for other families—just as it did for us." She waved a hand. "This is where

I want to spend my days, maybe someday raise my kids. I might even get back into Papa's gold studio during the long, frosty winter nights, see if I can create again."

"You always did have a flair for the unusual," Rowena said. "People still stop me to ask where I got this." She fingered the four-inch gold mask brooch she wore on her lapel.

"If it doesn't work out or I get tired of the solitude, I can always go back to the city. But moving here, this job—I have to try."

"Cathcart House is the perfect place to do it."

They sat together, each musing over the changes that had come into their lives.

"I keep expecting your grandmother to bring out a jug of hot chocolate and tell us to button up." Ashley sipped her tea, a half smile curving her lips.

"Last night I thought I heard your grandfather's snores." Rowena shrugged at their surprise. "What? Even I have normal dreams sometimes."

"They left Cathcart House entirely to you, Pip? You don't have to share it with your brother or anything?"

"They left Dylan cash. He never seemed to like the Bay, remember?" Piper shrugged. "I never understood that but he seemed happy enough with his share when I talked to him after their wills were read."

"Was your father at the funeral?"

"No." Piper swallowed hard. "At least, I didn't see him."

"It would be a bit much to expect him to show sorrow, wouldn't it? As I recall there was no love lost between your grandparents and him." Rowena tossed the rest of the tea over the side of the deck. "Though I must admit, I never heard them say a word against him."

"Gran always said God would handle him so she didn't have to worry."

The three remained silent for a few moments in sober remembrance.

"So you're not too concerned about your father or his plans?" Ashley asked, her forehead pleated in a tiny furrow.

Concerned, worried and a whole lot more. But Piper wouldn't say that or these two friends would fuss about her. She didn't want that.

"I want to be here to help with development if I can. That beach is glorious. There's no way I'm going to sit back and watch a Wainwright hotel ruin it."

"You're sure that's his plan?"

Piper nodded. "One of them."

"And if he sways the council to his way of thinking? What will you do then?" Ashley pressed, her face expressing her concern.

"Pray." Like praying had saved Vance's life. Piper pushed down the anger. God's will, not mine, she reminded herself.

"Changing Baron Wainwright would take an act of God, all right." Rowena snorted. "Other people's plans have never mattered to him. Did you hear about that Wainwright project in London? There are rumors that officials received bribes to pass some inspections."

"I hadn't heard." Piper sloughed off her gloomy feelings, determined that nothing would spoil her joy in having her friends visit. "Anyway, I'm going to do what I can here. This job means I'll be kept abreast of everything that goes on in Serenity Bay so, hopefully, I'll be one step ahead."

"Ever the optimist, that's our Pip."

"It's not optimism, Row. It's determination." She narrowed her gaze trying to make them understand. "I want to prove something and this is the perfect place."

"You don't have to prove anything to us, honey." Ashley rose, moved to fling her arms around Piper. "We already know you can do anything you set your mind on."

"Thank you." She hugged Ash right back. "But I have to prove it to myself, here, in this place. I didn't come back to see my grandparents as often as I should have when they were here. Maybe I can keep their dreams for Cathcart House and the Bay alive."

"Do it for yourself, Piper. Don't do it to prove something to your father," Row warned. "We all know he's not worth the effort, not after his behavior toward Vance. Just know that if this is what you want, we're behind you all the way."

"She's right. The Bayside Trio takes on tough challenges and rides 'em out no matter what. We're fearless females just waiting to vanquish our foes." Ashley thrust her arm above her head in the charge they'd chanted since grade nine. "Onward and upward!"

"Onward and upward," Piper and Row repeated, grinning as if they were fifteen again and the world was just waiting for them.

"Here's to your thirty-first year, Pip. You go, girl."

Rowena dumped a splash of the hated tea into her cup and the three friends held up their mugs in a toast. Their admiration went a long way toward reassuring Piper that she'd made the right decision. She drank to her own success, giggled at Rowena's jokes and answered Ashley's questions as best she could.

But that night, after the party was over and her friends had left to return to their own lives, Piper lay alone in the big house and let her thoughts tumble into free fall. It was time to face the truth.

She'd told Ashley and Rowena that she wanted to help the Bay grow, and that was true. But more than that, she wanted to stop her father from ruining the one place she called home. And he would ruin it. He ruined everything he touched. Her childhood, her relationship with her brother. Every summer that she'd returned here from boarding school he'd arrived to make a scene about her coming back to live with him. She'd gone back twice—and regretted both. She'd even tried to work with him once. He'd ruined that, too, treating her like a stupid child. So she'd left Wainwright Inc., built a name for herself.

And even after that she'd given him one more chance, a chance to make the difference between life and death, a chance to prove he loved her. He'd blown her off, refused to help.

Well, he would not ruin Serenity Bay. There would be none of the gaudy neon lights his hotels boasted, no famous rock bands blaring till four in the morning and leaving mayhem behind, nobody wandering the streets at all hours, causing a disturbance. Not here. Not while she could stop it.

Curious sounds so different from the city noise she was accustomed to carried down the cliff's side on a light breeze that fluttered the bedroom curtains.

Piper got up for a glass of water, and noticed someone moving across her property toward the peak of the cliff. At a certain point he or she stopped, removed something from a backpack and knelt down. A second later the figure had disappeared.

Lookout Point had always been a place where teens met for a good-night kiss. That's probably who was out there now.

She stood watching for a moment, her thoughts drifting to the mayor and the many plans he had for the direction the town should take. She'd never had a problem working with anyone before, but something about the way Jason Franklin had watched her respond to the council's questions made her wonder if he was as confident of her abilities as he'd said.

In her past jobs she'd been given a mandate and left to accomplish it, filing the paperwork, making her reports at the appropriate stages. But primarily she'd been her own boss. A tiny voice in the back of her head told her this job wouldn't be like that. Mayor Franklin had an agenda. He wanted the Bay to start growing and he wanted it to happen his way. From what he'd said, Piper was fairly certain he wanted it to happen yesterday. It might be hard to appease him when developers didn't immediately respond to her initial probes.

She smothered a yawn and padded back to bed.

Whatever happened, happened. She'd deal with it.

Maybe in doing her job she could coax Jason's diamond-blue eyes to come alive, maybe get him to loosen up a little. Piper had a hunch that somewhere under all that grit and determination, a guy with a sense of humor lurked.

Maybe the girls were right. Maybe Jason Franklin would turn out to be more than the mayor.

Maybe she could finally come to terms with why God had taken away the only people who'd loved her and left her with a father who couldn't see beyond his money to the daughter who wanted to be loved.

Chapter Two

When he'd handed in his resignation in Boston, he'd been told he wouldn't last a year in the sticks.

A lot they knew.

Not only had he endured, he was thriving.

Jason swallowed the last of his morning coffee, certain he'd never tire of this view. He had no desire to go back. Not to traitors....

Don't think about it.

He jerked to his feet. In his haste to escape what he couldn't forget, he almost crashed the foot of his chair into the Plexiglas panel surrounding the deck.

"Calm down," he ordered his racing pulse. "Just calm down. Forget the past. Let it die."

Easier said than done.

Originally he'd thought living on top of his marina store was the kind of kooky idea one of his former high-flying clients might have come up with. But after two years in Serenity Bay, he still relished his perch high above the water.

His neighbor to the left was an age-old forest whose trees sheltered him from the wind. On the right, Jason shared the view with the docks and a public beach.

Nobody watched him, and he only watched the water. A

little lonely, perhaps. But then again, he'd come to Serenity Bay for the solitude. At least that's what he told himself.

Today the sun shone, the water sparkled and sent the wind skimming over the land in a faint caress. Serenity Bay looked picture-perfect.

He squinted across the lake. That early sailor with two sheets billowing in the wind was bolder than most. The fun seekers he'd once hung around with wouldn't have endured more than five minutes of this cool April breeze blowing off the barely thawed lake before they'd turn back.

But this sailor didn't hesitate. The craft continued on a clear, invisible course directed by sure and steady hands, straight toward Jason. The streamlined hull pointed into the wind with gutsy determination. He liked the brashness of it—thrusting ahead on an unswerving course to get where you were going, no matter what.

That's what he was doing.

Fresh air, pure sunshine and a landscape only the Creator could have fashioned was about all anyone could ask.

Just about.

"Lucky guy." He wasted several minutes watching the pristine sailboat flit across the water like a butterfly set free from the cocoon of winter. Then he decided it was time to get to work.

He balanced his last cinnamon bun and a thermos of coffee in one hand, pulled the door closed with the other and descended the circular stairs into his office, unable to resist a glance through the wall of windows that overlooked the lake.

The sailboat was making good time. Obviously whoever was operating her knew exactly what he was doing.

At the height of summer when the days were heavy with heat and the promise of cool lake water beckoned, Jason often envied the freedom and peace a sailboat offered. But he freely admitted his knowledge lay in engines, the kind that sent speedboats tearing across the lakes, towing skiers or tube riders through the water. Or the kind that powered fishing boats and let them troll at a leisurely pace. Engines he understood. He could talk motors with the best of them.

But sailing? You needed money for beauties like that sailboat, and men who built marinas in small lake towns that development hadn't yet reached seldom found cash to spare.

A noise drew his attention to the dock and he stepped outside.

"Hey, Andy. Did you get those rentals all cleaned up?"

"Yes, sir." Andy saluted him, then grinned. "You find the customers, I've got the boats spick-and-span."

The kid looked like a double for an actor on *Gilligan's Island*. That effect was enhanced by a kooky sailor cap Andy loved, but which always slipped to one side of his shiny head.

"Ready to roll, boss. I also swabbed the decks, checked the minnow stock and measured the gas tank. We're good to go on all counts. Now I'll get at that painting."

"Good job." The boy was an employer's dream. He took pride in accomplishing his duties before being asked.

Andy reminded Jason of himself, long ago, before he'd learned that fresh-faced eagerness wasn't necessarily an asset in the corporate world.

"You see that?" Andy's gaze was also on the trim red craft and the pristine sails. "She's a beauty, isn't she?"

The sharp bow cut cleanly through the crest of waves, zooming ever closer, sails puffed out smooth. As they watched, the boat tacked left, turning in a perfect half circle as it headed into the harbor, straight toward them.

"I hope he knows how to bring her in. It'll cost a fortune if I have to get those docks redone."

Andy grinned, shaking his head.

"Don't worry, boss. The way that beauty's moving, there's no novice at the helm. Man, I'd love a chance to go out in her."

Who wouldn't? Jason pretended to busy himself, but he kept close watch as the sailor trimmed his sails perfectly and the delicate red hull slipped easily into dock. He turned away, refusing to let the owner of such magnificence witness his jealousy. Someday, when he retired, maybe he'd get a boat like that.

Someday.

"Ahoy, there. Mind tying me off?"

That voice was familiar. Jason twisted around, watched Andy snatch the line tossed at him and fasten stem and stern so that the sailboat was perfectly docked against Styrofoam buoys that would keep its hull mar free. Golden letters in a delicate font shone from the bow. *Shalimar.*

The sailboat's captain accepted Andy's hand and stepped onto the dock. Once the thick coat was unzipped and he caught a glimpse of her face, Jason realized the sailor was a woman.

Piper Langley.

She tossed her coat inside the hull, then drew the red knitted cap she was wearing from her head and flipped it into the boat, allowing her glossy black curls to dance in the breeze.

"Thank you, kind sir." She curtsied to Andy, then strode toward Jason. "Good morning, Mayor."

"Good morning."

He couldn't help but stare at her bouncy haircut. It had been a long mane of ebony when they'd first met. He'd dreamed about that hair. He couldn't decide which style he preferred.

Her ice-blue shirt and matching slacks managed to look

both businesslike and chic. The wool jacket added to her polished look, though her eyes weren't businesslike at all. He swallowed, rejecting the flash of interest that prickled whenever he talked to her.

"I didn't realize—that is, er…" He hesitated. "You'll need a car, Miss Langley. The area is large and our public transportation isn't up to big-city standards."

She frowned, obviously trying to decipher his curt tone.

"Please call me Piper," she begged. "I don't get to sail very often so I thought this would be the perfect way to commute across the lake. I left my car here." Her gaze brushed over the boat in obvious fondness, then she focused on him and the brown eyes darkened to almost black.

"I paid for the berth. Yesterday."

Andy hadn't told him. Jason wished he could time-warp back about an hour and do this all over again. Though it was a little late to explain, he gave it his best shot.

"I wasn't implying anything. I just wanted to be sure you knew you'd need a car." Idiot! How old was he that her appearance could knock him for a loop?

"I don't know whether or not I explained to you when we talked before, Mr. Franklin, but years ago I lived in Serenity Bay. I'm familiar with the need for wheels around here."

She smiled and it was a glorious thing. Her skin glowed, her eyes shone and her curls danced in the breeze. She was more beautiful than he remembered.

"No, I don't believe you mentioned that." *Otherwise, I wouldn't have made an idiot of myself talking about public transportation.*

Her gaze held his. A zap of awareness shot between them.

"Well, I did. Six summers, actually."

"Really?"

"They were some of the best times of my life."

Which meant—what? That she was here to recapture the past? That her life had taken a downturn and she'd returned to start over?

"That explains your enthusiasm for this place then." And her knowledge of the economic possibilities in the area.

"I guess." She continued to watch him, her scrutiny unflinching.

"What do you have planned, Miss Langley?"

"You're the boss. Shouldn't you be telling me, Mr. Franklin?" Heavy emphasis on the *Mr.*

"Actually I didn't think you would start till Monday."

"Why wait?"

She stood tall and proud, head tipped back, face impassive as her glance clashed with his. She shifted as if she were eager to get on with things.

Something was tapping. Jason looked down, noticed that her blue shoes matched the blue of her suit perfectly, and that the toe of one was rapping impatiently against the dock.

During his Boston years, Jason had known a lot of women. But he'd never met one who couldn't stand still for even a few minutes. Piper Langley pulsed with leashed energy.

She cleared her throat. "Mr. Franklin?"

"I prefer Jason. We're informal around here. Okay, Piper?" He smiled, showing there were no hard feelings. "Now perhaps—"

"Wait a minute. Jason. Jason Franklin. Man, I'm slow." The whispered words slipped through her lips on a breath of recognition.

He froze.

"There was a rather well-known Jason Franklin who

gained the reputation of finding fantastic recreation property that developers could evolve into spectacular tourism centers. He worked for a company called Expectations in Boston." She paused, searching his face while she waited for his response.

"Guilty," he admitted, heart sinking. "But that was in the past. Now I'm my own boss." *And I like it that way, so don't ask any more questions.*

"Of course." She nodded, obviously receiving his message loud and clear.

Immediately Jason wondered exactly what she'd heard, and from whom.

"It's a wonderful marina," she murmured. "We never had anything like this when I was here."

"Thank you. I've enjoyed putting it together."

Then in the blink of an eye, Piper Langley became all business.

"I've done some preliminary work since you offered me the job of economic development officer. I hope that's all right?" One finely arched eyebrow quirked up, daring him to say it wasn't.

"Great."

"Nothing too risky, but I thought one way to begin getting Serenity Bay on the map might be to initiate a fishing tournament, with a rather large prize. I realize it's only the first of April, but these things take a while to publicize and we don't want to miss the season." She glanced around, took in the lack of customers. "Do you have time to discuss some of my plans now?"

As mayor, he'd made her the offer on behalf of the town council, agreeing to hold the position until she was released from her current job. Her eagerness to get started was a far better beginning than Jason had dared expect.

He'd known she was the right one at their first meeting. Looked as though he was about to be proved correct.

"Now's a bad time?" The toe was tapping again.

Jason considered his schedule. Saturday. There would be very few people looking for a boat to rent this early in the season. Maybe a couple of guys would drop in looking for new rods and reels, but the majority of the cottagers hadn't opened up their summer homes yet and those year-round residents who weren't enjoying the sunshine were more likely to be planting what little garden they could, rather than visiting his marina.

"Now is good," he agreed. "Why don't you come inside, into my office? I've got some coffee already made."

"Great." She followed him. "Thank you."

Early on in life Jason had learned that tidiness was an asset with inestimable value. Today it proved its worth, especially when he found himself oddly confused by her presence in his personal space.

"Great office."

"Yes, it is." Jason checked for sarcasm but her appreciation seemed genuine. He castigated himself for suspecting her motives. Not everybody was insincere.

"I chose this side of the building specifically because of the natural woodlands next door. I don't have to worry about neighbors building over my view, or at least I hope I won't. The council hasn't approved the zoning yet."

"From here you can see across the entire store and down the marina." Piper trailed one finger over the metal filing cabinets that bordered his office, but did not obstruct his view. "Smart man. Do you live upstairs?"

"Yes." Why the sudden curiosity?

"It must be a dream to wake up to this view every morning."

"You wake up to the same thing, don't you?" He nodded toward the lake.

Her eyes widened in surprise. "Yes, I guess I do." She chuckled. "I keep forgetting that I'm here for good. Which reminds me—do you know what's happening up on Lookout Point? I went walking yesterday and noticed someone's been doing some digging."

"I have no idea. A telecommunications company has a tower near there, don't they? Maybe it's something to do with that. We've been begging them to install a higher tower to improve cell phone coverage."

"Maybe that's it." The brown eyes sparkled with interest. "You've put a lot of thought into a variety of aspects of development."

"Yes, I have."

"Good. You can give me some ideas." She rubbed her cheek with her thumb, then shrugged. "Seems a shame for land like Lookout Point to be used for something as mundane as a tower. It has spectacular cliffs and a view to die for. And some of the best wild strawberries you've ever tasted."

"I haven't been over there much. You're staying nearby?"

"At Cathcart House. It was my grandparents' and they left it to me. The land from Lookout Point once belonged to my Gran's family."

Jason hadn't lived in Serenity Bay for two years without hearing some of the old-timers rave about the parties at Cathcart House. There was a private beach, private docks, an oversize boathouse and a gazebo for parties on the lawns.

Piper Langley came from money. He probably should have figured that out, given her chic clothes and perfectly styled hair. It made her presence here in the backwoods even more curious.

"The house is far too big for one person, but—" she shrugged "—I love it. Every room is full of memories."

He envied her that strong sense of family identity. He'd never had it. Maybe that's why he pushed so hard for Serenity Bay to be the kind of place families could be together.

Most of the time the land acquisition team he'd been part of at Expectations seemed a thousand miles away, part of the distant past. Then he'd remember Trevor and that horrible feeling of being duped and he was right back there. Once he'd almost been willing to sell his soul to buy a piece of Expectations—so deep went his need to be part of something important and fulfilling.

Jason blinked back to reality when Piper swung a briefcase onto his desk. He hadn't even noticed her carrying it.

"I took the liberty of drafting up a few ideas for you to look over, Jason." She took a quick look at him over one shoulder as if to check he was listening, then spread charts and graphs across his desk. "I've been talking to several corporate heads and put together a list of those who might be willing to chip in as sponsors for different events I've planned for the summer."

The woman twigged his curiosity. According to her résumé, she'd had a great job in Calgary. Her boss had told him confidentially that when she'd resigned, she'd refused a substantial raise to stay, even given them rather short notice to come to Serenity Bay. Yet no one Jason contacted had said anything negative about her. Rather, they were very vocal with their praise of her skills.

Cathcart House couldn't be the only thing drawing her back. She could have kept that as a summer place, visited during her vacations. Instead she'd made a permanent move from the city to the middle of nowhere.

Stop questioning your good luck, Franklin.

"As you can see, I've scheduled events throughout the summer and fall. That way we can maximize the exposure without running ourselves ragged."

Jason hadn't heard all of what she'd said, but what he had absorbed told him her plans were ambitious. And clearly thought out.

"Piper. Why are you here?"

She feigned composure, but Jason caught the slight tremor in her hand, the way her eyes flickered before she glanced down.

"I'm here to do a job, to help make Serenity Bay a desirable getaway for those who want a healthy, natural vacation." She looked up, met his stare. "Isn't that what you wanted?"

Her voice was quiet, relaxed. And yet something nagged at him.

"Yes, it's what we want," he admitted.

"Do you want me to leave?"

"Of course not. We're delighted that someone with your qualifications is willing to take on the project." He paused, unsure of exactly the right words that would voice his feelings.

"You have doubts about my ability."

"Not really. It's just…I can't help speculating why you chose to return at this particular time. Your grandparents—?"

"They moved into a nursing home in Toronto about three years ago. They've since passed away."

"I'm sorry."

"Thanks." Piper's clear skin flushed. "If there's a problem with my references—"

He shook his head. "No, there's no problem."

She frowned, lifted one palm. "Then—"

He was an idiot to question the best thing that had happened since he'd been elected mayor. Everything he'd learned said she was great at what she did. That should be enough.

"Forgive my question. I've been told I'm a little obsessed when it comes to our bay." He smiled, hunkering down to peer at her work. "This looks very aggressive."

Piper didn't answer for several minutes, but when she did, a guarded note edged her voice in cool reserve.

"I thought that was the point. Didn't you want to start showing the world what treasures you have here in cottage country?"

"Yes, of course. Could you explain the first step?"

"It will be a weekend extravaganza, to whet appetites so people will want to come back."

Maybe Serenity Bay was her escape, too.

Jason nodded as if he'd understood. But he hadn't. Especially about that winter festival. He'd been thinking about promoting the Bay as a summer resort town and now she was talking about year-round development.

"Is there anyone you might know who could offer me some input on current local activities?"

He thought a moment, then nodded.

"The artists' guild is meeting this afternoon. They're the primary draw for outsiders at the moment. We have quite a number of local artisans. Weavers, painters, potters, stained-glass artists. Several earn a living from their work but most of them have to go to the other towns to capitalize on the customers that flood in during the summer."

"If we bring people in here, that will change. I can understand why they live here. The beauty stimulates your creative genes."

"Are you an artist, too?" He somehow couldn't imagine her spattered in paint.

"My grandfather was a goldsmith, my grandmother a jewelry designer. They taught me. I'd like to get back to it one of these days."

Gold. Yeah, that fit her perfectly.

"I see you have a tour program proposed," Jason said. "Some of the guild members would certainly go for that. Why not ask for volunteers to help with the extravaganza thing? That way you'd get to know them sooner."

"Yes, I'd thought of that." Her eyes glittered like black onyx. "This is going to be a very exciting time in Serenity Bay, Jason. I can't wait to see what happens."

"Neither can I." He cleared his throat.

"But?" She frowned.

"I'd appreciate it if you'd keep me in the loop about what you're doing. The council has several ideas of their own. We don't want to overlap."

"Don't worry, I'll keep you informed of whatever's happening. Thanks for your support." In a flash she gathered her papers and replaced them in her briefcase.

Five minutes later Piper Langley was walking down the pier toward a small red compact that sat in the parking lot.

Jason waited until he saw her taillights disappear, then he picked up the phone.

"Hey, Ida. How are you?" He chuckled at the growl from the town's secretary. Ida's bark was always worse than her bite. "Yes, I do know you're off work today. I just want to ask you something. Our new economic development officer is officially on the job. Can you let me know if she asks you for anything special?"

"Asks me for something? Like what?" Ida Cranbrook never skirted an issue. She claimed she was too old for that. "Pens? Paper?"

"You know what I mean. I just want to make sure she and I are on the same channel," he muttered. "We haven't got much of a budget. I don't want to see it squandered."

"You think she'll do that? A woman with her reputation?"

"Well—"

"You don't have to spell it out. I get it, Jason. You want to approve everything before she does it."

"You make that sound like a bad thing." Silence. Jason sighed. "I just need to know. Okay? Satisfied?"

"Not nearly." She cackled at her own joke. "You're the boss, Jason. If you want me to spy on the girl and give you daily reports, I suppose I'll have to do it. But I won't like it."

"I'm not asking you to spy on her."

"Ha!" Ida Cranbrook was no fool.

"Never mind. Sorry I bothered you, Ida. Especially on your day off."

"Doesn't matter a bit. Harold's nodded off to sleep in the middle of one of those car races, anyway. I just started spicing up some ribs for dinner. You interested?"

Interested in Ida Cranbrook's specially prepared, mouthwatering ribs? Was a fish interested in water?

"Just tell me when and where." His stomach growled at the thought of those succulent bits of artery-clogging pleasure.

"Six o'clock. And bring the girl. From what I saw at the interview, she looks like she could use some meat on those bones. Besides, then we can all watch her, make sure she doesn't pull a fast one on us." Ida barked a laugh, then hung up.

In one weak moment he'd confided his past and the betrayal that had precipitated his leaving Expectations. Now Ida could read him like a book—which Jason found extremely disconcerting.

So was inviting Piper Langley to go with him to Ida's. Piper of the iceberg-blue suit and immaculate makeup. He just couldn't envision her dripping in barbecue sauce and grease. Seemed a little like casting pearls into the mud to him.

Good looks and nice clothes had nothing to do with the person inside. He'd learned not to judge by exteriors and he couldn't afford to forget that lesson. Besides, he'd never yet met a person who didn't love Ida's ribs. Between Ida, Harold and himself, they should be able to find out more about the new owner of Cathcart House.

Jason drank the coffee he'd forgotten to pour for Piper wishing he'd told her straight up that he intended to be involved in every part of her plans.

Jason had compared her to a rose, but roses had thorns that could draw blood, cause pain. Fine. He could deal with that. But Serenity Bay's development was his chance to put his mark on the world, and he wasn't about to let anybody ruin that.

Jason had survived the shame of being duped by someone he trusted, had weathered whispers, mended broken relationships with each of his clients while he worked out his notice at Expectations and left a job he loved. He'd endured the sly looks at a wedding that should have been his by planning a new dream and praying for forgiveness while he struggled to trust God for a new plan for his future. He still wasn't certain he was where God wanted him, though he prayed about it daily.

Putting Serenity Bay on the tourism map without input from the major developers he'd once worked with would show anybody who doubted him that he could still make it in the big leagues.

He'd been duped once. But nobody, including Piper Langley, was going to fool him into trusting wrongly again.

Chapter Three

"I'm glad you asked me to join you tonight. I've never met Ida Cranbrook. At least, I don't think I have. I'm sure she wasn't around when I lived here before."

"She and Harold have only been here a little longer than me."

Piper climbed from Jason's truck and walked toward a cottage that looked like Hansel and Gretel's gingerbread house. She sniffed the air.

"Oh, that aroma is marvelous. I love ribs."

"You'll like them even more after you taste Ida's. She has this secret recipe. Every year more and more people try to copy it."

"Maybe I could wheedle it from her for the good of the town. You know, 'Come to Serenity Bay and sample Ida's ribs.' Something like that." Piper smiled at Jason, liking the way his hair flopped across his forehead. He was so different from the corporate stiffs she usually worked with.

"Nobody has managed to get it out of her yet, so you'd have a coup if you did." His fingers grazed her elbow as he directed her up the two steps to the front door.

"Hmm. I'll try hard, then."

"Ida's also the sounding board for the entire community. She knows everything about everything. What she doesn't know, she'll find out."

"Ah, an unimpeachable source. Good."

He laughed, rapped the door twice, then opened it.

"We're here," he announced in a loud voice, then motioned for Piper to precede him inside.

A man emerged from the room beyond, ducking his head to walk beneath the low, exposed beams.

"Don't call her," he murmured, shaking his head as he beckoned them inside. "She's at the crucial stage."

"Of what?"

"I don't know, exactly, but she says it's crucial." He held out his hand, smiled at Piper. "I'm Harold Cranbrook, Ida's husband. And you're the lady who's going to put the Bay on the map. Come on in."

"Piper Langley." She shook his hand. "And I hope you're right."

"Jason hasn't steered us wrong yet."

As far as she could tell, everybody liked Jason. That would make it easier to work for him. She hoped.

Piper glanced around. It was like walking into a doll's house. Everything seemed so tiny. How did a man as large as Harold endure living among all this china, crystal and dolls?

"Ida's out on the deck. Is it too chilly for us to join her?"

"Let's go," Piper agreed, relieved they'd be away from the fragile objects, at least for a little while. She eased left, leaving a wide gap between her leg and the tiny, blue china ladies perched atop a table, then blushed when Jason winked at her and followed suit on tiptoe.

"Hey there! I didn't hear you arrive. Come on out." Ida slid open the patio door, then wrapped her tiny arms around Jason in a hug. She did the same to Piper. "I'm glad you could come, Miss Langley. Welcome to Serenity Bay."

"Thank you. It was sweet of you to invite me."

"Jason told me you used to live here. We only moved here two and a half years ago, so I didn't know your grandparents, but I've heard a lot about Sara and Gordon Young from the old-timers on the Bay." She basted the ribs, pushed a fork against the meat, then shook her head and closed the lid. "People used to talk about how he'd sail her around the coves in that cute little sailboat. What's it called—*Shalimar,* that's it. Such an unusual name." Ida glanced at Jason, raised one eyebrow.

"Papa said it sounded like a faraway place you'd escape to. That's why he chose it." Piper noticed some kind of undercurrent running between the mayor and his office helper. She decided to wait and see what it was about.

"Piper uses *Shalimar* to get to work." Jason's gaze remained on the sizzling barbecue.

"Only when it's good weather," she said.

"Like today. I heard you've been talking to the guild." Ida glanced at Jason as if she knew something. "So has Piper given you her report yet?"

"What report?" Piper glanced back and forth, even checked Harold's expression. "Did I miss something?"

"Jason here is a bit obsessive when it comes to business in the Bay. Scratch that. He's a lot obsessive. Not that he doesn't have a good reason. Betrayal by your best friend is never nice." Ida patted his shoulder as if he were six. "If my hunch is right, and it is, he'll want to know exactly what you did this afternoon."

"But he already knows. I told him my plans this morning." Piper accepted a seat on a wicker chair, then glanced at Jason. He was frowning at Ida. Piper didn't blame him. Being betrayed by your best friend sounded horrible.

Maybe that's why he'd come to Serenity Bay, to prove to the powers at Expectations that he could handle more than one aspect of development. Maybe he hoped his work here would push him up their career ladder faster. *Please, not another Baron.*

"I am not obsessive."

"Ha!" The tiny woman sat down, crossed her arms over her thin chest. "You like to pretend you aren't, but you're totally obsessed by the Bay's future." She looked at Piper. "Controlling, too."

"Stop badgering the boy, Ida. We elected him to be concerned about Serenity Bay. I'd say he's doing his job perfectly." Harold turned to Piper, lowering his voice. "They're like two five-year-olds in a school yard. Best to change the subject. You got a boyfriend?"

Piper gulped. What ribs could be worth this?

"Don't answer that. Harold fancies himself a match-maker. You give him the least bit of information and he'll go hunting up a beau for you." Ida poked Jason's leg. "You read those test results?"

"What tests? I go to the boat show in Toronto for two days and you've got people doing tests?"

"I do my job." The older woman sniffed. "Public health said we had to have a water check. I got it done. No problem there."

"Good."

Ida stood and peeked under the barbecue lid, adjusted the heat.

"Ribs need a few more minutes," she explained. She wiped her hands on a towel hanging on the front of the barbecue. "Water's okay, but we do have a problem with some of the campsite facilities. He's going to let you know."

"Fine." Jason switched subjects, but he didn't meet her stare. "Piper thought someone was working up on Look-out Point. Know anything about that, Ida?"

"Nope. But the telephone people visit it in the spring

and the fall. Could be them." She turned to Piper. "What was Serenity Bay like when you used to come here?"

"Pretty much the same. Maybe there were a few more people but then I was mostly here in the summer. In the winter Gran and Papa went to Florida but only after we celebrated Christmas together at Cathcart House." She didn't want to talk about the past. "About the summer people—do you know the kind of radius you're drawing from?"

"We've done some surveys." Ida prattled on about the city dwellers who came north to get away.

"Would you be able to get me a list with addresses? I'd like to get an idea of our current market."

"Sure." Ida shrugged as if it wasn't important. "I'm in Tuesday."

"Do you always take Mondays off?"

"Unless there's something pressing. The town hasn't got enough money for full-time office staff in the winter." Ida plunked down on one of the patio chairs. "I'll start working full-time after Easter."

"Is there any new industry in the area?" she asked, looking for something to hang her plans on. "There used to be a sawmill—"

"It's been closed for years." Harold pulled out a map. "I heard that years ago some folks found a nice vein of copper up past the mill road—about there," he said, pointing. "Purest ever seen, according to the stories. Shone in the sun as if it had been molded into those rocks forever. People used to stop by, take little pieces of it. Few years of that and it was gone, too." He shrugged. "But it brought the place a minute or two of fame."

While he'd been speaking, Ida had hurried away. She now returned with a platter and scooped the ribs off the barbecue onto it and handed it to Harold.

"Time to eat," she announced.

Piper followed Ida to the dining room, where a long buffet table, six chairs and a huge black table were set.

"Piper, you sit there. Jason can sit across from you and Harold and I will hold down the ends. Good. Now, grace, Harold."

Harold gave thanks, then picked up one of the plates stacked in front of him and began to load it with ribs, creamy mashed potatoes and bright green peas.

"Oh, my!" Piper gaped when he placed it in front of her. "It looks delicious, but it's way too much. Perhaps you can make me a smaller plate."

"Nonsense! You get started on Ida's ribs, you won't stop."

Piper looked at Jason while searching her brain for some way to make them understand that she would never be able to eat what she'd been served. But Jason was busy eyeing his own heaping plate and spared her only a quick grin as he picked up a rib.

"Try them first," he advised, then bit into the succulent meat.

Since everyone else had begun to eat, Piper followed their lead. She picked up the smallest piece between two fingers and nibbled at the end. The spices hit her tongue like those candy Pop Rocks she and her friends used to buy for a quarter and leave on their tongues while the flavors fizzled and hissed.

Only better. Much, much better.

Silence reigned as the four of them enjoyed their meals. Piper waited until Ida had coaxed everyone into seconds before she asked her, "Have you noticed anyone looking around the town recently?"

"Oh, we get Looky Lou's all the time. Never amounts to a thing. Funny fellow with big glasses was in the office when Jason was away. Biggest brown eyes I ever saw.

Wanted to know about the beach. It's sand. What more could I say?" She croaked a laugh at her own joke.

So Wainwright Inc. *had* sent someone to check things out. It was strange Dylan was doing on-site research these days.

Piper realized Jason's blue eyes were on her. A smear of sauce dotted his cheek.

"Something wrong?" he asked.

"Not really. I just wondered if a corporation was already interested. I didn't see a hotel in town—"

"Exactly what I've been telling the council," Jason exclaimed. "The no-tell motel is hardly the kind of place we want to showcase, though it's clean enough. But Bart doesn't think there's any point in painting or modernizing the place, especially since business has been so slow. If he heard he'd have some competition, I imagine he'd sink some cash into his outfit pronto."

"So nobody's talked to you about building a hotel?" Piper had hoped for nonchalance but knew it hadn't quite come off when Jason's curious stare stayed on her. He couldn't know why she was asking, could he?

"To me personally? No." He turned toward the older woman. "Ida, you didn't get the name of this man, did you?"

Ida set down her fork, her forehead wrinkled.

"He gave one. I just don't remember what it was. Young fellow, really friendly. I might have written it down. I'll check on Tuesday." Her scrutiny shifted to Piper, grew more intense. "Why are you so interested in this guy?" she asked.

"If he was scouting locations, I'd like to talk to him," she ad-libbed. "Maybe the town can dangle a carrot that would encourage someone to build."

"We don't have much to dangle," Ida mumbled, her

face skeptical. She forgot the subject they'd been discussing, until later when Piper was drying dishes beside her.

"You know who was here snooping around don't you?"

"I could guess. I have a few feelers out with friends who suggested a company but I'll have to do more checking." She kept her attention on the glass she was drying.

"He kept asking about bylaws to do with the beach. You think someone wants to put a hotel right on it—like in Hawaii?" Ida swished the suds down the drain, then hung her dishcloth over the sink. "That might not be a bad idea."

Piper set down the last dry dish, searching for a way to express her concern.

"It could work, with a lot of input from the town council. But we don't want such a beautiful beach to be ruined."

"By pollution, you mean?" Ida shrugged. "I'm sure the government has lots of laws to control that sort of thing."

"Not just pollution. The wholesome atmosphere of the town has to be protected if we want to attract families. We don't want a bar near little kids playing in the sand."

"Goes without saying." Apparently her explanation satisfied Ida, who then busied herself filling the coffee decanter with water. "Stays light longer now. Would you like to join us outside and watch the stars come out?"

"They are beautiful, but don't make any coffee for me. Thanks, Ida. I have to be going. I sailed over and I need to get back before dark."

"Harold and I probably shouldn't be drinking coffee before bed, anyway. Harold always dreams." Ida pulled open the fridge and took out a jug of red juice. "Can I interest you in some cranberry juice? Made it myself."

"Could I try it another time?" Piper glanced at her watch, unwilling to believe the time on the kitchen clock was correct.

"You're welcome anytime. Bring Jason with you. He

says he likes his own cooking, but he doesn't cook much. Gets most of his nourishment from those cinnamon buns he buys at the farmers' market. I try to fatten him up."

If Piper was any judge, the fattening up would take a while. Jason Franklin didn't have a spare ounce on him. Rather, he had a polished, muscular look that made her think of a jaguar. From the state of his sneakers, she suspected he jogged to stay in shape. No wonder he could eat cinnamon buns whenever he wanted.

"Thank you very much for dinner. It was so delicious, I won't have to think about another meal for days. And if you ever want to let me in on your secret rib recipe…" Piper let the sentence trail away when Ida shook her head firmly.

"Can't do that, but you're welcome to share them anytime."

"Thank you. And you and Harold are always welcome at Cathcart House."

The dock was only a few minutes' walk from Ida's, but Jason insisted on driving Piper.

"I would have walked here with you, but I wanted to drop off Harold's motor." He hoisted the machine out of his truck bed and stood it against the workshop where Ida's husband waited beside the birdhouses he'd carved from driftwood.

They thanked the couple for the meal, wishing them good-night before riding back to the marina. Silence stretched awkwardly between them. Piper couldn't think of a thing to say.

"Are you going to be able to get back safely?" Jason asked as he unfastened her boat from its moorings.

The evening had grown cool and Piper tugged her coat from its hiding place in the hatch of the sailboat. "Oh, yes. I'll be fine."

Jason scanned the sky.

"There's a storm blowing in," he told her. "You could get swamped."

She tried to explain that she'd been sailing many times, and had handled her fair share of rough weather, but he refused to listen.

"I'll tie your boat behind mine. I've got an inboard that can weather anything. It won't take long to zip across the lake. Besides, I'll feel a whole lot better if I know for certain that you're home, dry and safe. The lake water is too cold to capsize in."

She couldn't talk him out of it, and so a few moments later Piper found herself seated beside him in his boat, watching the familiar coastline fly past. Truthfully she enjoyed the feeling of knowing someone cared. It had been a long time. Another thing she'd prayed about and it was still unanswered. Did God want her to remain single?

Jason asked her questions about her meeting with the guild and she told him some of what she'd learned and how she intended to use it.

He was obsessive, about the town at least. Well, maybe she could use that to her advantage.

They arrived in her little cove twenty minutes later, just as the last flicker of light sank behind the jagged cliffs of Paradise Peak. As she peered up through the gloom, Piper could see little of the familiar landmarks because the dock lights hadn't come on.

"Will you come up for some coffee?" she invited, once her sailboat was secured.

"Only if you make it hot chocolate," Jason said. "After Ida's high-octane sauce, my stomach will go into convulsions if I add coffee."

"Sure." Funny that his agreement brought such a flush of relief. She'd never worried about coming back late before. Piper led him off the dock and up the path to her home.

"You need some automatic lights. With all the clouds, it's quite dark along here. The trees keep out the moonlight."

She was suddenly aware of why she'd felt so uneasy. It wasn't just the dock lights that were out. There were no lights along here, either.

His hand grazed her shoulder.

"Piper? What's wrong?"

"I do have lights." She looked up, pointed. "There's one."

"Well, it's not working."

She raised one eyebrow. "Yes, I'd noticed. Thanks."

He grinned, then glanced around. "Looks like they're all out. What do you suppose happened to them?"

"I have no idea. Fortunately, I'm very familiar with this path." She turned and began striding along, confidence growing with each step she took. The next moment she was on her knees. "Ow!"

What was the willow chair her grandmother had always kept on the porch doing here?

"Whoa!" He was there, grasping her arm, helping her stand, his grip strong, reassuring. "What happened?"

"My pride just took a beating." She brushed her palms against her legs, feeling the prick of pebbles that had dug into her skin.

"Maybe I should lead." He lifted the chair out of the way.

"You've been here before?" she asked, staring at him.

"Good point. You lead, I'll follow. Just go a little slower, okay?"

"Right." Embarrassed, she picked her way up the path,

her mind busy with the light question. "Maybe a breaker's flipped or something."

"Maybe."

When she stumbled again, he took her hand, his warm, strong fingers threading through hers. "Let's just go slowly, make sure we don't *happen* over anything else."

At that moment the moon slipped out from between two black clouds and provided just enough light for her to see a shape move through the brush.

"Do you see him?" she whispered.

"Who?" He glanced at her. "I can't really see anything."

Then moonlight was gone. So was the shadow. Maybe she'd imagined it. Piper shook her head.

"Never mind. It's not far to the house now. This leads to the garden. Once we're past these roses, we take two steps up onto the deck." Her eyes were adjusting now, discerning familiar landmarks. "See? There's the arch into the garden."

He probably didn't need her directing him, but she did it anyway until finally they stood before her door.

"Now if I can just get the key inside." She slid it into the lock and twisted, unlocking the door and pushing it open. With one flick of her wrist the house entry and deck were illuminated. "Come on in."

She turned on lights as she walked into the house. Thank goodness she'd cleaned up the kitchen this morning.

"So all the power's not out. Just those lights." He raised one eyebrow. "Where's the breaker box? I'll check it, if you want."

"Thanks." Piper showed him the panel in the basement, then left him, intending to return to the kitchen and put the kettle on. Halfway up the basement stairs she stopped, taking a second look.

The old wicker furniture her grandparents had replaced

several years ago still sat down here because Piper had hopes of locating someone who would recane the seats and backs. But the furniture had recently been moved, and not by her.

Someone had been in her house.

"The breaker was off, all right." Jason slapped the metal door closed. "If you've got a timer, you'll have to reset." He stopped speaking, looked at her more closely. "Something else isn't right?"

"I'm not sure." She went back down the stairs, stepped between the two love seats and stared at the thick wooden door she always kept locked. When she tried to open it, the dead bolt held, but she could see faint marks on the wood where it looked as if someone had pried a screwdriver. Had it been done tonight?

"Where does that door lead to? A secret tunnel?"

"Kind of. I told you my grandfather was a goldsmith, didn't I? Well, he kept a workshop here after he retired." She saw the interest flare in his eyes and hurried on. "I've been catching up on what he taught me. Because of the chemicals we use, he always insisted his work area be kept hidden and locked up. I'm the same way."

"Sounds interesting."

"It is." Piper didn't want to say any more right now. She wanted to think about whether someone could have gone through her house, and why. "Thanks for fixing the breaker. It'll be nice to have lights again."

"Yes." He kept looking at her, though he said nothing more. He didn't have to; that stare sent a funny kind of zing up her spine.

"Let's go have that hot chocolate," she murmured, tearing her gaze away.

"Sure."

Jason followed her up the stairs to the kitchen and

perched on one of the breakfast stools, watching as she put the ingredients together.

"Are you telling me that you are a goldsmith, also?" he asked when the silence between them had stretched to discomfort.

"No. I just putter at it. Gifts for friends, things like that." She held out a mug. "Would you rather sit outside? There's a space where we'll be protected if it rains. We could watch the storm, though I'm sure it will only be a tiny one. The wind isn't blowing hard anymore."

"Outside sounds fine."

Before she could lead the way, the phone rang.

"Hey, there. I tried you earlier, but no answer. Were you out on a hot date with the mayor?"

"Um, I'll have to call you back, Ash. I've got company right now."

"So I was right! Rowena owes me ten bucks."

"Lucky you. Bye now."

Knowing full well that her friend would immediately call Row and the two of them would discuss her visitor made Piper uncomfortable, especially with the subject of their conversation so near.

"Sorry, that was a friend of mine." She pushed open the door. "You didn't have to come over here with me. The sailboat does have a motor."

"I'm glad I came. I was curious to see where you lived." He followed her through the French doors and sank down onto the chair nearest hers. "It's a beautiful view."

She tried to see the garden through his eyes. Her grandmother had ordered small, shielded lights installed high up which cast a wash of illumination over her favorite gnarled oak trees. Accent lights hidden by boulders would soon show off the glorious blues of delphiniums, bright-red poppies and candy-pink carnations. Buried in the beds of the soon-to-be fragrant and colorful rose garden were soft, romantic lights, and along the path oversize mushroom lights showed the next step on the path down to the lake.

"Sitting up here, it feels as if the world is far away. It must be a wonderful place to come home to."

"I never get tired of it." Piper wished he could see it on a summer day when Cathcart House was at its best. "Every day I thank my grandparents for leaving this to me."

"How did they die?"

"They moved to Toronto when Papa's heart needed an operation. But he was too frail to recover. They died within months of each other."

"I'm sorry."

"So am I."

"You didn't come back?"

"Not for a while. It hurt too much."

Low, growling thunderclaps rumbled their warnings across the water, and every so often a jagged slash of silver-blue lightning illuminated the rich, black-green forest across the lake for one brief space in time. A few droplets of rain spattered on the flagstones.

Why didn't he say something?

"When I sit out here and see all the beauty God's created, I can't help but think of that hymn, 'How Great Thou Art.'" It sounded silly, but Piper chalked her uneasiness up to the odd situation with the lights and the feeling that someone was watching them.

"I feel the same way," Jason admitted. "There are so many lovely places around Serenity Bay. That's one reason why I want to stay on top of the development we let in. It would be terrible to see the forests cut, the lake polluted and the coastline ruined in the name of progress. Know what I mean?"

She nodded. "Yes, I know. It's like we've been entrusted

with something precious, and while I do want others to see and appreciate it, I also want it to be here a hundred years from now."

"For your grandchildren," he teased.

"Yes," she whispered. But Piper didn't laugh.

Ever since that horrible afternoon she'd kissed Vance goodbye, she'd never allowed herself to think about kids. That only brought stabs of regret for what could never be. Her mother had clung to enough regrets for all of them. At twenty-three, when she'd left Wainwright Inc., Piper had made up her mind that she would never end up like her mother, pining for a man so consumed by making money he didn't know what his own family was doing.

To love someone so much and have him ignore you— until you lost the will to live— No!

Love best suited people like her grandparents. Vance's death proved that. Since he'd been gone, Piper had built a wall around her heart. She'd talked to her minister about it, talked to God about it, but somehow she couldn't risk letting anyone get too close in case she got hurt again. Maybe that's why she couldn't trust God when it came to her father. God's ways were slow and she had to stop Baron now.

"This has been great, but I think I'd better go now that the lightning has stopped. It's getting quite late." Jason stood, smiled down at her.

"You don't have a light on your boat?" Piper asked, rising, too.

"Oh, yes. I won't have any difficulty getting back."

"Oh." Obviously he was simply anxious to get away from her.

"I teach some boys a Sunday school class and I like to bone up on my lessons on Saturday night. They always have questions." He stepped down off the deck, then turned back. "You're very welcome to join us, if you'd like. It's

Bayside Believers Church, about half a block from Ida's. If you meet me on the dock at nine-thirty, I'll give you a ride. It's always easier to go somewhere new with somebody else, don't you think?"

His thoughtfulness touched a chord inside her. How was it he'd managed to read her so easily while he remained an enigma to her?

"Thank you. I'd like that. I'll be there."

"I'll wait for you then. Good night."

"Good night." Piper stood on the deck, watching as he wound his way down the path and climbed aboard his boat.

When he looked up, she waved, waited for the sound of his powerful motor to recede then picked up the two mugs and walked inside, carefully locking the door behind her.

She rinsed the mugs, but left them in the sink until morning. Right now there was something else she needed to do.

Piper quickened her step down to the basement. She grabbed a nearby flashlight and shone it on the door. Yes, those were tool marks. And they were new.

She moved back upstairs, checked the back doorknob. No marks. Same thing on the front. No sign of forced entry. Her entire body slumped in relief.

"Thank you, Lord."

Then she remembered.

"If you ever come and can't get in, we'll have a key hidden right here. Nobody will know about it but us."

Piper flicked on the outside lights, unlocked the door and stepped onto the deck once more. She trod lightly across the deck, stopped in one corner. Her grandmother's wishing well sat there, unused after the cold winter, cobwebs, dried leaves and dust frills gathered around the bottom.

The day she'd arrived she'd discovered one of her grandfather's diaries was missing. It contained her grandfather's thoughts from the last year of his life and it was the only one she hadn't read, thinking she'd leave it until the grief wasn't so fresh and it didn't seem as if he were sitting there, saying the words to her.

Piper bent, tilted the well and slid her fingers beneath, searching for the key. Nothing. She pushed and shoved the heavy wooden piece, propped it up with a piece of wood, then shone her flashlight beneath.

There was no key.

She'd come here once after her grandparents had gone into the home and again after they'd died. The key had been there then. So had the diary. She could close her eyes right now and see the gilt letters etched on the leather cover.

Someone had taken the key and the journal.

Someone like Baron Wainwright?

After a hasty survey of the garden, Piper stepped back inside, closed and locked the door. She made sure all the windows were secure before she phoned the police. Piper felt certain they would find little and she was right. The police left no wiser than when they'd arrived.

Even so, Baron was the top suspect on her list. He'd hated her grandparents because they'd shielded her when he'd tried to force her back home years ago. He'd hated her because she'd told him the truth—that her mother would never have condoned his hateful behavior toward them, threatening them with legal action and lawsuits, but stood up to him and demanded he leave them alone or she'd disown him. And because she wouldn't bow to his wishes.

Was taking Papa's diary his way of denying her the solace she might have found in those last beloved words? Or was it a trick, a way to get her to call him and beg for what was rightfully hers?

If he thought she'd come crawling to him, he was in for disappointment. Piper had nothing more to say to her father.

Soft rain began falling, muffling the world outside. Piper lit a fire and curled up in her grandfather's chair. She opened her briefcase and focused her attention on her plans for Serenity Bay.

But her thoughts kept returning to the tall, handsome mayor and the sense of gentleness she'd felt when he escorted her home.

Jason was a nice man. If she didn't disappoint him about the Bay they could be good friends. But that's all they'd be. Her heart couldn't risk anything more.

Chapter Four

Piper Langley was no slouch.

Except for weekends and the busy summer days when rentals were in demand and tourists milled around everywhere, Jason preferred to come in to the town office early to check on happenings from the day before. But on both Monday and Tuesday mornings Piper arrived before him. Today she was already on the phone.

"I know it's early for you, Jeff. But it's even earlier for me." Her light, musical laugh carried through the general office to the reception area. "I need to know if you're interested in making an investment. Serenity Bay. I sent you a fax. Of course you haven't heard of it yet. I haven't started publicizing it yet. But when I do—"

Jason moved quickly into his own office, sorted through the files Ida had left for him and began dealing with his workload. Piper's melodic voice carried to him periodically, her laughter bubbling out like a brook released from winter's grip. From what he'd overheard, she sounded awfully friendly with this Jeff person. But then someone who looked like her wouldn't be alone for long.

Checking the direction of his thoughts, Jason plowed through the pile of manila folders, then decided to start the coffee. Ida preferred hers the consistency of tar and wasn't averse to tossing out anything she declared dishwater. He needed a cup before she came in.

He walked to the kitchen, filled the coffeemaker and waited for the water to drip through the grounds.

"Tomorrow? Fantastic. Thanks a lot, Peter."

When the coffee was finished, Jason poured himself a cup, added some sugar and carried it toward his office. He was almost there when Piper flew out of her office and ran smack-dab into him. He jerked back to protect her and caught his breath as hot, dark coffee slopped over the rim and across his chest.

"Oh, I'm so sorry. I didn't realize anyone else was here. Come on, we need to get some cold water on this or it will stain."

She grasped his arm and half led, half dragged him toward the ladies' room. Bemused by her quick actions, Jason dug in his heels before she got him through the door.

"Umm…Piper…" he muttered.

Piper followed his stare to the sign on the door, blinked. "Oh, yes, of course," she murmured. "Just wait here and I'll get something."

She returned moments later with a wad of wet paper towels which she applied directly to his sweater.

He jerked back as the icy water contacted his skin.

"Hold still," Piper ordered.

"There wasn't any warm water in the tap?" he grated, watching as she dabbed then blotted the mark, her head tilted to concentrate on the task at hand.

"Cold works better." She kept up the routine until most of the color had been absorbed by her paper. "Just a little bit more," she said. "Stay here."

She disappeared into the ladies' room again before he

could argue that it didn't matter. Seconds later she was
back and the routine began again.

The dark curls of her hair bobbled and danced in the
light from above. A tiny pleat marred the perfection of her
forehead, her eyebrows drawn together in serious concen-
tration as she assessed her work.

"I think that's the best I can do," she murmured, tip-
ping her head back to look at him.

Jason got caught in her fragrance, a soft, light scent that
brought to mind warm summer nights when you could
smell roses bursting with beauty.

"Excuse me!"

Jason jerked back to reality, grimacing. Ida.

"I think your shirt's all right now." Piper acted as if she
hadn't even noticed Ida's appearance.

Jason knew he should have warned her about the woman's tendency to gossip. He loved her dearly but Ida took
great pleasure in being the first to know anything. And to
share it with everyone.

"I spilled coffee on my sweater. Piper insisted on cleaning it up."

Piper winked at him then turned to face Ida.

"Actually, he's being gallant. I came rushing out of my
office and forgot to check for cross-traffic. Not a very good
way to impress the boss, is it?"

"If it was that dishwater he usually makes, it wouldn't
have stained anything." Ida examined Piper's cream
sweater and slacks admiringly. "You're an early bird, too?"
she asked.

"Not really. I'm half-asleep most mornings. But there
was so much I wanted to do today—" she smiled "—I
couldn't sleep for ideas that kept bubbling up."

"Looks like they hired the right woman for the job then.
We could use some new ideas around here." Ida undid her

jacket. "About time I got to work, too," she said. "Otherwise somebody will want to dock my pay." She cackled then walked away.

"Sorry," Piper apologized. "I didn't mean to embarrass you."

"I'm used to it. That's Ida's favorite pastime." He grinned to show there was no ill will. "What are you working on this morning?"

"Sponsors for the fish derby. So far I've got three."

"Anyone I know?"

"Could be." She turned toward the staff area where the coffee machine was. "I think I'll get a cup of that. Want me to pour you a fresh one?"

He handed over his mug, trailed behind her wondering why Piper hadn't told him who the sponsors were. Was it a secret?

"Just in time," she mused as Ida picked up the pot. "If you're going to dump it out I'll have some first."

Ida poured both cups, made a face at the liquid. "Not a bit of body," she grumbled and tossed the remainder down the sink.

"Ida, could you get me a list of the dates for town council meetings?"

"Why do you need that?" Jason asked, accepting his mug.

Piper's surprise was obvious.

"I'll need approval from them, won't I? I mean, I can't just go ahead and put my ideas into action without some communication. We'll want to work together to make sure everyone is on the same page."

He felt like an idiot. Of course she would attend council meetings. He was getting paranoid. But that seed of distrust from the past still lay rooted inside, warning him not to be tricked again.

"Yes, of course. I wasn't thinking clearly," he told her. "Lack of coffee."

"My fault." She grinned, excused herself and went back into her office.

"Why are you acting so suspicious?" Ida scolded him. "The girl's trying to do her job, that's all."

"I'm not acting anything."

"Yeah, you are." Ida's gaze narrowed. "You're going to have to get used to working with her. It shouldn't be too hard. She's pretty."

"I never noticed."

"Liar." Laughing uproariously, Ida began filling the carafe with fresh water. "I saw the way your mouth was hanging open when she was cleaning your sweater. At church on Sunday when the pastor was talking about loving your neighbor, you kept sneaking looks at Piper. Never noticed, my foot!"

Jason sighed.

"Ida?"

"Yeah?"

"Get to work." Irritated beyond measure, Jason walked back to his office and this time he closed the door to shut out that laugh. But it took him a long time to read through the first sheet of paper.

A very long time.

"I love it, Ash." Piper leaned back in her chair and closed her eyes. "It's the most perfect job."

"With the most perfect boss."

"I'm not too sure about him," Piper admitted, remembering their encounter this morning. "One minute he's really friendly, the next he looks at me as if he suspects I'm going to walk out of here with the town payroll. It's weird."

"Especially after he took you to church and everything." Laughter lay beneath Ash's quiet voice.

"He didn't take me. I went with him. He introduced me around. But, yes, he was friendly then. But this morning—" A knock on her door cut short her conversation. "I've got to go. I'll call you later, okay?"

"Sorry. I didn't realize you were on the phone." Jason stood in the doorway.

Piper prayed he hadn't overheard that crack about the payroll.

"Is this a bad time?"

"No. It's perfect." She motioned toward the chair. "Have a seat."

"Thanks." He sat, his attention riveted to something on the floor.

"Something special you wanted to see me about?" she prodded, wondering about his stern look.

"I got a call this afternoon. At the marina. It seems you were talking to one of my suppliers about sponsoring one of your events—some kind of cup, I think he called it."

"The Vanity Cup is my working name for the project," she explained. "Yes, I did make some calls. Is there a problem?"

"I don't know." He named a well-known boat manufacturer.

"Peter Evans. Yes, I called him. Is something wrong?"

"Not *wrong,* exactly." He looked bemused, as if whatever he'd learned confused him.

To keep her hands still, Piper clasped them in her lap, waiting for the explanation. She couldn't have blown it twice in one day—could she?

"He wants me to arrange for a display of his boats near the marina this summer. His cost. If we sell them, he'll pay a hefty profit." Jason frowned. "Whatever you said to him must have impressed him a lot. He's never been willing to consign so much before."

"I take it that's a good thing?"

"Very good."

"Then I'm happy. Now if we can just get him to commit to some sponsorship stuff, I'll be even happier."

"He said to tell you 'yes,' whatever that means." He blinked when Piper let out a whoop of excitement.

"It means that I've got somewhere to start, a concrete commitment toward the boat and motor we're going to offer as a grand prize for the Vanity Cup," she explained. "It's not difficult to bring others on board when someone's already committed. Getting the rest of the prizes should be easy. I'll need some money to get the publicity rolling. I've worked out some figures if you want to take a look. Also, I want to get some advertising prepared."

A burst of excitement surged inside her. She'd prayed Serenity Bay was the right move for her and if this first success was any indication, God approved. Maybe He'd also help her stop Baron.

"Uh, yeah, I can take a look. But it's after six. Don't you want to get home now? You've been here for almost twelve hours."

"Really?" She checked her small gold wristwatch. "So I have. I guess it can wait for tomorrow."

At that precise moment, to her very great embarrassment, Piper's stomach growled loudly.

"Sounds like you're hungry." He chuckled.

Her cheeks burned. She picked up her jacket and thrust her arms in, surprised to feel his hands on her shoulders as he helped with her coat.

"Thank you." Her purse lay on the credenza behind her desk. She slid the strap over one shoulder and stepped toward the door.

"I don't suppose you'd want to share dinner? We could talk then."

Piper paused, surprised by the offer.

"The Lakeside Diner serves a great lasagna." He leaned against the doorjamb, waiting for her response.

"You're sure it's not an intrusion giving up part of your evening for work?" she asked, noticing that he'd changed his coffee-stained sweater for a gray one that emphasized the silver glints in his blue eyes. "Or maybe I should have said *another* evening. I'm sure that acting as mayor requires a lot of your time."

"Some months are more hectic than others. But developing Serenity Bay is important to me. I think it will be interesting to hear your plans."

"Great." But as she walked out of the building, women's intuition told Piper that Jason Franklin was more than just interested in what she'd planned.

"Do you mind walking?" He locked the door behind them then shrugged into a light windbreaker. "It's just a couple of blocks."

"Sounds great. I could use some fresh air." She turned her face into the wind, let it soothe the day's tension as she walked beside him. "The Lakeside Diner used to be a pizza joint when I lived here. We used to call for delivery so we could ogle the delivery boys."

"Your grandparents?" he asked, one eyebrow raised.

"No, silly, my friends. The Bayside Trio." She giggled. "We're still really close."

"And the delivery guys?" His eyes were bluer now, sparkling in the sunlight that still glittered on the water.

She grinned at his dour look. "None of us ever got up the courage to ask one of them out. We were really brave when we were talking about it, but once they showed up, our tongues got all twisted."

"Typical teenagers. Do your friends still live here?" Jason held open the door of the restaurant to allow her to walk through.

"No. We've all moved on. I did see them a few weeks ago, though. We make a point of getting together for an annual birthday bash. This year I hosted it here."

"Sounds like fun."

"Do you ever see any of your former coworkers?" she asked idly, taking stock of the homey interior of the restaurant. If the food went with the decor, the place must be busy in the summer.

"No."

His brusque answer surprised her. Piper studied him while he spoke with the owner. He introduced her, then followed her to the table. There were only two other tables occupied.

"I'm sorry," Piper murmured when they were alone. "I didn't mean to get personal. I'd forgotten what Ida said."

"It doesn't matter."

But it did. Otherwise why would he sound so gruff?

They ordered, then Jason leaned forward.

"Okay, tell me about the Vanity Cup. What have you lined up so far?"

Piper explained how she envisioned the plan working.

"I think we should make the Vanity Cup the final part of the Serenity Bay Fish Festival." She leaned back, waited for his response.

"But I thought the intent was to make this a family vacation spot. If we're catering only to fishermen—"

"We're not. We're going to have something for everyone. The events I'm planning will last throughout the summer—I've named it Summer Splash. Each weekend the art guild has agreed to sponsor a sidewalk sale in what I hope will soon be known as the town square. I have to talk to you about that."

He didn't look happy at that prospect but Piper plunged on, outlining events that would bring visitors in through the spring, summer and into the fall and engage people of all ages in ongoing contests, games and a host of other activities.

"The fall events will be connected under the banner of Fall Fair. That gives us Spring Fling, Summer Splash and Fall Fair. I'm thinking maybe Winter Festival, too. What do you think?"

He was spared an answer by the arrival of their food. Piper wasn't sure she could eat anything. Waiting for his response was like sitting on pins and needles.

"Smells great." He bowed his head for a moment. Piper followed suit, said a quick plea for help. Then Jason picked up his fork, then glanced at her, one eyebrow raised.

"Yes, it does." If he wanted to play it cool, she'd follow along.

"I like the ideas you've proposed," Jason said five minutes later. "There's a real diversity that will mean people want to keep coming back. But I'm somewhat concerned that you've contacted so many people without running this by me first."

"But you knew the basic idea," she said, stunned by his objection. "I showed it to you that first morning."

"This sounds much bigger than we first thought."

"That's the nature of tourism. It grows and changes." She sipped her water and tried to think of this from his perspective. "Some things that we try this year won't work the way we expect and we'll have to revise plans, even change midstream sometimes."

He nodded but she could tell he wasn't convinced.

"Is there something specific that bothers you?"

He lifted his head, stared at her. "Do I sound critical? I'm sorry. It's just that it's all a little overwhelming."

Piper nodded. "That's because I'm trying to get the ball rolling without the six to twelve months of prep work that should have gone before. We don't have time to lose if we want to see results this year." She fiddled with her napkin absently. "That is what you wanted, isn't it?"

He nodded. She continued.

"It's going to be hectic, but it's doable. Don't worry about details right now. It's more important to get the big picture in place. Once we've got things nailed down, once we know exactly what we can handle this year, who will sponsor what and how we'll handle whoever comes to town, that's the time to start getting the details in sync."

"But some of those details are going to affect what we can do this year. For instance, a hotel. We have a couple of motels, an RV park and a number of campsites, but we just can't handle the influx of people you're talking about without a major hotel developer."

"Yes, we do need more accommodation. But I doubt anyone can get a hotel built and operational before summer so we won't have to concentrate on that just yet."

"But that's the thing," he insisted, laying down his fork to accentuate his point. "Building a hotel takes time. I want to recruit a company who can provide the kind of amenities we're asking for quickly."

"Once Serenity Bay takes off, there will be any number of prospective developers knocking down your door. But most of them want to see some of the potential first. I'm sure you know that from your work at Expectations." One glance at his face had Piper wishing she hadn't said that. "There are lots of hotel builders, Jason." She heard a wariness creep into her own voice and paused. He didn't need to know her worst nightmare.

"There are. But I don't want just anyone. If we show them your plans, perhaps we can lure one here." Jason reached into his jacket pocket and pulled out a paper. "I drew up a list of those I think would do a good job for us."

Piper took the list out, read the first name and swallowed.

"I think we can cross off Wainwright," she murmured.

"But they are my first choice." Jason was clearly not pleased by her comment. "They've done lots of developing, they know how to make a project take off, they've got enough resources behind them to keep their commitments."

"They've also had trouble on several projects recently," she told him, remembering what Rowena had said about the London undertaking. "I don't want us to get tied up with a company that's dealing with serious legal issues elsewhere."

"Who are you suggesting, then?" he demanded, his gaze narrowed.

"I'm still checking into that. Ida mentioned a couple of local people who may be interested."

"Locals?" Jason's forehead furrowed. "I was hoping for someone with enough resources to make a big impact. I'm not sure a small local venture is—"

"It might be exactly what we want. The personal touch and all that. Besides," she reminded him, "we can hardly turn away their request for development. We don't want to be guilty of bias. The friendly, small-town aura a local would offer could be an asset, don't you think? Wainwright is known for their big, expensive hotels. Intimidating to some."

He didn't look convinced.

Piper changed the subject and by the time the meal was finished, Jason had completely forgotten about Wainwright—she hoped. She insisted on paying for his meal. After all, he'd listened to her ideas. She could tell Jason wasn't happy about that situation, either.

"I'll agree, as long as you let me buy next time."

"Agreed. Thank you." So there'd be a next time? Piper checked her watch. "I'd better head home. I've got a lot of notes to make. I don't want to forget anything we've discussed."

"You really get caught up in a project, don't you?" he asked, head inclined to one side.

"What can I say?" She grinned, spread her hands. "I love my job."

He walked her to *Shalimar,* waited while she stowed her briefcase. But the engine wouldn't start.

"That's odd. It was working well this morning."

"I didn't notice you sailing over," he murmured.

"You were probably still sleeping. I was in a bit of a hurry to get to work." Casting all your cares on Him for He cares for you. It was a promise of God's and yet she couldn't just leave her father to Him, could she? She had to stop Wainwright cold—before Baron got a foot in the door. She pushed the start button again. Nothing. "I wonder what's wrong."

"Can I take a look?"

"You don't mind?"

"Truthfully?" He waited for her nod, then climbed aboard. "I've wanted to check this baby out since the first day I saw her."

She unlocked the door to below, waved a hand, then chuckled at the speed he used to uncover and display the motor.

"I never would have guessed you were interested in her. Well?"

"When and where did you last fuel up?" he asked after

tinkering a few moments. He touched a spot of something, rubbed two fingers together.

"Yesterday. At home." She saw tiny bits of grit on his fingertips. "What's that?"

"If I was guessing, I'd say sugar. Or salt. Whichever, it's going to have to be cleaned out. Thoroughly. You can't go home in her tonight for sure."

"How would salt or sugar get in my gas?"

Jason held her gaze, his own open, thoughtful.

"Someone put it there."

"Someone…?"

He shrugged. "I doubt it happened here. Andy or someone would have noticed." He checked the lock on the boat's entry door to below. "Doesn't look like anyone's tampered with this. Maybe it's your tank at home."

"The whole tank?" She stared at him. "I just had it filled."

"Do you keep it locked up?"

"Of course. In fact, it's inside the boat shed. You have to have a key to get inside. Besides, I did cross the bay this morning. Could I have done that if it had been in the tank from Cathcart House?"

"No," he admitted with a frown.

Piper didn't like where this was leading. First someone had been in the house. Now her fuel had been sabotaged. She'd have to call the police again.

"Do you want me to run you home?" Jason closed up the motor and replaced the door, sealing it from the rest of the boat. "It's no problem."

"That's kind of you. But I have my car. I'll drive." She dug through her bag for her car keys. "Would you be able to fix the motor, maybe tomorrow? I've really begun to enjoy those trips across the water."

"Sure." He held out his hand for her to grasp, waited till

she'd stepped on the dock, then accepted the key for the boat after she'd locked up. "I'll get at it tomorrow morning."

"Thanks." His hand still held hers and Piper decided she liked it. Part of her wanted to keep her hand in his but the other part told her to act like a businesswoman. So she drew her fingers away. "Let me know when it's ready."

"I will." Jason's gaze held hers. An odd light glinted in his blue-grey eyes. "Drive carefully," he murmured.

"Uh-huh." Feeling utterly self-conscious, Piper walked across the lot to her car, unlocked it and stepped inside. She adjusted the rearview mirror, saw Jason had remained where she'd left him.

Calling herself a fool, she shifted into First and pulled away, but couldn't help fluttering her fingers in a last wave. Jason remained where he was.

Watching.

Piper drove the switchback road as twilight fell on the greening hills. As she gained the last crest, a small deer bobbed out from the bushes forcing her to slam on the brakes. Startled and slightly unsettled, she paused to draw a deep breath and settle her nerves before moving on.

Below her, Cathcart House lay nestled into the crook of the hill. The yard lights switched on as she watched, illuminating the budding rose garden her grandmother had coaxed to beauty each summer. Piper was ready to employ the lessons she'd learned to woo the biggest blooms from those bushes.

Her hand touched the gearshift just as Piper glimpsed a shadow by the hot tub move. Her breath caught in her throat as the figure lifted the lid, dumped something inside, then set the lid back in place. A moment later the intruder slipped into the darkened woods leaving no trace of a visit.

Call the police? Or check out the tub first? If it was nothing, just a nosy neighbor, she'd rather find that out for herself.

But a neighbour would have asked to use the tub first.

Piper sat in her car trying to imagine who would sneak into her yard. It had to be the kids from Lookout Point.

She put the car in gear and slowly glided down the hill.

"I'm an idiot, God. It's gotten so I suspect everyone. I want to get over that but with Dad—it's hard. Please help me."

She pulled into the yard. The place looked the same as she'd left it this morning.

Piper unlocked the door, carried her things inside, then moved to the deck. With a flick of a switch the entire area was illuminated.

No one.

"I need to soak in that tub and do some serious praying," she muttered.

She lifted the cover of the tub to turn on the jets and immediately stepped backward as a pungent odor filled the air.

Just then she heard a rustle behind her.

"You can come out now, Dad. And you can quit playing these silly games. It doesn't matter what you do. I'm not leaving Serenity Bay."

Piper waited for Baron to slip out from the shadows. Nothing could have prepared her for the sight of Jason.

Chapter Five

"What are you doing here?" Piper asked, her voice ragged, harsh-sounding in the quiet of the forest surrounding them. The tremble of her voice bothered him.

"After you left, I spotted some unusual lights flashing over here. At first I was going to ignore them, but then I thought about the salt in your tank and decided to check things out. Didn't you hear my boat?"

"No. I didn't hear anything." She sounded odd—confused as she glanced around as if searching for something—or someone.

"What happened?" He took her arm, guided her toward a chair and when she was seated, squatted in front of her. "What's wrong?"

"What makes you think something's wrong?"

He raised an eyebrow, glanced at her fingers clenching the side of the chair. "Call me intuitive?"

She made a face, then explained about the shadow and the excess chlorine. He noticed the strong odor as well.

"If you breathe in too much of the fumes they can do damage," she whispered. "Not to mention the effect on the skin."

He watched as she opened the small door of a niche,

pulled out a plastic box which held various chemical bottles. She chose a pack of test strips, threw open the lid and when the cloud of steam disappeared, dipped one strip into the water.

Then she compared the dark navy square with the normal shade on the bottle.

"Way too much."

He noted absently how the tub seemed to fit into the deck, as if it had been built when the original house had been erected, though given the age of the house, that wasn't likely. "Do you keep the chlorine out here?"

She shook her head. "Never."

"So they brought their own. Nice of them to think of it since they're using your tub." In Jason's opinion, Piper was too pale. "I'm going to call Bud Neely, ask him to take a look."

"There's nothing the police chief can do." She put the test strips into the box, returned the kit to its storage place.

"You don't know that." Something about her body language, the way she looked at him, pricked his curiosity. "Do you?"

He could hardly believe what he saw register on her face.

"You saw someone—a prowler's been out here before?"

"Yes. A couple of times, I think."

"When?" He thought a minute. "The night I brought you home?" Every hair on his arms stood up. "You mentioned seeing a shadow."

"Yes. I've seen something several times. But it may not be as bad as it sounds. I think my visitors have something to do with Lookout Point," she told him. "There are always kids going up there to meet each other. Even when I was a teen it was a popular place. I'm sure those were the lights you saw."

"Maybe. But, Piper, this isn't just a prank. It's danger-ous. If you hadn't noticed—" He stopped, hating to fin-ish the thought.

"Not necessarily dangerous," she amended. "Chlorine is one thing you smell as soon as you open the hot tub lid. After you add it, you're supposed to leave the tub open to circulate and off-gas. Since the lid was closed immedi-ately, the smell was kept inside. I'm sure I noticed some-thing wasn't right as soon as I lifted the lid."

She touched a button on the control panel that soon had the jets whirring. Clouds of steam rose upward. Along with them, the odor of chlorine dissipated into the night air.

"I'm calling Bud anyway. If he can't come out tonight, he or someone from the department can make a trip tomor-row and check things out." Jason frowned as he scanned the woods, saw the flicker of lights some distance away. "I don't think it's advisable to have Lookout Point open after dark. The terrain's rugged up here."

"There's hardly a reason to have a Lookout Point if you close it after dark," she murmured. "The lure of the place is the darkness. And the scenery, of course."

"What do you mean?"

"Teenagers. Moonlight. You can't have forgotten. You're not *that* old!" Piper smiled at him, her wide mouth tilted in a teasing grin.

Jason found himself blushing as he wondered what it would be like to go to Lookout Point with Piper. "Watch it," his brain warned.

"Thank you for your concern," she said, her voice back to normal. "You came a long way just to make sure. That warrants a reward."

"What did you have in mind?" he asked, his brain still busy with thoughts of moonlight and Piper Langley.

"I have some apple pie, if you're interested. And I could make some tea."

"You don't have to." Jason stopped when she cast a look behind her at the call of an owl. She was still nervous. "But I'd love some pie."

"Great. Come on inside." She led the way into the house, turning on lights as she went. "Make yourself comfortable."

After that first interview, before she'd moved here, whenever he'd thought of Piper, Jason envisioned chrome, glass and glittering stainless steel. Cathcart House was as far from that as the prairies were from Serenity Bay.

Big, comfy chairs and couches lay scattered around a room with vistas on three sides, hidden now by the night. Jason sat down in a leather recliner placed near a fireplace and found it exceedingly comfortable.

"I love this chair," he told her.

"So did my grandfather. Some of the chintz Gran favored went to the city with them and was later sold off, but that chair had to stay here."

"You said you stayed with them?" he asked, hoping his curiosity wouldn't show too much.

"After my mother died. I came here mostly for summers and Christmas. I went to a boarding school the rest of the time."

That tiny bit of tension in her voice only added to the questions he had about her past, but before he could ask more she was carrying in a big, brown teapot and two chunky mugs to match.

"Can I help?"

"The pie is on the counter. Help yourself."

He did, then returned to his seat. Once she'd poured the tea he sat back and savored the flavors of cinnamon and cloves he tasted, watching Piper light a fire.

"Did you bake this? It's great."

"Nope. Sorry. I went to a bake sale the art guild was having. I wanted to buy something to support them. The pie looked good so I chose it." She sipped her tea, watching him eat.

"I missed a bake sale?" He frowned. "I never miss bake sales. It's my one rule."

"Wow, you're lucky if you have only one." She giggled at his dismay. "I think I heard Ida say something about you holding a boating class that day. Don't feel bad. You can take the rest of it home if you like. I'm not much of a pie eater." Piper leaned back in the wing chair, her face lit by the flickering fire. "I was thinking about the hotel as I drove home. I have a couple of ideas floating around."

"Shoot."

Her head jerked up, her eyes widened. "Excuse me?"

"Go ahead. Tell me what you're thinking."

The dark curls bobbed back and forth as she shook her head. "I don't know if I can."

"Why not?" Jason put his empty plate on the coffee table, picked up his mug. "Is it some kind of secret?"

"No, of course not." Piper's attention was on the fire as she spoke. Her words emerged quiet, hesitant. "It's just… my brain doesn't work the way you might expect. I don't have a hard-and-fast schedule or plan. Nothing is concrete. For now they're just ideas."

"So?" Something was going on behind those dark eyes, something that made him curious and set a peculiar little nerve to twitching at the back of his neck. As if she was hiding something. "Tell me the ideas."

"It's not quite that easy, Jason." She raked a hand through her curls, tousling them even more. "They're more like nebulous thoughts, glimmers, if you will. I have to let them mull for a while. I ask myself a question, poke around. Things start to gel and then I can really plough ahead. Do you understand?"

He didn't. Not really. But he tried to sound supportive. "Why don't you tell me about your glimmers? Maybe we can brainstorm together."

Jason watched her closely, saw tinges of red dot her cheeks. He understood her embarrassment; the scoffing of some council members when he'd first presented his plan for the Bay still rankled.

"I'm not going to laugh," he promised.

Piper studied him as if assessing his truthfulness. After a moment she let out a pent-up breath and began speaking.

"This is purely brainstorming," she warned.

"I know."

"Serenity Bay is such a perfect name for this place," she murmured. "I mean, think about it. That word conjures up peace, relaxation, no worries—all the things you want a vacation spot to be. But it has to work for everybody. Moms, dads, kids, seniors, young people, rich, not so rich."

"Yes," he agreed, liking what he'd heard so far. Where was this going?

"The beach will take care of a lot of the kids' entertainment. Then, of course, there's the miniature golf course and I expect other venues will pop up as time passes."

"But." He knew he heard it in there somewhere.

"But I got dreaming about a real golf course. Is it feasible? Could the town chip in enough land or perks, something that would make it attractive for a developer to put in his hotel, include a pool, a couple of conference rooms and maybe nine holes of golf?"

Jason stared. He opened his mouth but she held up a hand when he would have spoken. Her smile held a hint of self-mockery.

"In the beginning I thought, not too luxe. But if a businessman or woman brought their family along, while attending a training seminar in the hotel's conference rooms—wouldn't having some nearby links make sense? You know—meet for a round of golf and not feel guilty because the rest of the family are enjoying their own activities. Think about Banff. That's their draw. The scenery, something for everybody. We have that right here."

"Wow!" He couldn't help admiring her ideas.

"I know you think it's too big, nothing like you were envisioning for a start. And I agree. It's just one of those ideas that's been floating around. Still, thinking ahead could save us problems down the road, if we plan carefully."

He liked the way she included him, as if they were partners in this venture.

"Wainwright Hotels could certainly offer all of that," he murmured, assessing her reaction.

Piper's head jerked the tiniest bit. She turned to look at him but her face gave nothing away.

"They could. But right now I doubt they're in a position to commit to that much development in an untried area. And they have labor problems." She held out a piece torn from a newspaper detailing the issues. "Look at this. It's unlikely we'd command their focus at the moment. I'd prefer to look into other options."

"You keep saying that. Who are these 'other options'?" he asked. He scanned the report, recognized the facts as those he'd already researched. He set it down, feeling that she was still holding something back.

Then something clicked.

"Piper, is there something you haven't told me? Some specific reason you don't want to work with Wainwright?"

She'd been peering at a notepad on the table but now she looked at him directly and blinked. "A reason?"

"Yes." He felt slightly foolish saying this but if there

was a chance… "Have you had some problem working with their team? Because—"

She shook her head, her curls bouncing wildly. "I've already told you my reasons. I don't think Wainwright is a good fit for Serenity Bay."

"Why?"

Piper fixed him with a hard look.

"This will probably sound sentimental and rather silly but this place was a haven for me. I found so much joy in Serenity Bay that I'm not sure I would have found elsewhere. I'd like to think I was passing it on." She tilted her head. "I feel like I've been given a kind of trust to help develop the Bay. That carries a certain responsibility. I don't want to ruin this beauty by allowing commercialism to overtake what God made. Do you understand?"

He nodded, feeling a hint of admiration.

"I understand very well. I think that's one of the reasons I tried so hard to interest you in the job. It's a goal we share." He kept his focus on her. "I've noticed that whatever you do, a certain flair, a special touch or attention to detail shines through. I think that's what makes each of your projects stand out from the others. You really care about the result. It's not just about money for you."

"No, it isn't. I think the same is true for you."

He nodded.

Their eyes met and held. A tiny flicker of current ran between them. Jason watched her moisten her lips, saw the way the fire caught the red undertones in her dark hair. Inside, a tiny ivy of interest sent down another root of interest and sprouted.

Piper could be trusted to help him accomplish this dream. Couldn't she?

She tried to hide her yawn but couldn't quite bring it off. Jason rose, carried his cup and plate to the sink.

"I'll go. You've got to be tired after such a long day."

"Thank you for coming to check up on me." She walked him to the door. "It wasn't necessary, but I do appreciate it."

They stepped outside into a spring fairyland. Her grandmother's lights twinkled in a misty breeze from the bay.

"I should have noticed the time sooner. I don't want you to get lost in the fog." She walked with him down to the jetty, pausing while he untied his boat. "Will you phone me when you get home so I don't worry that you're lost out there somewhere?"

Surprise ran through him. It had been a long time since anyone cared enough to ensure he got home safely.

"I'll call," he promised softly. Jason reached for her hand, held it lightly. "Thank you for an interesting evening. Whenever I talk to you I always come away thinking of more possibilities for the Bay."

"That's why you hired me, isn't it?" She chuckled, using the cover of her laughter to draw her hand away.

He didn't miss her reticence, but he didn't comment on it, either. Instead he climbed into his boat, started the engine and waved.

"I enjoyed the pie, too," he called. "Good night."

As he headed across the bay, Jason glanced back once. A single light illuminated Piper still standing at the end of the dock, facing into the breeze.

Then she quickly moved uphill and soon disappeared from sight. He revved the engine and headed home.

"As promised, I'm phoning," he told her later, relishing the low timber of her voice. "Home safe and sound."

"I'm glad."

"You're all right?" he asked. "No more visitors?"

"Everything's fine," she told him. "Good night."

But even after he'd hung up, after he'd talked to the police, after the lights were out and he was staring out his window over the water, Jason couldn't shake the niggling worry that everything was not fine.

It was more obvious than ever that Piper didn't want Wainwright Inc. involved with Serenity Bay and despite her protestations, he still didn't understand why.

"You're sure about this?" Piper held the phone pressed against her ear, desperate to hear the reassurance she needed. Even the May sun beaming through the window couldn't chase away her worries.

"As far as I've been able to ascertain, there are no concrete plans within the company to push ahead on Serenity Bay. Everything's been tabled."

"I see." Though she was relieved to hear it, questions bubbled in her mind. "Why tabled?"

"Mid-April, Baron ordered a halt on all projects until the problems in London can be investigated and settled. He flew over a week ago to do his usual hands-on checkup. He doesn't feel the company is sending the right image and you know how obsessive he is about Wainwright Inc. being the top in its field."

"Believe me, I know." Probably more than anyone realized. "You're sure he's still there?"

"Yes, of course. I've been sending my reports there every day. I'm still his personal secretary, Piper."

"And a very good one. Thank you for letting me know, Tina. I've been wondering and your call is very timely."

"Not a problem. How are you, Piper?"

A shot of warm affection went straight to her heart. Tina had always been like a surrogate mom to her, remembering her birthday, cheering her on. Piper often wondered if Baron knew how much his secretary had done for her.

"I'm fine, Tina. Thrilled to be back on the Bay. Working hard. In fact, our first big promo is scheduled for to-morrow. We're calling it a Spring Fling. We hope to get some interest from returning cottagers and those who are looking for a summer place."

"I'm glad. I just wish your grandparents could be there to witness your success."

"Me, too." The sting of loss eased a little each time she pulled out another memory, reassuring her that she'd done the right thing in coming back.

Jason appeared in the doorway.

"I've got to go, Tina," she said softly. "Thanks so much for everything. I appreciate it more than you know."

"You take care of yourself. And come visit soon. You can't keep hiding from him forever."

"I know. Bye." Piper hung up with a mixture of plea-sure that Tina hadn't forgotten her, and sadness that she wouldn't be able to visit anytime soon. She wouldn't walk through the doors of Wainwright Inc. again. Not as long as this knot of anger at her father still festered inside.

Let Baron come apologize to her. She was the one who'd been wronged. *Sorry, God, but I just can't forgive him. Not yet. Maybe not ever unless you show me how.*

"You look upset. Is it because of the forecast?"

She swiveled in her chair, glancing out the window. The sun was gone. Dark, foreboding clouds were replac-ing the glorious blue.

"What's wrong with the forecast?" she asked, frown-ing at him.

"I just heard on the radio. We've got a blast of arctic air coming down. Snow tonight and tomorrow. About two inches."

"Oh, no!" Piper groaned. "We can't have snow for Spring Fling."

"Not my first choice, I agree. But guess what? We are." He looked remarkably unruffled.

"You aren't bothered?"

Jason shrugged. "We've done the best we can. I've certainly spent a lot of hours praying. But I'm not in charge of the weather. If God thinks we need snow, I guess we need snow. There's nothing I can do to stop it, and I have to trust that He knows what He's doing."

"You're right. I suppose there isn't. It's just that we've spent so much time organizing everything to the nth degree. The weather's been fantastic. Now snow? What are we going to do?"

"We're going to handle this. The barbecue will work just as well in the rink. We can get tables set up there."

"Probably the best place for the kids' games, too." She caught his spirit and began writing notes to herself. "The sailing regatta?"

"Let's just wait and see what happens, I guess."

"Agreed. The artists are all showing indoors so there's no problem there. But I was hoping to showcase the potential of the area and snow was not in my plans." Piper tapped her pencil against her cheek, thinking. "We'll have to hold some events outside, otherwise we lose our impact. What's so funny?"

Jason's chuckles grew louder; his whole body shook with laughter.

"Serenity Bay—a place for all seasons," he sputtered, holding up the logo and artwork they'd approved to go on all the town correspondence and promo material. "Bet you didn't know how appropriate that slogan was going to be."

"Believe me, I had no idea," she grumbled, irritated by his easygoing outlook on this near disaster.

He laughed harder.

"You're not helping, you know." The ideas began to

whirl fast and furiously. She scribbled them down with little regard for neatness. *If you wanted to offer your assistance, Lord, we might make this work.*

"Stop laughing!" she hissed as Jason burst into another chuckle.

"Sorry. I'll try to control myself." But the grin remained firmly locked in place.

"If our Spring Fling is going to happen, I've got work to do." Piper grabbed the phone and started dialing.

"Me, too. I'll talk to you later." Jason took a note from Ida, grimacing. "This health inspector is getting far too chatty. Can't you block his calls?"

"No," Ida snapped as they left the room.

Piper concentrated on the task ahead of her. By the time Jason reappeared she had revised the schedule to accommodate any conditions the weatherman tossed their way.

"That forecast is not getting me down, you know. We'll have a snowman-building contest if we have to," she told him, leaning back in her chair and rubbing her neck to ease the knot of tension. "Whatever it takes, we'll make it work."

"Snow's the least of our problems." He leaned against the door frame, shoulders slumped in a weary pose.

"What now?"

"The campground. They're full with reservations. Some people have even begun to arrive."

"And that's a problem?"

"It will be. Their showers and bathrooms are operational only for summer. Thanks to the chill last night, the pipes froze and some burst. So far the units that have arrived are self-contained, but unless they all are, there won't be facilities for our visitors. Public health will shut the place down."

Piper winced, unable to believe that all their work would go for nothing.

"That's not the worst of it. The tenting area is completely flooded. Nobody can stay there no matter what their equipment. I've just gotten a revised forecast and more snow is due. I think we're going to have to call this off, Piper. I'm sorry."

Defeat. It washed over her in waves of disappointment and the realization that a major portion of her budget would be wiped out. For nothing.

What a waste.

"There's nothing we can do?"

"Short of tearing the place down and rebuilding it tonight, no. We'll have to cancel."

"Call me an eavesdropper if you want." Ida stomped into the room, her face more dour-looking than usual. "I can't believe you two are just going to give up."

"It's not our first choice, Ida. Piper's been on the phone all afternoon trying to work something out."

A river of warmth spread through Piper at Jason's quick defense and sturdy support. His style of management was as far from her father's taciturn orders as it could get.

"We can't manufacture bathrooms for this many people overnight, Ida," Piper murmured.

"Maybe you can't. But you've both ignored the biggest resource Serenity Bay has."

"We have?" Piper blinked, looking to Jason for answers. He shrugged.

"Serenity Bay was started by people who accepted the hardships of this place along with the beauty. People who didn't give up, didn't call it quits when the going got tough. The folks around here have hung on for a long time, hoping something would help this place." Her chin jutted out. "Jason came with his ideas and some of us caught a glimmer of hope that maybe the Bay could be a better place. Then you came along."

Piper shifted under the beady-eyed scrutiny. "Uh…"

"You put ideas in our heads. The painters and potters, the quilters and silversmiths, the glass artists—all of them, they thought maybe it wasn't too late for this place. That maybe they could live and work here, bring people in instead of chasing after a sale." Ida's bony finger stabbed the air between her and Piper's face. "We started to think big because of you."

Piper didn't know what to say.

"Do you know how many cottages were up for sale when you came? Do you know how many listings have been pulled since you got here?" Ida clamped her hands on her thin hips and glared at them both. "We had more than a hundred places for sale. That's down to less than thirty since the buzz about this place got out. People were just starting to think it wasn't quite time to write off the Bay. You quit now and you'll kill whatever morale there is in this place."

"I don't want to cancel, Ida. But what can we do?"

"Call a meeting," the woman declared, her eyes blazing. "Get the townsfolk together and decide what you're going to do. Find out their solutions. Give them a chance to be part of the new Serenity Bay."

As Piper watched the small, vibrant woman, her brain began to simmer with new ideas.

"Why not?" she asked Jason. "What have we got to lose?"

"It's their town," he agreed after a moment's pause. "It should be their decision."

They both turned to Ida.

"Where do we start?"

"I've got phone numbers here." She split the pages

among the three of them. "We'll call them all, tell them there's an emergency town-hall meeting tonight at seven o'clock. Tell them it's urgent they be there. If they fuss at you, mention canceling your Spring Fling."

Piper nodded, scanned the list of names. But her mind was busy with something else.

"Let's get to work," Jason said.

Before either of them could leave, Piper blurted out her idea, the receiver still clasped in her fingers.

"Wait!" They turned to stare at her. "You do know what could solve the biggest part of our tenting problem, don't you?"

Ida frowned; Jason looked confused.

"Wingate Manor."

Both faces registered skepticism.

"Doesn't open till late May, three or more weeks from now," Jason reminded.

"But someone has been getting the place ready so I know they're around." Piper glanced from one to the other, wishing they could envision what she did. "The brothers have been doing repairs for weeks now. Someone told me about their new catering plans. I tried to get an appointment to speak with the Wingates last week. When they didn't return my call, I drove out there. Have you seen the place lately?"

Jason shook his head.

"They've built a great canopied area out in the back that I understand will be used for some kind of summer theater. It's high and dry," she said quietly, watching their faces. "Perfect for camping."

"Camping? At Wingate?" Jason didn't look impressed.

But Ida caught on. One finger tapped against her bottom lip. "Wingate Manor does have a surplus of bathrooms," she mused. "The old house was used as a training lodge during the war."

"How do you know that?" Jason demanded.

"I know a lot of things you don't," Ida told him pertly. "I've been doing a little research for a local history book I'm working on. Also, Hank and Henry Wingate have kept the ground floor bathrooms updated. Do you know why?"

"No." Jason watched her, waiting.

"Because they've got their eyes on building their business. All those fairy lights in the summer aren't just pretty. Folks wander the grounds, look at Henry's lily ponds while they wait for their reservation. They don't mind waiting when there's so much to see. And those who have already enjoyed a meal often amble around afterward to take a look at the Wingate gardens—though they're not up to much yet."

"My friend Rowena's landscaping company had a call about working on a project there," Piper murmured.

"All part of the plan." Ida looked smug. "Most everybody who goes to Wingate ends up paying to dip something into that chocolate fountain they put out on the patio. Some folks even go to Wingate specially for the high-priced desserts."

Piper's brain began to percolate.

"Not that I'm saying it's a good thing, you understand." Ida scowled. "The prices those two charge, they should have a full orchestra and black-tux waiters to serenade everybody while they throw away their money."

"Smart men! The ground-level bathrooms would make it easy for people to stay on the property without bothering the restaurant clientele. Theater groups with facilities nearby would draw even more patrons." Piper looked at Jason, who was watching Ida.

"If people come just for the desserts, they don't have to

dress up for dinner so the chocolate fountain on the patio makes perfect sense." Jason nodded. "Very clever."

"And good for us if we can get them to let us use those bathrooms," Piper inserted. "Do you think the Wingate brothers will come to the meeting? I mean, they've been fairly reclusive. I'd hoped to include their place in our plans for the town but I'm not having a lot of success. Maybe if they came—" Piper glanced from Jason's sly smile to Ida's scowling countenance. "What?"

"They'll come—if Ida asks them."

"Oh?" She waited for a clue that would explain the flush of color on Ida's pinched cheeks. "Why?"

"The brothers want her rib recipe. Badly." Jason grinned when Ida smacked him on the arm. "Don't pretend it isn't true, Ida. Put them on your list to call. I'm not getting chewed out again by Hank for not repaving the road to Wingate Manor. He refuses to understand that we haven't got the funds right now."

"That's a good idea. I certainly don't think I should call, since I've never actually met them," Piper added.

"Don't think I don't know you two are in cahoots." Ida glared at them both then turned on her heel. "Fine. I'll call them. You two—start phoning," she ordered before stomping from the room.

Jason grinned. "You heard the woman," he said. "Let's get busy. Wouldn't hurt to pray while you're at it."

"I've been praying since you first mentioned snow," she told him dryly. *For all the good my prayers do. God isn't talking to me.* And she knew why. *Forgive me.* She saw him glance at her lists.

"Keep me posted," he added before leaving.

There it was again. *Keep me posted. Let me know. I'd like an update.* That constant reminder that he was always watching, always monitoring her every move irritated her.

It felt as if he didn't trust her. And that always brought to mind her father. Maybe Jason was more like Baron than she'd realized.

She was going to have to talk to him about that. Later.

Piper picked up the list Ida had laid on her desk, recognizing none of the names. She'd work from the top down and hope everybody was home. But not yet.

She set the list aside and pulled out the envelope she'd found by the deck on the far side of the hot tub the morning after the chlorine incident. So far she hadn't told anyone about this.

She pulled out the contents and unfolded them. The paper was legal size, a photocopy of detailed plans that were so small she'd needed a magnifying glass to identify the markings. What she saw made her catch her breath.

The plans bore the company stamp of Wainwright Inc. and were drawings of a hotel situated on the banks of Serenity Bay. A big, imposing edifice that would utterly block the view of anything in the immediate area.

Had her father taken a detour before going to London? Stopped by Cathcart House?

But that didn't make sense. Baron wouldn't bother to add chlorine to her hot tub, would he? He'd simply issue an edict and expect her to obey. If he bothered to speak to her at all.

Piper folded the paper, returned it to the envelope and tucked it under her organizer.

She was going to figure out what he was up to. That meant calling Tina again. And then she'd figure out how to stop her father from taking over *her* project.

No way was Baron going to horn in on Serenity Bay and spoil it like he had the other parts of her life.

Jason trusted her to find the best hotel developer. That's what she intended to do.

Wainwright Inc. wasn't even on the list.

Chapter Six

"Order. Let's come to order, please."

Jason rapped his gavel on a table, waiting for the voices to die down.

"So essentially what we're telling you is that unless we can come up with some way to look after the folks who'll show up here for our Spring Fling, we'll have to cancel the whole works. Wally's RV site just can't handle it all."

A grumbling murmur filtered through the room.

"Why didn't you think this through before you ran all those expensive ads?" someone hollered. More negative comments followed.

Jason needed to do something before this got out of hand. But he wasn't sure what. In a way they were right. They hadn't planned this out enough. But who could have expected such a huge response? Or snow?

After a moment Ida stood up.

"Order, please." Jason tapped his gavel again. "Let's be civilized about this. We have a question from the floor."

The furor died down once the group realized Ida was standing.

"Just how many people are we talking about?" she asked.

Jason could have kissed her. Ida knew the answer, of course. They'd strategized the logistics of this thing for an hour before the meeting. Obviously she hoped that getting the problem on the table would garner some fresh ideas.

"Piper, can you give us the facts and figures?"

She rose gracefully, checked the sheet in front of her then began to explain the categories of housing needed.

"At the moment we have over a hundred invitations on hold. If we're going to decline these people we need to let them know right away so they can make alternative plans."

"Don't know why we have to send away anyone who wants to see what this place has to offer," someone from the crowd said.

"Can you stand, please?" Jason asked, stretching to see the owner of that soft-spoken voice. "Ah, Henry Wingate. What are your thoughts on this?"

"My thoughts are that I've worked my fanny off for too many years trying to get folks to come to this town to see what we have to offer. Now they're on their way and we're talking about turning them away?" He shook his gray head. "How dumb is that?"

"Do you have a suggestion?" Piper asked.

"My suggestion is we welcome anyone who wants to come to Serenity Bay, just like we'd welcome our own family. Carter, you built that guesthouse of yours three years ago. Anybody ever use it?"

"Yeah, me."

The entire room burst into guffaws. Carter's proclivity for snoring, and his wife's objections, were well known all over the Bay.

"Okay, but for this weekend you rent it out. Boris, that RV of yours had been sitting in your driveway empty ever since you came back from California. It'd take care of a family for a few days. You could charge 'em if you wanted."

"Yeah, and what if they wreck it?" Boris objected.

"They want a place to sleep at night, not a party room. Keep it parked in your own yard, plug it in to your own power. You can keep your eye on it that way." Henry's quick response surprised Jason. So did the rash of responses that followed.

"I've got a couple of spare rooms at my place. I could put some of these people up. Be kind of nice to have the house full again."

"The Masons left me the key for their place. I'm sure they wouldn't mind renting it for a few days."

"I can put up some people."

Jason watched Ida scribbling down names with numbers beside them, trying to make a list. More than once she leaned over to speak to Piper, who was making her own notes.

"Okay, if that's what you want to do, we'll have Ida coordinate things. Each of you come up here after the meeting and tell her how many you can take and how much you want to charge."

"I don't want anything," Boris blustered. "This town needs a boost. If having somebody stay in my RV brings them here, I'll be glad to do it."

"He's right. This is our town. We've always pitched in to help each other out. Having all these folks show up is going to bring us business. Isn't that what we all want?"

"Long as we can make room, we won't turn anyone away." Boris grinned at Henry. "What's Wingate Manor gonna do to pitch in?"

Henry gulped, then looked at Jason. "Whatever we can," he said clearly.

Here was their opportunity. Jason glanced at Piper and caught her nod.

"We need campsites, Henry. With washrooms." He held the other man's gaze. "I understand Wingate Manor could help us out with that."

"I…guess." Fast-talking Henry wasn't quite so quick now.

"Talk to Ida about specifics." Jason scanned the room. "Anyone else have something to say?"

More people chimed in, suggesting even more ways of enhancing the town to receive their visitors with open arms.

Half an hour later they were done.

"People, you are awesome," Jason told them, meaning every word. "I can't thank you enough for pitching in this way. We appreciate all of your ideas and we'll promise to do our best to get them going. Maybe not this weekend but before the summer's out. Now we're going to need volunteers to assist Ida. If you can help, in any way at all, I want you to come up here and sign the sheets Ida's got laid out on the table. Everybody's going to have to pull together if we're going to carry this off."

He offered a few reminders, then adjourned the meeting. Two hours later the last of the townspeople had left. Piper was smiling, but she still couldn't believe what she'd just experienced.

"That was fantastic," she whispered.

"It was," he agreed with a grin. "Don't look so surprised. You prayed, didn't you?"

"Yes, I did."

"Didn't you expect God to answer?" He could see by her face that she hadn't expected what they'd seen. "Sometimes He goes above and beyond what we expect."

"Way above." She held up her folder. "I've only done a

rough count, but so far it looks like we've got fifty spaces more than we need. That's quite incredible considering our position this afternoon."

"That's God for you. Never a problem too big." He saw something dark flash in her eyes, and wondered at it. "Is something wrong?"

"No, it's just—" She paused, said good-night to Ida and waited until they were alone. "Can I speak to you about something?"

"Sure." He hooked a chair with his foot, pulled it close enough then sat down. "What's the matter?"

"Nothing." She bit her lip, blinking at him as if she expected him to yell at her. "No, that isn't true." She drew in a breath, then let it out. "Tell me, have I done something wrong?"

"I don't know. Have you?" He knew immediately that his teasing was misplaced. Piper was very serious. "Why don't you just tell me what's on your mind?"

She studied him, her brown eyes dark, unyielding. Finally she spoke.

"I feel like you're constantly looking over my shoulder, checking up on me," she told him baldly. "Every time I pursue an idea or have a meeting you ask me to speak to you about it."

"What's wrong with that?" He bristled.

"I feel like I'm back in high school! You don't have to keep telling me to consult you, Jason. I have no intention of excluding you from any part of this project. But I need some space to do the job you hired me for." Her face paled slightly as her fingers clutched the black folder she held. "It's unnecessary for me to come running to you every time I speak to someone or attend a meeting and I don't think you should expect that."

"You're mad because I asked Ida to include me in your next meeting with Peter," he guessed.

"No! I'm not mad," she grated. "I just don't see the reason for your constant hovering. It's starting to feel like you expect me to cheat the town, to go behind your back or deliberately evade the truth. I thought that by now you'd know that isn't how I work."

"You haven't really talked much about your ideas beyond Spring Fling," he reminded, watching her closely.

"No, I haven't." She wasn't backing down.

"Why?"

Piper glared at him and huffed out a sigh.

"Because they're not ready. That's not how I work. I've told you this before. I have to mull things over, get a feel for how I want things to work, toss around ideas that will lead to the goal, sound out people to see if they think something is plausible."

"What people?" he asked quietly.

"Friends, former coworkers, people who are in the same business or who understand the process."

"Why not sound them out with me?"

He could see the anger build. She set both feet firmly on the ground.

"No offense, but this isn't your area of expertise, Jason. You haven't done this before so you have no experience to draw on. The people I talk to have seen what's been done. They've even had some flops themselves and can help me hone my ideas so I don't make the same mistakes."

"Isn't that dangerous?"

"Excuse me?" She stared at him, eyes wide in surprise. "Dangerous? What are you talking about?"

"What if some of these colleagues, some of these friends—what if they take your ideas and run with them?" He felt a little funny, saying it out loud like that. But Jason was determined that Serenity Bay was going to be the model, not the copycat.

"Are you serious?" she asked, then jerked her head in a nod. "Yes, I can see that you are." She sank down on one of the hard plywood chairs, studying him, her whole body an expression of dismay.

"It's a possibility. One I don't want to deal with after we've invested a lot of time, effort and especially money into a promotional campaign for the Bay. I don't want someone to make us look like the stepchild of a bigger, brighter plan."

"If that wasn't funny, I'd be really angry," she told him softly.

"Go ahead, laugh at me. But the point is valid."

"No, Jason, it isn't." Her back straightened, and she set the folder down on the table, folding her hands in her lap.

He tilted his head, waiting for an explanation.

"This is what you don't understand. First of all, if I had gotten as far as a full-scale campaign, you can rest assured that nobody outside of a select few, you included, would know the particulars. But it's a bit too early for that."

He glanced at the notes he'd scrawled on a yellow tablet in his hands. "I thought that's what we've been doing for the past several weeks."

"No. At the moment we're trying to put on a few events, get a feel for what the area can handle, what goes over well, what doesn't. We're figuring out our market. All of that is going to impact our later decisions."

"And if someone copies us?"

She shrugged. "So what? By then we'll be on to something else. I've never been short on ideas, but if I were, I'm sure time and some deep thinking could generate new thoughts. Look how the problem with the tent sites and campers got solved tonight."

He nodded. "Yes, but—"

"No buts," she interrupted, stemming his words with a shake of her head. "I have to know that you trust me, that we're in this together, or I'm out of here. I will not work under a microscope, constantly being checked. You're going to have to believe that I'm looking out for the best interests of Serenity Bay. If you have a question, fine. I'll answer whatever you need. But I'm wasting time, your time and mine, by constantly reporting every time I take a baby step."

"I didn't mean to make you feel as though I don't trust you," he apologized honestly, wishing he'd been more careful to stem his questions. "I'm very sorry that my concerns came across as suspicions. It wasn't my intent."

"I know." She smiled. "I understand that this project has been your baby for a while and you're overprotective. I get that. But you have to back off now and let me do my job so that you can get on with yours."

"I do want to be kept abreast of what's happening," he said and then realized he'd just repeated the words that had irked her in the first place. "From time to time."

His word adjustment was not lost on Piper, who smiled again. But her eyes held no mirth as she assessed him.

"Of course. When I have something new or something concrete, I'll let you know. I promise. My reputation is riding on the success of Serenity Bay, too, Jason. I'm not about to jeopardize that by trying to pull some kind of a fast one."

"No. That would be foolish," he agreed. He rose, motioning toward the door. "I guess we'd better get out of here. It's getting late."

"Yes. By the way, I'll be going out of town tomorrow. I've got a meeting." She picked up her folder, walking with him to the door.

Jason couldn't help wondering where she was going. Nobody had said a word to him, including Ida, who was usually bursting to talk about Piper. Seemed curious that she'd plan an out-of-town meeting just two days before their big Spring Fling.

As he watched her car's taillights disappear into the dusk, a prickle of foreboding nudged him. He shoved it away and walked home. She was right—he was getting paranoid. Not everybody was like Trevor Johnson, pretending to be his pal while he secretly wooed his girlfriend and stole his accounts. Certainly Piper wasn't like that.

"Good to meet you, Mr. Gordon."

"Please, call me Ted." Ted Gordon motioned Piper toward a white leather sofa, and waited until she was seated.

"I can't tell you how much I appreciate this meeting."

"I owe your former boss a couple of favors so it's no problem." He sat down across from her and leaned forward. "Besides, I'm a little curious about this new job of yours. You've got a lot of people talking. Nothing like what you've done before, is it?"

"Not at all," she agreed with a laugh. "Which is probably why I'm enjoying it so much. We're aiming for the best of the best in Serenity Bay. That's why I wanted to offer Gordon Developments a chance to work with us."

"We usually develop our own sites," he reminded her, scratching his chin. "And we always want them to be year-round."

"I'm aware of that. We anticipate year-round activities as part of our plan."

"Really? So what do you have in mind for us?"

She'd rehearsed this carefully on the drive into Toronto. Now Piper laid out her pitch, emphasizing each detail that made the proposal worthwhile for his company.

"A golf course, huh?" He grinned at her. "You've got your conference market researched. Meeting rooms?"

"Of course. There are at least three conventions I'd like to approach. All of them would need meeting rooms. Once a hotel is in place, the possibilities for bringing in guests are endless." She let that statement dangle for a moment.

"I notice you've also included a spa in the workup. Are you sure that would be viable in a place like Serenity Bay?"

"Do you play winter sports, Ted? Ever pulled a muscle skiing? Spent the day ice fishing? Or snowmobiling? Doesn't a massage sound good?"

He burst into a guffaw of laughter. "I can see why Calgary didn't want to let you go." He chuckled. "You're good at persuasion."

"I just want you to consider all the angles."

He grew serious. "I'd heard Wainwright Inc. was interested in building there."

Piper caught her breath, turned it into a cough. Who was spreading that rumor?

"We've had no formal presentation, or any contact with Wainwright, as far as I'm aware," she said quietly. "Confidentially, I have some reservations about their ability to meet our timelines given their current...difficulties."

"Wainwright's had a spot of trouble but that won't stop them. Baron Wainwright always makes his deadlines," he said. "I've known him a while and I can tell you he's not a man who breaks his word."

You haven't known him as long as I have.

Piper did not want to go into her father's supposed virtues, nor did she want to talk about Wainwright, especially now. So she remained silent and after a moment he changed the subject, questioning her thoroughly on every aspect she'd thought of and some that she hadn't. An hour and a half later he finally rose.

"It's an interesting proposition, Piper. Very interesting." He watched her rise, motioning toward a board behind his desk. "As you can see, we're heavily invested in the Caribbean at the moment. We've got three new complexes going up."

"So I've heard."

"It would be pushing to start another venture before at least one of the others is complete. But what you're proposing is appealing. Very appealing."

"Then you'll think about it?" she asked, crossing her fingers behind her back.

"I will," he agreed.

"If you want a taste of what we're doing, come down for a day this weekend. We've planned a number of events as a first step to drumming up interest in the Bay. You can see our vision at work."

"I might just do that."

It was risky to invite him. Who knew what could happen with the weather and their constantly evolving plans. But they needed a hotel if they were to start fine-tuning their plans and Gordon Developments was top-notch.

He walked her to the door, sharing a story about her former employer. As they moved toward the elevator, Piper seized her opportunity.

"I have just one request," she murmured, glad no one else was nearby.

"What's that?"

"Everything I've told you is confidential. If you're not interested in the project, I want the opportunity to go in fresh to others. I'd appreciate it if you could keep my ideas and plans to yourself."

"Going to scoop them, are you?" He grinned. "Don't blame you a bit. Jason did a smart thing in recruiting you. Not that I'm surprised. That guy has his head on straight.

Couldn't have survived and started building an empire for himself after that mess at Expectations if he hadn't."

"You know Jason Franklin?" Surprise rushed over her.

"I should. I worked with him for a number of years. He's responsible for finding our properties in New Guinea and Bali, to name a couple." Ted rocked back on his heels. "Top-notch locator until that friend of his stabbed him in the back."

"Really?" Piper wondered if he'd explain.

"I don't suppose he's talked about it much. Can't say I blame him." Ted pressed the elevator button before continuing. "Trevor Johnson wasn't nearly as good at his job but Jason used to help him out, do extra research, suggest stuff for Trevor's clients. They were friends, had been since high school. Room-mates in college. I guess Jason got used to helping."

"There's nothing wrong with helping a friend, is there?"

"Not a thing. Not until Trevor approached me for a kick-back. Claimed he'd done the finding, that Jason took the credit for work that wasn't his."

This was far worse than anything Piper had suspected. As her stomach sank to her toes she struggled to keep her expression neutral.

"But our Trevor made a mistake trying to shake down Jason's clients. Developers have been around the block before. Most of us had been working with Jason long enough to know he was a valuable asset on our team. I'd been trying to coax him to come over for ages, but he was a loyal soul. Claimed Expectations had been good to him, that he liked working with his friend. He's not the type to claim credit for something that's not his."

"No, he's not." Piper couldn't imagine being in such a situation. "The whole thing sounds horrible."

"Believe me, it was. One of Jason's other clients con-

tacted me, asked if I'd been scammed, told me the lies
Trevor was spreading. He said the company was going to
sack him and leave him with a ruined reputation if somebody didn't do something. He wanted permission from all
of us who had been approached. Before he phoned Jason,
told him what was going on." He shook his head. "Wainwright was furious and he let the powers that be at Expectations know it."

"Baron Wainwright told Jason the truth?" She could
hardly imagine her father doing such a thing.

"Yes. The guy's reputation was on the line and Wainwright said he wasn't going to let it go down without doing
something." Ted shook his head. "All that talent—it was
sad. The treachery devastated Jason but he faced his best
friend, got a retraction about the lies. Wainwright and the
rest of us backed him up. Not that it did much good. Trev-
or's father was on the board. It was clear Jason couldn't
work there anymore. Anyway, I think the fun had gone
out of it for him."

"So he went to Serenity Bay." No wonder he'd spent so
much time keeping track of her, following her every move.
If you couldn't trust your best friend, who *could* you trust?

"I'd hoped he'd come to work for me. I know Wainwright approached him, along with a couple of others. But
when Jason found out the rest of the story, he decided to
get out of the business and lie low."

She was stunned that her father had done such a thing.
But then he'd always been more generous with strangers
than with his own family.

"Found out the rest of what?"

Ted shook his head. "I've said too much already. It's
Jason's business. Ask him."

As if to end the conversation, the silver elevator door
slid open.

"Thank you so much for your time," she murmured as she stepped inside. "I'll be happy to answer anything else you need to ask. My card's in the folder I've left. I hope you'll come down this weekend."

"We'll see. Thanks for the heads-up. I'll do some thinking. Goodbye, Piper."

Please let him sign on as the hotel developer. The prayer became a chorus that circled round and round in her head as she drove back toward the Bay.

She understood now why Jason wanted Wainwright. He felt he owed Baron. But if Ted Gordon took over the hotel project, Wainwright would leave the Bay alone and she wouldn't have to worry about her father anymore.

Her cell phone suddenly rang.

"Hello?"

"Hey, Pip. Just wanted to confirm that Ash and I will be there on Friday evening. Don't worry about us. You're busy and we know it. We just want to see what you've been up to. Help out if we can."

"I'm so glad you're coming, Rowena. Bring warm clothes because we're supposed to get a snowfall."

"How will that go over?"

"We'll manage." Something unspoken hung between them. Since Rowena never minced words, Piper knew it was bad. "What's wrong?"

"Tina's been trying to contact you for the past two hours. But your phone was off so she called me."

"About?"

"Apparently Dylan told her Baron is going to be in Serenity Bay this weekend. He's flying into Toronto tonight."

"But why?" Piper asked, her fingers tightening against the steering wheel as panic washed through her in a tidal wave. "What is he coming for? What does he want?"

"Like I would know how the great Wainwright's mind

works?" Rowena barked a laugh. "I just wanted you to be prepared."

"I'm not sure that's possible. But thanks, Row."

"You're welcome. Take care, Piper."

"You, too." She closed the phone and set it on the passenger seat as her mind entertained a thousand possibilities.

"What are you up to now, Daddy Dearest?"

Baron Wainwright wasn't coming to applaud any success she might have, that much was clear. There had to be some other reason to bring him to Serenity Bay, a place he had no love for, on the same weekend she'd spent weeks planning for. Had Jason invited him?

Immediately she pictured the paper she'd found, the drawing of Wainwright's hotel concept. Obviously Baron had decided to go ahead, to offer the town a proposal for his glitzy, Vegas-style hotel. One that would send the council members' eyebrows right into their hairlines, one that was as far from what she'd envisioned as parrots were from sparrows.

"Over my dead body," she sputtered indignantly.

"Where are you, God? Why don't you stop this? Don't you care?"

The silence was deafening.

Chapter Seven

Piper Langley was good—very, very good.

Jason stood in the shadow of the ice rink and watched as the last few stragglers arrived from the community worship service to join the lineup for burgers at the grill. When everyone had been served, he helped Ida refill coffee cups while Piper explained the treasure hunt to the kids eagerly gathered round her.

"When did that happen?" Ida wanted to know.

"About two-thirty this morning. Piper decided we needed a send-off for the kids that would have them clamoring to come back, so her friends and I stuck our heads together and came up with this."

"Smart." Ida asked someone to take over Jason's duties to free him to help Piper, then disappeared with her coffeepot, circulating among the visitors.

Jason focused on Piper.

"Each of you must stay with your leader. They're the ones to ask if you need hints or directions to a certain point. When you've located all the clues and found your treasure, you'll come back here. First team back gets the grand prize. Everybody ready?" Piper sent the children off in a buzz of excitement.

"She's not hard on the eyes, is she?"

"Ted?" Jason pumped the other man's hand knowing his grin stretched from ear to ear. "I didn't expect to see you here."

"Why not? The hype about this place is all over Toronto."

"Thanks to Piper." He motioned her over. "Piper, this is a friend of mine, Ted—"

"We've met," Ted interrupted. He held out a hand. "How are you?"

"Relieved," she told him, grinning. "That's the last event. By the time they get back we'll be ready to wave goodbye."

"Looks like you maxed out on attendance in spite of the weather."

"She's the queen of improvisation," Jason told him proudly. "We had three inches of snow the night before last, but we never canceled a thing. Modified, maybe, but no cancelations."

"We're getting requests for summer bookings, too," Piper added.

"Looking around you'd never know it was anything other than a gorgeous spring day in cottage country, except for the snow sculptures, and even they're melting fast," Ted said. "That sun's got some heat."

"Wait till summer. I hope you'll be here when we launch our Summer Splash," Piper said.

Her obvious comfort with his old friend had Jason wondering where and when they'd met. He'd have to ask her about that…later.

"If my kids have anything to say about it we will." He nodded at two teenagers, shaking his head when they loped across the street to join the last troop of treasure hunters. "I guess they're never too old to hunt for treasure. Jason, why don't you give me a tour, show me what you've got planned for this place."

"Sure." He turned to Piper. "If you need me, I've got my cell."

"Everything's under control," she said. "Take your time."

It became obvious after only a few minutes that Ted had been well informed about the Bay. His questions were pertinent and probing.

"This is where you're hoping a hotel will be located?"

Jason smiled. "I wondered if that's why you were here."

"How could I not take a look, especially after the pitch I got the other day? Your economic development officer is dynamite." Ted began to talk size, construction methods and access.

Jason had to concentrate on his answers. But at the back of his mind the questions formed—when had Piper contacted Ted and why hadn't she told him?

"Is the town prepared to offer any concessions?"

Jason focused on conveying his plan. He wasn't aware of the passage of time until his phone rang.

"You need to announce the winners and make your farewell speech," Piper reminded him.

"I'm on my way."

By the time Ted left, most of their visitors had, also. Volunteers were clearing the site, removing tables and putting the town square back to rights.

"Can I talk to you?" Jason asked Piper.

"Sure." She glanced around. "Want to find a park bench? I think I need to sit down before I fall down. Last night is catching up with me."

"Maybe we should do this somewhere private."

"Do what?" she asked, sinking onto one of the new cedar benches the town had paid for. She raked a hand through her curls. Her navy slacks and striped shirt were perfect for a day at the lake. For once she'd exchanged the heels he'd grown accustomed to seeing her in for a pair of pristine white sneakers, though how she'd kept them so clean was a mystery.

She gave him a veiled glance when he didn't say anything.

"Ted told you I went to see him," she murmured.

"He did. Why didn't *you* tell me?"

"There wasn't anything to tell. I presented the package, asked if his company was interested. He said he'd get back to me." She leaned closer, eyes sparkling. "So is he?"

"Interested?" Jason shook his head. "We won't know that for a while. Ted plays things close to the vest. If I were guessing, I'd say he hasn't made up his mind yet. I still think you should have told me."

Her eyes darkened. "We discussed this, Jason. Trust, remember?"

"Yes, but—" He decided to let it go. She looked too tired to argue. "Next time tell me before you hold one of those power meetings, will you?"

She didn't promise, just heaved a sigh and closed her eyes.

Jason reached out, lifted the strand of hair from her lips. "Your face is quite warm."

"I have no doubt. I got too much sun today."

"Piper?"

They both rose at the same time, bumped into each other. Jason reached out a hand to steady her and found himself the subject of scrutiny from two gorgeous women he now knew were Piper's best friends.

"Hi, Ashley, Rowena."

"Hey." They smiled at him.

"Listen, Pip, we've got to leave. Ash's flight goes out at seven so I think it's time we got on the road."

Something in the redhead's voice—Rowena, that was her name—made it sound as if she was warning him. Her eyes tracked his hand to where it lay against Piper's waist. He dropped it.

"Oh, I'm so sorry you have to go so soon," Piper apologized. "I should have spent more time with both of you. It was so sweet of you to give up your weekends to come out here and all I did was put you to work on that treasure hunt."

"Don't be silly! We loved helping with everything, especially the snow sculptures. Watching the polar swim today was a blast." Ashley smiled, including Jason in her warm, affectionate grin. "I think the old Bay is going to take off like we'd never have imagined all those years ago." She reached out and enveloped Piper in a perfumed hug. "Good work, Pip."

"From me, too," Rowena added, then grimaced. "I wasn't sure I'd ever see the end of the doughnut fryer yesterday but it has to be the best cure I've ever heard of. I'll never look at them in the same way again."

Another hug.

"It was nice to meet you, too, Jason. Pip's told us a lot about you."

Like what?

"Thank you both for your help." Piper smiled at them. "I hope you'll come back again soon—to relax."

"Try and stop us." Ashley consulted the gold bracelet on her wrist. "I'm sorry, Piper, but we have to leave now. I'll call you when I get home. I love you."

Moments later the two peeled out of the parking lot, gravel rattling under their tires.

"We need to talk about getting that parking lot paved,"

Piper mumbled, her face a darker tint of rose now than it had been before. "And about making some walking trails through the forest."

"We will talk about it. Tomorrow." She looked weary. "Right now I think you need to come over to my place."

"Your place?" Her eyebrows rose as she blinked at him. "What do you mean?"

"I'm feeding you tonight. In honor of your grand success with our Spring Fling."

"That wasn't just me. We all worked on it." But she didn't object when he wrapped her hand in his and began leading her toward the marina that housed his business and home. "But it did go well, didn't it? No major incidents, no delays, nothing we couldn't handle."

"A testament to your foresight." He opened the door, motioning for her to precede him up the stairs. "Welcome to Chez Franklin. Have a seat."

She chose the big chair by the window that overlooked the forest.

"This is beautiful," she murmured, gazing at the scenery surrounding them. "How clever to take up residence here."

"I'm very clever," Jason responded, thinking how little effort it had taken to get her here and how he'd wasted days trying to think up some excuse to have dinner with her again.

He searched the tiny cavern of his freezer, wishing something would magically appear. But even his stock of cinnamon buns was depleted. He closed the door, glanced around the galley kitchen and spotted the phone book.

He hadn't actually said he'd cook for her, had he?

"Piper, I—" He turned to ask her if she liked Chinese food and discovered she'd fallen asleep. Thick, dark lashes rested on her cheeks, the porcelain skin now glistening a rich rose. Her tinted lips parted slightly to allow even breaths to escape.

Jason marveled that the strong, competent woman who'd just successfully put together three days of nonstop activity for a throng of tourists could look so fragile. Her hands lay in her lap, pale white against the navy of her clothes. Those hands had pitched in everywhere, from mixing juice drinks for kids, to balling snow for the sculptures. She'd done it all. She deserved her rest.

He had so many questions about her. She'd lived with her grandparents. There was a rift between her and her father, he remembered from the spa incident. Was there no one else in her life but her two friends?

At first he'd thought Piper expected someone else to show up this weekend. She'd kept checking the list of attendees, constantly scanned the crowds even after her two friends had arrived. But as Friday night turned into Saturday, then Sunday, she'd relaxed. He decided to ask her about that later.

For now it was enough to lift a soft white throw from the sofa and place it carefully over her, shielding her from the faint breeze drifting in from the windows. Piper never stirred. Her cell phone rested on the arm of the chair. He picked it up, decided to turn it off once he'd left the room. She needed a rest.

But Jason paused in the doorway, studying her beautiful face. Even asleep she was gorgeous. At last he turned away, went downstairs to turn off her phone and make his call. Forty minutes later the food arrived but Piper was still asleep.

Loathing to wake her but knowing she needed nourishment, he squatted beside her chair, touching her shoulder.

"Dinner is served, sleepyhead."

She sighed, lifted her lids and stared at him as if bemused. "Jason?"

"That's me." He paused a moment while she took stock of her surroundings. "Dinner's ready. Think you can eat something?"

"Everything," she told him with a soft, sleepy smile that did something funny to his midsection. "I'm starved."

"Come on, then." He lifted the coverlet away and held out a hand to pull her up. "I hope you like Chinese food."

"My favorite." She blinked at the table setting. "You made all this?"

"I could lie. But Ida would tell on me and then you wouldn't trust me again." He held up one of the containers. "I ordered it. I'm very good with a telephone. Have a seat."

Jason held her chair, waited till she was seated, then offered up a quick grace. Soon they were savoring shrimp chow mein.

"Good thing I'm not allergic to seafood," Piper murmured, then giggled at his look of dismay. "Just kidding! I'm not. This is delicious. There was a Chinese restaurant here when I was a kid but we didn't have it very often. My grandfather was suspicious of anything that wasn't meat and potatoes."

"Did you live with them the entire time you were growing up?" He saw her pause, noticed the way she stared at her plate before answering.

"Actually I went to live with them the first summer after my mother died."

"Your father didn't want you?" He thought she was going to tell him to back off but after pressing her lips together for a few moments, Piper answered.

"Oh, he tried to insist but he was too busy, and boarding school was easy. We didn't get along well and I found it increasingly impossible to live with him watching my every move. Every Christmas, Easter and summer I spent at the Bay." Anger tinged her tones. She stabbed her fork into a piece of chicken with too much force and sent a spatter of translucent orange sauce across the plate.

"But surely that was his job, as a parent?"

"His *job*," she snapped, "was to love me, to help me grow into my own person, to nurture me."

"He couldn't do that?" He kept his voice quiet, watched a flurry of emotions rush across her face.

"Not unless I let him mold me into a carbon copy of him. And I didn't." She speared a piece of broccoli from her plate and munched on it. Then her head jerked up, her eyes meeting his. "How about you? Do you have family?"

He shook his head.

"I wish I did but there's only me. I grew up in several foster families. Nice people, but it wasn't like having your own kin."

"But you went to college. You got your degree."

"Yeah." He grinned. "I was one of those pizza boys you talked about. I had a reputation for getting the deliveries to the destination faster than anyone else the company hired."

"Why?" She leaned forward, her face rapt with curiosity.

"Because the tips are always bigger if you deliver on time."

"Ah." She grinned. "An entrepreneur even then. Was Expectations your first job?"

Jason swallowed, wondering how much she'd heard.

"The owner was the father of a friend of mine. We worked there together." He lifted some rice to his mouth so he wouldn't have to say any more. But Piper wasn't finished.

"You must have traveled a lot in order to scout out locations," she mused, playing with her fortune cookie. "Did you travel with your friend?"

"Sometimes. What is it you really want to know?" he asked, setting down his fork.

"Was I asking too many questions?" She smiled, reached across the table and covered his hand with her own. "I'm sorry," she murmured, squeezing his fingers. "Sometimes my curiosity gets the better of me. We've been working together all this time but I don't feel like I know a lot about you. I was just trying to rectify that."

Jason turned his hand to thread his fingers through hers.

"Funny you'd say that. I think I know quite a lot about you, Piper."

"Really?" She stared at him, eyes wide with surprise but a hint of wariness lodged in their depths. "Like what?"

"I know your perfume reminds me of Persian roses I once smelled in Tangiers. I know you're a night person, that you force yourself to come in early because you don't want anyone to think you're a slacker, but you'd prefer to sleep in." He smiled at her quick gasp. "I know you don't like onions," he teased.

She glanced down at her plate and the tiny pile of onions lying in one corner. "Too obvious."

"Okay." He debated a moment, then plunged in. "How about this? I know you like your job, but I also know you push yourself harder than anyone else ever could. And I think it's because you're trying to prove something— maybe to yourself or maybe to that father you talked about. You want people to value you for your own merit."

Her lips tightened a fraction, but otherwise Piper gave little away.

"Don't you?" she asked, drawing her hand away.

"Yes, of course. I didn't mean that in a bad way. I just

meant you're driven to succeed. That's probably how you've managed to make such a dent in the powers that be."

"Meaning?" She leaned back in her chair, ignoring the egg roll still lying on her plate.

"Meaning that Ted said he'd heard about your work here. I'm sure a lot of others have, too. That's because you don't aim for mediocre. I admire the way you took on my dream for this place and made it your own. It's a pleasure to work with you, Piper." He picked up his glass of ice water, clinked it against hers.

"I could say the same about you," she murmured, returning the toast.

"But you won't, because I'm obsessive and you don't want me breathing down your back."

"No, I don't," she admitted. "So…you're not angry about Ted?"

"Not angry," he agreed, savoring the last of the sweet-and-sour sauce on his plate. "Just curious about what he said. I realize I've been a little heavy-handed."

"A little?" She snickered.

"Okay, a lot." He set down his fork with a thud and glared at her. "Are you going to make me beg for information about your meeting?"

"It's a thought."

He scowled for the pure pleasure of hearing Piper's melodious laugh ring through the room.

"Seriously, there's nothing to tell. I laid it on thick with him, pointed out every advantage I could think of." Her slim shoulders lifted in a shrug. "He's going to think about it."

"He'd be a good choice, though not my first."

"I thought you said he was a friend?"

"He is, a good one. But I'd still prefer to have Wainwright on board."

She leaned forward, her face tightening. "I told you. They're not a good choice right now."

Jason nodded.

"I remember. I did some checking and while it's true that they're having financial problems with some aspects of their development, they seem like normal glitches for any major project. I don't think it has seriously hampered their ability to build what we need. I put a call in to their office when you were away. Someone should get back to us soon."

"You did what?" She flung her napkin onto the table and rose from her chair, her fingers fisting at her sides. "I especially asked you to let me handle this on my own time, Jason."

She was furious.

Jason watched her pace back and forth across his hardwood floors, and found himself grateful that she wasn't wearing heels.

"Do you think it's funny to go behind my back when I specifically asked you not to?" she demanded, eyes blazing.

"I didn't go behind your back," he said calmly. "You said you'd prefer not to work with them. I happen to feel they should at least be offered a chance to present a proposal."

She glared at him and he felt a modicum of regret that she hadn't been there when the call had come in from the company.

"Look, Piper. They've asked twice to present something. I've put them off both times because you were so hesitant. But they're eager to talk and I think that's a good sign. I want to see what they propose."

"I can tell you that without even listening to a Wainwright pitch," she hissed. "Big, splashy and out of place.

This is cottage country, not the Vegas strip. We want understated, friendly, not overpowering, neon blaze."

"I'm aware of what we want." He studied her, puzzled by her burst of anger, completely unlike the easygoing Piper who'd taken everything in stride this weekend.

"Wait a minute—they've called twice?" she whispered as her face drained of color.

"Yes. Why? Is something wrong?"

"Wrong?" She blinked. "I've told you about them over and over."

"I'm not talking about Wainwright. I'm talking about you."

"I'm fine."

Sure she was. He thought about it, then decided to tread on thin ice.

"Piper, were you hoping someone special would show up this weekend?"

"W-why would you ask that?" Her voice had dropped, her gaze veering away from meeting his.

"Call it a hunch," he said. Jason rose, walking over to stand beside her. "You've gone all out this weekend. It's natural to feel a little down if you were expecting someone to see your work and they didn't show."

"It's not what you're implying," she told him, a tiny smile curving her lips. "I don't have a boyfriend who didn't show. You won't have to nurse me through a broken heart."

Relief fluttered through him at this news but he ignored it.

"You were looking for someone," he insisted. "I saw the way you kept checking the sign-in sheet, scanning the crowds."

"And you want to know who?" She dragged a hand through her hair, ruffled the tousled curls even more. "If you must know, I'd been warned my father would show up. Thankfully he did not. He would have ruined everything."

He tried to read her expression but Piper avoided him by moving back to the table.

"I'll give you a hand with the dishes."

He laid his hand on hers, preventing her from moving anything.

"Not yet."

"Oh?"

"We haven't had dessert. And then there's the fortune cookie."

She did look at him then, in disbelief.

"You're going to put your faith in a fortune cookie?"

He laughed. "No way. My faith rests in God. But I usually find the sayings interesting. Scared?" He picked up the cookie, handed it to her.

"Why should I be afraid of a fortune cookie?"

"Because you might read a bit of truth?"

She snorted her opinion of that and sat down again. So did he. Jason waited while she cracked the cookie open and removed the small slip of paper.

"Well?"

"I think you planted this." Piper glared at him, but her eyes danced. "All right then. 'Man's schemes are inferior to those made by heaven.'"

"You see. Just because it's a fortune cookie doesn't mean it can't hold a wise saying."

"Yeah, yeah. Let's hear yours, Mr. Wise Man." She plopped her elbows on the table and cupped her chin in her hands. One eyebrow arched in a command to open his own.

He cracked the cookie, stared at the words.

"Well?"

"'War doesn't determine who is right, war determines who is left.'"

Piper burst into laughter.

"A fitting end to our disagreement on Wainwright, I think." She glanced at her watch. "Wow! I'm sorry to miss dessert but I've got to get going. I don't like driving those switchbacks in the dark." She began stacking the dishes, carrying them over to the counter.

"You don't have to do this. Go ahead. I can clean up."

"You worked just as hard as I did. Come on, the two of us should be able to make short work of this."

He didn't have a dishwasher but they worked together harmoniously, Jason washing, Piper drying. When the last dish was put away, she hung up the dish towel and smiled at him.

"This was fun. Thanks a lot."

"We'll do it again." He followed her to the door, remembered her cell phone and had to go back for it. "I turned it off when you were sleeping. I didn't think there'd be anything too urgent."

"Nothing that can't wait till tomorrow." She stepped outside. Jason followed. "My car's not far away."

"I need the walk," he told her, matching his step to hers.

"Would you believe from this warm air that we had snow a couple of nights ago?" She lifted her face, gazed at the heavens. "The sky is gorgeous. Look."

"I am looking," he murmured, but his attention was on her.

She caught him staring and turned away, quickening her step until she reached the car.

Without thinking Jason reached for the door handle. The door opened. He frowned.

"You leave your car unlocked?" he asked.

"No. I always lock it." She pushed the door closed, tried the remote. It worked. "I guess I didn't hit it hard enough this morning. I was sure it was locked."

He held the door for her, waited till she was inside, then pushed it closed. She started the engine and rolled down the window.

"Looks like you're taking work home with you," he said, leaning down to eye the brown-wrapped package on the backseat.

"What?" She twisted, blinked. "Oh, er, yes. Though I don't think I'll get at it tonight. I need an early night."

He was going to tell her to take tomorrow off, but he knew she wouldn't. So he stood there, staring at her beautiful face in the moonlight and wondering if he should follow his heart.

"Well, good night."

"Good night."

She pressed the button and the window began to move upward.

"Piper?"

It rolled down again. Her other hand rested on the gearshift. She turned her head to look at him.

"Yes?"

He could feel her breath against his skin. Her perfume filled the night air creating an intimacy that made him bold. Jason leaned in through the window, brushed her lips with his.

"You did a great job. Thank you."

She stared at him for a moment then nodded.

"You're welcome."

He stepped back, watched her car drive into the darkness. When it had disappeared he turned and strolled back to his place, the memory of her touch lingering.

It was probably not the brightest thing to do, given that he had to work with her. But he wouldn't regret that kiss.

For weeks now he'd been aware of the current between them. Tonight had confirmed that she felt it, too.

He stepped inside, whistling as he locked up.

Sure, there were some mysteries about Piper Langley. But that was going to make it more interesting to find out what lay beneath that mask she usually kept in place.

Very interesting.

Piper rolled out of town half-bemused by Jason's kiss. Every so often her hand lifted of its own volition, and her fingers touched her lips.

He was a nice guy, really nice. If only—

She glanced at the flash of lights behind her, glimpsed in the rearview mirror and saw that package lying on the backseat. Where had it come from?

She made a tight left turn, annoyed by the bright lights of the vehicle following too close behind. Edging over onto the shoulder, she waited for it to pass, but it didn't, which aggravated her even more.

Assuming it was one of their visitors who wasn't familiar with these roads she moved back into her lane and kept going, relieved when she could finally turn into her driveway.

Oddly, the vehicle turned, also, but then stopped and sat waiting when she drove into her parking space and shut off the engine. After a moment it backed out of the lane and drove away.

Disconcerted, Piper climbed out of her car and picked up the brown package. She carried it to the house, unlocked the door and laid it on the table. Once she'd slipped off her shoes and put the kettle on for a cup of tea, she began inspecting the parcel.

There were no marks on the plain brown paper, nothing to indicate either what it was or where it had come from. She slid a fingernail under the taped corner at one end and began unwrapping. Inside was a white box with the Wainwright logo on top.

She pressed her lips together and lifted the lid. A model sat inside—a hotel model. She lifted it out, found a small card underneath.

Proposed development for Serenity Bay.

It had to be her father. Obviously he'd come to town and when he'd found her car unlocked he'd slipped this into the backseat, too chicken to face her outright.

Piper set the model down, grabbed the phone and dialed the number from memory. Her father never went anywhere without his cell phone.

As soon as it was answered she burst out.

"How could you? How dare you? This is my project. Keep—" She paused.

"—leave a message," his voice ordered in that gruff, overbearing tone. A beep, then silence.

Piper thought for a moment then slowly hung up the phone.

She wouldn't give him the satisfaction. If he wanted to know where she was, his company spies would soon find her. If he wanted to talk to her, let him do the calling.

Suddenly she recalled those bright lights. Her stomach sank. It had been him. She was sure of it. He'd hung around, then followed her home. But he hadn't had the guts to face her.

She walked over to the mantel, picked up Vance's photo and stared into his beloved eyes.

"Why couldn't you have talked to me then, Daddy?" she whispered, her finger sliding over the precious cheeks, so gaunt from cancer treatments that hadn't worked. "Where were you when I needed you most?"

Several moments passed before Piper set the frame back on the mantel. Vance was gone, pain-free, in heaven, with God. And Baron was still out of her life. Apparently that's the way he wanted it. There was no point in getting trapped in the past again. She'd come to Serenity Bay in search of the future.

The kettle whistled and she made herself a cup of mint tea, pinching the leaves before she dropped them into the strainer, just as Gran always had. While it steeped, she studied the small model her father had left.

The main floor lobby lay open to the street level, a kind of piazza fronting it. She could imagine people gathered there, sipping lemonade on a hot day, admiring an ice sculpture in winter. The perfect place to hold all kinds of events.

The second floor restaurant and dining room overlooked the water with big Palladian windows, their arches emphasized by molding that lent it a European style. Each of the rooms had a balcony large enough for two chairs and a table.

When she turned the scale view around she could see where the spa was located, the treatment rooms. An indoor pool had been included. It was bounded by huge glass doors that could open to a terrace with steps down to a rose garden and lawn below. A tiny sign indicated tennis courts, horseshoes and a golf course beyond. It was not the usual Wainwright style.

It was exactly the kind of hotel Jason wanted for the Bay.

But there was no way he could see this. To let Baron create this hotel, here, in Serenity Bay, would be a sacrilege to her grandparents. They'd savored happy times with their daughter here, stayed to mourn after her death.

This had been their paradise, a pure, unspoiled place

of natural beauty untouched by greed, manipulation and anger—everything Baron Wainwright stood for. Even if he created everything he showed in the model, which Piper didn't believe he would, she didn't want him here, leaving the Wainwright impression on the only place she called home.

Piper knew she should destroy it, get rid of the evidence now and find someone else to build. But she couldn't bring herself to crush the tiny edifice that must have taken hours to create.

So she returned it to the box and stuffed it into a closet, out of sight, just as the phone rang. She glanced at the caller ID and froze.

"Piper? It's your father. Are you there?"

She couldn't move. Even her gaze stayed riveted to the phone.

"I saw your number when I turned my phone on. I'm glad you called. We need to talk."

No, they didn't. Not now. Not ever.

"I wish you were there. I have so much to say to you." Baron's voice sounded different, quieter, more introspective. "Okay, well, if you want to talk, you know how to reach me. Bye, honey."

The machine beeped then clicked off, its tiny red light flashing a reminder. In order to erase it, she had to listen to the message again. Tears welled but she gritted her teeth and got through it, then hit the erase button.

"Why, Dad? Why couldn't you have been the father I needed? Why can't you say you're sorry?"

Finally she turned and walked to her bedroom.

There were no answers.

Tomorrow morning she'd accelerate her hunt for a hotel developer.

Chapter Eight

He'd done it again!

Jason walked through the door and took his place at the meeting table as if she'd personally invited him—which she had not!

This was no time to pitch a fit but Piper decided that once they were finished she'd lock herself in her office until she came up with a plan to force Mayor Franklin to back off. His need for control exposed his similarity to her father more now than she'd ever imagined. And that was not a good thing.

She held her temper and called the meeting to order. When it was finally adjourned she was ready to hit the roof.

"Thank you all for coming. Let me know if you run into problems."

"Good meeting. This recreation board seems to be eager to get started on your ideas now that we're into the heat of the summer." Jason leaned against the board table, his smile appreciative. "You look beautiful, by the way," he said, for her ears only.

"Thank you." She felt the heat rise to her cheeks as he assessed the white silk jacket and skirt she'd chosen for today. She needed to think of something to get him off her case and she couldn't think with him in the room.

Thankfully, Ida chose that moment to enter and hand her a pile of messages.

"The top two are urgent," she grumbled. "I'm going to lunch."

"Thanks, Ida." Piper scanned the first one, realizing it gave her the excuse she needed for privacy. "Excuse me, Jason, but I need to answer these."

He followed her out of the room, but when she turned to close her door, he stepped back, one eyebrow lifted.

"I'm sorry, Jason, but this is personal."

"Sure. When you get a minute, I'd like to talk about an idea I have. Call me at the marina. I've got bookings all afternoon."

"Okay, I'll do that." Piper closed the door, leaned against it and heaved a sigh. Then she walked to her desk, picked up her cell and dialed. "Can you talk?"

"Sure. I'm on a lunch break. What's wrong?"

"Nothing's *wrong,* exactly. Can't I just call you?"

"Sure." Rowena's voice brimmed with laughter. "But you sound steamed. So what's going on?"

"*That man* is going to drive me around the bend!"

"That man being the mayor, correct?"

"Oh, don't sound so smug." Piper swallowed her last words before she said something else to give herself away.

"What did he do now?"

"Most recently? He waltzed into a meeting I was having with a group who's thinking of establishing a summer camp for the mentally disadvantaged. Anyway, they'll be located about ten miles from town, but they wanted to see what we had to offer. Jason just sat himself down and took over the meeting."

"What's wrong with that?"

"Nothing's wrong with it, except that all the questions he asked, I already knew. I was hoping to get more details about other plans they have. Two hundred campers renting town facilities of any kind would certainly bring in some money, particularly because they have an autumn camp and a spring camp—traditionally slow seasons around here."

Piper slapped a pile of reports Ida had left onto her console in an effort to suppress her ire. "He's driving me nuts!"

"So get him something to do." Rowena's voice sounded muffled.

"Are you laughing at me?"

"Pip, would I do that?"

"Yes!" She thought for a moment. "He's already busy. The fishermen are coming by the boatload, excuse the pun. The fishing derby we sponsor seems to be a big draw."

"He's not busy enough or he wouldn't be at your meeting. Didn't Ash tell me you said he did the same thing last week, twice?"

"Yes, he did."

"But you were more forgiving then because he'd fed you dinner and kissed you, huh?"

"I wish I'd never told either of you that," she grumbled, her face on fire. If Ida walked in now—

"Too late. We know. And we're going to use it against you." Rowena chuckled. "Seriously, Pip, he seemed like a nice guy. He sounds a little obsessed, maybe, but if this is his dream, as you've said, he probably just wants to make sure nothing spoils it."

"You know, I have done this kind of thing once or twice before. And I'm working my fanny off to make sure his dream comes true. I can't make him trust me."

"No, you can't do that." The sound of a crunch transmitted over the line.

"Where are you, Row?"

"In a very posh part of Toronto, seated in the back-yard, on a rich lady's lawn, eating an apple. She's watching me out the window. I think she's been on the phone to my boss but she's only emerged once and I don't think she'll do that again."

"Why? What happened?"

Rowena snickered. "I asked her to help me with a juniper. A seven-foot one. She got dirt on her fresh manicure. And on her poodle."

Piper could imagine her friend doing exactly that. She had to laugh at the mental picture it created.

"I can imagine she hightailed it out of there fast. Poor thing. Just because you like grubbing around doesn't mean everyone does."

She closed her eyes, imagining Rowena, never happier than in a garden, clad in her favorite tattered jeans and a T-shirt that said, The Earth Laughs in Flowers. After studying gardening in England, Row took a part-time job and parlayed it into manager of landscaping for a well-known nursery. Now her designs were winning awards all over.

"Don't feel too sorry for her, Pip. We finished her pool and hot tub yesterday. She can rinse her nails off in there." Rowena said something to someone then came back on. "I've got to go. A truckload of bedding plants just arrived and I want them planted in a certain way so I guess I have to do it myself. Call me tonight and we'll think up a new strategy."

"It's okay," Piper murmured as an idea blossomed. "I think you've given me the best advice I could get. Don't work too hard."

"I will. Bye."

Piper set the phone aside, pulled her calendar near and scoured it with a tiny smile.

"Mr. Franklin, you're about to become more involved than you ever imagined."

* * *

"Sorry, boss. You never said you wanted me to work today and I've got a date. Her family's here on vacation," Andy said.

"Wish I was," he muttered.

"Huh?"

"Never mind."

"Okay. See you tomorrow."

Jason frowned. The kid was far too young to date. Muttering about the irresponsibility of youth, he pulled off the top of an outboard and started tinkering with the spark plugs.

Just when he'd almost got it, the phone started ringing. Again. He turned to pick it up, knocking his screwdriver into the water.

"Franklin's," he growled into the receiver.

"Hi, Jason. Is something wrong?"

Wrong? What could be wrong? He'd been locked into meetings for four hours this morning, breathing in Piper's exotic perfume and watching those elegant fingers take notes while some company discussed upgrading the town's boat launches or the kind of seed a golf course would need or how many people it would take to rejuvenate the kiddie park.

After lunch Piper had included him in a meeting with government officials who asked a heap of silly questions ten times over, and took more notes than any bureaucracy could ever use.

He was heartily sick of meetings.

"I'm sorry if I'm bothering you, Jason." Her voice was too soft, too sweet.

"No bother."

"Good. Well, you said you wanted to be kept up to speed and I've scheduled a meeting with some magazine people who are going to help plan an ad campaign for our reunion next year. I know you want to be involved so we're thinking we'll meet about eight tomorrow morning. It's an all-day thing."

"All day?" Seventy-eight degrees, a little breeze and bright sunshine. He was supposed to toss all that to sit in an office and discuss advertising?

"Maybe two days," she corrected.

"Listen, Piper. Don't think I don't care, but we're getting into my busiest season and I have to be at the marina more. If you could handle this, I'd sure appreciate it. Just this once."

"Well," she temporized. "If you're sure. I don't want you to feel left out or anything."

Why suddenly so meek? She never...suddenly Jason got it.

"Okay, you can stop now. I'm on to you."

"I don't know what you mean."

But he heard the laughter underneath that velvet tone.

"Just for that, *you're* buying me dinner tonight."

"Well." She giggled. "If you think you can get away—"

"Six-thirty," he ordered. "Here. And don't think I'll settle for some puny salad like you're always munching on. I've been slowly dying in your boring meetings, and killing myself trying to keep up here. I need sustenance. Red meat is the only acceptable peace offering."

"Have you got a barbecue?"

"Piper—"

"Never mind. It was a silly question. How about if I pick up a couple of steaks and we grill them at your place. I don't expect you've got time to come to mine?"

"You're right about that." His mouth was already watering. "Have you got time to grill steaks?"

"Jason," she chided in a teasing tone.

He laughed. "Never mind. Silly question. Nobody who's as good at juggling seven different balls would find fitting in a meal difficult. Six-thirty?"

"Deal."

She was as good as her word. She arrived promptly at six-thirty and started grilling two steaks. She wouldn't let him help, so he fixed three engines while succulent aromas drifted to his nose.

"They're ready."

"Perfect." He scrubbed his hands, washing away the grease and oil with his special cleaner. "Another hour and the fishermen will be coming back. Lots of time to eat."

Piper had shed her jacket to display the sleeveless burgundy tank top underneath that showed off her delicately tanned arms. Her legs were bare and shoeless beneath her skirt, displaying her red toenails. In his mind red had become her signature color—the red of long-stemmed roses.

"You sit down, I'll serve."

He sat and watched, amazed by her ability to create this feast in such a short time.

"New potatoes, fresh garden asparagus, biscuits and the pièce de résistance—steak. Medium. I hope."

"Wow." He savored all of it, remembered he hadn't had lunch and that cinnamon roll for breakfast seemed a long time ago. "This is great. Where did you get all the vegetables?"

"My place. Gran always had a little garden patch so I planted a few things. I ran home and picked them up after work. I actually picked the asparagus last night."

"You planned this?" he asked, pausing with his fork halfway to his mouth.

"I was hoping you'd cave in pretty soon." Her eyes sparkled with fun, her curls danced with an electricity that turned them as black as coffee without cream in the soft overhead light.

He opened his mouth to protest, then closed it. He'd been an idiot.

"Are you mad?" she asked hesitantly, as if afraid to hear.

"Furious." He chomped down on another bite of steak, closed his eyes and let the flavors hit his tongue. "Enraged," he added after swallowing.

"I did try to tell you," she murmured, watching him from beneath her lashes.

"Yes, you did. But I have this thing about trust. I should have listened to you. I'd get twice as much done. I apologize for ever questioning you."

"You don't have to." She picked at her own meat, a tiny portion a quarter the size of his. "It's just—" She laid down her fork, looked him straight in the eye. "It's important to me, too, Jason. I won't do anything to jeopardize Serenity Bay's future. You can believe that."

"I do."

The moment stretched between them.

Jason could have stared at her forever, but in twenty minutes, half an hour tops, there'd be a horde of fishermen returning his boats, so he kept eating until his plate was clean.

"Thanks for making dinner. It was great."

"You're welcome." Her smile stretched from ear to ear. "But we're not finished yet. I made a cake last night. Coconut. Do you want some?"

"Silly question," he said.

She giggled.

"Okay, here it is." He stared at the confection she presented to him. Fully three layers high, covered in white icing and golden, toasted coconut, it begged to be sampled.

She cut a slice, laid it on a plate and handed it to him. "Tell me if I goofed."

He lifted a bit on his fork, placed it on his tongue and let his taste buds decide.

"Is it bad?" she asked, her brows drawn together. "I haven't made it in a long time. I guess I'm out of practice."

"Terrible," he agreed. Then he took another bite.

"You don't have to eat it. I'll throw it out." She rose, lifted the cake, her face drawn, slightly pale.

He grasped her wrist, lifted the cake away and took her other hand.

"Teasing, Piper. I was teasing. It's great. Light, fluffy. It's perfect."

"It's my grandmother's recipe." She stood, her wrists encased by his hands, and met his stare. "She always made a coconut cake every time I came home." Her voice dropped. "She said coconut is to celebrate happy times and being together."

"I agree with your grandmother," he whispered before he bent his head and kissed her. Forget the fishermen.

She froze for a moment, her slim body straight, unyielding. Then she was kissing him back. Her hands slipped from his to wrap around his neck. Jason shifted his grip to the narrow curve of her waist to ease her closer. The other hand he pressed into those tantalizing dark curls. She was light and fresh and he allowed his starved senses to revel in her.

When Piper drew back, she stared at him, her brown eyes huge in her face. She rested one hand against his chest, smoothing the fabric of his chambray shirt between two fingers.

"Why did you do that?" she whispered.

"I've been wanting to do that since the night of the

Spring Fling," he told her honestly. He grazed a knuckle against her velvet cheek.

She chuckled. "Ida would be appalled."

He shook his head. "I don't think so."

She tilted her head to one side. "Oh?"

"Ida doesn't miss much." He shook his head, brushed his knuckles against her cheek. "Could we please forget about work?"

She nodded. Jason kissed her again. She was so beautiful.

"This has been brewing for a while," he whispered.

"Yes," she whispered.

When she nestled her head against his chest, he prayed, *Please don't let her shoot me down.* "What about you?"

"Me?" Her sigh drifted upward. "I think I've been running away for a long time."

"Why?" He tipped up her chin, struggling to read the emotions fluttering through her eyes.

"Love hurts, Jason. I'm not sure I'm ready to get involved again."

"Meaning you were before? In love, I mean."

"Yes. But he's gone now. Almost three years."

Gone—meaning he'd abandoned her? Or was it a mutual parting? Jason couldn't quite interpret her meaning. But he heard the tiny yawn she struggled to smother.

"You're tired. Come on, I'll—" Noises from the dock interrupted him. He glanced out the window, saw his renters returning. "Bad timing," he muttered. He brushed his lips across hers once more, then smiled. "I'm sorry, I've got to go sign these guys in."

"Go ahead. I'll clean up."

"No. I'll do that later. I insist," he said, holding up one hand when she would have protested.

"Okay." She moved away from him, found her shoes and slipped them on. "Mind if I go down with you?"

"Not at all." But he had no idea why she wanted to. Checking in rented boats filled with smelly fish wasn't exactly thrilling.

She followed him downstairs, stood to one side while he spoke to the men. After his introduction, she greeted them but added nothing else. Her attention seemed to be on the group of women and families waiting for their men. After a few moments she moved toward them and began chatting.

Jason wasn't stupid or naive. He could see the men's interest in her. In a green patterned skirt with a red top she was a summer rose, beautiful yet fragile at the same time.

His thoughts startled him and he ordered himself to concentrate on business. When the last of his renters was gone, he glanced around. Piper was still standing on the end of the dock but this time her gaze rested on him. After a moment she walked back.

"Can I ask you a question?"

"Sure." Her eyes narrowed in the way they always did when she was mulling something over. He waited.

"Do you ever get requests for rides around the bay? I don't mean fishermen, I mean regular people who just want some time on the water."

"All the time. Some rent the boats just to sightsee, but my fishing boats aren't the best for that sort of thing."

"Why not?"

He glanced at his fleet.

"Too shallow and too small. They're built to accommodate a guy trying to get his fish, not a lot of people. A tour boat is a different proposition. It can usually carry a bigger load—group outings, reunions, that kind of thing." He paused, then decided to tell her part of his dream. "I hope that in a couple of years I can expand to reach that market."

"What if I could guarantee you a full month of book-ings if you had a boat that would sleep six?"

He smiled at her optimism.

"Piper, I appreciate the thought and it would be a great start, but it takes forever to get those boats. Peter has a waiting list a year long to supply three major outfits on the Great Lakes."

She didn't seem fazed by his comment. Instead she wrapped her hand in his arm and tugged him toward the door. "You do have a computer, don't you? And you're hooked up to the Internet?"

He nodded.

"Show me."

He led her to his office, opened his laptop. Piper said nothing, merely accessed her e-mail account.

"I had a phone call today just as I was leaving."

Where was this going?

"A gentleman from Pine Bluff has called several times, an older fellow. He's lived in the area for sixty-odd years but he's moving away now, going to live near his daughter on the West Coast. But he doesn't want to leave."

"Piper, what—"

"Mr. Higgins was wondering if I happened to know of anyone who'd be interested in purchasing his fleet."

Jason perked up, scrutinized her face and waited for the kicker. Piper watched him, giving nothing away.

"His fleet?"

"He sent me this e-mail. Read." She pointed to the screen.

"Two houseboats, a floater, two cruisers and three ski boats." His heart did a nosedive. "I can't afford all this, Piper."

"I know." She smiled, touched the corner of his mouth

with her fingertip and pushed up. "Don't look so sad. I haven't quite finished."

"Okay." He straightened, slid his hands down her bare arms. "I'm interested. Hit me with the rest of it."

"As we've been developing the Bay, I've received a number of requests. Everything from an ice-cream shop to a place to board pets. I keep them filed by subject so that if I ever need to contact someone I have the information handy." She smiled slowly. "It so happens I have quite a large file on people seeking rentals on which they can overnight. In other words, a houseboat."

"But if I'm touring around in a houseboat, I won't be here and it's imperative that I be here. I can't leave everything to Andy."

"How old is Andy?" she asked, tracing his jaw with her fingertip.

"Eighteen."

"Does he have his boater's permit?"

He nodded, distracted by her touch against his skin.

"Couldn't he be trained to take a group out?"

"I guess."

"Mr. Higgins told me today that he'd consider some kind of partnership. He might even be persuaded to stay on for the summer. And of course, some houseboats are rented unaccompanied, meaning the renters drive themselves around the lake."

He burst out laughing at her smug look.

"What do you think of me now, Mr. Mayor?"

"I think you're a jewel beyond price." He kissed her, then set her away. "How do you feel about taking a trip tomorrow?"

"To see Mr. Higgins? I'd love to. I'll call him tonight, make sure it's okay."

"Good. After church we'll have a picnic on the way to his place. You can help me negotiate."

"You're going to do it?" she breathed. "Really?"

"I'm going to try. A houseboat or two would give the place a boost and it's about time I did a little expansion." He brushed the tip of her nose with his fingers. "Thank you."

"No problem. I don't know why I didn't put it together before. Of course, I haven't seen his inventory, but tonight while I was talking to those families and they mentioned a houseboat vacation they'd taken in the Shuswaps, a lightbulb went on."

"I like your lightbulbs," he murmured. "And your dinners."

"Does that mean you're bringing the picnic tomorrow?" she asked archly.

"Of course. Do you like dill pickles and peanut butter?"

"No."

"Too bad. I love them."

Piper made a face and scooted upstairs to retrieve her jacket and purse. "I'd better get going."

"It's too dark to sail," Jason said when they were outside. A slash of lightning jagged across the sky as if to emphasize his opinion. In fact, high waves splashed against the dock as if to warn them. "I'll take you home in the truck."

Piper cast one look at the whitecaps dotting the bay and agreed. Five minutes later they were on the switchback.

"I hope you make it inside before the rain starts," he said, peering through the windshield. "You'll ruin that suit."

"Clothes aren't important. People are. I don't like that you'll have to drive back in what could be a deluge."

"I'll think about you. Time will fly."

They made it to Cathcart House as the first droplets began to splatter the screen.

"Come in and wait it out," she invited. "There's no point trying to negotiate the road when you can't see."

Because the black clouds looked ready to explode, and because he wanted a few more minutes with her, Jason nodded, climbed out of the truck and grabbed her hand. They raced across the yard with the wind whipping at their clothes and hair. Piper unlocked the door, stepped inside and flicked on the lights.

The heavens crackled, light blazed. A second later the power went out.

"Wouldn't you know it?"

"Is this a ploy to get me alone?" he teased, bending to whisper against her neck.

"You wish." Piper wiggled away from him. "Wait there. I've got some candles ready."

Jason closed the door behind him, waited until the faint flicker of a candle turned into the glow of several.

"Come on in. You can light the fireplace, if you want. That'll take the chill off things. I'm going to change." She disappeared.

Jason knelt in front of the fireplace, chose a match from the brass container and lit the already-set tinder. It caught immediately and he fed it with bits and pieces of wood until it was safe to add a small log, then two. Satisfied that the fire would not go out, he put the fire screen in front.

"That's better." Piper emerged wearing a red, bulky sweater and jeans that emphasized the length of her legs. "Fortunately my stove is gas so I can make tea. Or would you rather—"

The sudden break in her voice sent Jason hurrying to the kitchen where he found her staring at something on the table, her fingers clenched around the kettle handle.

He turned to look, reached out a finger to touch the tiny hotel model.

"Where did this come from?"

She sank onto one of the stools.

"That was the package in my car after the Spring Fling. I don't know where it came from or who put it there." Her dark eyes held secrets. "I'm pretty sure my car was locked that day, Jason."

"You're saying someone broke into your car?"

"And into this house." She scanned the room, shivered.

"What do you mean?"

Her attention shifted to the windows, to the yawning darkness beyond.

"Piper?"

She turned her wide-eyed gaze on him. "Yes?"

"What do you mean someone broke in?" He took the kettle from her, set it on the stove. "Tell me."

"I'd put the model in a cupboard," she whispered. "It wasn't on the table when I left this morning. I'm certain of that. Which means someone has been in my house when I wasn't here. Maybe they're still here." *Oh, God, why is this happening?*

Jason hugged her then reached for the phone to summon the police. He checked the main floor and upstairs. Nothing. He returned to the kitchen, found Piper hadn't moved. Her face was pale, her eyes robbed of their usual sparkle.

He filled the kettle and turned it on. Then he located the hot chocolate and made a cup, which he insisted she drink. By the time Chief Neely came she'd regained her equilibrium. But he lost his as she described several other incidents, none of which she'd discussed with him.

"Well, I haven't seen much evidence. It's useless to look outside with all this rain. And in here you say there's nothing out of place?"

"Not that I've noticed. Everything seems as I left it this morning. Except for that model." She kept staring at it, as if she could get a hint if she watched long enough.

"Not much point in dusting for fingerprints then. We wouldn't know where to look." Chief Neely offered a sympathetic smile. "Most I can do is have regular patrols go past, check things are okay. It might help if you changed the locks, and maybe look in to getting a security system."

"A security system?" She shook her head. "We never needed that before."

"Well, there's lots of folks coming and going these days. Could be someone on Lookout Point just snooping around, but I'd say it's a little more personal than that. Maybe someone doesn't like your ideas for the Bay." He stuck his pencil in his notebook, thrust it back in his pocket. "Even with a security system, if you were working in town and they broke in, you wouldn't get here in time to stop 'em, but at least you'd know when it happened. You'd feel safer coming home at night."

"I'll think about that," she told him. "But I'll definitely have the locks changed. I meant to do that a while ago."

"Okay then. That's the best I can do, ma'am." He started toward the door, then paused. "Say, you wouldn't know if someone's been buying land up here, would you?"

Jason caught Piper's start of surprise.

"Someone's buying property up here?" he asked.

"I'm surprised that as mayor, you don't know about it. Had a complaint about digging, reports of unusual traffic on the road. Thought maybe somebody was building a house."

"We'll look into it on Monday," Jason promised. "Thanks for your help."

"No problem." Bud left a few minutes later, after promising to check on the house throughout the night.

When he'd left Jason crouched to look into Piper's eyes. "Are you going to be okay? Would you feel better camping out at Ida's?"

"No, don't be silly. I'll be fine. It's just someone playing silly games." She offered a nervous laugh that didn't quite come off.

"You don't know who it is, do you?"

"No, I don't *know*. It just seems it has to be someone playing tricks. An ordinary thief would have taken something. Right?"

"Yes." She didn't sound sure of that.

"I guess."

"I'll be praying for you, Piper. Asking God to protect you. You can trust Him."

He kissed her good-night and left shortly after that, scanning the ditch and every side road as he returned to his place. Once inside he phoned to tell her he was home, but also to check on her.

"I'm fine, Jason. Don't worry about me. I'll see you tomorrow at church."

"You wouldn't prefer me picking you up?"

"Don't be silly. You'd come here and have to turn around and go back. I'll be there."

But after he'd hung up, he sat in the dark, watching out the big picture windows as the storm puttered out and the clouds scattered. A while later the stars emerged.

"Something's not right, Lord. I can feel it." He squeezed his eyes closed, trying to put his finger on the thing that had set his radar flashing. But he couldn't put the pieces together.

Neither could he get the picture of that model hotel out of his mind. He hadn't had much time to examine it, but at first glance it seemed to represent everything he'd been hoping for. Piper must have known that when she first un-wrapped it. Yet she'd said nothing.

Trust.

"I'm trying, but please, don't let me make another mis-take," he whispered, the sting of a past betrayal flickering to life. "Don't ask me to go through it all again, Father."

Piper closed and locked the front door, waiting till Ja-son's car lights were obscured by the valleys and hills. Then she walked to the table, picked up the model and turned it over and over, searching for the wooden *W,* Wain-wright Inc.'s distinctive logo. It had been glued on the front, above the entry. Now it was not there.

She searched the cupboard where she'd hidden it, fin-gered everything in the drawer, wondering if it had fallen off. Nothing. That left just one possibility. Someone had removed it when they'd set the model here.

Her father?

What was it Jason said—that Wainwright had called *him?* Other than calling her father directly she knew only one way to check out her suspicions.

"Dylan? It's me."

"Hey, sis. How are you?"

"Okay. You?"

"Same as always. Running circles for the old man. Don't you wish you were back at Wainwright?"

"No."

He laughed.

"No, I don't suppose you do." She heard him talking to someone. "Listen, Piper, I've got company. Could I call you back, say tomorrow, sometime after sunup?"

"Sorry," she murmured. "I know it's late. I just need to ask you a question."

"Shoot."

"Where's Baron?"

"Why? You want to talk to him?" He sounded shocked.

"No. I just need to know if he's in town."

"Supposed to be in Montego Bay, but you know Baron. He does what he wants, when he wants." His voice grew softer. "I'm coming, Susan. It's my sister. I won't be long."

"So he's back from Britain?"

"Oh, sure. He's been all over North America in the past two weeks. We've had some company problems. Is that all you wanted?"

She drew a deep breath. "W-would he have come to the Bay, Dylan?"

"What bay?" He paused, choked. "You mean Serenity Bay? I doubt it. Why would he? I think he had dinner meetings scheduled in New York last night."

Relief. Piper swallowed, let out her pent-up breath. "Okay, thanks."

"Are you okay? Do you need to talk to him?"

"I'm fine. And no, I don't want to talk to him." She was about to hang up then thought of one more thing. "Dylan, is Wainwright working on a hotel project for the Bay?"

"We're interested but Dad called a halt until we can get to the bottom of some other problems. He's not in a hurry. He thinks there will be lots of time before you call for proposals."

"So you don't have an active, workable plan? And you're not buying up land around here?"

"Not that I know of."

"And you would know, wouldn't you?"

He laughed. "I'd better. Look, Piper, much as I love you, I do have another life besides Wainwright. I'll call you tomorrow, okay? We can talk then."

"No, it's okay. Take a day off. Goodness knows you deserve one with the pace he keeps you running at." She thought of her big brother. How she wished he could break free of Baron's grip on his life and walk away. But Dylan wasn't like her. He needed that approval.

"I took today off, Piper. That's the best I can do at the moment."

"I know," she murmured, understanding what he hadn't said. "If you need a longer break, come and stay with me. The Bay's great for reorienting your priorities."

"Is that what you're doing there?" Dylan didn't wait for her response. "Maybe I'll see if I can work something in later on but right now I have to go, Piper. You take care of yourself."

"You, too. I love you."

"Uh-huh."

She hung up, leaned against the counter and surveyed the model.

Either Dylan didn't know as much as he thought he did or someone else wanted her to think Wainwright was ready to pitch. Didn't matter which, though; she wasn't comfortable with knowing someone had been in her car, in her house, found the model and left it out.

Somebody was trying to tell her something. But what?

As she turned from rinsing her mug, Piper spotted the *W* sitting on the shelf over the sink, right beside the photo of her grandparents. She retrieved it, turned it over and over, thinking.

Had Jason seen it?

If so, why hadn't he said anything?

What's going on here, God?

Sunday's sermon echoed in her mind. How many times should I forgive my neighbor? Seven times seven? Seventy times seven, Jesus told him.

Forgive.

"I can't," she whispered.

Chapter Nine

"We can't stop Wainwright from approaching the town council with an idea, Piper. That wouldn't be fair. Anyway, why would we?"

"Because we've already ruled out Wainwright, Jason," she said, tired of the argument they'd wasted weeks debating. "Why bother?"

"*You* ruled them out," Jason said quietly. "I haven't. For all we know they may have come up with something we want, something that will meet all our needs." He held out a file. "These are notes from a brainstorming session the Chamber of Commerce held when you were away yesterday. I think you'll find some things of interest."

"Okay. Thanks. How are the houseboats working out?"

He grinned. "Purring like kittens. Higgy has tuned them purr-fectly. He's a great mechanic."

"Higgy?" she asked, one eyebrow raised.

"Andy calls him that and so do I. He prefers it." Jason sat down. "You look tired. Is everything okay?"

"No. I've been checking in to recent land sales. There have been several transactions for property near Cathcart House. All to the same company. Ida and I have been trying to find out who owns it, but so far all we've got is a never-ending paper trail which looks like it leads to some offshore conglomerate."

"Well, they can't build anything without a permit and it's zoned residential. Since we haven't received a request to build, I don't know if you have much to worry about."

"Maybe not." Piper slid her hand into her pocket, felt the whisper of paper against her fingers. The Wainwright invoice she'd found in Gran's rose garden was burning a hole in her pocket, but this wasn't the time to blurt out her concerns. Besides, she didn't want to rehash the old arguments between her grandparents and her father, or get into his threat to someday buy Cathcart House and force them out of the Bay.

She'd tell Jason about her own past—sometime, but not now.

"We had another development yesterday."

The strange note in his voice brought her head up sharply. "Oh?"

"Wainwright asked to make a presentation at the council meeeting tonight."

"What?" Piper couldn't believe he'd said it. "Who called?"

"I don't know." Jason gave her an odd look. "Does it matter? Someone spoke to Ida, asked to be included on the agenda. So she did."

"At the last minute? Aren't there other important matters already scheduled?" Irritated, Piper glared at him. "You could have put them off."

"I told you. I didn't talk to them. Anyway, what's more important than a hotel for this place? You know how hard it's getting to house people who want upscale accommodations." He leaned forward, grasped her hand where it fidgeted with papers. "Piper, what's wrong?"

The concern in his eyes melted her heart. She grasped his hand, squeezed, then let go.

"Nothing. I'm sorry. It's just—you know my objections to Wainwright." She shrugged, tried to summon a smile. "I've been working so hard to coax Ted. I don't want him to be scared off just because Wainwright wants to make a play."

"Ted won't be scared off if he really wants it. Besides, isn't competition good for us?"

"Not necessarily. If Ted thinks we've been courting him and then learns we're also talking to Wainwright, he could feel like he's wasted his time."

"Who were you talking to yesterday?" he asked, then blushed at her look. "I'm not distrusting you, I just wondered if it was another hotel expressing interest."

"No. The corporate head of a fast-food company phoned me night before last to ask for a meeting. They wanted to know about available land within the town limits."

Jason grinned, slapped his hand on the desk. "Yes! I knew we'd start getting some attention. What's next?"

Piper shook her head, held up one hand.

"Whoa! Let's not get ahead of ourselves. This was an expression of interest. We talked possibilities but it's a long way from a done deal, Jason. You know how land development works. You were involved in locating parcels. You must know the ins and outs of negotiations."

"Uh-uh. I was never involved in any of that." Jason rose, moved to the window. His back was to her as he spoke. "I scouted locations, concentrated on finding the properties best suited to my clients. Once they were satisfied, I moved on to the next search."

"You never went back to see what had become of the property?" She frowned, sensing he was holding back.

"I did go back, once."

"And?"

"You could say the visit didn't meet my expectations. I saw my girlfriend there. With another man."

"I'm sorry." This was what Ted had hinted at that day by the elevator.

"Yeah, me, too." He turned, offered her a lopsided smile. "Shortly after that I quit and moved here."

"I'm glad."

"So am I." He touched her hair with gentle fingers. "Otherwise I'd never have met you."

"Did you care about her very much?" she asked.

"I'd planned to ask her to marry me the following weekend. It's a good thing I didn't. She married him instead."

"Oh, Jason." She rose, wrapped her arms around him and held him close. "I'm sorry."

"No, it's okay. I'm over it. I realized that I didn't really love her. I loved the idea of marriage." He pushed her bangs off her forehead, cupped her face in his palms. "That's why I'm paranoid about trust, I guess. In here—" he tapped his chest "—I know you're not like her. But it hasn't quite penetrated up here." He touched his head. "But working with you is teaching me."

He was telling her he trusted her, that he'd stopped suspecting her every move.

A flicker of guilt pinged inside her head. But Piper ignored it, lifting her face for his kiss.

A gentle rap on the door soon had them separating. Jason touched her cheek then walked to the door and opened it.

"This just arrived from Wainwright Inc. I thought you'd both want to take a look at it before council meets tonight." Ida handed Jason a long tube, took one look at Piper and grinned before she hurried out of the room.

Jason removed the end and let a roll of papers slide out.

"Artists' renderings," Piper murmured as he unfurled them. She held her breath, stared down at the drawings. "They're not the same," she breathed.

"As that model you have? No, they're not." He looked at her with an odd expression. "Did you think they would be?"

Piper shrugged, avoiding an answer. She grabbed a pad and began making notes of changes to the hotel that would have to occur before it would fit in with the town's plans. There were many. An hour later, she leaned back in her chair, rubbing her forehead.

"It's too much. They'll never go for what we want."

"You don't know that."

He wanted it badly. She could see the excitement in his eyes.

"Why is this hotel so important to you, Jason?" She should have asked that long ago. But now Piper couldn't contain her curiosity about his answer.

"Because the town can't really move ahead without it."

"It's more than that, though, isn't it?" she said, noting the way he avoided her gaze. "You've been pushing hard to get one here ever since I came. Tell me why."

He sank down in the chair across from her. Silence stretched for a long time before he finally spoke.

"Have you ever wanted to be part of something really great? To see your ideas at work, watch other people benefiting and know that you had a big part in making it happen?" He grimaced. "Of course you have. That's what your job is all about."

"Never mind me," she said, realizing that until now he'd never really exposed his innermost feelings. "I want to know about you."

He sighed, leaning back in his chair.

"A while ago you asked me about Expectations. My job

there involved a lot of travel and I loved that. But after I found my girlfriend and my best friend together, my world came crashing down. I realized that I'd never really taken in the whole picture. I'm not talking about my girlfriend."

He was quiet for a moment then spoke again.

"Maybe seeing them together forced me to realize that I wasn't committed to anything. I looked around that resort and thought 'I'm a part of this, I helped create this.' That experience changed the way I began to assess property. I decided I wanted to be more involved in the end result."

"I see."

"When I learned about Serenity Bay and began re-searching it, I couldn't help feeling that if I recommended it and some developer moved in, stuck in one of those cheap-lodgings-and-not-much-more places that would do little to help the town, that would be my fault, too." He rested his elbows on his knees. "I fell for this place the moment I laid eyes on it. Then things blew up at work. I quit and decided to come here, to see if I could help change things for the better, make a difference."

"To make it something more than just another cheap and tacky tourist town," she murmured with a smile. "Believe me, I understand. But I feel that way because I used to live here, because it was my refuge at a time in my life when things were really bad. What's your excuse?"

He studied her silently for several moments. When he spoke, his voice grew solemn, utterly serious.

"Because it's my fresh start." He searched her eyes, his face showing a defensiveness she'd only glimpsed before.

She knew there was more to it than he'd admitted.

"Why did you need one?"

"Because I'd made so many mistakes." A crooked smile lifted one corner of his mouth. "I doubt you could under-stand what it was like, Piper. You had your grandparents to love you. You never had to struggle to matter, to fight to achieve recognition, to be valued just because you're you."

If he only knew. Piper understood only too well.

"I didn't have terrible foster homes. They never abused me." He raked a hand through his hair, mussing it so he looked like a forlorn little boy. "But I was very aware that when I left, there'd be another boy to take my place, another kid to fill my shoes. I doubt if any of them even remembered me a year later."

"I'm sorry."

"That sounds like self-pity and I don't mean it to be." He rose, pacing the room. "I went to school on full academic scholarships, won the top prize offered. That got me a big mention, but there were a hundred other kids in college who'd accomplished the same thing. Big deal. It benefited me, but it didn't mean I'd contributed anything."

"And Expectations?"

"The debacle there was an awakening. I started to understand that I needed more to fill me inside than just finding a good piece of property. I wanted, needed, some personal involvement in any project I worked on." He shrugged. "I own a marina now, make half the money I used to. I don't have high-powered lunches or fraternize with the money guys. But I'm doing something important here. Or trying to."

What she'd heard had touched Piper deeply, but it also concerned her. She, more than most, knew the folly of looking for fulfillment in work. She'd seen it in her father, watched it overtake him, all in the name of helping God help him succeed.

"Jason, you don't have to prove yourself." She rose, walked around the desk and stood beside him, her hand on his shoulder. "It's not what you do that makes you a good person. God loves you, He cares about you whether you put Serenity Bay on the map or not. It's not about what you can do, it's about what He does," she reminded.

"Yes, yes. But surely what God wants is for me to succeed, to do the best for the Bay." He glanced at his watch. "I've got to get back. Andy's taking a group out to The Bowl."

The Bowl was the fishermen's name for a spot where some of the best and biggest northern pike could be found. Jason gave her a quick kiss then ran out the door. Piper watched him go, troubled by what he'd just said.

It was obvious Jason thought he had to prove himself, which made her wonder if that wouldn't contribute to his eagerness to accept Wainwright's proposal. She'd have to call Tina, find out what was going on.

But the afternoon slipped away too quickly. There was no time to do more than answer calls and make her notes in readiness for the meeting ahead. She ordered a sandwich to give her a few more minutes to prepare, ate it, then walked into the council chambers, hoping she was prepared to meet her father.

To her surprise no one from Wainwright was in attendance. The meeting proceeded without incident for an hour. Then a knock came at the door and Dylan appeared.

"I'm sorry I'm late," he apologized, the grin that had gotten him out of so many scrapes firmly in place. "It took a little longer than I expected to get here. I'm Dylan Wainwright."

"Come in." Jason introduced everyone. "We have nothing else pressing at the moment. Why don't we hear what Mr. Wainwright has to say?"

Since the council was in agreement, the pitch began.

Dylan didn't even glance her way, for which Piper was glad. He lifted the huge portfolio he carried onto the table and began Wainwright's proposal.

"As you can see," he wrapped up twenty minutes later, "we've gone to a great deal of trouble to make this hotel a premiere jewel in the Wainwright chain."

"Our economic development officer, Piper Langley, and I took the liberty of examining the drawings you sent this afternoon. Perhaps she has some questions," Jason responded.

"Hello, Piper." Dylan grinned at her, his bad boy grin firmly in place.

"Dylan."

"You two know each other?" Jason asked.

"Of course." She looked at him, then refocused on her notes. "We've got a couple of problems with the concept, Dylan. The golf course won't work where you're indicating because we're hoping that in the winter we can use the greens for trails for cross-country skiing."

She listed the deficits one by one. Dylan took it gracefully, nodded occasionally, making notes for himself.

"You're asking for a lot," he said when she was finished.

Piper nodded. "But we're offering a lot of concessions. We want this hotel to fit exactly right with the Bay. The developer will be getting prime access, prime positioning and some lucrative tax breaks. In exchange we want a complementary structure."

The council members began to voice their own considerations. Lively discussions covered every imaginable topic until Jason called a halt.

"Order. Folks, we're way over time. I'd like to thank Wainwright Inc. and Dylan for taking the time to explain all that."

"No problem." Dylan began replacing the charts and drawings in his portfolio. "I'll get together with Dad and we'll come up with some changes." He glanced around the table, oozing charm. "Wainwright Inc. is committed to meeting your needs, folks. We want to hear your concerns, and if at all possible, we want to address them. When we make a commitment, it's for the long term."

"We appreciate that."

The meeting was adjourned. Piper caught up with Dylan outside a few moments later as he was loading his case into his SUV.

"Are you angry that I shot holes in the proposal?" she asked quietly. Their father was the problem, not Dylan.

"Of course not. All part of doing business." He turned to face her. "You don't think we get a contract on one presentation, do you?" He laughed. "Come on, Piper. You know better than that."

"Yes. But I also know how much time you put into each presentation, especially when you told me you had nothing going."

"You know Dad. Pulls things out of a hat."

Or plans them way ahead. *Forgive.* Piper shook off the anger. "It's a great hotel, Dylan."

"Just not for here."

"No." She decided to be honest. "I'm not sure Wainwright can do the kind of hotel we want for here."

"My concepts aren't good enough for you, Piper?"

She was stunned at the bitterness she heard in those words and laid a hand on his arm.

"Your concepts are fantastic, Dyl, and you know it. I just meant that this is a poky little lakeside town—not your usual forte."

"I'm an architect with a master's degree in business administration. My forte can stretch to anything it needs to," he said, his voice icy. "That's why Dad made me second in command of Wainwright Inc."

"I know. I'm sorry. I didn't mean anything. Please don't be angry," she begged, exactly as she had when they were children and she'd hurt his feelings with a snide comment about her father.

He glared at her, then like lightning, he was her big, charming brother again. "Sorry, sis. Put it down to the grueling drive here. You folks need some roadwork done."

"We're working on that." She stood on tiptoe, brushed his cheek with her lips. "Want to stay at Cathcart tonight, get an early start in the morning?"

"No."

The abruptness of his rejection dismayed her. But then Dylan had never appreciated the Bay and especially her grandparents' home. He'd hardly ever visited after she'd moved in with them, and then only with her father. Dylan had witnessed the same bitter feud she had.

"Okay."

He sighed. "I'm sorry, sis. I just meant I can't. I've got three early meetings tomorrow. I have to get back tonight."

"You should have flown."

"You should have an airport," he countered.

"We're working on that," Jason said from behind Piper. "She's got her finger in so many pies I'm amazed she doesn't get confused."

"She's a wonder all right. Best development officer in the biz." Dylan touched her cheek with one finger, squeezed her hand. "See you, Piper. Jason, it was nice to meet you. I'm sure we'll be talking in the coming days."

"I look forward to it." He stood beside Piper, watching as Dylan drove away.

"He seems nice."

"He is," she agreed. "I hope we didn't dash his hopes too much. I know he put a lot of time into that proposal." She glanced at Jason. "What did you think of it?"

He held her gaze. "Do you really want to know? Or are you just being polite?"

Piper frowned. "What do you mean?"

"It's pretty clear you've already decided to throw a negative light on Wainwright's ideas, no matter what they are."

He was right. Even if Dylan had brought in that perfect model she had at home, Piper knew she would have found fault. But she couldn't admit it.

"That's not true."

"Sure it is." Jason thrust his hands in his pockets, but his gaze never wavered from her face. "There's something else going on here, Piper, and I'd like to know what it is. I'm not denying you might have a legitimate reason for distrusting the company, but we can't let that past experience impinge on what we're trying to do here."

"You thought the ideas he presented were what we wanted?" she asked, deciding a counterattack was better than defense. "You approved that plan? Because that isn't the impression you gave this afternoon."

"I didn't say I approved all of it. But there were some really good features. The ability to open out one side and make a patio café for the pool—that was excellent. The materials and the decor—they're very close to what we'd hoped for."

"Yes," she admitted.

"You never said that. You jumped hard on all the negatives." He glanced over her shoulder, lowered his voice. "It came close to an attack on Wainwright. I'll be surprised if he comes back to us a second time and that's not good for the Bay, Piper. We need a broad variety of interest and if Wainwright can give us what we need, I see no reason not to choose them."

I do, she wanted to scream. But she silenced that inner cry by gripping her briefcase a little tighter. A twist of anger coiled inside her stomach. Where was God in all of this? Did he honestly expect her to welcome Wainwright to her sanctuary?

"You're telling me to back off," she said.

"I'm *hoping* you'll get past whatever grudges you're carrying and see the possibilities in every presentation," he said softly.

"I was *hoping* we were aiming for top-notch and not settling for the first idea that came along," she murmured. "My mistake. Next time I'll note my concerns and hand them over for you to check before I say anything." She slid the strap of her bag over one shoulder. "I need to get home now. Good night."

But he wouldn't let her go so easily, insisting on walking beside her to where *Shalimar* was tied.

"What's really wrong?"

She ignored him, slipped out of her heels and into the deck shoes that would save the glossy wooden surface.

"Talk to me, Piper."

She straightened, met his scrutiny and decided to tell him.

"You hired me, presumably, because of my skills at economic development. But every time I offer an opinion, every time I try to do my job, for the benefit of Serenity Bay, you challenge me. Maybe I'm not the person you need to do this job, Jason."

He grasped her elbow so she couldn't leave.

"You're the only person who could do such a good job for us and you know it. But this—" he jerked his head toward the town office "—this wasn't about your job. It's about something else and I want to know what is going on." His voice dropped; he touched her hair, brushed it out of her eyes. "Tell me the truth, Piper. Maybe I can help. Is it Dylan? Was he the problem—something in your past?"

"No."

It would be so easy to release the memories that flooded back—dark, painful snapshots of seventeen-year-old Dylan begging her to go with them, angrily asking her to stop antagonizing their father, to stop causing a fuss. Her prayers that always went unanswered. Her secret fear that if she stopped fighting her father, she'd never be her own person again.

Piper could use words to describe the long days and nights after her father had taken Dylan away, the months he'd refused to allow him to visit, the long, lonely nights when she'd despaired of ever having her big brother close again—but words alone wouldn't help Jason understand how abandoned she'd felt. Letting him see the hole inside would only make her appear weak.

Dad needs you here with us, Piper. He needs his family. We haven't got anyone else but us you know. Wainwrights stick together.

But Baron hadn't needed her; he'd wanted to control her—just as he did everything else in his world. Just as he'd controlled and manipulated Dylan into becoming a replica of himself. Besides, Baron Wainwright had not been there when she'd needed him most.

Forgive.

How could Jason possibly understand that?

"Just talk to me," he whispered, reaching out to draw her closer.

But Piper backed away.

"I'm tired. I'm going home. You decide if you want me to stay or if you'd rather I left so you can get on with courting Wainwright."

She heard his hiss of exasperation but ignored it by casting off. Free of the dock, she revved the engine and took off across the water, in no mood to sail tonight.

The calm bay waters accelerated her progress and soon

Shalimar was inside the boathouse. She climbed the stairs to the house. The lights were on, casting a yellow glow up the hill where Cathcart House lay waiting. Having the locks changed made coming home less of a worry, something the new security system enhanced.

Once she'd changed clothes and made herself a cup of mint tea, Piper curled up on a deck chair and searched the night sky for answers. Was it time to leave the Bay, to give up on the plan that had brought her here?

Why don't you ever help me when I need it, God?

I demand that you love each other as much as I love you.

"I do love him," she admitted at last, "but I hate him, too."

God is love.

"If you love someone, you will always believe in him, always expect the best of him, always stand your ground in defending him." She could almost hear him reciting the passage from Corinthians.

"He hurt me." She wept. "He hurt them. And he didn't come when I needed him. How can I forgive him?"

Let love be your greatest aim.

"I can't love. It hurts too much."

But that wasn't true. She thought of Jason, of leaving as she'd suggested. Of never seeing him again.

A soft sigh of sadness filled her at leaving the friendly souls she'd grown to care about. Abandoning her work plans wouldn't be half as bad as not seeing Jason again.

She was in love with him.

The realization surprised her, left her shocked.

Cared about him, yes. Wanted him to succeed, yes. But loved him?

She thought for a moment, comparing this love to her love for Vance. The soft, sweet rush of love she'd felt for him was nothing like what she felt now. With Jason it was different, more like a tiny fire that flared to life when he was near. Her breath caught whenever he walked into the room. Her heart skipped a beat when he winked at her in that audacious way he had. She found herself wanting him to wrap her up in his arms. To forget about Wainwright and hotels and the Bay and simply enjoy his presence.

But Jason was like Baron. He was consumed by his plans for the Bay, so much so that he was willing to cave on the rest of his dream if it meant getting the hotel he so desperately wanted.

She thought of Jason discovering the girl he'd cared about in the arms of another man, learning that his best friend had betrayed him. Perhaps he was coping with that betrayal by using the Bay to prove himself.

Hadn't her father used his work to compensate in the same way after Piper's mother had died?

Her parents had seemed close. Certainly her mother had never been shy about giving Baron her opinion on anything. They argued. They made up. Until he'd started that last project, the one that had overtaken his entire life. Nothing her mother had said then seemed to make a difference to him. He was gone for long periods of time and when he came home they'd argued. Then she'd died. Baron had become more controlling, more demanding.

And Piper had left home.

Tears trickled down her cheeks at the death of a family. Why had God let her mother die?

"Piper?"

She blinked. Jason stood in front of her. "What are you doing here?" He leaned down until his face was level with hers. He reached out to wipe the tear from her cheek.

"I had to come back," he whispered. "I'm sorry."

The simple words touched a spot deep inside that she'd

thought long dead. Piper put her hands in his, rose and leaned into his embrace.

"I didn't mean to hurt you," he whispered, hugging her tightly. "I'd never do that. I only wanted to help. Instead I upset you. I'm so sorry."

She said nothing, simply laid her head on his chest and slid her arms around his waist, allowing his quiet words and gentle touch to heal. His kiss asked nothing in return but offered sweet comfort. How could she not love a man like this?

After a long time he turned her so they could both watch the stars.

"Why were you crying?"

"I was thinking about my mother, about how different things might have been if only she'd lived. I never understood why. Our lives were ruined."

"Sweetheart, your life isn't ruined." His words held a certainty she envied. "I know it hurt and I know the pain never totally goes away, but you coped, you kept going. You've made a difference. I'm sure your mother is very proud."

"Do you think so?" She watched a star skate across the sky. "I have a hard time believing that."

"Why?" He rested his chin against her shoulder.

"Has to do with my idea of heaven, I guess. Or rather God in heaven. I feel like he punished us and her by taking her too early, for no reason. I've always felt that God is sort of like a stern judge, sitting up there, peering down at us, waiting for one little misstep. In my head I know that's wrong. But inside—" She sighed.

Jason was silent for several minutes, then he coaxed her to sit down. He crouched down in front of her.

"Piper, God didn't punish you by taking your mother. He had other plans for her and for you, but He made sure you had grandparents who loved and cared for you. He gave you a wonderful place to live, and two very good friends. And then He brought you back here because He loves you. He has so much in store for you. You can't even begin to imagine." He touched her cheek. "He's not a God of hate. He's a God of love. He's your Father."

She made a face. "Maybe that's my problem. God as a father is one analogy that doesn't work for me. My real father is bad enough."

"Tell me about him."

"What do you want to know? He's driven, arrogant, controlling, demanding, pushy, manipulative if he has to be, and he thinks he does." She shook her head, tossing away the pain. "I don't think he ever saw me as anything other than an extension of his own ambition."

"Now tell me about your grandfather."

She smiled, closed her eyes and tipped her head back against the chair.

"Papa wasn't any less demanding than my father, but he had little time for arrogance. He was interested in everything and everyone. Any time you wanted to talk, if you needed a story or a hug, he had time. He listened, really listened. And he never told you what you should or shouldn't do. He'd hear you out, then help you put things in perspective. You know?" she asked, blinking to look at him.

Jason nodded. "You felt as if he really cared about helping you achieve your goals?"

"Yes! I miss him so much." Tears ran down her face. "I have no one to talk to."

"Oh, Piper." A sad little smile lifted his lips, and his eyes rested on her in a comforting way. "That isn't true. You can always talk to God."

She frowned, trying to understand what he was telling her.

"Don't you see? God knew your father wasn't what you needed, so He moved you into a position where you'd know and love a man like Himself, a man who taught you God's ways. A man who loved you and, more than anything, wanted what was best for you. If you need an analogy for God, use your grandfather, think about his open arms, his welcoming smile. God is just like that—always there, always ready to listen, offering His love."

"I never thought of it like that before," she whispered, staring at his hands holding hers. "But you're right. Papa was the way the Bible describes a loving father."

He smiled, patted her cheek, then rose. But he stood there watching her.

"Can I say one more thing?"

"Sure."

"Don't hang on to your bad feelings against your father."

"You don't understand—"

"No, I don't," he interrupted. "Nobody can know what drove him but your father. He lost his wife. His daughter left his home. I'm not saying he didn't deserve what he got, I'm just saying that maybe it's time to cut him a little slack. Who knows what he was thinking of, or how your mother's death affected him. Maybe losing her hit him harder than anything he'd ever experienced."

"He threatened my grandparents, you know." She glared at him, the pain alive and burning in her heart. "He actually told them he'd take this house and all the land from them."

"He never did it, though. He was hurt and angry, lashing out at someone in his pain." Jason shook his head. "Can't you forgive him after all these years?"

For that—maybe. But there was something for which

Piper would never forgive Baron—not as long as she lived. She tried but—

"Think about it, Piper. Think about what hanging on to the hurt does to your life." He tugged on her hand, drew her up. "Believe me, I know what I'm talking about. Having your best friend try to ruin your name and then marry your girlfriend isn't easy on the ego. But they love each other very much. I wasn't the man she needed. I have to believe God knew what He was doing."

She stared into his eyes, saw the same gentleness she'd glimpsed in her grandfather, a respect and care for others that was more than merely words.

"Thank you," she said, reaching up to brush his cheek with her lips. "You didn't have to come all the way over here. I would have come in to work tomorrow."

Jason chuckled. "Yes. But I would have missed this."

He wrapped her in a snug embrace and told her without words that he cared about her. And Piper kissed him back.

When he drew back, his eyes sparkled.

"That was definitely worth the trip." Jason glanced at his watch. "But I'd better get home."

Suddenly he bent, lifting something.

"What's this?" he asked, holding out a book.

Piper caught her breath.

"It's my grandfather's diary. It's been missing since I moved back. Someone must have returned it."

Someone like…Baron Wainwright?

Chapter Ten

"About time, boss!" Andy's voice bellowed above the roar of the houseboat motor as Jason eased the craft into its mooring.

"I hope you enjoyed your trip, folks. Step carefully now." He gave the boy a warning look, nodding when Andy held out a hand for the ladies to grasp as they stepped off. "I believe your lunch is waiting for you, if you'll follow Mr. Higgins. Come again soon."

The small group of day-trippers was the third that week. Jason hoped there would soon be many more boat tours. They took time, but they more than paid for themselves in word-of-mouth publicity among seniors' groups in the area.

Once they were out of earshot, Andy captured his attention.

"What is it, Andy?"

"Ms. Langley wants you up at the town office, ASAP."

"Did she say why?" Jason asked, stifling his groan. Not that seeing Piper was a hardship. But the day stretched ahead with a hundred things to do and none of them included the town office until the council meeting at seven tonight when Wainwright Inc. would address them again.

Maybe Piper's call had something to do with Dylan's re-appearance. After last week he wasn't sure what to expect.

"Couldn't really understand what she was saying but I think it's important. She came down here herself a few minutes ago. Wanted to know why you didn't answer your cell."

"Okay, thanks." He finished tying off the boat. "Can I leave you to clean her up?"

"Of course." As Jason walked away Andy muttered sotto voce, "If it were me, I'd be moving a little quicker than that to see a babe like her, but I guess when you get that old—"

"Hey!" Jason threw him a withering glare. "I'm not deaf, you know. Not yet."

Andy didn't look the least bit daunted.

"She's got a good-looking guy with her. Holds her arm when she walks, smiles at her constantly. I wouldn't waste my time talking to me if I were you."

"You're right. I won't." Jason strode up the dock and crossed the street, heading for the town office. He rapped once on Piper's door before entering. "Piper?"

She looked flustered, totally unlike cool, competent Piper.

Jason crossed the room to stand beside her. "Anything wrong?" he asked, keeping his voice low.

"Everything's just fine," she said gaily, her fingers touching his in the lightest brush. "Jason, I'd like you to meet Quint Gilroy. Mr. Gilroy, this is our mayor, Jason Franklin."

They greeted each other. Jason glanced at Piper, discerning from her carefully modulated tone that this man was important to them.

"Mr. Gilroy would like to speak to the council to-night, Jason. He's interested in purchasing land in town to build some rather lovely condos." Excitement glittered in her eyes.

Jason didn't blame her. It was more than they'd ever hoped for. Immediately his mind swung into overdrive as a mental picture blossomed.

"Wonderful," he enthused, shaking the other man's hand. "Let's sit in the boardroom. We've a wall map there that might help us. What kind of land are you looking for?"

He listened as Gilroy described his project, struggling to keep his mind from blowing everything out of proportion.

"I don't do huge projects," Gilroy stated. "I'd like to start with two buildings of ten units but have enough room to expand down the road by adding more complexes as the idea takes off."

Piper waited, but when Jason didn't offer any suggestions, she drew attention to a parcel of property that had been empty as long as Jason could remember.

"Jason has a lot more experience with the needs of your kind of development than I, Mr. Gilroy. But this particular plot does offer the benefit of a water view on three sides."

It was enough to get the ball rolling and as ideas mushroomed Jason took over, falling back into an old pattern as he emphasized the location, the amenities and the possibilities. He wasn't sure how much time had passed before he noticed Piper's glare.

"I'm sorry. Was I rambling?"

Gilroy rose, grabbed his briefcase as if he couldn't get away fast enough.

"There's no way I can accommodate that kind of development," he said hurriedly, edging toward the door. "I appreciate that you once worked with the big boys, Mr. Franklin, but I haven't got that kind of money. I'm a small investor who happens to own a construction company. We could have begun immediately but your ideas are a little too rich for me." Gilroy gulped, glanced at Piper and forced a smile. "I'm sorry to have bothered you."

Jason tried to backpedal, caught the tiny shake of her head Piper gave him. He shut up while she did damage control. In the end Gilroy calmed down enough to go with her to the site she'd proposed to look around.

"I know you're very busy, Jason," she purred sweetly, "so we won't detain you. Mr. Gilroy and I can talk at our leisure." The look in her eyes told him not to argue.

"Nice to meet you, Mr. Gilroy. I hope you find what you're looking for." He watched them leave, Piper soothing as she walked with him.

"What happened?" Ida asked, her head tilted to one side like a curious bird.

"I think I just blew it." How many times had Piper warned him to slow down, not to push so hard?

"A little aggressive, were you?" Ida's snort earned his glower. She didn't back down. "When are you going to relax, Jason?"

"I don't know what you mean. Developing Serenity Bay has been my first priority for quite a while now. I thought you knew that."

"I do. But does it all have to happen this month?" Ida poked her pencil tip into the automatic sharpener on her desk and let it whir until the pencil was just a stub. "You're grinding us down with your pushing, Jason. Piper's lost about five pounds since she got here, from stress. When are you going to learn to trust?"

"I trust Piper!" Indignant at the accusation, he leaned his elbows on the counter and glared at her.

"I wasn't talking about Piper, though some other time I might dispute that comment—like when you're pressing me about her whereabouts." She let him digest that for a moment, then sighed. "I was talking about God."

"God?" Now that didn't make sense at all. God was the only one he did trust.

"You act as if He's out to wreck whatever you do," she said. "If you trust someone, you have to have faith in them. Doesn't the Bible say that God will give you the desires of your heart if you devote yourself to Him?"

He nodded. His Bible study this morning had been about that very verse.

"Isn't developing the Bay your heart's desire?"

Yes, it was. Proving himself was a deep-seated need that grew whenever he thought about the past.

"Don't you believe that God wants this place to progress, that He'll work all things together?"

Did he? Jason searched his inner heart and realized she'd hit on the truth. Maybe he wasn't so sure he had God's approval, maybe he knew, deep down, that success with the Bay had more to do with shoring up his own shaky self-esteem. It was time to examine his motives.

"Does Harold know he married such a smart woman?"

"He should. I tell him often enough." She laughed.

"You keep telling him." He checked his watch, then made a decision. "Ida, I'm unavailable until the council meeting tonight. If somebody needs me, send them to Piper or put them off."

"You've got it, boss," she said, then she winked.

As he walked back to the marina, Ida's words reverberated through his mind. He gave Andy his jobs for the rest of the day, got in his truck and took off for the depths of the forest where nothing and no one could interfere with his thoughts.

Piper had tried to warn him but he wouldn't listen. He'd wanted the Bay to flourish so badly that now he was risking losing investors by pushing them too hard for what they couldn't or wouldn't give.

But if he didn't, if he just sat back and waited, what would change?

Maybe nothing. And that was his biggest fear.

So what was he trying to prove here—that the foster kid who'd never mattered to anybody was important, that the Bay couldn't get along without him at the helm?

He delved deeper into the truth, then finally faced it head-on.

It didn't matter what level of success he achieved for the town. He could never erase the hurt that came from knowing she'd chosen someone else above him.

He'd told Piper he'd never loved Amber, that he'd realized she wasn't the woman for him. That much was true. But the realization had only come after she'd dumped him for Trevor. And it had come on the heels of learning that Trevor had chosen money and achievement above their friendship.

Jason claimed he'd accepted God's will in that matter. Was that true?

Not really. He saw that he'd clung to the pain of it, searched for a way to erase it. What he hadn't done was let God wash it away.

Who was he to talk to Piper about letting the past go?

He'd thought he'd dealt with it but it'd been there, underneath, eating away at him all this time.

What about Piper?

He thought of her now, her gorgeous face surrounded by that mop of unruly curls that expressed her mood of the moment. Gorgeous, confident, accomplished. She answered to nobody and forged her own path, depending on herself to achieve her goals.

Piper was everything Amber hadn't been. Was that why

he'd found her so attractive, because she outshone his former girlfriend?

Jason hated the thought, hated what it implied about him—a shallowness he'd never imagined. But he faced the possibility because what he needed now more than ever before was to face the truth.

Was Piper important to him because of what he felt for her, because of the place she filled in his life? Or because he needed to prove that a beautiful, strong woman could care about him, that he wasn't unlovable?

He closed his eyes and tried to imagine Serenity Bay without Piper, but a thousand images filled his brain. Piper at the helm of *Shalimar,* her face utterly serene as the wind whipped past. Piper struck with a fit of the giggles in the middle of a snowball fight at Spring Fling. Her melted-chocolate eyes darkening black with temper when she took him to task for interrupting her meetings. Tears plopping from those black lashes onto her silken cheeks hiding a wealth of hurt she kept tucked inside.

The Bay without Piper? It didn't compute.

He loved her.

Jason leaned back against a tree and let that sweet knowledge flood over him. It wasn't about comparisons. With Piper he'd found something he'd never known before—acceptance. She hadn't flinched when he'd told her his sad little story, didn't seem to care that he was only a glorified mechanic. When he was with Piper he felt at home.

So what was he going to do about it?

Nothing.

Oh, he'd be there, as much as she'd let him after today's debacle. He'd make sure she knew that he cared for her. But he wasn't going to push her, force her into something she might regret.

This time, Jason decided, he was going to sit back and let God take over.

Even if it killed every plan he'd ever made.

Where was he?

Piper kept her seat, forced her hands to remain still and scanned the notepad in front of her but every nerve in her body was attuned to the sounds around her and the expectant faces waiting for Jason to appear at the town council meeting.

Dylan wasn't here, either, but she knew he'd show. Once her father decided on a project, he was like a dog with a bone. He'd keep pushing until he got his way. Rather like Jason, she mused grimly as she smiled reassuringly at Mr. Gilroy.

"I'm sure he'll be here momentarily."

A rush of footsteps outside the room signaled Jason's arrival. He burst into the room, tousled, slightly dusty and meekly apologetic.

"Sorry. I was out in the forest and I got a flat tire. Shall we begin?" He picked up the agenda. "Mr. Gilroy is here to talk about his desire to build some condos in Serenity Bay. Go ahead, Mr. Gilroy."

Piper swallowed her surprise as the condo builder rose and began a halting speech. Jason asked several questions which soon loosened the man's tongue and his presentation became much more interesting. Asked for her opinion, Piper reinforced what Gilroy had said. At the end the council's interest was palpable and an offer was tabled.

Satisfied with that development, she glanced around, realized Dylan had arrived while she was speaking. He smiled at her, but she could tell his focus was elsewhere. She found herself gripping her notepad a little too tightly as Jason called on him next.

"Wainwright Inc. has taken your concerns under advisement and made significant changes to our proposal. We are hopeful that what you see today will offer you greater perspective into our future plans."

Piper studied each aspect as Dylan presented it, wishing she'd seen it first. Several things sent up immediate red flags and she scribbled notes to herself for later comment. She couldn't help studying Jason during the presentation. He seemed remarkably calm. Perhaps too calm?

His disappearance this afternoon left a lot of questions, and the possibility that he'd met with Dylan. Jason's aggressive stance on the hotel was no secret, so it wouldn't be surprising if he'd sought an opportunity to meet outside of the council.

But he said he'd been in the forest. Doing what?

"We'll now open the floor for questions. Piper, anything you want clarified?"

Surprised that Jason had called on her first, she gathered her composure and rose.

"It's a good proposal," she said, her focus on Dylan. "Well thought out and carefully planned. But there are still several issues that run counter to our plans for development of the beachfront and the immediate area." She listed the problems, illustrating how they would alter plans already moving forward for other aspects of development.

As she spoke, Piper waited for Jason's rush of argument. But he remained silent. It was Dylan who pressed her.

"We have to have some leeway to fulfill the needs of the hotel," he argued. "We can't build something this massive only for the town's benefit. Wainwright has an investment to recoup, after all."

"Naturally," she said quietly. "But our investment is also great. In two or three years, when Serenity Bay is ready to pursue another phase of our plan, we don't want to be in the position of having to reorient some of our projects, or perhaps even cancel them, because we didn't plan for the contingencies I've noted."

"So what you're saying is that we're close, but still not quite there yet," one of the councilors muttered.

"Yes." She met Dylan's glare, knew he was frustrated and felt a twist of shame that she'd hurt him. But if that's what it took to defeat Wainwright…

"Okay then." Dylan began taking down his work. "I'll take that as a no. I should warn you that I'm not sure Wainwright is prepared to come back with another offer. We do not usually accept such a large amount of—er, guidance when we submit a project and we have already made a number of concessions to fit your needs."

"I'm sorry we've been so difficult," Jason chimed in.

Piper could hardly believe he had said that. She'd expected him to be furious but he looked almost resigned as he thanked Dylan for his work. As Dylan left the room, Jason called the meeting back to order and suggested they go in camera—retire to privacy where the general public was not present—to deal with the rest of the issues.

Thus excused, Piper left, caught up with Dylan as he placed his briefcase inside his car.

"You're not in a rush to get back again, are you?" she asked quickly, needing to make him understand her position.

"Why?" He paused, turning to look at her.

"I put a chicken in the slow cooker. I thought you might share a meal with me." She widened her gaze. "You haven't eaten, have you? You never used to before a presentation."

His brows lifted as if he was surprised she'd remembered.

"Come on, Dyl. It'll be just us two. I'd like a chance to catch up with you."

After several moments he shrugged. "Sure. Why not?"

"Do you want to come with me, or follow me to Cathcart?"

"I'll have to leave and for that I'll need my truck. I'd better follow you. It's been so long I'm not sure I remember how to get there."

"You'll remember once we get going." She reached out and hugged him. "I'm across the street." She pointed.

"You're still driving that thing?" he asked, but a hint of softness lay underneath the words.

"I couldn't get rid of my little roadster. Vance loved it. So do I. Besides, it runs like a dream." She grinned, then hurried across the street, thanking God for the opportunity to reconnect with her brother outside of the business arena.

She drove quickly, eager to share what little time they had together. At the house Dylan told her he'd been up since five and asked if he could take a quick shower. By the time he returned Piper had everything ready.

"I remember this meal," Dylan murmured as he served himself more of the golden chicken. "We'd come back here after church for Sunday dinner," he guessed.

Piper nodded.

"Then you and I would run outside to play."

"Yes." She smiled at the memory of that happy time before her mother had died. "You used to tease me with garter snakes you found in Gran's garden."

"And you never told. Why?"

Piper shrugged, smiled. "I thought you wouldn't play with me anymore and I loved playing with you. You were always the best big brother, Dyl. Nobody could have had more patience."

He ignored that, concentrating on his food. But the furrow between his brows grew deeper.

"Why did you come back here, Piper? Why didn't you sell the place and get on with your life?"

"I tried," she told him honestly. "After Vance died I buried myself in work, took on way too much and pushed myself to keep going. But I lost my joy." She pushed at the two peas left on her plate. "Gran and Papa were gone so I came back here, spent a weekend clearing out, dealing with stuff. When the day came to leave, I knew I'd rather stay. I felt a peace here, a certain comfort of happier times that I wanted to hang on to. So when I saw the want ad for economic development officer—" She shrugged. "That was my chance."

"Dad tried to contact you in Calgary," he told her.

Piper gaped. "Why?"

"He's had some health concerns, Piper. He's not as young as he was the day you walked out."

The anger in his voice shocked her until she recalled those visits her father had made to Cathcart demanding she return home. Dylan had begged her to come back. Baron had made both of them miserable.

"Oh, Dyl." She reached out to grasp his hand. "I'm sorry I had to leave you alone with him, but I just couldn't take it anymore. You were older, starting college. I doubt if you knew just how overbearing and demanding he'd become."

"Are you kidding?" An angry smile lifted the corners of his mouth. "I took the brunt of it the day you disappeared. I still do."

She tried to console him but Dylan shook her off. After a moment she coaxed him into the living room and served coffee there.

"Why don't you leave, Dyl?" she asked quietly. "You're smart. You could sell your stock, work for someone else, or set up your own company. Why do you keep taking it?"

"Why?" He barked out a laugh. "Because one of these

days Dad is going to retire. You don't realize how much he's aged, how much I actually do around there, Piper. Every day he depends on me more and more. And one of these days I'll be taking the reins. I deserve it. I've worked long and hard, and I intend to be CEO of Wainwright Inc. Then I'm going to implement some of my own ideas."

"Good for you." But she didn't think the benefit was worth the price he'd paid.

"You don't care?" Dylan asked, obviously puzzled by her attitude.

Piper shook her head.

"Wainwright Inc. has only ever meant unhappiness to me. He insisted I work there and I tried, really tried. But I had no autonomy. I couldn't think for myself. It was stifling. Far better for me that I left. For Vance, too," she reminded.

"Funny how Dad never took to him." Dylan shook his head. "I guess he never forgave him for stealing you."

"If it hadn't been Vance, he would have found another reason. Now tell me about some of your projects, something you're really excited about."

His eyes lit up and he began to discuss an idea he hoped to present to their father soon. But as Piper watched him her mind drifted back to Jason and his face when Dylan's hotel idea had been scotched. He'd looked forlorn, as if someone has just kicked him. She vowed to redouble her efforts to find a developer.

Before Dylan returned with an idea that she couldn't punch holes in.

Jason secured his boat to Piper's jetty, then climbed the stairs, anxious to share his decision to let God take control of everything now that his meeting was finally over. He slowed his steps as music wafted down the hill, the sound of voices laughing, teasing.

Piper had company.

Two more steps and he'd reached the rose garden. He looked in through the big windows. Shock held him immobile.

Dylan Wainwright lay sprawled in her grandfather's easy chair, his face wreathed in a smile as he stared at a picture Piper held up.

"I can't believe you kept that after all these years," Jason heard him say.

They shared an intimate chuckle, then he saw Dylan glance at his watch.

"I've got to get moving, Piper. It's a long way back."

"I'm glad you came for dinner, Dyl. It gave us a chance to catch up." She reached out and hugged him. "Don't be such a stranger."

"I'll try." Dylan hugged her back as if he was used to it, brushing a hand over her hair. "I like it like this. Makes you look younger."

"I feel better than I have in a long time. You should try living here for a while."

He couldn't hear any more. Jason turned on his heel and moved back down the slope, not caring that he was going too fast and could slip. He jumped into his craft, gunned the engine and took off across the water, turning the words in his mind over and over.

What did it mean?

"You two know each other?"

"Of course."

He should have figured it out earlier. It wasn't her father Piper had been waiting for during the Spring Fling. It was Dylan—a man she clearly cared about. So why was she so determined to shoot holes in his project?

And if she cared about Dylan, what was going on between himself and her?

Nothing made sense. Jason eased into his slip at the marina, secured the boat then took the stairs two at a time up to his perch. He didn't bother with lights, simply sat there, staring into the black water.

I said I'd turned it all over to You, but— The idea stole in as silently as the mist that now began to creep across the water.

Maybe it had all been a test. God only wanted him to surrender to show he could give up control. Now that he had, maybe Jason was supposed to act, do something to ensure Wainwright would come back to the table with something new.

Only, what could he do?

When the mist turned to fog, then a light shower, Jason finally moved inside. But the mental snapshot of Piper laughing with Dylan, her hand on his arm, kept Jason awake all night.

By morning he'd come up with a plan. He went to the office at the crack of dawn, searched Piper's Rolodex and came up with a number. Once Andy was busy with his duties for the day and the fishermen had left, Jason locked himself in his office and made a call.

Piper was great at her job, no question. But some things you just had to do yourself.

Chapter Eleven

"I appreciate the appointment, Mr. Wainwright. I know you're a busy man."

"Nonsense, Jason. I've always got time for you." The firm grip closed around his with a strength the almost-white hair belied. "You look better, my boy."

"I feel great."

Baron brought him up to speed about Expectations and they talked freely about his time there.

"Have a seat, son. I know I'm going to."

"Thank you."

"Now tell me what brings you here."

"I was hoping we could discuss your ideas for Serenity Bay. You've shown us two projects, but neither have quite met our hopes. I'm wondering if there's something I can do to ensure the next one is a winner."

"Serenity Bay." Baron shook his head. "That's Dylan's department. I don't have anything to do with it." The tanned fingers clasped and unclasped his custom-fitted pant leg, the dark brown eyes never quite meeting his. "Perhaps I should call him, though I don't believe he's in the office today."

"It's not necessary. I was hoping we could just talk for a few moments."

"I'm mostly a figurehead at Wainwright Inc. these days, Jason. The old man getting ready for the pasture. You should have made an appointment with my son."

He said it with a laugh but Jason could hear the pain behind the words.

"Wisdom doesn't age, sir." Jason took a deep breath. "Besides, I'm sure Dylan has other things to do. He's given us such a lot of his time already. Maybe you and I could brainstorm for a few minutes without him."

He laid out the diagram Dylan had forgotten on the board table two nights ago.

"This is the last conception we looked at."

Baron Wainwright leaned forward, traced the building with a fingertip. "It's a beauty, isn't it? The boy has real talent. I don't tell him that enough. What's your concern?"

"Do you know Serenity Bay, sir?"

Baron smiled and his whole face transformed.

"I should. Spent almost every summer there for many years. My wife grew up there. She loved it." The smile faded, the eyes dimmed. "But that was a long time ago. I don't go back anymore."

"Maybe you should, sir. You could see how much it's changed."

"I like to remember it the way it was when my wife was alive." He pointed to the drawing. "So what aren't you happy about?"

Slowly, precisely, Jason laid out each of Piper's points. And with a sharpness he wouldn't have imagined, the head of Wainwright solved every one. Though Baron looked somewhat older than he remembered, his mind was obviously as sharp as ever.

"It's a matter of perspective, primarily. No doubt Dylan

believes the restaurant is best located here. But if it was shifted, you could get what you're after and we'd free up another vista point without ruining your beach."

It was so simple. Jason couldn't believe they hadn't thought of it before.

"I can't thank you enough, sir," he murmured, staring at the lightly penciled lines the old man had drawn in. "I think this is something everyone will approve."

Wainwright rose, motioned to the coffeepot his secretary had just set on his desk. "Are you in a hurry, Jason?"

"Actually I'd love a cup. I didn't get my morning dose."

"Got up too early, I suppose. It's a long drive in to Toronto." He handed Jason a porcelain mug.

Jason took a sip, turned to sit and found himself staring into Piper's face from an eight-by-ten glossy framed in gold. She was younger, her hair was long, but it was definitely her.

"Will Piper approve of this change?" Baron Wainwright asked, sitting down behind the desk. "I can't imagine my daughter is exactly thrilled about doing business with my company, especially not in Serenity Bay."

"Your...daughter?" Every ounce of breath left his lungs.

"You didn't know?" Baron inclined his head to stare at the picture. His whole face seemed to sag with sadness. "No reason you would, I suppose. We don't exactly communicate anymore. Piper hates me."

"I—" Jason struggled to recover. "I'm sure that's not true, sir."

"Yes, it is. And I deserve it. After her mother died— well, let's just say I made some mistakes."

This was the man Piper loathed? Jason couldn't get it through his brain. Baron Wainwright was decent, honest and not above standing up for what he believed in. Something must have changed him.

The door burst open.

"Dad, Tina's not at her desk and—hey, Jason. What are you doing here?" Dylan thrust out his hand, glanced from one to the other. "Everything okay?"

"Of course. Don't fuss." Wainwright's gruff tone surprised Jason. "We were just talking turkey."

"I was worried that after our last meeting you'd be tempted to toss your ideas for Serenity Bay in the garbage and get on with your life," Jason interrupted. "I couldn't reach you so I contacted your father. He's come up with a brilliant idea to satisfy both our needs."

"Indeed."

Jason caught the dark look of pure anger Dylan tossed his father's way, though he recovered quickly.

"Well, let's see what you've got," he said, moving toward the table.

"It's your concept, of course, and I wouldn't dream of asking you to change it except that I thought we might save each other a whole lot of frustration and time," Jason remarked diplomatically.

"Does Piper know you're here?" Dylan asked.

"No, I'd prefer to tell her about this trip myself, in my own way." He saw Dylan understood.

"She's not going to be pleased you went behind her back, you know," Dylan mumbled, his attention on the drawing.

"That's an understatement."

Dylan glanced up, grinning.

"In fact, she's going to tear a strip off you a mile wide. Piper is very independent. You can't believe how long Dad and I debated even presenting a Wainwright idea."

"I'm very glad you did, because this idea is one of the best hotel concepts I've ever seen."

"Thank you." Dylan glanced at his father, rose quickly and moved behind the desk. "Dad? What's wrong?"

"Nothing, son. I'm fine. Just a bit dizzy. Don't fuss," the old man barked. "I'm fine, I said."

"Okay. Okay."

The tender tones of care and compassion in Dylan's voice surprised Jason. He'd always seen the man as hard-nosed, fixated on business. Yet the other night with Piper, and now with his father, his feelings lay exposed on his face.

Dylan lifted his father's cup, sniffed it.

"You're not supposed to be drinking coffee, Dad. You know what the doctor said."

"Phooey! At this age, what am I saving myself for? It's not like you're providing me with grandchildren." Baron glared at Dylan. He brushed his fingers against the picture of Piper.

Dylan took away his cup, moving to stand beside Jason.

"I'll get the changes to you at your next council meeting," he murmured. "I think it would be better if we left my father now. He's been overdoing it and he's tired."

"Certainly. I'll just say goodbye." Jason thanked the older man then quietly left.

Outside the office, Dylan plunked down the cup on the secretary's desk and gave her an angry glare before turning back to face Jason.

"I'm sorry to involve you in family problems, Jason. I'm not sure what my father told you but he and Piper haven't spoken for several years. I'd prefer it if you didn't mention that you came here and saw him."

"But surely she should know that he's failing?"

"I've told her." He frowned, then continued. "Dad will rebound. Baron Wainwright always does." A lopsided smile added to his sad look. "What I don't want is a confrontation between them. It's better if things go on as they have for now."

"You *don't* want them to reconcile?" he asked with a frown.

"I'd like nothing better. This position as go-between isn't fun. But every argument, every hurtful word only diminishes him more. For now it's best that they live their own lives." He sighed, raked a hand through his hair. "I'm trying to shield Dad as much as I can, take the load from his shoulders, though he doesn't like it. But both of them have hard heads."

"I understand. I won't lie to her, but as far as is possible, I'll keep my meeting here to myself." He walked beside Dylan to the elevators. "You'll be up next week with the revisions?"

"Count on it."

"Maybe when the hotel's done, your father will come and see it."

Dylan shook his head, his eyes dark and foreboding. "Don't count on that, Jason. Going back there—it could kill him."

Then he walked away.

All the way home Jason could think of only one thing— Piper Langley was Baron Wainwright's daughter. He'd trusted her completely and she'd kept that one most important truth from him. The woman he'd come to trust, to care about.

To love.

Pain at her deceit boiled inside, but he tamped it down, told himself to remain calm. Better to go along as if nothing had happened, find out what else she was willing to lie about. Then he'd expose her—and she'd leave.

That was for the best, wasn't it?

As Jason rolled down the last hill into town, a new question bubbled up.

When and why had she changed her name? Was that all part of the plan?

Something was wrong.

Though she couldn't put her finger on it exactly, Piper knew that Jason had changed. What she didn't know was why, or how she could fix it.

He was unfailingly polite, he listened to every idea, worked with her on each project as willingly as she could have asked. But all the time there was a barrier between them, a chasm that, no matter how hard she tried, she couldn't breach.

She longed to hide out at Cathcart House. But the council meeting lay ahead of her tonight. According to the agenda, Dylan would be there with a new idea. She wondered how many more times she'd have to shoot down her brother's ideas, watch the haunting sadness of disappointment fill his eyes, and know that she'd put it there to protect herself. What kind of a sister did that?

Not that she didn't have the best interests of Serenity Bay in mind. She did. Tweaking his last idea would have been easy. She could have made the suggestions herself if she hadn't been too afraid to allow Wainwright to build here.

For the tenth time today she wondered about her father. Last night during dinner, Jason had alluded to an article he'd read that claimed Baron was declining in health, that he'd begun to leave more details to Dylan. At first she'd thought he was hinting at something, but that feeling had been chased away by a flurry of new ideas they'd worked on. Then he'd calmly wished her good-night.

Piper pushed away her half-eaten sandwich and asked

the waitress for her check. Fifteen minutes and then it would start again.

You don't have to hurt Dylan. Why not trust Me?

The chiding of that still-small voice had grown louder in the past week, reminding her that once she'd believed that God would work all things together. What had become of that faith? When in all the pain and hurt had God become synonymous with Baron Wainwright?

Piper didn't know anymore. All she knew was that a lump sat in her heart and every time she thought of her father, it ached a little more. Why couldn't he have been a real father, loved her the way a man was supposed to care for his own daughter? Failing that, why couldn't she have continued the life she'd loved in Calgary, the one Vance's death had ended?

Discontented with questions that had no answers, Piper left the restaurant and strode down the street to the office. Inside she stored her bag in her desk, gathered up her notes and, after combing her hair, took her usual seat in the council room. Jason and Dylan arrived together a few moments later, teasing each other about their fishing abilities.

When had they become so friendly?

The evening started out badly as a council member pointed out the mistakes in two ads that had run last week. Piper tried to explain it was a printer's error but the member wouldn't let her finish a sentence. Finally, after waiting to no avail for Jason to intervene, she gave up and remained silent.

After making short work of the rest of business, Jason then asked Dylan to present his new ideas.

"I think you'll agree we've hit the nail on the head this time," her brother said, passing around artists' renderings of the newly revised hotel. He went into great detail explaining the changes and how they aligned to each problem she'd outlined last week.

Tension inched up her spine as Piper scrutinized the plans for problems. There were a few but they were minor and she knew it. She offered her half-hearted objections but they were quickly shot down. Everyone seemed to favor this new proposal.

Piper felt as if the sand were sinking beneath her feet. Relief swamped her when Jason finally adjourned the meeting. She rose, intent on escape.

"Hey, Piper, we're going for coffee. Want to join us?" Dylan sounded happy, probably buoyed by his good presentation.

"I can't, thanks. I have to get home." She rose on tiptoe, kissing his cheek. "I'll have to take a rain check."

He shook his head at her, his fingers trailing down one cheek. "You can't live in the past, sis. You've got to look ahead."

She smiled, hugged him, then left without saying anything more.

Jason stood on the sidewalk, watching *Shalimar* push across the blue water.

"She didn't look well. Is everything all right, do you think?"

Dylan turned from the truck where he'd stowed his belongings.

"With Piper? She's all right. Her problems have more to do with the date."

"The date?" Jason searched Dylan's face for an answer. "July 22 is a bad day?"

"For Piper it is. Her husband died on this day three years ago."

Husband? She'd been married?

"Vance was a nice guy, and they really loved each other. Then he got brain cancer. They tried every treatment but nothing helped. By the time he died, it was a blessing to everyone. He suffered terribly. That's one of the reasons Piper and Dad don't speak."

"Why?" Jason choked out, his anger rising. "What did your father do?"

"As far as I know, nothing. I don't really understand it, but after Vance's death, Piper refused to ever speak to him again. And she hasn't."

So she'd lost her mother, her grandparents, her husband and cut herself off from her father. Why?

"Dylan, I'm sorry, but I'm going to have to take a rain check on that coffee. Do you mind?"

"No, no problem. To tell you the truth, I should go straight back, anyway. I'm up to my ears at work."

Jason waited until he saw the taillights of Dylan's truck fade away, then he climbed into his boat and raced across the water, uncaring that he soaked himself by pushing against the waves too hard.

How could he have been so stupid? How could he have let it happen again—duped by the only person he'd dared trust? Anger seethed in his soul, fueled by the pain that stabbed far deeper than anything Amber had caused.

Once his boat was tied to the jetty, he took the stairs two at a time, stomped across the deck and pounded on the door. It opened seconds later. Backlit by the kitchen, Piper stared at him.

"Jason? What's wrong?"

"Why didn't you tell me you were married?" he shouted, clenching his fingers around the door frame.

Her mouth opened in surprise, her eyes darkening to huge pools that threatened to draw him in, drown him in their depths.

"Why? Because my husband died a horrible, painful death that upsets me to think about, and because it's no-body's business but my own." She stepped outside onto the deck, glaring up at him, the oval of her face lit by the fairy lights dancing in the breeze. "If divulging personal information was a job prerequisite you should have in-cluded it in the application process. Does your knowing about Vance make me less capable at my job?"

"Stop that!" He knew she was angry, but so was he. "It's not the knowledge. It's the secrets. I don't understand why you couldn't have said something."

"Like what? 'Oh, by the way, I'm a widow'? Why should I have to? I came here to start over. I haven't cheated you of anything, haven't worked against the Bay."

"Haven't you?"

She looked so innocent, standing there in her bare feet, her hair tumbling over an unmade-up face. Jason dropped his voice, trying to hide how deep her dishonesty had cut. "Why didn't you tell me you're Baron Wainwright's daugh-ter, Piper?"

She looked stunned by the question. "But I—I as-sumed you knew. I thought you understood that Dylan's my brother."

"You didn't think there might be a tiny conflict of in-terest there?" he snapped, infuriated that she offered no argument.

"Conflict of interest?" A rueful smile twisted her mouth. "Hardly. I've deliberately avoided anything to do with Baron Wainwright for ages. I'm trying to stop my fa-ther's company from building in Serenity Bay, Jason, not gouge a big profit for them. Where's the conflict?"

"The conflict arises, Piper, because you deliberately worked against me," he growled. "I thought we were both trying to do something special for Serenity Bay."

"I am!" She clamped her hands on her hips, met his stare. "In every way that counts I am *not* my father's daughter, Jason. What I've done, I've done for the benefit of the Bay. Wainwright is wrong for us."

"Why? Tell me that." He leaned in so his nose was mere inches from her. "What do you have against Wainwright Inc. aside from an old feud with your father, Piper? And don't give me any garbage about them not serving our interests. That's nonsense. The hotel Dylan proposed tonight will fit our needs perfectly."

"So you've decided, have you? You know enough about hotels to know what will work best in this town, what will help achieve the goals we've set?" She laughed bitterly. "Be careful your eagerness to get your name on the map doesn't trap you into trusting the wrong man."

"You don't trust Dylan?"

"I'm not talking about Dylan." She turned her back to him to stare into the night. "My brother does his best, but whatever he promises, he is unable to fulfill without my father's backing. And Baron Wainwright cannot be trusted."

"Why Piper? Tell me why."

"Leave it alone." She whirled around, her eyes flashing with anger and pain and a thousand other emotions he couldn't decipher.

"I can't." He touched her arm, waited for her to meet his gaze. "I don't understand why you did this, Piper. I trusted you. I believed you when I haven't believed anyone for a long time." He lowered his head, touched her lips, unable to break free of the magnetic pull he always felt around her. "I care about you," he whispered.

"If you care about me, drop Wainwright." She didn't move, didn't flinch under his stare.

"I can't. You know how important the Bay is to me. I can't just write off someone as big as Wainwright Inc.

without a very good reason." He settled his hands on her shoulders. "Tell me why, Piper."

Her shoulders sagged under his grip. He felt trembling course through her and knew she couldn't take the stress much longer.

"You want to know why you shouldn't trust Baron Wainwright?" she whispered so quietly he had to lean in to hear.

She drew back, settled herself on one of the chairs perched on her deck and motioned for him to do the same.

When he was seated across from her, she spoke.

"Baron Wainwright let my husband die."

Chapter Twelve

"His name was Vance Langley. He was a decent, honest man who wouldn't hurt a flea. He taught track in a high school. He loved kids, poured his heart and soul into helping them train, fulfill their potential, reach their goals. You couldn't have found anyone who was healthier. At least that's what we thought."

Piper prayed for the composure that would let her get through the story without breaking down. She kept her focus on the floor in front of her and forced the words out.

"My husband contracted a rare form of cancer. It progressed very fast. Vance was in horrible pain and there was not one thing I could do about it."

Her voice broke but she cleared her throat and pressed on.

"We'd almost given up the day I learned of an experimental treatment that had worked on other patients in a situation as desperate. It was being offered in Italy but it cost a great deal. Our insurance had run out, I'd spent our savings, borrowed from friends, done everything I could. We had nothing left. Even our house was gone."

"Dylan?"

"He helped out as best he could but he's on a salary

and he didn't have a lot of ready cash." She pushed her hair off her face. "I couldn't stand watching Vance suffer any longer. I hadn't spoken to my father at all since I left Wainwright Inc."

She caught his surprise and managed a faint smile.

"I'd worked there for almost a year, trying to mend fences between us. But my father wouldn't accept that I was an adult, that I could contribute to his company in my own way. The third time he went behind my back to change a deal I'd made we had a huge argument. I left, and I never went back."

"But surely—"

"Vance was in agony. I had to do whatever I could to stop that, so I phoned my father. Baron didn't answer so I left a message. I begged him to loan us money so I could get Vance to Italy." She twined her fingers together, staring at them, reliving those hours of waiting, praying, hoping. "He never called me back."

"I'm sorry, Piper."

"I couldn't understand why he didn't call back. I tried again. After the third message I phoned Dylan, begged him to talk to my father, ask him to help. My father never called us back. Vance died soon after."

She looked up through a wash of tears.

"Do you understand, Jason? He let him die. He could have helped, he could have talked to me, visited Vance, anything. He chose to ignore us, to punish me for leaving his company. That's how I know he isn't to be trusted."

Piper rose, walked to the door and pulled it open.

"If that's the kind of person you want to do business with, go ahead. But understand that I won't be a party to it. I can never forgive him."

She was almost through the doorway before the hand on her shoulder stopped her.

"You have to forgive, Piper."

"How can you say that?" Bitterness welled up inside her. "He was my father and he couldn't be bothered to help the man I loved."

"I understand what you're saying, sweetheart." Jason gathered her into his arms and held her as the sobs racked her body. "I know you went through agony. I don't pretend to understand it. But I do know you have to forgive Baron Wainwright or it will suck the life from you. I couldn't move on until I forgave Amber and Trevor. That's the way God made us."

"It isn't the same," she argued, easing away until the night air replaced his embrace. "God wasn't there. Only my father was. He's supposed to be there for me, no matter what. He didn't care enough. How do I get past that?" She pulled open the door. "I don't want to talk about it anymore. Good night, Jason."

"Good night."

She didn't watch him leave, didn't wait for the sound of his boat or pick up the phone when he called and left a message that he'd arrived home safely. Instead, Piper slipped on her swimsuit and immersed herself in the soothing waters of her hot tub.

She'd never felt so alone.

Jason read the hastily scribbled note left on his desk the next morning, wishing he'd ignored the querulous renter who'd kept him occupied for too long. He hurried out to speak to Ida.

"When did she go?"

"I'll assume you're speaking about Piper?"

He inclined his head.

"I have no idea. There was a note on my desk when I came in saying she'll be out of town for the next three days. If I have questions I'm to contact you." Her stare narrowed. "I have questions."

He did not want to face Ida's acerbic wit today. But escape wasn't an option now. He leaned his elbows on the counter.

"What's the problem?"

"Piper's notes say there's a delegation from a tour company coming today. She wants you to host a barbecue on the houseboat after you take them on a tour of the bay." Ida tapped a pencil against her notepad. "Apparently she's been coaxing them to come out here with their tours and they perked up when she mentioned you had houseboats for rent."

"Really?" The news stunned him. To be included on a prepackaged tour was a coup he'd never imagined happening so soon. Piper had mentioned nothing about interest from a tour company.

And he knew why.

A wave of shame rushed over him as the knowledge penetrated. She'd been afraid he'd mess it up, get too aggressive and turn the prospective clients off. It had happened before, though she'd warned him over and over to relax and let people get a feel for the area.

"She says that if you can't handle it, I'm to figure out something else. I need to know if you can handle it, Jason."

Last night came back with a vengeance. He'd accused her of pursuing her own agenda yet here was proof positive that Piper Langley was committed to getting Serenity Bay on the map.

"I can handle it," he muttered through gritted teeth. "What time?"

They sorted out the details then Jason left to get Andy started on cleaning the houseboat to within an inch of its life.

Piper had given him a chance to prove himself. He wasn't going to mess it up.

Now if only he knew that she'd be coming back.

"Thanks a lot, Row. I don't know what I'd have done if I couldn't hide out here for a few days."

"Like you haven't done the same for me a hundred times. I just wish I hadn't been so tied up with work and we could have spent more time talking." Rowena slammed the trunk. "You're really going to call Baron?"

"Already have. He wasn't in so I left a message. I guess he'll call me when he gets it." Piper shrugged. "The Bible tells us to forgive as we want to be forgiven. At this point, I'm not sure I can do it, but I have to try."

She searched her friend's face, saw the doubts rush across it. Rowena reached out and hugged her, then stepped back.

"Of course you do. Don't mind me, Pip. You already know I have a problem in that department."

"I realize now that part of what Jason said is true. I have been letting my anger and hurt toward my father cloud my life, until it'd begun to take over. My focus has been sidetracked from God. I don't want to become a bitter old woman hiding away from life."

"You won't." Rowena trailed behind her, waited till she had the car door open. "What about Jason?"

"I don't know." The sting of his accusations burned too deeply to brush off. "He doesn't trust me, Rowena. It's pretty hard to have a relationship with someone who constantly suspects you."

"You want to have a relationship? With him, I mean?"

"I love him," Piper admitted.

Rowena nodded.

"What's happening with the hotel?" she asked.

"I haven't been able to find out much. Tina's on holiday so my source is dried up for the moment."

"Dylan?"

"He's been unreachable." She decided to confide something she'd kept to herself. "The morning I was leaving Serenity Bay to come here, I could have sworn I saw his truck parked on a side road."

"Dylan? What was he doing—camping?"

"He hates camping." Piper shook her head, checked her watch. "There must be lots of those trucks around. It probably wasn't him at all. Anyway, I've got to get on the road." She took a deep breath. "I'm going to stop by my father's before I leave."

Rowena's eyebrows rose high on her forehead. "You're kidding?"

"No. I want to get it over with. If he doesn't want me there, he'll have to say so. Then I'll know I've done the best I can. Then I'll be able to put it to rest."

"Call me," Rowena ordered after hugging her once more. "Let me know. And don't take any of his garbage."

"Thanks, Row. You're a good friend," Piper said as she climbed into the car. She prayed silently as she wove her way through the streets, deserted at this early-morning hour.

Sunday morning. Baron should be having breakfast on the terrace by the pool about now.

The house looked the same. Elegant, stately. Two massive pots burgeoned with cascading flowers—pansies, babies' breath, lobelia. Her mother's favorites.

Forgive.

"I'm trying, God."

Piper swallowed the lump in her throat, climbed out of the car and walked to the massive door. Whispering one last prayer, she lifted her hand and pressed the buzzer.

The door swung open, but it was Dylan who stood there.

"Piper? What are you doing here?"

"I came to see Dad," she said simply.

He stared at her for a moment. His eyes flashed with surprise but he quickly recovered.

"I wish you'd phoned first. He isn't here."

Somehow she hadn't prepared for that. "Oh."

"Do you want to come in? I'm just leaving but I could manage another cup of coffee."

"No, thanks." She couldn't face the memories right now. "I'm on my way back to the Bay. I guess I might as well get on the road."

"Okay." Dylan closed the door behind him and walked with her to the car. "Did you like my idea?"

"The hotel is great, Dyl."

"Not the hotel." He frowned. "Didn't Jason tell you?"

"No, why don't you tell me?"

"I gave him a concept for a community center. It would be perfect at the edge of town on that vacant plot by the bush."

Piper listened as he went on and on, detailing his ideas of concerts and events that would tax the little town. Her heart sank as she realized Dylan had drawn Jason into his dream.

"We're nowhere near that stage yet, Dyl. We haven't even got enough accommodations right now."

He glared at her. "Why do you always have to pour cold water on everything, Piper? Are you mad because you didn't think of it first?"

"No! I'm sorry, Dyl," she apologized. "I didn't mean to do that. It's a great idea. We're just not ready for it yet."

She'd hurt him again and now he was pouting. Piper sighed, stood on tiptoes to kiss his cheek, then got back into her car. Home was the best place for her.

"I love you. Tell Dad I want to talk to him, will you?"

He nodded, rocking back on his heels. "Sure. Soon as I see him. Take care, Piper. The roads will get busy with all the cottagers coming back after the weekend. I don't want to hear about my sister in an accident."

"I'll be fine," she said. She waved then left, eager to escape now that the confrontation with Baron had been averted. The more she thought about it, the stupider the idea seemed.

Anyway, the ball was in his court now. If he wanted to talk to her, all he had to do was call.

The rest was up to God.

Jason stood inside his marina and watched Piper dock *Shalimar*.

Two weeks and nothing had changed. She was still keeping him at arm's length.

She laughed and joked with Andy while retrieving her briefcase from the hatch of the boat. On the surface everything was fine. But he didn't miss the way she tossed a quick glance toward him, as if she knew he was standing there, watching her. Or the quick, hurried walk that got her away from him.

He prayed endlessly about her, apologized several times, until she'd told him to stop. He'd done everything he could think of but the chasm remained there between them— a widening gap of distrust that had cost him more dearly than he'd ever imagined.

For once Jason was tired of the endless round of tourists that swarmed the Bay. He was putting in eighteen-hour days just to keep up with things. Higgy was an answer to a prayer. He took on most of the houseboat tours now. But yesterday he'd pulled a muscle in his back, leaving Jason to manage on his own.

He checked his calendar. Today looked relatively clear, thank goodness. Maybe he'd have time to take a break after lunch.

But it didn't happen that way. Piper's summons had him curious and anxious at the same time. He walked into the town offices at ten after one and found her on the phone.

"I can make that," she said, beckoning him inside. "It's not a problem at all. What information will you need?"

No cheery smile to warm him. Jason missed that. He closed the door behind him, sat down in front of her desk and waited for the call to finish.

"All right. I'll see you tomorrow morning. We'll count on talking for the full two days. Thank you." She hung up, leaned back in her chair and rubbed the corner of one eye.

"Tired?"

"Not really. Just a little frazzled."

Jason kept his lips shut. If she wanted to explain, she would, but he sure wasn't asking.

"That was a man from Toronto who develops strip malls. They've been looking around Serenity Bay apparently, though no one contacted me until today."

A strip mall? He almost let out a yell of excitement. Until he caught the look in her eye and reminded himself that it was just a phone call.

"Do they need more information?"

"No. Apparently they've almost decided to begin purchasing land." She rose, moved to a town map. "Here," she said, indicating a block that would coincide nicely with structures already there. "I'm to meet with them tomorrow to answer more questions about the town's future plans."

"Great!" He kept an eye on her, trying to assess her. It wasn't easy. Piper had always kept her emotions under wraps, more so now. "Do you want me to come along?"

She shook her head.

"It's not necessary, thanks. I'm assuming that if and when they have something to decide, they'll approach the town council."

His heart sank. He wanted to be included in the discussion, but how could he say that without making her think he was shadowing her?

"I'd really like to go, Piper. I promise I'll let you do the talking. I'll only answer what I'm asked. But I'd like to hear what they have to say."

A sad little smile tipped her mouth.

"Still don't trust me, eh, Jason?"

"Of course I trust you." He leaned in, held her gaze. "Can't you understand what a shock it was to learn you were a Wainwright and that you'd been married? I thought we were beginning to share our lives."

"I never deliberately kept either from you," she murmured, her face pale. "I assumed you knew my maiden name, but even if you didn't, I never thought it would matter. I left that behind a long time ago."

"Really?" He watched her closely. "I think you're still carrying it close to your heart. I think that's why you never came right out and asked me if I knew—because you're afraid to face the truth."

Piper shook her head.

"I know exactly what I feel for my father," she told him, her tone icy. "I even thought it was my duty to contact him, to try and repair the rift. I thought that's what God expected me to do." She stood in front of the window, peering out.

"It is."

"Is it?" Piper whirled around. "That was two weeks ago, Jason. Since then I've heard nothing. My father hasn't even so much as left a message for me, that's how little he cares about me."

"I don't believe it." He frowned as he rose, holding up a hand to stem her protest. "I'm not calling you a liar, but something must be wrong. Have you spoken to Dylan?"

"This morning, as a matter of fact. Dad is fine. He's quite capable of picking up a phone. In fact, he's been working long hours trying to get the London project up to speed. It's just his daughter he doesn't have time for."

"I'm sorry." He wrapped his arms around her and drew her close, waited for the shower of tears to abate. "I'm so sorry. I thought for sure that if he—"

"You know a different man than I do, Jason. You know the charismatic businessman who swings the big deals and spreads his charm on everyone around." She drew back, sniffed. "I know the man who doesn't have time to waste on the girl who wouldn't do as he wanted."

"But it doesn't make sense."

"Let it go, okay?"

He nodded, snuggled her head against his chest and let her recover, but his mind couldn't synthesize the two men. Baron Wainwright had known the name of every single locator at Expectations. If they were married, he knew their spouses' names and often asked after them. He remembered illnesses, anniversaries and any other information you told him. He'd taken pains to make each encounter warm and personal.

Could someone just shut that off when it came to his own family?

"You said you used to work with him," Piper said, lifting her head to look into his eyes. "How come you didn't know Dylan?"

Jason shrugged. "I don't know. He never came to Boston with your father, I guess. I never made any trips to Wainwright's offices so I wouldn't have seen him there. But I've gotten to know him better since."

"What do you mean?"

"He was here on Saturday. We went for a boat ride, barbecued some steaks, talked. He stayed at my place."

"What did you talk about?"

"Dylan has big ideas, Piper. I get the feeling that he never really discusses them with anyone else. He knows Serenity Bay very well. He's given me a couple of ideas."

She tilted her head to one side.

"Why the funny look?" he asked, tugging one of her curls.

"I always thought Dylan hated the Bay. He wouldn't come here much after I left home. Now you're telling me he knows it? I just find it odd."

"I find it odd that you're in my arms and I'm not…"

Jason leaned his head down and kissed her gently.

He hoped he'd convinced her that he loved her, but Jason decided he wasn't leaving anything to chance. He couldn't go through another two weeks of agony.

"Piper?"

She blinked at him, as if her mind had been elsewhere. "Yes?"

"Will you forgive me? Will you believe me if I tell you I love you, that I have for a long time? That I want to go back to the way we were?"

She wore a troubled look.

"I don't know if we can." She met his stare. "You didn't trust me, Jason. Even after all the time we've spent together, after all the things I've worked on, you actually thought I'd betray you. It's hard to rebuild."

"No, it isn't. You just trust that I've learned my lesson, that I know I was wrong and that I'll never make the same mistake again. I'd trust my life with you, Piper. That's how much I believe in you."

She wanted to believe him. He could see that. But she was holding back.

"What can I do to prove I trust you?"

"I don't know."

"Would it help if I said I have no intention of going to that strip mall meeting you're holding?"

She chuckled. "You can't. You have town council tonight, remember?"

"But it's supposed to last two days. I could go tomorrow." Her expression changed and he hurried to correct himself. "But I'm not. You're the person who handles development for the Bay. When you're ready to talk to me about it, I'll be here."

The phone rang. She answered it, jotted down notes, said she'd call back. Then she looked at Jason, her eyes dancing with excitement.

"What?"

"I don't think you can go tomorrow, either."

"Why?" It was something good, he could tell that much.

"The Freemont Society just phoned to say they want to talk to you about an idea they have. They want a conference call with you tomorrow morning at nine. You're to call them back at this number to set it up."

"Shouldn't you be in on that?"

She shook her head. "They're interested in working with Franklin's Marina, not Serenity Bay."

"The Freemont Society—don't they run that summer camp for disabled kids?"

"Yes."

"So what do they want with me?"

"You'll have to ask them tomorrow. I've got to get busy assembling packets for my meeting." Piper picked up a file from her desk, then turned to look at him over one shoulder. "You're sure you're okay with not coming?"

He forced his head to nod. "You go get 'em."

"I will." She opened the door, paused, then quietly asked, "Do you want to have dinner tonight?"

Jason shook his head.

"I'm sorry, I'd love to but I'm hired out for a seniors' picnic cruise this evening and Higgy is off. His back is still bad."

"Okay, well another time then." She smiled then followed him out of the room.

Lunch would have been good, too. Any time that they could spend together would have. Jason decided to phone her tonight, after he got back.

As it turned out Jason did have a dinner partner. Dylan dropped in just as Jason's pizza delivery guy left.

"Want to share?" he invited.

"Yes. I'm starving," Dylan said.

They shared the pie, consuming every last bit as Jason told him about the possibility of an outside tour company taking him on.

"Sounds like you're going to make some people very happy."

"I hope so. It could mean a great deal to the Bay if we had regular tours."

"Of course." Shortly after that Dylan left.

Jason picked up the phone, glanced at the clock and hung up again. Too late to call Piper now. His questions would have to wait.

He loved Piper. He'd told her that.

One of these days he was going to find out if she felt the same way about him.

Chapter Thirteen

If the first day of meetings hadn't gone well, the following morning rated as a major disaster.

Piper excused herself for the lunch hour, picked up a sandwich and drove to a nearby park to take a break.

She was putting off calling Jason and she knew it.

Her cell phone rang. It was him.

"Hey! How's it going? I'd hoped to hear from you last night." He sounded in a good mood.

"We talked till midnight. I thought it was too late to call." Suddenly no longer hungry, she put the sandwich back in the bag and sipped her coffee.

"So?"

Truth time. "Don't get your hopes up on this one, Jason."

"What's wrong?"

"Nothing's *wrong*," she said, bristling. "They're asking too much. They think that because we're small, we should concede on every point. I'm trying to illustrate the benefits of the first location but now they're asking for the waterfront. We just can't do that."

"Maybe I should come down."

Fury lit a fire in the pit of her stomach. *Here we go again.*

"No, Jason, you should *not* come down. This is my job. This is what I do. Remember? But I don't expect to win everyone I talk to. We may have to walk away from this, wait until we're further along." She drew a calming breath. "What did The Freemont Society want?"

"They'd like to take some kids on a houseboat cruise tomorrow morning. An all-day thing. If it works out well they'll book once a week for as long as their camps run. It's a kind of reward for the ones who push through their rehab."

Piper frowned.

"You don't sound that excited. It's quite an opportunity, isn't it?"

"Yes, of course. The steady income will be welcome."

"But?"

"But the opportunities from that mall would be even more welcome," he said quietly.

Piper gritted her teeth, rose and tossed the uneaten sandwich and half-finished drink in the garbage.

"You're doing it again," she complained. "I leave for one day and you're right back second-guessing me. When are you going to stop trying to control the world, Jason?"

"I'm concerned, that's all. This is a big thing for the Bay. If we lose them we don't know when the next opportunity will come along. It could be years."

"It could be tomorrow." Inside the car now, Piper closed her eyes and leaned her head back against the headrest. "Look. You've been teaching that boys' class at Sunday school about God's plan for their lives. Well, don't you think he's got one for yours? Do you really believe what you're telling those kids—enough to follow it in your own life?"

Silence. He was probably furious.

Tough. So was she.

"Trust is a two-way street, Jason. If I can't trust your faith in me, if it fluctuates with the circumstances, what kind of a relationship are we going to have? You said you care about me."

"I do," he insisted.

"Prove it. Have some faith that I'll do the right thing, whatever it is." She swallowed hard, then gave him the ultimatum. "More than that, have some faith that God didn't bring you this far to kill your dream because of one strip mall. In fact, I'd say He's trying to give you your dream."

"What do you mean?"

"You'll have a heaven-sent opportunity waiting on your boat dock tomorrow morning. What are you going to do—blow it off to race here and try to persuade a group of men to do something they don't want to? Or grab what your Father has given you and make it work?"

Piper waited a moment then closed the phone. It was time to go back to work.

"They're all wearing life vests?" Jason waited for Higgy's nod. "Okay then. Let's cast off."

He left Higgy to steer out of the bay while he made sure everything was secured. Andy waved goodbye and the kids waved back, in high spirits and ready to savor this new adventure.

"Couldn't have asked for a better day," one of the group leaders said.

"It is gorgeous out here, but I hope you've got lots of sunscreen. This sun can be hard on the skin."

Assured that each child was protected, he moved into the galley and started preparing the hot dogs they'd roast later on the beach. The atmosphere was stifling hot down here with barely a whisper of air despite the open windows.

Peals of laughter echoed across the water.

Too bad Piper wasn't here.

Her call yesterday had caused him a sleepless night of soul-searching. By five he'd admitted the root of the problem—he wanted to tell God how things should go and God wasn't listening.

As Higgy said, "If you want to hear God laugh, tell Him *your* plans."

It wasn't about Jason Franklin, though. It wasn't his plans that were important. With the dawn's early light had come the last vestige of surrender. God was in control.

He heard the engines slow as he finished his prep. That meant they were at The Bowl. The kids would need help with their rods and reels.

For the next three hours he baited hooks, removed fish and took snapshots. If this continued they'd have enough fish to fry for dinner.

Complaints of hunger had them moving on toward Carroll's Cove, a pretty picnic spot easily accessible for the children with wheelchairs and those with locomotion issues. Jason pulled, tugged and lifted while Higgy went ahead and got the fire going. Then there were coolers of supplies to be transported. Everybody was hot and thirsty.

"I never would have imagined I'd enjoy the day so much," Higgy murmured later as the supervisors helped those who wanted to swim into the water. He held the soda can against his cheek trying to cool it. "Looking at these kids. It makes me feel shame to know I don't give thanks enough for my life. Look how hard they work just to get to that water."

He was right. Once they'd packed up the food, Jason and Higgy relaxed on the banks under a willow tree and watched the impromptu water volleyball game. Then it was time to push toward Fairview Falls.

It was four-thirty before Jason thought to check the

weather report. The news was not good. He motioned Higgy in.

"Tornado warnings are out."

"Makes sense given the heat and humidity," Higgy murmured. "But I've never heard of the Bay being hit before."

"One touched down five miles out last year. Close enough for me. I think it's time to head back."

"Gotcha."

They got everyone on board and Higgy steered them back toward Serenity Bay. But they were a long way out when the wind picked up and began tossing waves that pushed them too close to shore.

Then the motor died.

"What's wrong?" he asked Higgy.

"I think we're out of fuel."

"Impossible. Andy filled her last night. I checked to be sure." Jason did his own check and couldn't believe what he saw. "The spare?"

"Empty. I'd say someone doesn't want us going home."

They looked at each other for several minutes.

"Find a place along the shore. The waves will push us in and we can dock. Then we'll get the kids off. We can probably shelter them on board, but I'd feel better if we found a cave or something off the water," Jason said.

A crack of lightning had Jason reaching for the radio. He issued a distress call while Higgy edged them inward. Suddenly he realized the radio had died.

Reality stung. He was on the water, in the midst of a storm, with a group of kids who would need a lot of help to get off the boat. By the looks of the sky, the houseboat was about to be deluged, perhaps even tossed onto the rocks.

Jason pulled out his cell phone and dialed. No signal.

The distress beacon—they could set it. He opened his

mouth to tell Higgins, saw the open panel, the empty space. The beacon had been removed.

They were on their own.

The weather bulletin ended as Piper parked her car. Her skin prickled with warning. Jason's houseboat trip was today.

She climbed out and raced for the marina. Her heart hit her toes at the sight of the empty berth. The houseboat was not in its mooring.

Inside the building, Andy was on the phone.

"I'm telling you, I can't reach him and he's two hours overdue. There's no response on his radio and his cell phone isn't working."

She pulled out her own phone, called Ida.

"He's not here, Piper. I've already called for help."

"Good. He's got that group of disabled kids with him. If they've had mechanical problems we'll have to pray they made it to shore. Who's searching for them?"

Ida's silence sent a shiver through her.

"What's wrong?"

"Water search and rescue was called over to the next county to help there just after lunch. We've got a couple of launches out looking but I'm pretty sure Jason intended to take the group a long way down, make it a real tour. If that's the case—" Ida didn't finish.

She didn't have to. Piper understood exactly what she hadn't said. He'd never make it back in time before the second storm hit.

"Is there a way to get someone up in the air? If they could fly over, spot them, we'd know exactly where to send the boats. The wind is dying down, I think," she added, studying the wind sock Jason had fastened to the end of the building.

"We don't have air support up here, Piper. It will take at least three hours to get something from the city. My other phone's ringing. I have to go."

Piper hung up as the truth sank in. At best, Jason was stranded. At worst, he could be lying somewhere hurt, unable to protect his passengers.

Have some faith that I'll do the right thing.

Her angry comment returned with haunting clarity. She'd told him to trust her. Now it was time for her to prove that she was worthy of that trust.

There had to be someone with a plane or a helicopter who could help them.

Like a dream, an old memory of her father landing his helicopter at Cathcart House flew across her mind. He still had one. She knew that. She'd seen a news clip in which he'd climbed down from the powerful beast.

Maybe—

This was no time for hesitation. They needed help and they needed it fast. Piper pulled out her phone and dialed the office. Baron was at home. She dialed the house. Dylan answered.

"Dyl, this is an emergency. I need to talk to Dad."

"He's not here, Piper. Did you try his cell?"

"Not yet."

"What's wrong?"

She explained the situation as quickly as she could.

"It's urgent that I talk to him. The winds are down for now but the weather station says they'll pick up later. The Bay is going to get lashed by a very heavy storm. I've got to find Jason and those kids."

"Okay. Well, if I hear from Dad I'll get him to call you."

She nodded, hesitating.

"Anything else, sis?"

"You couldn't come, could you? Just to be here. I'm so scared."

A static-filled pause hung between them.

"I would if I could, Piper. You know that. But I'm too far away. I'd never make it there before morning."

"Of course. I should have thought of that. I'd better go, Dyl. I want to keep the line free."

He said goodbye and she hung up.

Though Piper kept the line free, her father did not call back and hurt sent a deeper root into her heart. She'd told him it was urgent, explained how badly they needed his help. Why didn't he answer?

"I tried, God. I tried to forgive him. But this is exactly like before, with Vance."

She turned her attention to the group of volunteers who'd gathered at the marina to help organize the search effort. Most of them had friends or family on the water, searching. But nobody had reported a sighting.

"Waiting's the hardest part," Andy told her as minutes ticked into hours. He handed her another cup of coffee though she hadn't finished the first one he'd already given her. "We've only got a small window of opportunity here, according to the weather forecasts. If we could just get something in the air to search…"

Piper's cell phone rang.

"Dad?"

"Piper?" The beloved voice sounded faint.

"Jason! Where are you?"

"…help. Boat…ran out of fuel…stranded. Send help."

"It's coming," she promised. "Just hang on. Jason?"

But there was only static, then the line went dead.

She couldn't lose Jason, too. She hadn't even told him that she loved him.

Two more boats chugged toward the marina. The room

fell silent as the men walked inside, shaking their heads at the unasked questions.

Piper knew then what she had to do. The past could not be repeated. She wouldn't let it. The old arguments and bitterness had prevented her from pleading, begging, doing everything possible to get Vance what he needed. She'd caved in, let anger and hurt interfere when she should have demanded help no matter what the cost to her pride.

She clicked open her phone and dialed. When one avenue didn't work out, she tried another. Dylan was still no help but after seven calls she finally reached Tina.

"Thank goodness! Tina, I need to speak to my father. I've been trying his cell, the house. I can't find him. Do you know where he is?"

"We've just come out of a meeting, honey. He's right here. Hold on."

"Piper?"

The sound of his voice grabbed her heart and squeezed until tears pooled in her eyes. She loved him. She couldn't fix the past, couldn't undo what he'd done. Right now it didn't matter that he'd hurt her and maybe would do so again. This was her father and she needed his help. No matter what.

"Daddy?" she whispered.

"I'm here."

"I need help."

A soft, slow sigh, then the voice came back. "Tell me what's wrong, sweetheart."

Piper quickly poured out her story.

"It's really bad, Dad. Jason's got kids on the boat. Disabled kids. We've got to rescue them."

"I have an old friend who lives about an hour from the Bay. He's got a big chopper he uses to bring his family to their lake home. Let me see if I can reach him."

"Will you let me know, Dad?" she asked softly.

"As soon as I do. And Piper?"

"Yes?"

"I love you."

Joy sprang up inside her, a fountain of happiness she couldn't suppress.

"I love you, too, Daddy." She closed the phone and found Andy at her elbow.

"Was that the answer to a prayer we've been waiting for?" he demanded.

"I hope so." She hugged him, whispering a heavenly plea. *Please, God?*

Jason tied off the lines as best he could, hoping it would be enough to keep the boat from ramming against the rocks and destroying the hull. But that was the least of his worries.

"Did you find anyplace we could shelter?" he asked Higgy.

"A cave, of sorts. If we can get everyone off before it starts really pouring, those with wheelchairs might have a hope of making it. Otherwise, we'll have to carry each of them. I started a fire already in case we need to dry some things out."

"Good enough for me. Let's see if we can get a ramp ready. You man the controls, try to keep us steady while I help unload everyone."

"Okay."

A clap of thunder had some of the kids whimpering.

"Hey, this is just another part of the adventure," he told them with a grin. "Don't you worry. Cap'n Higgy and I have everything under control."

What a joke. He was utterly powerless and Jason knew it. No matter what he did, it was only a stopgap measure until—*if*—help arrived. The arrogance of trying to impose his will on the universe hit him full force. He was no more in control than a flea controlled the dog it sat upon.

He looked into the trusting faces of his passengers and turned to Someone who knows all things.

God, forgive me for thinking my way is best. Show me what to do.

"Okay, mateys. We're almost ready for our first expedition. I want you all to pay attention to your leaders. They'll give you each a number. When your number is called, it's time for you to get off this boat. There's a storm coming so the waves will bounce us around a little, but don't you worry. You're all going to be just fine."

"Are you sure, Captain?" A little redheaded boy who looked about nine tipped up his freckled face and peered into Jason's eyes. "Certain sure?"

"I'm positive, son. You're number one," he said, then glanced at the supervisor to be sure she'd heard. She nodded and Jason went back outside.

He jumped off the edge into the water and secured the ramp as well as possible with the waves lashing against him. They'd have to move fast.

But with that thought the storm seemed to intensify.

"You are in control here, Lord. But if you could give us ten minutes, I'd sure be grateful. Give us a break in the weather for ten minutes so we can unload these kids and get them safe."

Nothing happened. The wind continued its raging, the water soaked his pants, splashed his face. Then a soft whisper inside his head asked, *Do you trust Me now?*

"All the way, Lord. Your will be done."

A quiet sense of calm filled him. God was here. All

Jason had to worry about was the task before him. Rain pelted his upturned face, but he ignored it.

"Number one. Come on down."

Chapter Fourteen

The chopper blades whipped the bay into a frenzy. To Piper it was a glorious sight.

She stood under the eaves of the marina building, watching for the pilot to emerge. To her surprise her father stepped out of the cockpit and jogged across the parking lot.

"Daddy?" She tumbled into his arms and hugged him back. "What are you doing here?"

"I came to help." He grinned. "Had to fly to Don's house. He's away but he said we could use his chopper. So I brought it. Are you ready to go?"

"We have some supplies—blankets, extra clothes, stuff that might help if the kids have been exposed to the elements. Also a nurse, just in case." She didn't want to even think about injuries.

He nodded. "How far out is he?"

"We're not sure. Probably a long way since no other boats have spotted them."

"Okay, let's get loaded. It's going to get worse before it gets better."

Less than ten minutes later they were airborne, carrying an extra passenger, a volunteer who'd insisted on coming, in case Jason needed help. The other two sat in the back. Piper sat across from her father, watching as he touched the controls that carried them over the water.

"Thank you for doing this," she said quietly, knowing the softness of her words would carry through the headset.

Baron reached out and touched her hand.

"Sweetheart, I've been waiting for so long for you to ask me for something. Your call today was an answer to a prayer."

"It was?" She adjusted the earphones to be sure she wasn't dreaming this.

"Of course." His smile reached out to warm her. "I've wanted to talk to you for a long time but you would never listen."

"But I phoned you and you never answered." She cut herself off, holding up her hands at his protest. "No. You know what? Let's not do this. Vance wouldn't have held a grudge and neither do I. I've forgiven you. Let's just move forward."

"Vance?" Baron's head jerked around from his scrutiny out the side window. "What grudge?"

"Forget it, Dad. Let's just concentrate on finding Jason."

She turned to stare out the window as the angry feelings threatened to take over again.

"I am concentrating. But I want to know what you meant that Vance wouldn't have held a grudge?"

"That you didn't help," she said simply, swallowing down the tears.

"Vance never asked me to help him."

"No, he didn't." She lifted her head, looked at him. "I did. I begged you, Daddy." She could barely squeeze the words out. "You never returned my call. Vance believed you'd call, Dad. He died waiting."

"Piper, listen to me. I never got a call from you. Not

once." His face had paled, his eyes swirled dark with turmoil. "If I had, I would have sent whatever you needed, done whatever you asked."

"But you must have. I left a message with Dylan. He said he'd passed it on to you."

Baron glanced at her, then stared through the windscreen.

"This message—what exactly did you tell Dylan to say?"

"That I needed your help. That Vance would die unless we could get him to Italy for a new treatment. You must know."

He shook his head, his face haggard.

"Don't you think I would've come if I'd known my own daughter needed me?" he grated. "I thought you hated me."

"I thought I did, too. I was wrong. But this doesn't make sense."

Baron nodded.

"I remember—I was in Europe then. I never even knew Vance was gone until two weeks after his funeral. If I'd known you needed me—" He frowned at her. "You told Tina you'd been trying to reach me today."

"Yes. I left messages at the office, at the house, on your cell. I even called Dylan, begged him to tell you." She stopped, touching his arm. "You're very pale. Are you ill?"

"No." He dropped several hundred feet to get a better look at something on the water's edge. "Piper, I spoke to Dylan about ten minutes before you called me today. He said nothing about your call."

"But that doesn't—" She leaned forward, peering down at the tiny island off to her left. Her heart leaped to life, sending a rush of joy.

"There, Daddy! I think that's Jason's boat. Higgy painted the top just the other day."

"I need a patch to land on. See if you can spot a clearing." Baron's voice was stronger now, his face purposeful as he concentrated on his machine. "And Piper?"

"Yes?"

"Pray."

The noise echoed into the cave. The kids looked up, eyes wide.

"Is that the elephant you were telling us about?" the smallest asked.

Everyone burst into laughter.

"I think it might be. I'll go check. Don't let those marshmallows burn."

Jason motioned to Higgy to wait then he stepped outside, scanning the sky. A helicopter was circling the island, preparing to set down on the grassy knoll fifty feet away.

Piper had come through for them.

He hurried back inside to tell the supervisors what was going on.

"Didn't I tell you the adventure wasn't over yet?" he teased the children.

Their laughter had Jason thanking God that none of the day's events had traumatized any of them. He was certainly in control.

He returned to the cave opening, watching as the massive machine came to rest. Rain fell in sheets of gray but he could make out the figures of four people moving toward him.

"Piper?" He wrapped his arms around her and held her tight. "You didn't have to come all this way."

"Yes, I did." She kissed him, then leaned back, her wet hair hanging in her eyes. "Are you all right? Is anyone hurt?"

"No. But I'd like to get them out of here while they still

think it's a game." He blinked in surprise at Baron's appearance. He reached out to shake his hand. "Thanks for coming, sir. I take it the transportation is courtesy of you?"

"A friend," Baron told him. "But that's not important." He pointed up. "I asked some friends to follow. I hope you don't mind. Let's get your passengers loaded as soon as they're landed. We're going to have to do it in one trip. The wind is getting too high to risk another trip back."

Jason nodded, squeezing Piper's hand.

"I'm glad you called him again."

"There's something you should know, Jason." Piper stopped speaking when Higgy interrupted.

"Gale force winds are predicted."

"The storm looks like it's worsening," Jason told her. "We've got to get moving. We'll talk later, okay?"

Piper nodded. "Go and do what you have to," she whispered.

With Baron's help, Jason soon had teams formed. Together they moved all the kids aboard the three choppers. After a last look at the houseboat, he joined the others, motioning for Baron to follow them home.

Piper tried to give him her seat but he shook his head. "Tell them a story," he said, then moved to the second chopper. He'd keep the kids calm, make it an adventure. Hopefully they'd never realize the perilous situation they'd been in. To keep them busy Jason launched into another story that left them hanging until the helicopters finally landed at Serenity Bay.

"Hey! How are we gonna find out what happened?" his carrot-topped friend demanded.

"Guess you're just going to have to come back next week." Jason grinned. "Okay, the ride's over." He glanced at Piper, who stood waiting.

"Everyone's to go to the community center," she explained. "We've got a chicken dinner and lots of games. With prizes."

The excited kids could hardly wait to exit the helicopter before hitting the power buttons on their wheelchairs and zooming off, supervisors jogging to keep up. While Piper was busy with one of them, Jason turned to Baron.

"Thanks hardly seems enough."

"Forget that. What happened with the boat?"

"I'm pretty sure somebody sabotaged it." He explained the problems. "Higgy checked the beacon last night. Everything was fine." He swallowed, hating what he had to say. "I've been trying to think who could have done it. Dylan was here, Baron. We had dinner then I got a phone call. He said he was going to wait outside."

"I was afraid of that." Baron looked upset.

"Why?" Jason frowned, his surprise deepening as he heard about Piper's attempt to reach her father through Dylan. "But why? Why would he do that?"

"I don't know. But you need to speak to the police. Now. They'll want to examine the boat."

"And Piper?"

"She and I have some talking to do," Baron told him. "I love my daughter, Jason. Even though I've acted like a jerk, I always did. It kills me that I wasn't there when she needed me." His eyes clouded. "For her to lose Vance like that—" He shook his head.

"You're here now. I think that means a great deal."

"I messed up, Jason. I messed up a lot."

He patted the tired father's shoulder.

"We all did. But we serve a God of second chances."

Baron nodded but he said nothing more, content to feast his eyes on Piper, who was speaking to several officials. She looked over one shoulder, winked at them and grinned.

Jason longed to hang on and never let her go, but he

couldn't. Not yet. Not until he'd apologized to the Society's director, not until he talked to Bud Neely.

Then he'd find her. And with God's help he wouldn't let her go.

Piper slipped her arm into her father's and walked beside him to her car. She could hardly believe he was here, that he loved her, that he always had.

"Where's Jason?"

"He had some things to do." Baron pressed the hair out of her eyes. "I need to talk to you, honey. Can we go for a coffee somewhere? I could sure use one."

"Get in. I'll drive you." She switched the heat on then steered out of the parking lot toward the town's only drive-through. After she'd ordered and picked up two coffees, she pulled into an empty space on the lot. "I'm so thankful you came. I don't know what we would have done."

"God would have worked something else out." Baron sipped the steaming liquid. "Piper, I need to apologize. I acted like a boor and an oaf after your mother died. A hundred times I've wished I could take it back and a hundred times I've prayed for God's forgiveness. Now I'm asking for yours."

"Why did you do it, Daddy? What changed?"

"Everything." He tilted his head back, closed his eyes. "I always thought I'd die first, never her. When she was gone I couldn't accept that God would do that. I got bitter and very, very angry."

"You were hurting," she agreed. "We all were."

"It was worse than that. I let fear take over."

"Fear?" Piper had never imagined her father was afraid of anything. To hear him say it shocked her. "Fear of what?"

"Of messing up. Of not doing the right thing. Of being

a horrible parent." He dragged one hand through his hair. "She was so good at it, a natural-born mother. I should have let her teach me but I got caught up in making money. As if that mattered after she was gone."

"You did your best," she offered quietly, wondering at the anger that had faded now that he was here.

"No, Piper, I didn't. What I did was try to dictate every move you made."

"Why did you do that?"

"Because I was stupid. Because I was stubborn, too stubborn to know your grandparents were exactly what you needed. Because I was terrified something would happen to you and you'd leave me, too. Just like her." He blinked rapidly, then stared into her eyes. "I loved your mother more than my life, Piper. But in those days I was young and brash and I scorned God. I certainly didn't think I needed Him. I'd decided I was going to raise you all by myself, my way. I was going to turn you into a woman your mother would be proud of."

"Oh, Daddy."

He reached out to touch her curls, laid his palm against her cheek.

"She would be proud, Piper. So proud of her brave, strong, true little girl." He patted her shoulder. "Even though I took my loss out on your grandparents, accused them of taking away my daughter, even though my incessant demands drove you to them and kept you from the home your mother had made, even though I wasn't there to help you as she would have wanted, you've come shining through. Your mother would be so proud of you. Just as I am."

Piper set her cup into the holder, leaned over and wrapped her arms around him.

"I didn't understand, Dad. I wanted you to hug me and

hold me and you were trying to live through your own grief." She relaxed in his embrace for a few moments, then risked a look into his eyes. "But you were much harder on me than Dylan. Why?"

He let her go, and shrugged.

"I felt that Dylan was older, that he'd already made so many decisions, chosen his path. I didn't think he was as vulnerable."

"Dylan needs to know you love him, Dad."

He nodded. "I should have told him more, I know. Instead I've taken him for granted. And now there are problems."

"What problems?" The concern etching his face sent a shaft of fear to her heart. "Dad, is there something wrong at Wainwright?"

He nodded.

"There have been a number of—irregularities—all involving him. That's why I've been traveling so much. I've been trying to catch them before—" He paused, refusing to say any more even though Piper begged him to continue.

"I've got to go, honey. I promised I'd finish what I started and I can't stop now. Can you drive me back to the helicopter?"

"Of course." She swallowed the last of her coffee, switched the engine on. "But you'll come back, won't you? You'll come and stay so we can talk and get caught up with each other. I have so many things to tell you."

He smiled. "I'll be back, honey. Nothing in the world could stop me."

Satisfied, she drove them back to the marina. The rain had stopped for the moment. They stood together on the windswept lot and embraced, saying without words everything that needed to be said.

"Take care, sweetheart," Baron murmured, kissing her cheek.

"You, too, Daddy." She hugged him tight, then let go. "Come back soon."

"Yes." He turned to walk away, then paused, turned back. "When Dylan shows up, find a reason to keep him here and then call me, will you?"

She nodded. He gave her one last look, then walked to the helicopter, climbed in and was gone.

Piper checked Jason's shop, but he was not inside. They needed to talk but it looked as if that would have to wait. Once she'd made sure the children had left and she was no longer needed, Piper returned to her car, intending to head home. But when she was inside, she remembered her father's words and puzzled over them.

Why would Baron ask her to keep Dylan here when Dylan wasn't even in town?

She'd have to ask him when next she saw him.

Piper turned her thoughts to Jason, a tiny smile lifting her lips. She wanted to see him, to tell him how much she loved him.

But not like this.

She decided to go home to Cathcart House. She'd cut some roses, fill the house with their heady scent. A bubble bath, fresh clothes and then she'd start dinner.

And maybe, if everything worked out just right, Jason would show up. Then she'd tell him what she'd been afraid to say before.

Now she knew why God had brought her to Serenity Bay.

"I forgive," she murmured. "Please forgive me."

The rush of peace assured her God did. She could hardly wait to tell Jason.

Chapter Fifteen

Jason huddled in his chair, desperately praying for God's help. Once more his life was out of control.

Outside a car stopped, a door clicked. Footsteps padded to the door. It opened.

"Dylan? Hey! What are you doing here?" Piper paused with one hand on the screen door, scanning her brother's lounging form in her grandfather's chair. Her gaze rested on Jason, widened at the gag in his mouth, the ropes binding his hands and feet. Her body sagged, her shocked whisper carried across the room on the wings of fear. "What have you done?"

"*Me?* What have *I* done?" Dylan lurched out of his chair, his voice a notch too high, speech a tad too quick. "Shouldn't that be what have *you* done?"

A gun appeared in his hand. He waved Piper into the room.

"I don't know what you mean." Piper moved forward, dropped her bag on a chair but kept going until she stood in front of her brother. "Dad said you never passed on my message, Dylan. Not today when Jason needed help, not when Vance was sick. Why?"

"Why?" The stark pain brimming in his voice echoed around the room.

"Do you really have to ask, Piper?"

"Yes." She sat down in front of him, ignoring the gun barrel aiming directly at her midsection. "I have to ask because I don't understand why you'd do such a thing. I love you, Dyl. You're my big brother. I thought you loved me, too."

"I did." For a moment the dark eyes softened. A wistfulness flickered across his face. "I do. But it costs me too much. I'm sick of paying. Now it's your turn."

Jason knew the exact moment she realized the truth.

"It was you! All those incidents, the model hotel, the chlorine in the tub, the plans so conveniently dropped. You did all that. Even the salt in *Shalimar's* fuel?"

Dylan nodded and Jason wished he could spare her this. But there was nothing he could do except pray.

"Jason's boat?" Her eyes flared with anger at the response.

"Yes!"

"Why?"

"Do you know what it's like to be second best? To always fall short, to never feel like you've quite managed to meet the bar? That you'll never be able to do enough, say enough, work hard enough to get your father's approval?" He shook his head, snorted. "Stupid question. Of course you don't. How could you? You were always the apple of Dad's eye. 'Piper this. Piper that. When Piper comes back.' Blah, blah, blah. On and on he went. I could count on one hand the number of times I heard my own father say, 'Good work, son. Well done. I appreciate your effort.'"

"Oh, Dylan." Tears washed down Piper's face as the hate-filled words poured out. "You have no idea."

"Don't I?" He jerked his head, scanned the room. "Look

at this place. Even here you were the favored child. I got cold, hard cash. You got the place they loved."

"Because they thought you didn't like it here, Dyl. You took Papa's diary. Did you read it? He loved you, they both did. But you never seemed to want to stay at Cathcart. Not after Mom died."

"Why would I? To compete with Perfect Piper?" He glared at her, his face red. "I read the diary, read all about how proud they were of you. You're right there. I kept as far away from this place as I could."

"I'm far from perfect." She shook her head. "But why Vance? What did my husband do to you that you would stop Dad from helping us?"

"He would have bled the company dry looking for a miracle. I knew there wasn't one. Not for him. Not using the company I'd been breaking my back to keep on solid ground." Dylan touched her arm. "I was sorry about Vance, Piper. But in reality his chances weren't good, anyway. According to my information he wouldn't have made it through the treatments. And when he died, Dad would have felt he had to console you by offering you a job at Wainwright. I wasn't going to allow that."

"I feel like I don't know you at all," she whispered.

"You don't."

"And Jason? What is his crime? How did he threaten you?"

"He didn't. But you fell for the guy. His business is here. That meant you'd be staying. I couldn't have that." He jerked the gun toward Jason. "I figured that if he died on the water somewhere, you'd get out of here fast. Then I could get on with my plans."

"Your plans?"

Jason had never seen Piper so white. Her fingers

clenched around the arm of her chair as she struggled to remain calm.

"Your *plans* could have killed innocent children, Dylan. Your greed and hate could have stolen their lives. You would have been a murderer!"

Dylan paced, agitated and angry.

"I didn't know they'd be on that boat! He never said anything about them. He only said he was going out in the morning. How was I supposed to know? How could I know?"

The plaintive wail hit a nerve. Jason felt a wash of pity for the boy so desperate to gain love he'd resorted to such extremes.

"It couldn't have been just jealousy, Dylan. What you did to me, to Jason, to those kids—there has to be more to your actions."

Dylan nodded, his eyes emotionless, his face very calm. "There is."

Piper rose, moving forward until she stood directly in front of him—as if she intended to protect Jason from that gun. His blood ran cold and he wiggled hard, thumping the chair on the wooden floor.

Piper's eyes begged him to be silent. Dylan grew agitated.

"Shut up or I'll shoot you." He turned back to Piper, grabbed her arm. "You want to know why? Look. I'll show you. Then maybe you'll get it."

He pulled a folder lying on the table toward him, flipped it open.

Piper bent, staring at the contents.

"This is the hotel model you left in my car," she whispered. "It's beautiful, Dylan. But what—"

He didn't let her finish.

"I own all the land around Cathcart House, Piper. All of

it. Once you sell me Cathcart I'll be able to start construction. The hotel in town will look like a dump compared to this place. *My* place. When you're gone and construction is complete, then everyone will know, especially Baron, that I'm worthy of the Wainwright name, that I deserve to run the company."

"When I'm gone?"

Jason knew how hard she struggled to keep calm, to say the words through the fear. He'd never felt more proud or more grateful to God for giving him a chance to love this woman. If only—

"I don't want to kill you, Piper. I won't have to if you'll promise never to come back here. Never."

"Why? You could have built this in town, Dylan. You could have brought the model in to the council. They would have passed it in a heartbeat." She touched a finger to the file. "It's beautiful, the most fantastic work you've ever done."

"Really?" He was like an eager boy, his smile hopeful, begging for a soft word.

"I didn't tell you, Dyl, but I've kept track of your work. You have an amazing talent. *Builder's Digest* was right when they said your work will only gain more accolades." She smiled, but it was a sad smile, one filled with regrets. "You could have done it in town. So why here, Dyl? To ruin what Gran and Papa built? To spoil my dream?"

He lost his smile; his eyes burned with anger.

"Isn't it only fair? You've managed to ruin mine."

"How?"

"After Christmas last year, the old man had a physical. His heart isn't right. He got scared about dying and had a new will made out." Dylan's face altered into a hardened mask of fury. "He left you half of Wainwright Inc. Half of everything I've worked so hard to build. Half of what you walked away from and left me holding the pieces. I had to show him I was worth loving, worth holding on to."

"I do love you, son." Baron eased into the room and stepped forward, one hand held out. "God has been dealing with me about the way I've treated you."

"God!" Dylan jerked away from Baron's touch. "Mom used to say God is love but after she was gone I never felt it. I used to come home at school breaks wishing she'd be there to hug me. I was all alone, Dad."

"I know." Baron nodded. "You shouldn't have been. That was my mistake. I have to ask your forgiveness, Dylan. I was not the father you deserved. You are the best son a man could have asked for and it took me too long to appreciate that. I love you. With my whole heart I love you, son."

"You can't." Dylan bit his lip as his father removed the gun from his hand, dropping it onto the floor. "I did some things at Wainwright, Dad. Bad things."

Baron nodded. "I know. I forgive you. Because I love you."

"Are you sure?" Dylan murmured, hesitant yet to believe.

"Positive." Baron drew his son into his arms and held him as Dylan wept, clinging to his father like an anchor. "I love you more than my life."

"I love you, too, Dyl," Piper added a few minutes later, wrapping an arm around his waist. "You're my big brother. I'll always love you."

Jason's heart got stuck in his throat as he watched a family reconnect bonds that had been ripped apart by hate and anger and jealousy.

If ever he'd needed proof that God was in control, he had it now.

Baron signaled and Chief Neely and another officer

stepped through the door. Bud picked up the gun, tucked it into his belt. Then they cut Jason's restraints. Jason rose, stretching his limbs.

"We have to go with the police now, Dylan. But don't worry. I'll go with you. I'll be there to help you. I don't know what we'll face, but we'll do it together." Baron met his son's gaze without flinching. "We have to tell them the truth now, son. All of it."

"I know." Dylan lifted his head, nodding at the officers. He glanced at Jason. "I'm sorry." He held out one hand. "Forgive me?"

Jason took it, squeezed hard. "Of course. After all, God forgave me."

"Thanks." Then it was Piper's turn. Dylan's face fell as he stared at her. "I'm so sorry, sis."

"It's okay." She hugged him, then sniffed. "You go with Dad. He'll take care of you. I love you."

The police walked him out of the room to a waiting squad car outside. Jason moved to one side, giving father and daughter space.

"I've got to go with him, honey. He'll probably go to jail but I have to help." Baron's eyes begged her to understand.

Piper smiled, touched his cheek. "I know. You go, Daddy. Do what you can. When you want to talk I'll be here. Waiting."

They embraced then Baron hurried away. Jason stepped forward, eager to get Piper to himself. But the police had other ideas.

"If you'll come with me, Jason, I'd like to get your statement. Piper, you go with this officer."

"Sure." She looked at him directly, summoned up a smile. "Talk to you later?"

"Count on it," Jason confirmed.

Epilogue

By ten o'clock, Serenity Bay lay in a pool of darkness with only a small, yellow flicker here and there.

Seated on the deck, Piper's gaze rested on the surrounding forest. She ignored the chilly breeze whispering across the land.

Waiting was the hardest part.

"Piper?" The warm hand on her arm made her smile. "Are you all right?"

She turned her head to look at Jason and nodded. "Yes."

"What are you thinking about?" he asked, sinking down beside her.

"God. My father and Dylan. Love. Forgiveness. His leading."

"God led me here to teach me how to trust." His fingers grasped her chin, urging her to face him. "I believe He led you here, too."

She nodded.

"I came for the wrong reason," she murmured. "But He turned that into good, showed me a side of fatherhood I'd never seen before." She threaded her fingers with his, staring out across the water. "God is like the bay, I think. Ever changing, ever new. Sometimes demanding but always there, always waiting to wrap you up and hold you close."

Tears rose but she ignored them.

"I saw God in my father today. Tina's been filling me in on what Dylan's done to Wainwright. To my father. Dad knew everything, Jason." She blinked away the tears and smiled. "And yet when the time came he wiped it away, loved my brother in spite of it all."

"He did the same for you," Jason reminded.

"Yes. I misjudged him so badly and yet he forgave me. Dad was there, waiting for me all along. Just like God. Only I couldn't see it, I couldn't experience the love because I wouldn't trust in it. I guess He brought me here to teach me trust, too." She smiled at him as the peace settled like a blanket on her heart.

"I love you, too, Piper. I think it began the first day you showed up at the town office. You looked like a winter rose to me."

"A rose?"

"Mmm." He laid his index finger against her cheek, let it glide across the skin. "You were wearing red and I remember you reminded me of a long-stemmed rose, the kind a man gives a woman he loves."

Jason leaned over, plucked a deep-burgundy rose from her grandmother's arbor and brushed it against her cheek.

"I love you," she whispered, sitting very still as he tucked the bloom in behind her ear. "When I thought there was a chance you might drown out there, I knew I couldn't go another day without telling you how much you've meant to me these past months. Everything I've worked to achieve, I couldn't have done any of it if you hadn't been there."

"Even though I pushed you too hard?" he asked with a lopsided grin.

"Even though you constantly challenged me to try harder," she agreed.

He slid an arm around her waist, drew her so close only a whisper separated them.

"We make a good team when we work together, Piper. Will you keep working with me, keep reining me in, keep teaching me to trust? I think God has lots in store for Serenity Bay. Together we're strong enough to accomplish whatever He sends." His lips brushed hers. "Someday soon I'm going to ask you to marry me, be my partner for the rest of our lives."

She tilted her head a fraction to the right, tracing the lines of his face with her eyes.

"Someday soon I'm going to say yes. After we help Dad with Wainwright Inc. Think you can work with me there?"

"Think I'll love it." They kissed, sealing the promise of a thousand tomorrows. Across the bay a shower of gold sparks lit up the night sky.

"What's that?" Piper asked, blinking as one after another, an array of fireworks dazzled them.

Jason groaned.

"I forgot to tell you. We were invited to Ida's for ribs again. She caught me just as I was coming over here. She knows I love you, Piper."

Piper burst out laughing.

"After today, I'm pretty sure she knows I love you, too."

Another boom resounded across the valley and the sky filled with a soft, golden glow. Jason picked up Piper's hand and squeezed it.

"What's next on your Serenity Bay calendar?"

"The Summer Splash will be over soon, but then we've got the Fall Fair." She reached up, pulled his head down and told him wordlessly how much she loved him. "Then it will be time for the Winter Festival."

"Piper, the mayor probably shouldn't say this, but you are the number one priority on my to-do list."

She laughed, snuggled her head against his shoulder and thought how wonderful it was that God had planned for her to love this man.

"I think I might be free on New Year's Eve, Mayor Franklin. Does that fit in with your schedule?"

"It's pretty far away." His chin rested on her head. She could hear the rumble of laughter from deep down in his chest. "But I'm learning that good things come to those who wait. I'll wait for my winter rose."

* * * * *

Dear Reader,

Welcome to Serenity Bay. Though this pretty tourist town is a total figment of my imagination, it's as real to me as my own backyard. That's because it's not so much a physical place on the map as it is a destination for the soul, a place where wounded hearts can run to find healing, help and friends who will be there no matter what.

I hope you've enjoyed Piper's search for forgiveness and the revelations it brought. Jason had his own quest to learn to trust. That's not an easy thing when those to whom you're committed most have betrayed so deeply. Isn't it good to know that no matter how many mistakes we make, our loving heavenly Father is there with open arms and a heart brimming with tenderness to show us He never gives up on us?

Please join me for Ashley's story in *Apple Blossom Bride*. I wish you peace in your relationships, joy in your everyday life and the fullness of a love that grew in the heart of God to be shared with His children on Earth. I pray you find an abundance of it, enough to pass on to those you touch today.

Lois Richer

APPLE BLOSSOM BRIDE

I am holding you by your right hand—
I the Lord your God—and I say to you,
Don't be afraid; I am here to help you.
—*Isaiah* 41:13

This book is dedicated to my dad. I love you.

Prologue

Seventeen Years Ago

"How can they do it, Pip?"

Ashley Adams scrubbed at her cheek, struggling to eradicate tears that wouldn't stop flowing. Sobbing made her hiccup. She had to pause to catch her breath before she could get out her next question.

"My parents promised to love each other until death parted them and now they're getting a divorce. How can they do that?"

"I don't know." Piper Langley sat down cross-legged beside her on the fresh spring grass, her forehead creased in a frown of perplexity. "I don't understand adults at all, Ash. I wish I did."

"Me, too. We'll be teenagers pretty soon. We're supposed to get smarter about this love stuff but I don't get it. I don't want to have two homes. I don't want to leave my dad or Serenity Bay." She wept. "I just want my family together."

Piper, good friend that she was, silently shared her grief.

"At Bible study last week Mrs. Masters said love is a decision." Ashley sniffed as she plucked the tumbling apple blossoms off her sweater. "My parents could *decide* to love each other, they could *decide* to stay married."

"If they told you about their decision today, it doesn't sound like they're going to change their minds," Piper warned. She checked her watch. "I've got to get home. Gran told me not to be late today. I want to stay with you," she hurried to explain, "but if I'm any later they'll worry."

"It's okay." Ashley sniffed, managed a weak smile. "I understand. You go on. I think I'll stay here for a little while."

"Don't stay too long or you'll be completely covered in apple blossoms." Piper jumped to her feet, black pigtails bobbing. She bent, hugged Ashley once in a tight squeeze, then grabbed her backpack, climbed on her bike and pedaled down the road toward her grandparents' home.

Ashley wished she could follow. Pip was so lucky. Her grandparents loved each other, and her. They would never make her choose between them.

You're away at school most of the year, anyway, honey. You'll spend the summers with me, and Christmas and Easter with your mother. Or would you rather have it the other way around?

Who cared? The point was she wouldn't have a home. Not a real one.

A moment later her friend had disappeared from sight and Ashley was all alone in the churchyard with only the tumbling blossoms to listen to. Behind her, the woods rustled as the wind tickled newly sprouted leaves, but she paid no attention.

"I trusted you, God. I prayed and prayed, but they're still getting a divorce. I'm scared."

The words sounded worse when she said them out loud. She laid her head on her arms and wept for everything she was about to lose, uncaring that the afternoon sun weakened, unseeing when it let fingers of gloom creep in.

A rustle behind her drew her attention. But, before she could check it out, hard fingers locked on to her arm, pinching so tight she dropped her tissue.

"Get up. Slowly now. Don't make a sound."

Ashley blinked, startled by the command of a man who looked like a storybook hermit. She obeyed automatically, thinking she must know him. A friend of her father perhaps?

But when they reached the curb and he opened the door of a battered station wagon, her confusion gave way to uncertainty, concern, then full-bodied fear. She opened her mouth to protest but he thrust her inside, then climbed in beside her.

Panic gripped her so fiercely she couldn't breathe or make her legs work. The sensation of spiders crawling over her skin made her scratch at her arms. But that was nothing compared to the wave of dizziness that rose inside when she glanced over her shoulder and saw two suitcases on the backseat of the man's car.

You have to be careful, Ashley. Her mother's constant refrain accompanied the warning bells that were filling her brain.

She hadn't been careful. Now she was being kidnapped.

"Stop!"

But he didn't stop, and before she could scramble out of the car he'd already shifted into gear and roared past the church, past the apple blossom tree where she'd always found sanctuary.

"Let me out," she whispered, pressing herself against the door. Her throat was so dry she could hardly speak. "Please let me out."

He didn't seem to hear her. His attention was on his

rearview mirror, his foot heavy on the gas pedal. He was moving too fast for her to jump out of the car.

They neared the center of town. Surely someone would notice that Ashley Adams was in a strange man's car?

But the stores were closing, the streets almost deserted. Only the coffee shop still shone its bright neon lights onto the street, welcoming people into its cozy interior.

"Let me go!" she pleaded. "I'm supposed to be at home now."

He ignored her. Perhaps he knew that her parents were too busy with their divorce plans to notice she hadn't been home all afternoon. Maybe that's why he'd taken her—maybe people could take one look at her and know that she was going to be like the kids in school she'd always felt sorry for.

As the car whizzed over the road Ashley tried to pray, struggled to think about God and those loving arms Mrs. Masters always talked about. But she couldn't feel them. All she felt was alone and very scared.

The man hunched over the wheel, his face set in a forbidding angry mask. Every so often he'd glance in his rearview mirror. Then his lips pinched together and his fingers squeezed the wheel so tightly they turned pasty-white. Anger emanated from him like smoke from a fire ready to ignite.

She had to get out of this car!

They approached the only traffic light in town, a yellow light which quickly turned red. It was now or maybe never. Ashley slid her fingers around the door handle and prepared herself. When he jerked to a stop she yanked the door open, hurled out of the vehicle and raced across the street to Mrs. Masters' coffee shop.

"Hey! Wait. I'll take you home," the man yelled after her.

Fat chance!

Ashley didn't look back nor did she stop running until she reached the coffee-shop door. Using both hands she dragged it open, burst into the pungent warmth that surrounded her as she drew deep gasping breaths into her lungs. She glanced from face to face, searching for an ally.

There were two customers at the counter. Mrs. Masters was laughing with them, but she stopped when Ashley locked the café door. By the time her sobs gurgled out, her Sunday school teacher was there, holding her.

"What's the matter, honey?"

"A man." Ashley clung to her capable hands as if to anchor herself. "A man tried to take me away. In his car."

"What man?" Mrs. Masters peered through the coffee-shop windows, shook her head. "I don't see anyone."

"He was there. I was at the apple tree by the ch-church and he grabbed me. He was trying to k-kidnap me." She was shaking and didn't know how to stop.

As if through a fog she heard Mrs. Masters speaking, felt herself being pushed down onto a chair. Someone pressed her hands around a cup. It warmed her icy fingers so she clung to it while people came and went.

"She said a man took her." She felt their stares and looked away, locking her gaze on the table, the chair, anything but the street in front. A while later her father came and took her home. To the home she wasn't going to have anymore.

That night the dreams started: nightmares so real Ashley could feel those bony fingers pressing into her skin, hear the gravel rattling beneath her feet as he pulled her across it, feel the biting odor of freshly cut spruce sting her nostrils and the hard metal pressure of the window handle against her back when she crouched in the car and waited for a chance to escape.

And every time she'd wake up, shaking, crying, knowing that some time, someday, somewhere he'd come back. And that when he did, she wouldn't be able to leave.

Chapter One

Ashley shoved open the door of her Vancouver condo with her crutch and hobbled inside, absorbing the stale odor of a place too long uninhabited. She let the door swing closed behind her, made sure it was locked, then concentrated on inhaling deep breaths.

She was home. She was safe.

The mail sat neatly stacked on a side table, thanks to her landlord. But Ashley ignored it, coaxing her body to move a little farther into the room.

All she really wanted was to run. Which was sad when she'd spent so much time and effort dealing with her panic attacks, making this her safe haven. The accident with Kent had only proven what she already knew—there was no safe place. As if to emphasize that point, the fear that had assailed her in the elevator a few moments ago now ballooned and wouldn't let go.

The phone rang.

"Ash?" Piper's familiar voice soothed her fractured nerves. "I thought you'd be coming home today. How are you feeling?"

"Battered and bruised, Pip. My ankle's weak so I'm on

crutches for a couple of days. But I'm okay." Would she ever be okay again?

"And Kent?"

"Walked away without a scratch. It was my side of the sportscar that was hit." She debated whether to explain, then decided there was no point in pretending. "He kept going faster, though I begged him to stop. He told me he could handle it, that he knew what he was doing with such a powerful car. He lied about that. He lied about everything."

"Oh, Ashley. I'm so sorry."

She couldn't handle the rush of sympathy. Not now. Not today.

"I'm not," she said steeling herself against the pain she knew would follow the words. "It wasn't me he really wanted. It was the money. It's better it happened now, before we're married, than finding out two years down the road."

"Yes, it is," Piper agreed quietly. "When do you go back to work?"

"I don't. Ferris let me go when I had to cancel out of the exhibition."

"The rat! You couldn't help the accident."

"I should never have believed Kent when he said he knew how to drive a race car. He admitted at the hospital that he'd never even been inside one before."

"Yes, but—"

"Ferris was in a tight spot with the gallery expansion and he was depending on me to help. Being in the hospital because I was stupid and let myself get talked into something isn't an excuse."

"I suppose Kent left the bill for that car for you to pay, too, didn't he?" Piper waited a second then groaned. "Oh, Ash. The greedy—"

"Believe me, it was a cheap escape. Anyway I don't want to talk about him, Pip. I'm tired." Ashley leaned against the wall, rubbed the throbbing spot at the side of her head. "I guess I need to rest."

"Then as soon as you feel up to it, you should come here. The autumn colors are always gorgeous around the Bay." Piper's voice changed, softened. "Cathcart House is made for visitors. You know that. Think of it—you could sleep in every morning, take long walks when you're better, think about your next move. You could even help me plan my wedding. Or you can just relax if you want. Please say you'll come."

Piper sounded so happy, so at peace with her world. Ashley swallowed a tinge of envy.

"I should really be looking for a job, Pip."

"Don't tell me you've emptied your grandfather's trust account already? You were supposed to be recuperating in that hospital, not buying stuff online."

Piper and Rowena were the only two people Ashley would allow to tease about her recent inheritance. Piper's taunt brought back happy memories of other times they'd shared in Serenity Bay.

"You're awfully quiet, Ash. You'd better fess up. Just how many pairs of shoes can one woman buy?" Piper demanded.

"Since you're the queen of shoes, you tell me." Ashley glanced down at the scuffed and dirty sneakers she'd worn home from the hospital. Looked like she'd have to go shopping. She wanted no lingering memories—of Kent or the accident.

"Ash?"

"I'm here," she murmured. "Just thinking."

"Why not come visit me?" Piper pushed.

Ashley could picture exactly how Serenity Bay would

look. The water always seemed darker, deeper in autumn. The sky switched to a richer shade of cerulean. The hills cloaked their rolling sides in the finest burnt orange, fiery red and forest green.

And the people—she doubted many of them would know about her broken engagement, even though Serenity Bay was so small everybody knew everyone else's business.

"Rowena's coming down for the Labor Day long weekend," Piper wheedled. "We'd have a chance to reconnect."

The last weekend of summer. It was too tempting.

"Okay I'll come," Ashley agreed. "But just for a few weeks. I want to work, Pip. I don't want to be one of the idle rich."

The snort of disbelief carried clearly down the line.

"Like that would happen, Ms. 'Frenetic Pace' Adams. When can I expect you?"

Ashley glanced around. There was nothing to hold her here.

"A week—no, two. The doctor said I'll need a few days for my ankle to strengthen. It will take me about five days to drive there. Say…two weeks from today?" she suggested.

"Yes!" Piper cheered. "I can hardly wait."

"Listen, I know you're busy. I don't want to interfere with your work there, or get in your way."

"You won't. The busiest part of the summer is over. It went better than we could have imagined. Now if I could just get my winter plans to work."

"Winter plans?" Ashley yawned, suddenly tired.

"You're exhausted. I can tell." Piper chuckled. "Never mind my brilliant ideas. I'll tell you all about it when you get here. Go rest, Ash. Dream of all the things we'll do together once you get here."

"Yes. It'll be great." But she didn't hang up. Instead Ashley clung to the phone, needing to share what lay so heavily on her heart. "What's wrong with me, Pip?" she finally whispered.

"Absolutely nothing," her friend stoutly insisted. "You just made a mistake."

"Two of them. I thought I knew Parker. And yet I had no idea that he was in love with someone else."

"He should have said something earlier." Piper's voice wasn't forgiving.

"I should have listened better."

"Does it matter now? Your engagement to Parker only lasted a couple of days before you learned the truth and corrected things. It's not your fault. He wasn't honest about his feelings for someone else."

"Maybe. But what about Kent? I thought I could trust him. I thought he was everything I wanted in a husband." She hated saying it out loud. It sounded so silly, but why deny the truth when Piper knew it anyway. "All he wanted was my money, Pip."

"I'm sure that isn't so. But even if it is, he's gone now. You're starting over."

"Yes." She chewed her bottom lip. "Don't tell anyone, okay, Piper?"

"About the engagements?" Piper's soothing tones did wonders for Ashley. "Of course not. No one will care anyway. One look at you and the men will be knocking down my door."

"I doubt that." She chewed her bottom lip for a moment, then admitted what was really on her mind. "I suppose people know about my grandfather's oil money but I hope nobody asks about it."

"I can almost guarantee that someone will. After all, your dad lived here till he died. Some of the old folks will remember him, and you. What's wrong with that?"

"Nothing if that's all it is. But sometimes when people find out about it they change, ask me to do things, insist I help them. It can be rather scary." She felt silly admitting that but it was the truth. "Last week a woman who said she knew my grandfather came into the gallery and asked me to pay for her son's rehab. I was lucky Ferris came back from lunch early but even then he had to call the police to make her leave. I've been on tenterhooks ever since, hoping she won't accost me on the street."

"I'm sure no one here will do that. Mostly I've found that people here are as friendly as you are. Just like when we were kids. The only thing is I've already told Jason about Kent and all the rest," Piper soothed. Her soft voice brimmed with happiness. "We don't have any secrets."

"Jason's okay. You trust him, so I do, too."

"Yeah, I do trust him. Totally. Which is why I can hardly wait to marry the man."

"I'm happy for you, Pip."

They discussed how long it would take to drive from Vancouver to the cottage country two hours north of Toronto.

"It's an awfully long drive to make alone, Ash."

"It's the only way. I can't fly. Last time was horrible."

Piper sighed. "I was hoping you were getting over those panic attacks."

"Some days I think I am. Then something happens and it starts all over again."

"That's an even better reason to come to the Bay. You know you're safe here."

Not quite true, but Ashley wasn't going to get into it. She promised to call Piper every night she was on the road, then hung up. Because her ankle ached she sank onto the sofa she'd bought with her first paycheck, the one Kent hated so much—the one she loved because to her the pale-blue suede said *home*. She gazed at her watercolor of Serenity Bay.

Would she be safe there?

She was older now, had learned how to take precautions. Therapy had helped her deal with the panic attacks. But most importantly, *he* wasn't there anymore. She'd been back to the Bay several times and never once had she seen the man who'd grabbed her that spring afternoon so long ago.

Thinking about him made her anxious, so Ashley closed her eyes and let daydreams of happier times take over— until the familiar nightmare cut in. Then she rose and changed into her nightgown. From the vial in her purse she took out one of the sedatives that would guarantee a deep, dreamless sleep and swallowed it.

Snuggled into bed, she refocused on Serenity Bay and the good times she'd once found on its shores.

Michael Masters gazed at the cherubic face of his sleeping daughter. Tatiana was so small, yet she held his heart in that grubby little fist.

He touched a fingertip to the cloud of hair as dark as his own, felt the silken texture of one fat curl wrap against his skin. He'd never imagined he would experience weak knees and palpitations all because of one four-year-old girl.

Lest he disturb her afternoon nap, he tiptoed from the room, monitor in hand. If she made a squeak he'd be back in here in three seconds. But he hoped she'd nap for an hour, long enough that he could get some work done.

His studio, if you could call it that, was at the back of the house, far from her room. It was an addition roughly thrown together, a place to work in his spare time.

Spare time. Ha! A joke. There was never any spare time, not since Tati had whirled into his life.

Michael stepped inside the room, breathed in. Pine, spruce, cedar—they mingled together into a woodsy blend that made his fingertips itch to get to work. Once he'd checked the volume on the monitor, he set it on his work table, picked up the oak piece he'd begun two weeks ago and grabbed a chisel. In his mind he visualized what he wanted to create, then set about releasing the face from the wood, bit by hardened bit.

He was almost finished the left side when it dawned on him that he'd heard nothing from Tatiana's room. He glanced at his watch, blinked.

Two hours? Tati had never slept that long in all the time she'd been with him, no matter how he tired her out.

He set down his chisel, touched the wood with one scarred thumb, then placed the carving on the table, too. As he made his way quietly through the house he chastised himself for not being a better father. Maybe Serenity Bay wasn't the best place for his daughter to grow up. Sure, his mom was here and she'd gladly offered all the mothering one small grandchild could want, but Serenity Bay was the back of nowhere. There was no ballet school or children's theater here. Maybe Tati was missing out on something.

He pushed open the door of her room, ready to tease her awake.

His heart dropped like a stone.

The bed was empty.

He scanned the room, noticed her shoes were missing, as well as her doll. The window was pushed up, curtains fluttering in the warm autumn air. Surely she hadn't gone outside by herself?

Oh, Lord, keep her safe.

He raced through the house, then outside around the back to the window of her room. Tiny footprints had rearranged the flowers he'd so painstakingly planted last spring, but Michael didn't care about that.

"Tati?"

His heart hit overdrive as he pushed through the woods, found her hair band on the other side of the bridge. Thanks to a dry summer the creek down here wasn't much more than a trickle, but farther up… He raced along the trail until he came to the old stone church he worshipped in every Sunday.

Where was she?

He stood for a moment, eyes narrowed, assessing the view. Finally his heart gave a bump of relief when he spotted the familiar dark curls beneath the apple tree. She had her doll with her, the one her mother had given her. A red wagon, the one Tati dragged everywhere she went, was turned upside down, forming a stool for her bottom.

Anxious not to scare her, he fought to control his breathing as he listened to her discussion with the beautiful bride doll she never let out of her sight.

"You mustn't run away again, Princess," she said in soft admonishing tones. "Daddy doesn't like it and Mommy can't follow you. I know the other children come here sometimes and you want to play with them, but you have to ask me first."

His words exactly. So she knew she was in the wrong.

"Tati?" He stepped closer, crouched down beside her. "What are you doing here?"

"Playing. Princess and I like to catch the leaves. You know, Daddy, for our book." She pointed to a stack of curled up reddish leaves spread out at her feet.

He remembered the big books she'd stacked on the floor. Ah. Presumably there were leaves between the pages. He'd have to take them off the shelf and put them back before she discovered he'd moved them.

At the moment there were more important concerns.

"Yes, your book is nice. But Tati, you know very well that you are not allowed to come here by yourself."

"I wasn't alone, Daddy. Princess was with me." She blinked that guileless expression that punched him right in the gut. "You didn't say Princess couldn't come, Daddy."

"I didn't say you *could* come. I said you had to ask me before you went anywhere. You didn't ask. That's disobeying." Michael struggled to keep himself from weakening when those big brown eyes met his. Staying firm with her was the hardest part of being a father. "I was worried about you when I saw that you weren't in bed, Tatiana."

"I wasn't tired anymore and a bird was calling. I'm sorry, Daddy."

"I know you are. But that isn't the point." He brushed the curls off her forehead, tipped her head up so he could look into her eyes. "It's dangerous to go through the woods yourself, especially in the fall. Sometimes there are animals around. That's why I said you have to ask me."

"Okay, Daddy."

He'd have to get a fence up around the yard, fast.

"That's not enough. I told you not to go outside by yourself."

She kept staring at him. Michael reached down, grasped the handle of her wagon, praying she'd move, that he wouldn't have to physically force her to comply. He wasn't good at the battle of wills she occasionally set him.

"Come on, now. We have to go home. And next time you may not come here unless you ask me first."

He hated bawling her out but many more disappearances and he'd be grayer than the oldest man in Serenity Bay.

"I'm *not* finished playing." Her chin butted out in that determined way that told him she was ready for a battle.

Michael's heart sank but he knew he couldn't give in.

"Yes, honey. You *are* finished. We're going home. Now." He waited a moment, and when she didn't move he gently lifted her off the wagon, turned it right side up and stacked her leaves in it. "Climb in. I'll pull you back."

Tati shook her head, curls flying. She began picking at her doll, tugging off the tiny socks. Before he could react she'd headed for the brook—and it wasn't a trickle there.

"Princess wants to wash her feet in the water."

"Stop!" He gasped as he fought to control his breathing. "Tatiana, you may not *ever* go in that water without me. Do you understand?" Panic assailed him in a wave that sent his hand out to grasp her shoulder. "Never. Come on. We're leaving. Now."

"No!" She jerked away from him, her dark eyes blazing with temper. "I don't want to go."

"I'm sorry about that but we have to. Get into the

wagon, Tati. I'll give you a ride home." Before she could argue any further he wrapped his arms around her fore-arms and lifted her off the ground.

"No!" she bellowed, her face a rich angry red. "I won't. Leave me alone."

She struggled against him, her shoes making painful contact with his midsection while her elbows dug into his chest.

"I don't want to go with you. Let me go!"

"Stop this right now. You're coming with me if I have to force you—"

"Put her down!"

The fury in that voice commanded his attention. Mi-chael glanced around, saw a tall, slim woman with a cas-cade of silver-gilt hair glaring at him. She stood a few feet beyond his reach, her stance alert as if she might race away any moment. Or attack him.

"Excuse me?" Michael frowned, noted the way her hands curled into fists at her sides.

"I said put her down. And I meant it. Do it now. Other-wise I'm calling the police." A cell phone appeared in her fingers, flipped open.

Tati had gone completely still. Michael took one look into his daughter's curious face and knew he had to get this settled, fast. Before the little girl found a new way to create chaos in his once-normal world.

"Look, Miss Whoever You Are. You have no idea—"

"My name is Ashley Adams, if that matters." She stepped an inch closer, touched Tati's hand with a gentle brush. Her eyes rested on his child, softened for a moment, then returned to him.

The softness dissipated. Now her eyes glittered like

rocks. Her other hand slid into her purse. She looked like a city girl, which meant she was probably carrying some kind of protection. He prayed it wasn't a gun.

"You're the one with no idea, buddy. Put that child down on the ground and do it fast. Then get out of here. I don't care how you leave, but you'll only take her with you over my dead body."

She was serious. So was the can of Mace in her fingers.

Michael took a step backward, opened his mouth to explain. Tati struggled against him. Deciding it might be wisest to argue his case without clutching her wiggling body, he set her gently down on the ground but clung to one tiny hand. After a moment, as if to emphasize her power, Tati dragged that hand out of his.

He would have held on, but the woman's stern glare warned him to let go. A puff of angry frustration boiled over.

"Look, er, Ashley. This isn't what you—"

She ignored him, crouched down to look into Tati's eyes.

"Hi, honey. Are you all right?"

Playing the part of the maligned child to the hilt, Tati nodded, thrusting one knuckle into her mouth in a way that always aroused sympathy in the grocery store. What chance did a mere man have against those wiles? Her thick dark lashes fluttered against her chubby cheek as if she was ready to burst into tears.

Michael almost groaned. Consummate actress. Just like her mother.

"What's your name, sweetie?"

"Tati—Tatiana."

"Why don't you come with me, Tatiana? We'll go get the police to help us find your mom. Okay?"

Tati frowned, shook her head. "We can't."

"Why not, sweetheart?"

"'Cause Daddy said Mommy's in heaven. Didn't you, Daddy?" Tati's hand slid back inside his as if she'd accepted that he was her main protector now.

"Daddy?" The woman's almond-shaped eyes opened wide. "You're her father?"

Michael nodded.

"Guilty," he admitted, amused by the look on her aristocratic face. Half belligerence, half embarrassment. Served her right.

"Well, for goodness' sakes, why didn't you say so?" Her sharp high cheekbones bore dots of bright red.

"You didn't actually give me a chance to explain." He squatted down, grasped Tati's chin. "Grab Princess and get into the wagon," he said clearly. "We have to go home. Now."

"Okay, Daddy," she sang agreeably, as if there had never been any other option. "Can I have one of the chocolate cookies Granny made?"

"After disobeying?" He gave her an arch look. His daughter had the grace to look ashamed. "Get in the wagon, Tati," he ordered quietly.

"Look, obviously I misjudged the situation. I'm really sorry." The woman followed his stare to her hand, shoved the Mace and her phone back into the peacock leather purse that hung from her narrow shoulder.

"No problem. I guess I should be relieved that you didn't call the police. I'm Michael Masters, by the way. You've already met my daughter." He thrust out one hand, shook hers, noticing the faint white line on the ring finger of her left hand where it clutched her bag.

He caught himself speculating about the reason she'd interrupted him and Tati, and ordered his brain to stop.

"Wait a minute—Masters?" She blinked. "Mick—I mean *Michael* Masters?"

"That'd be me." He hadn't heard that nickname since high school. Which meant she knew him—but he couldn't remember anyone from those days who looked like she did.

"Oh." Her expression altered, her eyes widened. A moment later her mask had dropped back into place and he couldn't quite discern what had caused the change.

She drew herself erect. "I'm Ashley Adams. As you already know."

"Nice to meet you, Ashley Adams."

"Yes, well." She gulped, risked a look at him then quickly looked away, toward Tati. Her voice emerged low, with a ragged edge. "I'm really sorry. I shouldn't have butted in. It's just that I heard her yell and it reminded me of—never mind."

"It doesn't—"

"Sorry," she whispered. "I'm really very sorry." She rubbed her left hand against her thigh, half turned as if she wanted to race away. But she didn't.

Michael blinked. Instead model-long legs encased in cream silk pants covered the distance toward a sleek sports car at a careful pace. How on earth could she walk in those spiky shoes—with a limp, nonetheless?

"Why didn't you ask that nice lady to come for cookies, Daddy?"

Michael turned, saw the glimmer in Tati's eyes and sighed.

"You're not having cookies, remember? Anyway, she didn't exactly give me a chance," he told her as he grasped the wagon handle and began tugging it toward home.

"Next time I'll ask her. I don't think that lady likes you, Daddy."

Too bad. Because Michael was interested in that lady. And in what had made her rush to Tati's rescue.

Most of all he wanted to know what made her stumble over his name.

Chapter Two

She was bored.

Ashley perched on the deck of Piper's gorgeous hillside home two weeks later and stared down into the smooth clear waters of Serenity Bay without really seeing a thing.

Her ankle still ached if she walked too much, her ribs weren't totally healed, but after two weeks of sitting around while Piper rushed off to work, she was sick of waiting for a return to normalcy—whatever that was. She'd expected to find peace here. Instead the same old sense of unease clung.

She needed to do something.

"Maybe I'll go into town," she told the crow perched on a deck railing.

Maybe you'll see Mick Masters again, a little voice whispered.

She pushed it away, but the damage had already been done.

A perfect likeness of Michael filled her head. Neither the brown-black eyes, nor that flirting diamond sparkle that dared you to smile, had been dimmed by the years. His hair was exactly as she remembered—maybe a little shorter now than it had been when she'd fallen for him in her fifteenth summer, but still a bit shaggy, emphasizing his rakish charm.

He hadn't recognized her. There was a lot to be thankful for in that. Heat scorched her cheeks remembering how she'd trailed after him when his mother had held parties for the church youth group at her house. Ashley had attended the group every week that summer just to catch a glimpse of Mick.

That summer shone golden in her mind. Her friends, the bay with its silken sand beach and Mick's teasing grin to hope for—a thousand girls would have envied her. But they didn't know that she was only pretending to be normal.

Ashley rose, walked inside, sweeping away the memories in a rush of busyness. But dusting Piper's pristine living room was a wasted effort and soon she was gazing out the windows again.

"Might as well go into town and get it over with," she told herself.

She hadn't been back since the first day when she'd embarrassed herself. Grabbing that little girl—what was she thinking?

Simple. She'd been thinking about the past, about the day anxiety took over her life. Over the past ten years Ashley had consulted counselors, psychologists, medical personnel of all kinds, but no matter what she tried, the panic attacks continued. They'd grown worse lately.

A Bible study leader in one of the small groups she'd attended suggested that the sense of fear Ashley had asked them to pray about was a result of not trusting God, that she had to let go and let Him handle things. Like she hadn't tried that a thousand times!

The woman meant well but she didn't understand. How could she? Ashley couldn't explain where the fear came from. She'd carried it around with her for so long it had become part of her. So she found a way to deal with it.

Everything in her life was deliberately planned, carefully organized and carried out, minimizing the chance for that paralyzing terror to swamp her. That she'd let her guard down with Kent and endangered herself was too scary. That's why she'd been so ready to leave Vancouver. It didn't feel safe anymore.

Ashley remembered the look on Mick's face when she'd ordered him to put his daughter down. It would have been funny if it hadn't been so pathetic. Well, she'd just have to run the other way if she saw him. She was thankful that he hadn't seemed to recognize her. Maybe he wasn't aware of her teenage crush, or he had forgotten how she'd hung on his every word. She hoped.

Serenity Bay looked the same as it always did after the summer cottagers had gone back to the city. Barrels of flowers still burgeoned with cascading blossoms, fairy lights hung from red-gold maples in the town square, a few balloons clung limply to the lamppost outside the ice-cream shop. The welcome banner still stretched across the main road.

The biggest difference was the abundance of empty parking spaces on either side of the narrow streets.

Ashley pulled in front of the Coffee Pot. Through the huge glass windows she could see Mrs. Masters, her round face as unlined as it had always been. A spurt of warmth bubbled up at the welcome Ashley knew she'd find inside. She pulled open the café door with a flutter of excitement.

"Ashley? Ashley Adams, is that you?" Strong arms pulled her close, enveloping her in a cloudy aroma of yeasty bread and summer's last roses. After a minute, Mrs. Masters drew back, peered into her face. "My goodness dear, you look like a New York model. If it wasn't for those big gray eyes of yours I'm not sure I would have recognized you."

They chatted for a few minutes. Mrs. Masters insisted she share a cup of freshly brewed coffee and a piece of fresh apple pie which Ashley picked at.

"Is there something wrong?" her hostess asked, frowning at the mangled pie. "You used to like my apple pie."

"No. It's delicious. And I still do. I'm just not very hungry, I guess."

"You really need to take care of yourself, my dear. You're so thin. And there are dark circles under your eyes."

"I was in an accident. I guess it's taking longer to heal than I thought." She smiled to ease the other woman's concern. "I'm going a little stir crazy just sitting around at Piper's. It was very kind of her to invite me, but I'm used to being active and Serenity Bay isn't exactly buzzing at this time of year."

"A museum or something—wasn't that where you worked?"

"Actually an art gallery," Ashley corrected. "But I'm not there anymore."

"No, I don't imagine you're up to working after crashing a race car." Her eyes twinkled. "All right, I'll confess. I had heard about the accident. Remember, there are no secrets in a small town." Mrs. Masters paused, tapped one finger against her bottom lip. "I wonder."

"What are you wondering?" Ashley murmured, then questioned whether she should have asked. Mrs. Masters was a busybody—a nice one, but a busybody all the same.

"The art teacher up at the high school was in for dinner last night, bemoaning the fact that the school board can't afford to provide the students access to galleries to see the new styles today's artists use. She's got some creative souls in that class who she thinks would flourish if they could just have their interest piqued. I don't suppose you still carry around your slide collection?"

Ashley nodded. "Yes, I do. In fact, they're in my car. I brought them specifically to show Rowena when she was here for Labor Day. We had some wonderful things come through the gallery this summer and you know how she loves to scout out unusual pieces for those landscapes she designs."

"Yes, I do. I also think I know some high school kids who'd appreciate seeing those slides." Mrs. Masters scanned Ashley from head to foot, nodding. "One look at you and I know they'd sit up and listen. You are what they aspire to be. Talented, gorgeous, smart, interesting."

"Me?" Ashley raised one eyebrow. "I don't even have a job at the moment."

"That's not important right now. Your health is what matters most. But if you're bored, helping at the school might fill your day." Mrs. Masters pulled out a pad of paper and a pen. "Take this to the school. Jillian Tremaine is the teacher's name. Tell her I sent you."

Three men pushed through the doors of the coffee shop. Ashley gave them a quick check, her heart racing. Nope. Not him.

"You've got customers. I'd better go." But Ashley couldn't leave until she'd learned what she really needed to know. "How is your family, Mrs. Masters?"

"We're all fine. My girls have moved to the east coast for their jobs but Michael's back in town. He lives below the ridge with his daughter. She's a darling." A fond smile tilted her generous mouth.

"I didn't know he'd married." Understatement of the year.

"Yes, but he's single now. Tati is a godsend." Her eyes lit up. "We love that little sweetheart so much."

"I'm sure."

Mrs. Masters's attention wavered to her now-seated customers.

"Excuse me, dear. I've got to get back to work. You be sure to talk to Jillian." She patted her shoulder absently. "I hope you're feeling better soon."

"Thanks for the pie."

"Oh, *pfui!* You take care of yourself."

Ashley waggled her fingers and left, mulling over the idea of showing her slides. A few hours a week at the high school—it might just keep her busy enough to prevent getting involved in Piper's winter festival plans.

Not that Ashley had anything against a winter festival in Serenity Bay. Her father had been part of a group who'd self-published a community history book on the trappers, hunters and fishermen who'd originally settled the bay. Piper's plan to resurrect some of those old skills into a modern-day festival sounded like loads of fun.

But Ashley wasn't ready to tie herself down here. Not yet. Not since a tiny sprite with black curly hair had demanded to be free, stopping her heart and reminding her that the past wasn't dead and buried.

Her focus shifted to what Mrs. Masters had said about Mick. So he'd been married. Hardly surprising given that half the tourist girls that had visited the Bay every summer went gaga over Mick's bad-boy grin and heart-melting winks. Ashley had come back to visit her father every summer after her parents had split, and her fifteenth summer had been spent hoping and praying Mick would notice her.

It had never happened.

Mick never chose one female over another. He preferred hanging out with a group of friends—both boys and girls. Of course she'd never really been part of his set. He was three years older for one thing. And employed. While she'd played with Piper and Rowena, Mick had helped out his dad in the garage and his mother in her coffee shop. Then one summer Ashley arrived to find he'd left the Bay. She'd never seen him again.

Until the other day at the apple tree when she'd let the past intrude.

She was more certain than ever that Michael had probably never noticed her gaping at him from afar. Good thing, because it meant she wouldn't feel doubly embarrassed if she met up with him again.

Which she had absolutely no intention of doing.

Ashley started the car, shifted into first and headed toward the school.

"I can't tell you how relieved I am that Mrs. Masters asked you to talk to me." Jillian Tremaine pressed a hand to her upsweep, pushing a pin in place.

"Oh?"

"I've been at my wits' end trying to get these kids interested in expressing themselves with visual arts. Unless it has to do with computers they tune out, you know. And somehow the curriculum books just don't cut it. But you and your slides—" She smiled. "They're going to enjoy their time with you and I'm going to enjoy putting those busy little minds to work."

"I hope you're right—about the slides, I mean."

"I am."

Ashley chatted with her for another few minutes, agreeing to show up Monday after lunch. She left as the bell rang for the next period.

Students filled the halls, laughing, talking and shoving each other good-naturedly as they went. One or two of the boys gave her the once-over. Ashley had to smile.

She was almost to the front door when a hand closed

around her arm. Every nerve tensed as she jerked free, whirled around, prepared to defend herself. Her jaw dropped.

"You!"

"Yep. Sorry if I hurt you." Brown eyes melting like chocolate in the sun lit up Mick's face. His mouth tilted into a crooked smile. "I didn't mean to grip so hard. I called out a couple of times but with this mob I don't suppose you heard."

"No, I didn't." Why had he stopped her? "Are you leaving, too?"

His nose wrinkled. "I wish. I have a class this period."

"You're teaching here?" She couldn't believe it. The last thing she'd expected Mick Masters to become was a teacher.

"Started this month. Shop class for grades ten to twelve. You don't want to know how dangerous it is to pair up a teenager with a saw." He grinned. "Most of my students are accidents waiting to happen."

Ashley honed in on the bandage covering his thumb. "Apparently not only the kids."

He had the grace to look embarrassed.

"A misbehaving chisel. I chastised it thoroughly, don't worry."

"Uh-huh." She zipped her jacket. "Good to talk to you again, Michael. I'd better not keep you."

"You're not. The kids aren't allowed to touch anything unless I'm in the room. For that reason I try always to be late." He said it without any sign of an apology, but his eyes danced with fun. "Can we have coffee sometime?"

"Why?" She held the door open, wishing her brain would function. She wasn't prepared for this, not at all.

"Why?" He frowned, tilted his head to one side. "Well, because I've never had coffee with a fashion model and because it would greatly improve my status with the two terrors watching us from upstairs."

"I'm not a fashion model." Ashley glanced up. Both boys were ogling her and Mick.

She shifted uncomfortably, her fingers tightening against the metal.

"Besides, I wanted to thank you for going out of your way to make sure no one was hurting my daughter. Not everyone would pay that much attention to a child's cry," he said quietly.

"It was a mistake. I should have minded my own business. I have to go now. Goodbye." She scooted through the door and strode down the steps toward her car. Seconds later she'd left the school—and Mick—far behind.

When she saw the sign for Lookout Point, Ashley pulled into the parking area, shut off her motor and sat there, staring across the valley, the sound of her heartbeat echoing in her ears. She hadn't answered him about the coffee but no doubt he'd gotten the message. Mick wasn't stupid.

And yet, it wasn't Mick she'd met again.

This was no boy, definitely not the teenage heartthrob she'd spent hours daydreaming about. Michael Masters was a grown man, with a daughter and responsibilities.

He'd been married once, now he had a child.

That alone was a good reason not to go with him for coffee. She'd already made two mistakes trying to achieve a relationship where she completely trusted her partner. One where her heart wouldn't be at risk.

Young Mick Masters had been anything but safe. Michael Masters the man would be no different.

"I don't know how you do it, Mom." Michael savored the last bite of apple pie his mother had saved for him. "You work a much longer day than I do yet you still manage to make a home-cooked dinner and entertain Tati when I can barely keep one foot in front of the other. Amazing."

"No, honey. It's just years of practice. And owning a restaurant." She chuckled as she picked up his plate, set it in her dishwasher. "Things will get easier for you, I promise. When you and your sisters were little your father and I were walking zombies. But we learned how to cope. You will, too."

"The difference is you had Dad. I sometimes wonder if Tati's suffering without her mother."

"Has she said something?"

"No. She seems fine at the daycare. But it's hard to leave her there with strangers all day. Thanks." He accepted the tea she handed him, watching out the window as Tati climbed the old slide and whizzed down it just as he and his sisters had done.

"Tatiana is adjusting well. She has a stable home now, a daddy who loves her. That has to be better than gallivanting all over the globe with Carissa. Children need security. You're providing that. Cut yourself some slack."

"I guess." He mulled that over as he got up, dried the pots and pans she had washed, then resumed his seat. Tati was busy in the sandbox so he had a few minutes to talk. "I wanted to ask you about someone I met. A woman— tall, blond. She looks like a movie star or something. Her name is Ashley—"

"Adams." His mother nodded. "You should remember her. She used to live in the Bay. She was in my Bible class before her parents separated. Her mother moved away, but Ashley came back every summer to stay with her father, Regan Adams. Remember him? He died several years ago—a salesman who traveled a lot. Ashley's a good friend of Piper Langley's."

"Wow. Do you also know her shoe size?" He stared at her in admiration. "Nothing gets past you."

"Remember that," she teased.

"She was at the school today."

"Of course she was. I sent her there to talk to Jillian about showing her art slides." His mother stored the last of the pots away. "Ashley used to work in a fancy gallery in Vancouver. She keeps a collection of slides from noteworthy work she's handled. If what I've heard is correct, they're perfect for Jillian to show to her students."

"A gallery?" He sat up straight. "You said 'worked,' not 'works.' She's not there anymore?"

"She was in an accident. She came to Cathcart House to stay with Piper and recuperate. I don't know if she's going back or not." His mother gave him "the look." "If you'd spoken to her, you could have asked her."

"I tried. If I'd known about the gallery gig, I might have tried harder." He checked the backyard, saw Tati hovering by the fence. "Uh-oh, she's restless, which can only mean trouble. I'd better go. Are you sure she didn't ruin your tablecloth? That juice is a pain to get out."

"After surviving you three my linens are indestructible to childish spills. Besides, it wouldn't matter a whit if she did," his mother insisted. "I can buy another tablecloth. But that sweet child will only be four years old for a very short time."

"True. The question is whether I can last till five." Michael rose, massaged the tense cords in his neck. "Thanks again for dinner. I appreciate not having to cook."

"Are you going to work tonight?" his mother asked. She tapped one knuckle on the window to get Tati's attention, shook her head. Apparently Tati obeyed.

"Tonight I have to check over some homework I stupidly assigned last week." He groaned. "Teaching takes up so much time. I never imagined I'd be spending so many hours at it. It makes it hard to find time—" A squeal from outside drew his attention. Michael sighed as he went to investigate. "We'd better go. It's almost bath time."

Teaching, Tati and trivialities—that's what took up his time nowadays. Frustration ate at Michael as he fastened her into the car seat, but a pat on his cheek from her little hand tamped it down. He'd choose Tati over his silly dream every time.

His mother waved them off while Tati chatted merrily about her friend Wanda at day care. Tales of Wanda filled the entire drive to the house he'd purchased a few short months ago. The place had seemed the right decision then, but on days like this he wondered about all his choices.

Michael struggled to engage Tati in their nightly bubble war. Though she was up to her eyebrows in the iridescent globes and only too willing to douse him as well, she wasn't entirely happy about something. He didn't press. She wouldn't tell him until she was good and ready anyway. At least he'd learned that much about her.

His attention strayed too long. The bubble bottle slipped and it took ages to clean up the slippery mess. Another half hour to clean Tati off, get her into pajamas and dry her hair.

But once she was tucked in bed, pressed against his shoulder as he read her a favorite story, Michael couldn't begrudge her one second. This was worth everything.

"Wanda says daddies and mommies are supposed to live together. Is that right, Daddy?"

"That's the way God planned it, sweetheart. But sometimes things don't work out like that."

"Because my mommy is in heaven?"

"Uh-huh." He so did not want to get into this tonight.

"Well, I don't like it. I want a mommy to do things with me like Wanda has. Do you know her mommy made her a pretty dress for her birthday? I want to have a pretty dress, Daddy. One that's white with frills and lots of ribbons. Just like Cinderella's."

Tati wouldn't last two minutes in frilly white, but Michael only smiled and nodded. "Very pretty, honey."

"Can I have a dress like that, Daddy?"

He studied the picture she indicated, wondering what the right answer was.

"Those dresses are for special occasions. Like Christmas and stuff. They're not very good for finger painting, or for playing in Granny's sandbox."

"I know." She flipped through the pages until she found the one she wanted. "Can I have a dress like this for Christmas, Daddy?"

He stared at Snow White's layered organza perfection and wondered if children's clothiers even made such a thing anymore.

"Tell you what, Tati, we'll have a look in the store when they get their Christmas clothes in. But that's a long time away. You might change your mind. How about if we think about it till then?"

"I guess." She tilted her head back to study him. "Wanda says 'We'll think about it' means her mommy won't do it."

"I'm not Wanda's mommy," he told her wishing the four-year-old fount of wisdom his daughter played with would, just once, run out of answers. "We'll both think about it. And when it gets nearer Christmas we'll talk about it again. Okay?"

"Okay, Daddy. I love you." She reached up to encircle his neck with her arms and squeezed as tight as she could. "This much," she grunted as she used all her strength to show him.

Michael closed his eyes and breathed in as he wrapped

his own arms around her tiny body. "I love you more, Tatiana," he whispered.

They outdid each other in hugs for a few minutes until he caught her yawning. She said her prayers then hugged him once more.

"Goodnight, sweetie. Sleep tight. Don't let the bed bugs bite."

She gave him one of her old lady looks. "Wanda says there are no bed bugs in Serenity Bay."

"Oh, yeah? What's this then?" He gently pinched her leg under the covers, grinned at her squeal. "You tell Wanda she better watch out."

"You're silly, Daddy."

Michael leaned down, brushed his lips against her forehead. "I love you."

"G'night." She yawned, then curled into a ball under the pink bedspread covered with ballerinas. "Tomorrow for dress-up I'm going to be a lifesaver," she murmured just before her eyelids dropped closed.

"You already are." He flicked off the lamp so the nightlight shed its pale glow. He checked the window, made sure it was locked, cleared a path in case she got up in the night. Then Michael left the room, pulling the door almost closed, so he could hear if she called out.

He reached out to get the monitor from the dining room table, realized he'd left it in his studio. Again.

Michael unlocked the workroom door, pushed it open and flicked on the light. He paused for a moment, studying his work.

His critical focus rested on the last two carvings he'd done. These faces were his best. It had taken more than four years to get comfortable with his own particular style, but it had been worth the effort and time he'd spent to perfect his craft. His carvings now were nothing like those from his New York days, ones his mockers had called kindling.

He'd need another six or seven months to get enough of them to mount a showing in the city. Of course he had no idea how to go about something like that, but Ashley Adams might. Maybe that's why God had sent her here, put her into his path—so he was one step closer to make his dream of working as a full-time carver come true.

The telephone rang.

He hurried to answer it, praying it wouldn't wake Tati and regretting the intrusion, but happy to hear Piper Langley's voice.

"Hello, Piper. It's nice to hear from you. I enjoyed the fireworks display you organized for Labor Day. You received high praise from my daughter, too."

He listened as she spoke, outlining a plan that, even for her, was big.

"Sounds like fun," he agreed when she'd finished describing her winter festival ideas.

"I'm hoping I can persuade you to get more involved."

"Me? How?"

"I'm using the history book of the area as a resource guide to organize some of the events. It was done several years ago and though we don't have many trappers or woodsmen around anymore, I'm bringing in some people who can show folks what it was like."

"Sounds like a lot of work."

"Eventually we want to have dogsled races, trapper contests, the whole thing. For this first year, though, we're counting on a few big names, maybe make some spectator events like snow sculptures and dogsled pulls for kids."

"Okay." He still didn't get how it involved him.

"As a windup for the week of the festival, we plan to

have a live theater event in the school auditorium on the last night."

"Piper, I can't act worth a hoot. And when it comes to costumes—"

"We need a set builder," she interrupted. "For the play. There aren't a lot of sets to be built and the hardest work will be painting them, for which I've already found volunteers. But we need someone to put them together. Jason and I thought that since you're the shop teacher and already at the school, you might be able to help."

"Harmon McTaggert would be a lot better at it than me," he muttered.

"He's willing to help you whenever he can, but a recent health scare has him taking things easy."

"Morley French?"

"He's organizing two of the events. And Steve Garner is working the publicity end." She sounded apologetic. "I've exhausted my list, Michael. The only person I haven't asked is you."

"It's a great idea, Piper, and I'd really love to help."

"Great!"

"But I'm going to have to refuse," he added quickly, before she got started thanking him. "I'm sorry, I wish I could take it on but it's just not possible."

"You're sure?"

"Sorry, but yes."

"I see. I'm sorry about that. I'd really hoped to persuade you." She sounded tired. "I was just telling Ashley about the bins you helped the kids put together for the recycling program. It's a great project."

"Thanks."

Ashley. Her name kept coming up. In his mind's eye he could see her, slim and elegant, her hair looking tousled and windblown around those big gray eyes, though it had probably taken a salon hours to create the effect.

"Really, I wish I could do it, Piper. But with Tati to take care of and working at the school—I think I've bitten off just a little more than I can chew."

She laughed, a soft musical sound that carried across the wires.

"Tati's a sweetheart. One look from those big brown eyes and I'd be lost. I don't know how you can ever say no to her."

"I can't," he admitted.

They traded a few more words then Piper let him go, but not before asking him to dinner after church on Sunday.

"Nothing big, just a few of our friends. Jason and I want everyone to meet Ashley."

"Oh, we've already met," he told her. "Didn't she tell you? She was going to call the cops on me."

When they hung up Michael was grinning.

Let Ms. Ice explain that.

Chapter Three

"Everything for the winter festival is coming together so well. If I could just figure a way to get those sets built."

"You will."

Piper tossed her briefcase on a chair, flung off her shoes and smiled at Ashley.

"Such faith. Thanks, pal." She sniffed. "Something smells wonderful. I love it when you cook on Fridays. Jason says it's like the kickoff to a great weekend."

Jason says this and Jason says that. During the month Ashley had been at Cathcart House, barely a sentence had left Piper's lips that didn't include her fiancé. Ashley felt a faint prick of envy for the couple. Theirs would be a wonderful marriage.

"Shrimp cocktail for starters. Prime rib and roasted potatoes. Corn from the farmer's marker. Coleslaw from the cabbage in your garden, and apple betty crumble for dessert. How does that sound?"

"Like I should have brought another three guys." Jason walked through the door, kissed Piper, then waved a hand. "Come on in, buddy. Hey, Ashley, I found Michael heading for his mother's coffee shop and invited him to join us. Since he missed our Sunday get-together, I figured we owed him. Is that okay?"

Like she could say no now, with him standing there, grinning at her.

"Of course. The more the merrier." Ashley sent a half smile in Michael's direction then busied herself thickening the gravy. "It won't take a minute to get everything on the table. I made some punch if anyone's interested."

"I ask you, could I have found a better roommate than this?" Piper poured four glasses, handed them round, then walked out onto the deck with Jason, laughing over something that had happened that day.

Ashley prayed Michael would follow, but God apparently had other plans. Michael leaned one hip against the end of the counter and took a sip of his drink.

"Cranberries, raspberries and a bite," he guessed, licking his lips. "Cinnamon and bitters?"

She nodded.

"For some reason the changing leaves always make me think of cinnamon. Is it too strong?"

"It's perfect. Like you." He ignored her uplifted eyebrow. "I mean it. Look at you, after slaving all day in the kitchen your hair looks as if you'd spent the day at the spa. Your dress hasn't got a spot of grease on it and as far as I can tell you haven't broken a sweat."

She had to laugh.

"It's not exactly hard labor you know. All I did was cook a few things and set the table."

"To me that is hard labor. Mostly I hope my mother invites us for dinner so I don't have to go through the agony of cooking. Tati even asks Wanda to invite her so she won't have to eat it."

It was hard to tell if he was joking or serious. She began to dish up the meal. Without being asked, Michael carried each porcelain container to the table. When he saw her lift out the meat, he went to the door and called the other two.

Jason helped Piper be seated. Michael winked at Ashley as he held her chair, then promptly sank down in the one closest to her.

"Honey, do you want to say grace?" Piper asked, reaching out for Jason's hand on one side of the table and Michael's on the other.

"Sure." Jason held out his hand for Ashley's, watched Michael take the other one, then bowed his head. "Thank you God for friends and food and your love. Bless us now we ask. Amen."

Jason released Ashley's hand immediately but Michael held on so long she had to tug her fingers from his. He made a face.

"Couldn't you think of a longer prayer, Jason?" he asked.

Piper and Jason chuckled. To hide her red cheeks, Ashley rose to retrieve the carving knife. As she handed it to Jason her gaze rested on Michael.

"It's very sharp," she said clearly. "You'll want to be careful it doesn't slip and hurt someone."

Michael inclined his head. "She means someone like me," he explained in a loud whisper.

Ashley pretended to ignore him and concentrated on her meal, listening as Piper expounded on her winter festival plans.

"Things are falling together so well. So far we've had a great response. It looks like we'll have entries in every category. The trapper's dinner has been taken over by two women who used to run a catering business, which is a huge relief." She leaned back in her chair, her forehead wrinkled. "If it wasn't for that play—"

"Still nobody to build the sets, I'm guessing." Michael sipped his water, looked at Jason. "How about you?"

Jason's head was shaking before he'd finished asking.

"Give me a motor and some tools and I can do great things. But with a hammer I'm a liability."

"He's telling the truth," Ashley vouched, trying to smother her smile. "If you look above the piano you can see where he was going to hang a picture."

They all turned to stare at the damaged plaster. Jason endured their teasing good-naturedly until Ashley cleared the dishes and served dessert. The subject changed to the timing of the festival.

"It's got to be in January," Piper explained. "We need the ice and snow to carry off the ice-sculpture contests. And the lake will still be frozen, which will allow us to have our family skating day and the community bonfire out there."

"Not to mention the ice-fishing tournament." Jason set down his fork. "I don't know when I've enjoyed a meal so much. Thank you, Ashley."

"Me, too," Michael added, scooping up the last bite of apple betty. "You should sell this recipe to my mom. She'd pay a lot to serve this."

"It has to be the spices," Piper decided, savoring the taste on her tongue. "I know there's cinnamon, but you've added something else that makes me think of apple trees just starting to form the apples. It's delicious."

"A hint of nutmeg. Thank you all." Blushing, Ashley rose, began removing the dessert dishes.

"Oh, no. You cooked. We clean." Jason lifted the plates from her hands. "Isn't that right?" he asked Piper.

"Absolutely. Why don't you take your coffee out on the deck, Ash? It's a gorgeous evening. Jason even lit a fire in the firepit, just in case it gets cool."

"I'll go with you to make sure you won't have to stand out there alone and stare at the stars by yourself," Michael offered, grasping her elbow as if to lead her. "You understand, don't you, guys?" he said over one shoulder, winking at Piper and Jason.

"I'll let it go this time because I get to spend some more time with my girl, but I'm warning you, man." Jason shook his head. "There will come a day when that smooth tongue of yours is going to fail."

"Envy is a terrible thing." Michael let Ashley tug her arm out of his grasp, and poured two cups of coffee from the decanter she'd left on a side table. "After you, madam."

She went with him, because to refuse would be to create a scene. Besides, Piper and Jason needed time together without her in the room.

"You and Jason sound like you've known each other forever."

"That's what it seems like. Jason could be the brother I never had," Michael admitted. "We clicked the day I arrived back here and he offered to help me move in."

"He is a nice guy. I'm glad he and Piper found each other."

"You two have been friends for a while, I take it?"

"The three of us, Piper, Rowena and I, were inseparable as kids." She smiled. "We all came from here, went to boarding school together and stuck by each other through thick and thin. We still try and get together as often as we can. And we phone a lot."

"Nice." Mick handed her a cup. "This deck has the most fantastic vista." He remained beside her, staring across the treetops. "Years ago people considered the view and built accordingly. Now it seems like we raze everything to the ground and then try to recreate nature. Most of the time we don't do nearly as good a job."

"Why won't you help Piper with the play sets?" she asked, refusing to dance around the issue any longer. "She's worked so hard on this, trying to get Serenity Bay on the map so people can live here year round and earn a good living. It can't be that hard to build a few sets."

Michael kept staring outward, as if he were ignoring her.

"Are you against the winter festival or against bringing more tourists to town?"

"Neither." He did look at her then, surprise covering his face. "I'm for both. The more the merrier. I think Piper's done a fantastic job of developing Serenity Bay."

"But you're against development, is that it?"

"Not at all." He shook his head, frowned at her. "Why do you say that?"

"Well, you're not helping, so—"

"It's not that I don't want to. I think the winter festival is a great idea. Bringing back some of the old ways to teach the kids, showing them firsthand how trappers worked— all of it is going to be very educational and fun. That's the way kids learn best."

"Not to mention the people it will bring to town just to see the contestants," she murmured. She kept her focus on him. "So what's the problem?"

"The problem is time. Actually a lack of it." He sipped his coffee, then reached out, plucked a tumbling leaf from her hair. "I don't have enough of it. I teach full-time. I have a young daughter to raise and a house to clean. I'm already struggling to keep up in all three of those areas, Ashley."

It wasn't the answer she wanted, and Ashley had a hunch it wasn't the whole answer, either. There was something Michael wasn't saying. What was he hiding?

"I finally remembered you," he said quietly.

"P-pardon?"

"From when you lived here before. Ashley Adams. You lived in that big silver-gray house on the waterfront. I used to envy you."

"Me?" Ashley turned to look at him. "Why would you ever envy me?" You had parents and sisters who loved you, a stable home."

"That's easy. You could get up in the morning, walk a hundred feet and dive into the water," he explained.

"So could you. Serenity Bay is almost surrounded by water."

"Ah, yes, but I had to bike to get to the beach. You lived right beside it. You could swim anytime you wanted. For someone like me who is addicted to water, your house was perfection. It's up for sale, did you know?"

"No, I didn't." The house she'd once loved had become a cold empty place. Her father wasn't home much during the year so he'd only kept the sparsest of furniture. Summers he spent in the backyard or on his boat. By an unspoken mutual agreement, neither of them spent more than the necessary amount of time inside.

"Well, it is. I looked at it when I moved here last spring. It might need a bit of work but the location is still its biggest asset."

"You weren't tempted to buy it? Access to water and all that?"

"I wish." Michael shook his head. "I couldn't afford it. Anyway, it's a place meant for a big family to enjoy and right now there's only Tati and I."

"She's a beautiful child."

"Yes, she is. Beautiful and headstrong with a tendency to spill stuff."

Ashley remembered her own childhood. "Aren't all kids clumsy, to some extent?"

He snickered. "You don't know Tati very well. *To some extent* doesn't begin to cover my child."

There were several comments Ashley could have made just then, but none of them seemed kind. So she kept her mouth shut and after a couple of minutes of silence Michael described his daughter's attempt to "help" him make dinner two nights before.

"Every smoke alarm in the place was ringing. I had to toss the toaster outside eventually. That's when I found out she'd put cheese slices on the bread she'd buttered before she put it in the toaster. The house still smells."

"Accidents happen," she told him, suppressing her laughter.

"Once could be called an accident but yesterday I had to take my DVD player apart."

"She put something in it?" Ashley asked, trying not to stare at him as his expression changed from chagrin to laughter.

"My socks. Tati claimed she was trying to make a video for her grandmother."

"A video of socks?" Ashley frowned.

"To show Granny the holes so she could get me new ones for Christmas," he admitted. "Tati's a little focused on Christmas at the moment. She has her special Christmas dress all picked out."

"Smart girl. It's good to be prepared."

His shoulder brushed hers. Since Ashley was in the corner of the railing she could hardly move away. Leaving would only prove—to herself most of all—how much he affected her. So she stood there.

"It must be fun to have a child in your life."

"Fun, yes. Also very scary. Since you knew me back when, you might remember I was never an A student when it came to responsibility. Being the youngest kid does that,

I guess." He studied her. "Are you cold? Would you like to move nearer the fire?"

Ashley nodded, followed him to the lounge chairs. He waited till she'd sunk into one, then sat down on the end of it.

"What about you? Do you want children?"

"Someday." She panned a look. "I'd like to get married first, though."

"Smart lady." He flicked her cheek with one finger, chasing away a mosquito. "If I remember correctly, you were always popular with the boys."

"You remember incorrectly," she chided, peeking up through her lashes. "Or you'd remember me hugging your mother's ficus plant in the corner at her parties. I was usually the wallflower. Too shy, I guess."

"You don't seem the shy type."

"But then you don't know me that well." She reached for the soft shawl she'd dropped on a side table earlier.

"I'd like to," he said simply, meeting her gaze. "Know you better, I mean. Maybe we could go out for dinner one evening."

"You're too busy," she reminded archly. "You can't even find a moment to work on the sets."

"Tati and her grandmother have a standing date on Friday nights. I'm free as a bird then."

Ashley shifted uncomfortably. "I'm not really interested in dating right now," she murmured, feeling hemmed in. "I came to Serenity Bay to relax and recuperate for a little while."

"After your accident. My mother told me. Do you want to talk about it?"

"No."

"Okay, then." Michael folded his hands together in his lap, stretched out his legs and glanced around like an eager tourist taking in the sights. "Nice weather we're having, isn't it?"

She couldn't help but chuckle.

"Now there's a sound I haven't heard in a while. Ashley laughing. I like it." Piper walked onto the deck behind Jason who was carrying a tray with two mugs and a plate of cookies on it. She sat down on the swing, patted the seat next to her then accepted her cup. "What are you two talking about?"

"The weather."

"Ashley not dating."

Their simultaneous responses had the other two grinning.

"Maybe we should go back inside and let them settle this," Jason said.

"Oh, I'd rather let them continue. We'll just listen in." Piper leaned back against Jason's arm, slung across the back of her seat and passed the cookies. "Ashley needs a challenge, Michael. She's kind of stuck in her ways. That's why I've been begging her to help me with the festival. Did you know she contacted her former boss about setting up a gallery to display local artists' work in town?"

Michael shifted, his attention intent on Piper.

"I didn't know," he said. He turned to Ashley. "Any luck?"

"No. He turned me down without even seeing some of the things that are produced here. But that's okay. I'll find someone else. I'm good at getting backers for artists who need to get their work to the public."

"Are you?"

"Have you heard of Terrence Demain?"

"Who hasn't?" Michael nodded, eyes wide. "Mosaics. Gorgeous walls of fantastic color."

"Exactly. A friend of mine commissioned his first wall.

The critics couldn't get enough of his work and he took off."

"That's what Ashley does, you see. She finds the talent and then brings it to the light. Her former boss could tell you how good she is if he hadn't fired her." Piper smiled at Ashley. "How many times has Ferris begged you to come back, Ash?"

"I've lost count."

"You don't want to go back to your old job?" Michael studied her.

"Maybe. Sometime." Ashley kept her face expressionless as she scrambled for excuses. The intensity of his stare was unnerving. "I need a break first. I'd been working nonstop for ages. It feels good to relax, putter around a bit. And Piper's a peach for letting me come here. There's nowhere like the Bay for reorienting yourself."

"Mmm." Michael tilted his head to one side, shrugged. "I guess."

She watched him closely, framing her next words with care.

"You probably thought the same thing yourself. I mean, isn't that why you've come back, after all these years? To start over with your daughter?"

"I guess you could say that."

If she hadn't been watching Ashley might have missed his wince. As it was, she couldn't help but wonder what had caused it and why he was staring at her as if she held some secret he needed.

"Anyway, I'll probably leave in a couple of weeks."

"But you have to be here for our wedding, Ash," Piper protested. "You and Row are my bridesmaids and I'm not getting married without either of you. I've got your dresses all picked out." She threaded her fingers through Jason's, her engagement ring flashing its fire. "Christmas isn't all that far off, you know."

Michael choked on his coffee. One look at his face and Ashley burst into laughter.

"What is so funny?" Piper asked.

"Apparently you're not the only one who's looking forward to Christmas," Ashley told her.

"Or thinking about fancy dresses," Michael added.

"Oh." A furrow appeared across Piper's forehead. She glanced from him to Ashley, then shrugged. "I'll assume it's a private joke."

"It is," Ashley assured her.

Michael winked at her, then rose.

"I'd better get going," he told her, holding out one hand to Ashley. "Walk me to my car?"

She could hardly refuse. Ashley placed her hand in his and rose. "I thought you said you had Friday evenings free?"

"I do. I gave my students a test last week and promised I'd have their marks ready on Monday. People think teaching is nine to three but they have no idea about the overtime."

"I guess not."

"Thanks for hosting me, Piper. And Jason, anytime you want another dinner guest, give me a call."

"Will do." Jason and Piper stood together, arms wrapped around each other's waists. "You know you're welcome. Bring Tatiana next time."

"We'll see." He walked toward the door. Ashley followed. "Good night," he said as he stepped outside. "Thanks again."

They waved. Ashley walked with him to his car without saying anything. Dusk had fallen. Across the road, some sixty feet away, a doe and her fawn were enjoying an evening lunch on a patch of grass. She touched his arm, pointed.

Michael watched for a while. Then he faced her.

"It was a great meal," he said. "I enjoyed talking to you. Are you sure you won't have dinner with me sometime, so I can repay your generosity?"

She shook her head, smiled. "I don't think so. But thank you."

"Why?"

The bald question took her by surprise.

"Because."

"That's not an answer." He shoved his hands into his pockets, kicked at a stone on the ground before meeting her gaze.

"I'm not trying to trap you into anything, Ashley. I'm not looking for anything more than a friend I can talk to." He shrugged. "Tati's great but sometimes it's nice to talk to another adult, discuss something other than her friend Wanda at day care."

She smiled at the frustration that gilded his voice.

"I'm sure there are lots of adults you can talk to."

"But not you?"

She shrugged. "I won't be here that long. I'm going to spend some time helping Piper while I search for another job." She struggled to explain. "I'm sure your mother told you I broke off my engagement recently. I guess what I'm saying is that I need time to put my world back together again."

He nodded, his dark eyes melting with empathy.

"Believe me, I understand that." He thrust out his hand. "If you get a moment and want to talk, phone me."

"And you'll make time in that busy schedule of yours?" she murmured as her fingers slid into his.

He held her hand, stared down at it cradled in his bigger rougher one, then looked at her. Ashley stared into his eyes, unsure if the zip of current she felt was only her imagination.

"I'll make time for you," he answered quietly. He lifted her hand, brushed his lips against her knuckles. "Good night, beautiful. I hope we cross paths again soon."

Then he was gone and Ashley was left with the imprint of his lips on her skin. But it wasn't only that he'd touched her physically. Something in her spirit recognized that he was seeking solace, just as she was.

She didn't understand how or why she knew that, but Michael Masters's effect on her was no different than the first time she'd visited the Louvre. Her knees were weak, her palms damp and she couldn't quite catch her breath.

Sort of like a panic attack. Only better.

All the more reason to stay away from him.

Chapter Four

"Will you get me another mommy?"

Michael jerked out of his thoughts, found Tati staring at Carissa's picture in the silver frame he'd placed on a shelf in her room. He regrouped quickly, picked up his daughter and hugged her.

"I don't know if I can do that, sweetheart."

"'Cause my mommy was special." Tati nodded like a wise owl. "I know. She danced the best *Swan Lake*."

She never failed to amaze him. "How do you know about *Swan Lake*?"

"Wanda." Tati's busy fingers brushed through his hair. "She said her mom didn't believe my mommy was a ballerina so she looked on the Internet. Wanda's mom said my mommy had rave reviews. Are rave reviews good, Daddy?"

"I'm very sure they are," he murmured, kissing her cheek. But they didn't compare to holding your child in your arms. "Did you get all your toys put away?"

"Uh-huh. Can we go to the Dairy Shack now?"

"We can." He swirled her around until the giggles he loved to hear burst out of her, then he set her down. "How about getting your jacket?"

"Daddy." Her eyes brimmed with scorn. "It's boiling outside."

"It is now," he agreed, brushing her nose with his fingertip. "But it might not be so warm on the water later."

Tati squealed with delight. "We're going on a boat?"

He nodded. "The houseboat. Like we had for Granny's birthday, remember? We've been invited to go for a ride with Piper and Jason."

Her face glowed with excitement, but she said nothing more, simply headed for her room and her sweater. Moments later they were on the road and Michael was fielding her incessant questions, punctuated by expressions of delight. Tati would finally have something interesting to talk about at show and tell.

"Can I catch a fish?"

"I don't know, honey. We'll have to see."

"I hope it's a giant fish. A whale."

"We don't have whales in Serenity Bay, honey."

"It could happen," she insisted stubbornly then turned to stare out the window. "Wanda says lots of strange things happen."

Wanda would know. Michael drove through the shedding trees, crunching over dry red and gold leaves toward the ice cream shop. His mind grappled with the same old problem. Assuming he could get some pieces finished by next summer, how and where could he arrange a showing? And was that God's will or his own?

"Look, Daddy. Aren't the flowers pretty?"

"Where?" He followed her pointing finger to a shiny convertible sitting next to a gigantic plastic cone advertising fifty-one flavors. Something about that car seemed familiar.

"In the window of that car. The nice lady's there."

Michael pulled into a parking spot, turned his head and

saw Ashley Adams seated behind the wheel of her black sports car, facing straight ahead. A transparency of Van Gogh's big yellow sunflowers had been stuck on the back side window.

"Let's go say hello." Michael released Tati from her car seat, took her hand as they walked toward Ashley. Though the roof was down, all her windows were rolled up. He tapped on one.

Ashley jerked, slowly turned her head to face him. Her face was a pasty white, her eyes stretched wide with fear.

"Are you all right?" He waited, and when she didn't respond, reached over the window to unlock the door. He opened it, touched her shoulder. "Ashley?"

Her whole body jerked at the contact.

"Yes?" Her voice emerged a thread of sound.

"Is something the matter?"

"Is she sick, Daddy?"

Tati's squeak of inquiry seemed to break the bubble Ashley had been trapped in. She drew in a deep breath and released her fingers from their death grip on the wheel.

"I'm fine. Thank you for asking."

"You don't look fine," he told her bluntly. She cast furtive glances to the left, then right, as if searching for someone. Or something.

"What's wrong?"

"Wrong?" She blinked, swung her legs from the car. "Nothing's wrong. I came to get a carton of ice cream. I'm going for a boat ride with Piper and Jason."

"So are we!" Tati squealed in delight. "What kind of ice cream are you going to get?"

"What kind would you like?"

Her recovery happened faster than he expected, but it wasn't complete. Michael knew from the way she closed the car door then checked the street that she was looking for something. Or someone.

"I like chocolate chip cookie dough. And tiger-tiger. And strawberry cheesecake and pistachio and—"

Ashley laughed. "Maybe I should have asked what kind you *don't* like."

"Oh." Tati frowned, grasped Michael's hand. "What kind of ice cream *don't* I like, Daddy?"

"I don't think there is one." He motioned to the store. "Shall we go inside and look?"

"Sure." Ashley walked along beside him. She wasn't wearing her usual high heels but the cream linen pants and matching silk sweater still screamed money. Even her toes, poking out of woven rope sandals, were perfectly manicured and polished a soft blush pink.

Michael held the door, waited for her to pass in front of him.

"Your hand is shaking," he said, softly enough that Tati couldn't hear. "I wish you'd tell me what's wrong."

"It's nothing." She tipped her head back to stare into his eyes. "Just some bad memories that won't go away."

Her hair was bundled onto the top of her head and held there by a silver comb, though wispy ringlets broke free and framed her face. A few longer tendrils caressed the long smooth line of her neck like an expensive pewter frame. She was gorgeous.

"I didn't realize you'd be going on the houseboat today."

"Or you would have begged off?" He smiled at her faint blush. "I can cancel if it will bring back that killer smile of yours."

"Don't be silly. Tati would be devastated." She inclined her head toward the little girl peeking over the ice-cream freezer trying to choose her favorite. "You have a beautiful daughter."

"Yes, I know. I thank God for her every day." Since they were early Michael insisted on buying them each a cone, then suggested they wander across the street to the park to eat them.

"Color coordination down to a T," he murmured, watching as she nipped at the top of her ice cream.

"What do you mean?" Ashley blinked, stared at him.

"Just thinking aloud."

"Oh, no, you don't," she said. "Tell me the truth. What did you mean by that?"

"Okay, but just remember, you asked me." He wrinkled his nose, glared at her ice cream. "Vanilla? Of all the flavors you could have picked you chose boring old vanilla? I assumed you chose it so that it would blend in with your clothing."

"You think my clothes are boring?" She lifted one eyebrow like an imperial queen questioning a servant.

"No." Michael shook his head. "See, I knew I'd blow this. Your clothes are perfect. You're perfect. But vanilla ice cream is boring. Not like you at all. I would have thought you'd choose something subtle but definitely flavored, like butter pecan."

She glanced over at Tati who seemed happy to sit on the bottom of the slide and lick her double chocolate chip ice cream.

"I'm not big on pecans. See. You don't know me that well."

"Sure I do. You're the girl who used to hide behind my mom's plant."

"You didn't remember that." Ashley shook her head, her smile faint. "I told you."

He tried again, scouring his brain for some other memory. "You never used to say much. The silent type."

"I told you that, too." She looked him straight in the

eye. "You don't remember me at all, do you, Michael? Not that you should. I don't think I ever said more than fifteen words to you. We never had anything in common."

"Of course I remember. You came here to spend summer with your father after your parents split. You and Piper and another girl used to hang around together a lot." He struggled to recall some detail his mother had let slip. "Anyway, you had the best house in the neighborhood."

"You said that before." She glanced down at her cone, dabbed at the white glob that dripped on her wrist. "It really doesn't matter. Just accept that I chose vanilla ice cream because I like it."

"Why?"

Ashley gave him a testy look, shrugged her shoulders.

"I don't know. It's simple, uncomplicated. The way I want my life to be."

He almost laughed—until he saw how serious she was.

"Ashley, unless you're a monk in a monastery, I don't think that's going to happen."

"Why not?"

"Because life isn't like that. It's messy and challenging and full of surprises. And that's good."

"Why? I don't like surprises."

From the dark clouds scudding across her face, Michael got the distinct impression she'd just made the understatement of the year. He waited, hoping she'd expound further.

"I like my life organized, not chaotic. I like to wake up knowing what I've planned for the day and then do it. I don't like wondering what tomorrow will bring."

"It scares you," he guessed quietly. "I suppose an accident, losing your job and breaking an engagement can do that to a person. But you'll get past it. You'll want challenges in your life again."

She tilted her head to one side.

"Are you analyzing me?"

"Hardly." Like he was qualified to help anyone when his own life was such a shambles. "I'm just saying, why not cut yourself some slack? You've obviously gone through a lot. You need some time to just let the wind blow the cobwebs away."

"Is that what you do?"

He glanced around, found Tati kicking sand in the sandbox. "Not lately," he admitted.

"But you'd like to spend more time with your daughter?" Now she was analyzing him.

"I spend as much as I can with her, but sometimes the mornings are so rushed." He shrugged. "As the days get shorter, daylight comes later and it feels more and more like I'm dragging her out of bed at the crack of dawn to ship her off to day care."

"Doesn't she enjoy it there?"

"Oh, yeah." Michael smiled. "Tati's always been around a lot of people. Keeping her at home alone wouldn't be an option."

"So why the guilt?"

He studied her wide gray eyes, found only empathy. That was probably why he let the words pour out.

"I want to give her everything," he explained softly. "I don't ever want her to think back and feel like she missed out on something because of me or remember that I wasn't there when she wanted me. I don't want to be too busy for her, but—"

"But you have a lot of things to do and it's not easy to divide your time between them. I understand. And I really wasn't going to press you about the set building again." Ashley tossed the rest of her cone into the trash can, dabbed her fingers against a napkin and tossed it in, too. "Piper's very good at recruiting people. She'll find someone else. I hope."

He laughed at her last remark.

"Hint taken. I'll think about it, okay? Now no more guilt," he decreed. "Let's go for that boat ride and enjoy the afternoon. It'll be something to look back on in January when it's twenty below and the snow's up to our ears. Come on, Tati."

She came trundling across the leaf-covered grass, legs churning as fast as they could carry her, chocolate smears covering her face, her T-shirt and her jeans.

"You need a bath," he told her, grimacing at her grungy fingers. He glanced at Ashley. "Could you watch her while I run across to ask for some damp napkins?"

"No need." Ashley reached inside her cream purse and lifted out a small zippered bag. She removed two small packets, handed them to him. "Wet wipes. They should do the trick."

"Thank you." Michael sighed. She's a lot better prepared than you. One step at a time.

Once Tati was as clean as they could manage, they trooped back to the cars. Michael couldn't miss Ashley's surreptitious scan of the area.

"I wish you'd tell me what's wrong," he murmured quietly as Tati climbed inside her car seat and buckled herself in.

"Why do you keep saying that? I'm fine."

"Is that why you keep checking over your shoulder?"

She stared at him for a moment, bit her lip. "I thought I saw someone," she finally admitted.

"Someone you don't want to see, I assume."

Ashley's spun-silver hair jerked as she nodded. "Someone I never want to see again."

The vehemence in her voice stunned him. Who did she mean?

"Your former fiancé?"

"Kent?" Surprise filled her eyes. She shook her head, her smile lopsided. "No worries there. He's off looking for other fish to fry."

"You don't sound upset by that." He studied her face, searching for the remnants of pain. He found none.

"I'm not." Her eyes hardened for a moment, then she shrugged. "I made a mistake. A marriage between us never would have lasted."

Since she didn't seem averse to sharing, Michael dug a little deeper. "Why not? Didn't you love him?"

"I thought I did. Turns out he loved something more than me."

"You mean *someone*, don't you?"

She chuckled. "Actually I don't, Michael. I mean some-*thing*—as in money. My fiancé wanted to be kept in the style to which he'd become accustomed. When I objected to being his meal ticket, he decided it was time to cut all ties." Ashley's indifference to that decision was visible. She pulled her sunglasses off the dash of her car and twiddled them in one hand. "He's probably found someone else by now."

"And you don't care?"

A tiny flush of color tinted her pale cheeks. "It's a little embarrassing, but once I get past that, no, I really don't care. Actually I think I'm glad I found out when I did. I can't imagine living the way he wanted. I like to work, to be busy. I'm not good at lounging."

"I wouldn't mind trying it for a while," he admitted.

"Are we going now, Daddy?"

Michael raised his eyebrows, inclined his head. "See what I mean?"

"Yes," Ashley laughed, her gray eyes agleam with fun. "And I think it's wonderful. She's a great little girl. You're very lucky."

"Then maybe you'd like to share my good fortune and ride with us to Jason's marina? I could bring you back afterward."

He thought she'd refuse but after a moment she nodded.

"Sure. Just let me put up the top and lock my car."

Michael stood back and watched, envying her the luxury of such a beautiful car. That meant she had money, right? Must have, to afford something like this.

"She's a beaut," he told her, sliding one hand over the fender, unable to decide if it was last year's model or not. "You have good taste in cars."

"Oh, I didn't choose this," she told him, her eyes wide with surprise. "I don't know anything about cars. My grandfather bought it just before he died. He left it to me."

"Nice grandpa." By comparison his old wagon was an oxcart, but Michael held the door for her, waited while she stepped inside, her long legs swinging in with a grace he admired.

"Are you a car afficionado?" she asked once he'd started the engine.

"Mostly I admire them from a distance." He caught her stare and grinned. "I like nice cars but I also like having a roof over my head and three square meals. In the scheme of things I guess a new car isn't all that important to me."

"Daddy had a nice red car but it got made into lemonade." Tati's chirping voice carried clearly.

"Lemonade?" Ashley twisted to study him. "Did you crash?"

He burst out laughing. "No, nothing like that. I had a sports car, but I sold it, bought this one and pocketed the extra cash. It wasn't roomy enough for Tati and her friends and this one will be more practical when the snowdrifts come. Besides, it gave me a bigger deposit on the house so my payments aren't as high."

"But how—"

"Lemons make lemonade," Tati explained, reaching forward to pat her shoulder. "Daddy says that's just how life is."

"Okay." Ashley smiled at the little girl but it took her a few minutes to make the connection. "When life hands you lemons," she said eventually. "I get it."

"Exactly." He grinned as if they'd just shared the formula for world peace. They arrived at the marina to find Piper waiting for them.

"I'm so glad you could come but there's been a hitch," she explained. "Jason had one of his rentals break down and he's had to go after it. Since there's nobody to stay at the shop in case they come back, I have to wait here. But you three can go on your own. You've handled the Zephyr before, haven't you, Michael?"

"Yes, I rented it when we took Mom out for her birthday in July. But are you sure we shouldn't wait for Jason? He won't be that long."

"Oh, yes, he will. He said at least three hours and by then the sun will be cooling. You go ahead. Take Ash with you. She hasn't done anything but hang around the house and show her slides at school." She wrapped her arm around Ashley's waist, hugged her. "You can trust Michael. He's good at everything he does but maybe you can help with Tati."

"I don't need help." Tati planted her hands on her hips. "I'm a big girl."

"I know it. I think you've grown two whole inches this summer." Piper swooped Tati up into her arms and hugged her. "You've got spots," she said, wrinkling her nose.

"Choc'late chips from the ice cream. Daddy thinks I'm a mess."

"A very pretty mess."

Tati wiggled free, moved beside Ashley, her fingers grasping the long slender ones. "Can you help me with my life jacket?"

"Um, sure. I guess."

Michael watched a silent message flutter from Ashley to Piper and wondered if she'd back out. Not if he could help it.

"Is everything ready to go, Piper?"

"Jason said to tell you the tank is full and everything's operating perfectly. I tucked a picnic in the galley for later and there are some CDs next to the stereo. Just get back before eight. It gets dark fast lately."

"Wait!" Tati tugged her arm. Ashley leaned down so his daughter could whisper something in her ear. Ashley listened, smiled, nodded then straightened.

"Ready now?" Piper asked with a grin.

"Ready." Tati wore the happiest grin he'd seen in hours, which made Michael just the tiniest bit nervous.

What was she up to?

"Well, ladies, shall we?" He waved a hand toward the vessel hopefully. He'd spent months trying to figure out God's plan for his future and since wisdom hadn't yet arrived, he'd no doubt spend plenty more. But surely God wouldn't begrudge him an afternoon with a beautiful woman on this glassy lake.

"We shall," Ashley said as if she sensed his thoughts. Then she pointed her nose in the air and strode across the deck as if she were a princess. Tati followed, copying her snooty stance.

Michael looked to Piper who was trying to conceal her grin.

"Come along then, Captain. Let's get this rig moving." Ashley tilted one imperious eyebrow as if questioning his hesitation.

"You have your orders, sailor." Piper saluted him smartly.

"Yes, ma'am." He saluted back then marched across in proper servant form. He started the engine, waited till Piper cast off, then eased them out of the berth and across the still blue water.

"Ta ta," Ashley called, offering a queenly wave. She and Tati both wore life jackets and sat in the front of the boat on the most comfortable chairs.

Michael pushed the throttle a little harder, watching as the two heads, one silver-bright, one dark as night, pressed together. Even over the sound of the motor he could hear their singing.

So that was the secret. Tati loved to sing.

He shoved his sunglasses down over his eyes and smiled. Life didn't get much better than this.

"It was a great afternoon," Ashley murmured as Michael lifted Tati from her lap and carried the sleeping child ashore. "Thank you very much."

"Thank you for coming. It wouldn't have been nearly as much fun without you." He'd already tied off the boat, so he handed her the keys. "If you could take those into the marina, I'll put Tati in the car."

"Sure." She strode to the store well aware that his eyes followed her progress. Only when she was inside did she peek over one shoulder. He was heading for his car.

"Everything okay?" Jason asked as he took the keys.

"Everything was lovely. Tell Piper—" She stopped, smiled as she saw her friend sitting behind him. "The lunch was lovely, Pip. I don't know how you managed to find fresh strawberries at this time of year."

"I have my sources." Piper raised one eyebrow.

"What's the look for?"

"Oh, nothing." Piper's dark eyes sparkled with interest. "So you enjoyed your afternoon with Michael? And Tatiana, of course."

Suddenly Ashley got it.

"No, Piper. Don't get any ideas. It was a nice afternoon, but I'm not interested in becoming anyone's mommy." As the last word left her lips, Ashley heard a noise behind her. She turned. Michael stood there, his face tight.

"Excuse me. Just wanted to say thanks for a great afternoon." Michael didn't even look at her. "Tati and I both enjoyed it." He turned and walked out of the building, toward his car.

"Rats!" Ashley glared at Piper. "This is your fault. I'll talk to you later."

"I look forward to it," Piper said with a knowing glint in her eyes.

As she followed Michael to the car, Ashley searched for the appropriate apology. But how did you apologize for a faux pas like that?

He held her door, politely waited until she was inside, then closed it with great care so as not to waken his daughter. But as he walked around the hood and got into the car, she saw that all the fun had drained away.

"It won't take a minute to get back to your car," he said quietly.

"Look, I'm sorry you heard that." Ashley bit her lip, tried again. "I didn't mean it exactly the way it sounded."

"No?"

He wasn't cutting her any slack. Ashley tried again.

"No. Piper's in this blissful state because she's in love with Jason and she thinks it should be the same for me."

"Uh-huh." He kept his gaze straight ahead.

She could almost feel the ice.

"Look. I'm sorry. Really. But your life is full with your daughter and your work, Michael. You told me that yourself."

"Yes, I did." He glanced at her. "I don't recall suggesting I was looking for a mother for my daughter. Or anything else."

"No, you didn't." She shifted uncomfortably. "But Piper's thinking that way. I was just trying to stop her before it went too far."

He turned the corner, pulled up beside her car, then turned to face her.

"What's too far for you, Ashley? Friendship? An afternoon on a boat?" His mouth tightened. "I'm not going to abduct you, you know."

She blanched at his words, pressed her spine against the seat. "I know that."

"For your information, just so we've got everything straight—I was divorced. Her idea, not mine, but our marriage ended shortly after it happened. Several years ago actually." He glared at her, a self-mocking, sardonic smile twisting his lips. "I guess I wasn't as bright as you. I didn't see the problems early enough to bail."

"Michael, please. I didn't mean—" She stopped. The hole was only getting bigger.

"You see, that's the problem, Ashley. I don't know what you mean. I don't understand you at all. One minute you look like you're enjoying yourself, the next you've thrown up this iron fence around yourself as if you're scared you might let go and let somebody see the real you." She opened her mouth, but he held up a hand. "Don't bother to deny it. You were laughing and enjoying yourself today. What's wrong with that?"

"Nothing." She glared through the windshield, irritated by his manner.

"Then why do you act as if you're afraid?" His voice dropped. "For a little while you forget. You poke your head out into life for a few minutes, let yourself enjoy what's happening. But then something changes and you pull back in like a scared turtle. Can't you tell me why you keep freezing up?"

"I'm not doing that," she insisted.

"Yes, you are." He held her gaze, his own solemn. "I thought we could be friends, but you put up barriers, like you expect something bad to happen. As if you expect *me* to do something. What did I do to make you think that?"

"Nothing."

"Then…" He opened his eyes wide, waited for her to speak as he parked beside her car.

She wanted to pretend, but Ashley knew exactly what he was talking about. Because she *was* afraid, she had been for years. But she wasn't going to admit it here and now. Especially not to him.

A flickering memory from the past reminded her that he'd always championed the underdog. He would want to help, to give her advice or reassure her. But Ashley did not want to be Michael's next project.

"I've ruined everything and I never meant to," she apologized quietly. "I was trying to stop Piper from matchmaking and I blurted out the first thing that came to mind. It was rude and I regret it. Your personal life is entirely your own business."

"Sounds like there's a *but* coming."

"I had a wonderful time with both of you. It was fun. Tell Tati goodbye for me, will you?"

Before he could say a word Ashley eased out of his car, closed the door and unlocked her own. A moment later she drove down Main Street, headed in the wrong direction, but who cared? Anything to get away.

But as she drove the familiar streets, Ashley realized she was driving toward her childhood home, the one she'd returned to each summer to live in with her father. She paused, prepared to turn around and then suddenly, she changed her mind.

Maybe it was time to face the past. Part of it, anyway.

She drove slowly, savoring the maple-lined streets, the big spacious lawns with bikes on the sidewalks. Then she was home.

Home. What an odd word. She hadn't really felt at home for years.

There was a sign on the lawn. Open House. She stared at the sign, let the idea spark into life. What could it hurt— just to look?

Ashley climbed out of the car, walked up the cement sidewalk her father had put in when she was about four.

"Hello. Are you here for the open house? You're just in time. I was about to close up. Come on in."

The agent held the door. Ashley walked inside.

It was different.

It was the same.

The entry was big, showcasing an oak banister she'd slid down more than once. Someone had painted the wood a gruesome shade of green and covered the hardwood floors with broadloom, but otherwise the layout was the same.

"It's a beautiful house. Needs a little work, of course. No one's lived in it for several months."

"The owners moved out?" Ashley asked, pausing to study the living room and the huge bay window where she'd sat mooning over Michael all those summers ago.

"They separated in the spring. Here's the study."

Ashley followed her, listening as the woman described features already engraved in her mind.

"It's a gorgeous study. There's a little fountain outside that window that the birds just love. And here's the dining room. Perfect for entertaining. You'll love the kitchen, too. Updated, but without ruining the views and the layout toward the family room. The lake view is perfect, isn't it?"

"Yes, it is." Ashley stared out the wall of windows toward the jetty her parents had built together. It had probably been repaired over the years, but if she cleared her mind, she could almost see her mother standing there, calling her, Piper and Rowena to get out of the water and eat supper.

"There's a back staircase tucked under here providing access to the bedrooms from both ends. It's well laid out." The woman led the way upstairs. "Here's the master bedroom. Very spacious. And the bathroom's been refinished."

Ashley gave it only a cursory look then moved on to the room at the back, her room.

"I think this is the best room in the house. Just look at that view."

Ashley was looking, drinking it in like someone dying of thirst.

"The window seat is perfect, isn't it? Water view, hills, the garden below. See the tree house?"

"Do you mind if I spend a few moments here? By myself," she added when the woman looked as though she'd stay. "I know you want to close but I'd just like a bit of time to think."

"Take all the time you want. There are two other bedrooms to see, as well. I'll be downstairs."

"Thank you."

Two other rooms that should have been filled with

brothers and sisters that had never happened. Her mother had claimed one as her sewing room. Ashley had used the other for her paints and watercolors.

In the blink of an eye her surroundings became her room from the past. White organza curtains billowing at the windows, white carpet on the floor, a white eyelet spread on the bed. Even after she'd left to come back each summer, it had stayed the same. Piper and Rowena had lounged on the red chairs while she stretched out on the bed.

For a few moments the happy times flooded back, but then the pain intruded. With a wistful sigh, Ashley turned and walked downstairs.

"Are you interested? I'll give you my card, just in case. Feel free to call at any time. Here are the specs if you need them."

"Thanks for letting me look." Ashley tucked the paper into her purse, then walked back to her car, the sadness of the place haunting her.

Why am I still here, God? What is it I'm trying to find in Serenity Bay that will let me get back my life?

She could easily find herself another job. She had the experience and the credentials—it wouldn't be hard. And yet a tiny tug in her heart told her she should wait. A verse Mrs. Masters had taught them echoed back from the past as it had twice before.

Be still and know that I am God.

Be still—Was He trying to teach her something?

But before Michael came, at the ice-cream shop—I saw him. I know I did. She'd never forget that face, no matter how long she lived.

Which meant that either her abductor had returned or he'd never left.

"How can I stay if he's here?"

As she drove to Piper's, Ashley heard only one answer.

Know that I am God.

Chapter Five

After three weeks of using every possible excuse she could find to avoid running into Michael Masters again, Ashley's luck ran out the Friday an early snowstorm sent school students home ahead of schedule.

"Hello, Michael," she said when she had to pass by him to get her coat from the staff room.

He nodded, stepped back to allow her to pass. "Ashley."

She retrieved her coat, wound her scarf around her neck, buying precious minutes until he left. But Michael didn't seem inclined to leave quickly. He thrust his arms into his jacket, waited until the other teachers left the room. Then there were only two of them.

"How are you?"

"Fine." She risked a look at him, found his focus centered on her. "You?"

"Can't complain." He kept watching her. "You're still here."

"Yes." She shrugged. "I promised Piper I wouldn't leave until after her wedding. Except for Christmas. I'm going to Hawaii for that."

"Nice."

"My mom lives there." Ashley drew on her gloves,

wishing he'd move away from the doorway. She didn't want to push past him and there really was little more to say.

"What's keeping you busy?"

"Nothing much."

"Somehow I don't see you content to think about nothing much which means you've been up to something." Michael's mischievous grin flashed then disappeared. His voice grew edgy. "Sorry. It's none of my business."

"It's not a secret." She sighed, pressed the strap of her purse over one shoulder. "Look. I messed up. Big-time. I offended you and I know it. If I say I'm sorry again will you forgive me and forget about my big mouth?"

"It's *why* you said it that bugs me."

She'd known that was coming. Ashley met his gaze and admitted the truth.

"You make me nervous, Michael."

"Nervous? Me?" He blinked. "Why?"

"Shades of the past, probably. I guess I still think of you as the most popular boy on the Bay and I feel like the dumb klutz I was, hiding behind your mother's plant. Sometimes my mouth gets going before my brain is in gear, like that day when I—you know. I feel stupid."

"Then we're even," he murmured.

Ashley frowned. "What do you mean?"

"I look at you and see a classy polished woman who's traveled around the world, wears designer clothes, has mingled with some of the twentieth century's best artists, and I feel like a country bumpkin. And then there's the connection."

Connection? What was he talking about?

"I know it probably sounds cheesy to put it like that, but there *is* a connection between us, Ashley. You must have felt it."

She might have told herself he was teasing but for his serious expression. And for the fact that she had felt a zing of electricity the moment she'd first seen him. That had grown stronger with each meeting.

"You're not saying anything. That's a bad sign."

"I don't know what to say," she admitted.

"Just talk to me."

"I like you, Michael. I like Tati very much. But coming back to Serenity Bay—well, it's brought back a lot of stuff I'd rather forget. None of it particularly pleasant." She hoped he wouldn't press for details.

"So where do we go from here?"

"What if we just agree that you're no country bumpkin and you say you'll forgive me saying and doing the wrong thing at the wrong time."

"Done." He thrust out his hand and grasped hers, shaking it as if they'd struck some deal. "So what have you been doing lately?"

"If I say you're like a dog with a bone, will you be offended?" She chuckled at his growl. "If you must know, I've been assembling a sort of inventory of the artists in the area."

He frowned. "Why?"

"Probably because of all Piper's talk about getting Serenity Bay on the map. She thinks there could be a real explosion of interest here once tourists find out there are so many talented people doing such a variety of work. Frankly, I think she's right. But nobody's going to know unless the artists get some exposure."

"You know a way to do that?"

"I know some gallery owners," she said, wondering what had put the glint back in his eyes. "I've contacted a couple of them who are willing to look at some pieces on spec."

"You don't look pleased by that."

"I guess it's a first step, but I was thinking more in terms of setting up something here. If a well-known gallery had a satellite place in Serenity Bay, they'd have first shot at the pieces and the city galleries might accept that the work that's produced here is worth coming to see." She rubbed her neck, aware that a tiny headache had begun there. "A win-win situation."

"But your gallery people don't want that."

"To them a place here would be a money loser. The area's tourism isn't built in yet so they say what's happened so far might be a flash in the pan. Piper's plans for the winter look good on paper but until the Bay starts attracting people and revenue, I don't think anyone is going to sink that big an investment for return that only lasts a few months in the year."

"I see."

She ducked her head to look outside. "The snow's getting worse. I'd better go."

"Yeah." Still he didn't move. It was almost as if he wanted to say something but couldn't quite get the words out.

"Would you let me pass, please?"

He opened his mouth as if to say something, but after a moment shook his head and stepped aside. "Of course. Drive carefully."

"I always do." She eased past him, catching the scent of his aftershave that made her think of a summer long past when she'd seen Michael riding his motorcycle. Her heart skipped.

Oh, yeah, there was a connection between them.

"Have a good weekend."

Ashley fluttered her fingers then hurried down the hall, pushed open the door. Noon's brisk autumn breeze had become a raging gust that ripped at her hair and dashed snow against her cheek. If this kept up, it wouldn't be long before the roads were covered with snow drifts. She tossed her purse onto the passenger's seat, saw a slide fall out and remembered that she was supposed to have given it to a student in her class who was studying that artist's work.

"Blast!"

Ashley pulled out her cell phone and called Jillian to get directions to the girl's home. Then she eased out of her parking spot and onto the street. The sky darkened to lead as the wind caught falling snowflakes and hurled them into the air, making visibility difficult.

"Just give me enough time for one stop," she begged, peering through the windshield. "Just one, then I'm home."

She found the outlying street without any trouble, but the house was set far back on the property and she had to drive the car down snowy ruts. She could have waited, of course. But the essay Jillian had assigned was due next Wednesday and Ashley had already forgotten once.

She left the motor running, grabbed the square of film and trudged to the door. After a hurried explanation she handed it over to the girl's mother. As she hurried back to her car, she slipped twice. The temperature had dropped. The storm was getting much worse.

Back on the street Ashley found her exit blocked by two cars that had hit each other head-on. She backed up, took a side road, biting her lips as the undercarriage of the car rubbed over the ice and snow ridges.

"Just get me home, baby. That's all I ask."

The road Ashley turned onto wasn't familiar. These houses were set on larger plots of land, far back from the road, hidden from view.

"They must all drive four-by-fours," she muttered to herself as she corrected yet another swerve of the car. A truck behind her moved in a little too close so she eased to one side, hoping he would pass and let her to drive at her own speed.

He didn't pass.

Ashley gripped the wheel tightly as she steered. The truck stayed on her tail, only now the driver was honking. The familiar quaver of panic began in her stomach, pinching its way to each nerve as she crept along, her wheels slipping and sliding over the icy surface, trying to find traction.

What if? What if—

Finally, at a crossroad approach, the truck roared up beside her.

He was going to pass. Ashley drew a calming breath, felt the pressure ease. Everything was fine. She was safe.

"Good riddance to you, too," she agreed when the truck blasted one last honk before it roared ahead of her.

But the flurry of white it left behind caused her to lose sight of the road. Too late, she realized she was heading for the ditch. Trying to correct, she oversteered. The car spun round and round and all she could do was hang on as memories of another crash took control of her mind.

Except this time there was a soft *poof* as the car slid into a pile of snow.

She wasn't hurt. She was fine. Nothing had happened.

Ashley pressed the gas pedal. The tires spun uselessly. She tried Reverse—to no avail.

Great. She was totally stuck on the side of the road in the middle of a freak snowstorm.

"Wonderful," she grumbled, reaching for her purse. "Not only don't I know exactly where I am but my cell phone probably doesn't work out here."

It didn't. Hills loomed on either side. Which, of course, blocked the signal.

"Perfect." Reminded of warnings against carbon monoxide poisoning Ashley switched off the engine. Immediately the howl of the wind whistled around her. The rag-top wasn't built for this.

At least she had on her low-heeled boots, a warm sweater and her heaviest wool coat. She could walk if she had to. Somebody had to live at the end of the lane across the road—which meant there should be traffic on this road. She turned on her flashers and decided to wait it out.

The heat from the car dissipated in minutes. Ashley drew her collar up around her ears, tightened her scarf around her neck. She'd give it ten minutes. If no one came by then, she'd get out and walk. Locking the doors made her feel a little better.

Time ticked by so slowly.

A forgotten sweater lay on the backseat. She reached back to grab it, heard someone rap on her window. Heaving a sigh of relief she struggled to unroll it, trying to see through the misted glass.

Her breath caught in her throat as a face she'd never forgotten loomed before her.

"Get out." Same words, same gruff tone.

The terror of those moments rushed back, snapping the paralysis that had kept her silent.

"Go away," she screamed as she grabbed the handle and rolled up the window. "Leave me alone!"

He tapped on the window twice more but Ashley ignored him, her body shaking as she prayed for help. She pressed the horn, once, twice. He yelled something, rapped one last time then finally left. She tried to see where he'd gone as her heart pounded furiously. Finally a rusty truck pulled onto the road and passed her.

It wasn't the same vehicle she'd been pushed into so long ago, but then it wouldn't be, seventeen years later.

Ashley clutched the wheel, closed her eyes and fought against another wash of fear by pulling in slow deep breaths, just as she'd been taught. It took a while but finally she felt able to critically assess her situation.

No way could she get out and walk now. He could be the one who lived down that lane. But neither could she wait here forever. The radio said the storm could last all night. She'd be buried by morning. Already the light was fading.

Fears that had hung in the wings of her mind tiptoed forward, encouraging a host of worries to follow.

Piper and Jason were away. No one would miss her. If the snow and wind continued, her car could be buried, or hit by a snowplow. She could die out here!

Oh, God, I'm scared and alone and I need help. Please send someone.

"That's Ashley's car."

Michael frowned, dared to glance away from the road for a second. "Where?"

"Up there. See, Daddy. The sunflowers."

"Yes, I see, honey." He followed her pointing finger, saw the car half buried at the edge of the road. What was Ashley doing out here? "I'm going to talk to her. You stay in your seat and keep your belt buckled," he ordered as he edged over onto the side of the road. "Don't get out of your seat, Tati. I mean it," he emphasized as he set his hazard lights.

"Yes, Daddy."

Michael tugged on his gloves then stepped out of the vehicle, struggling through the accumulation of snow to reach her. The car was going to need a tow truck.

He rapped on her window.

"Leave me alone!"

Uncertain that he'd heard the words correctly, he tried again, pulling on the door handle as he spoke.

"Ashley, it's Michael Masters. Are you all right?"

The window rolled down a crack. "Michael?" she whispered.

"Yep, it's me. Unlock the door and I'll help you out."

"I'm stuck."

"I can see that. You're going to need a tow truck and they're really busy with the storm. You can come to my place to wait. It's just down the road."

"Okay." But she didn't move.

"You have to open the door, Ashley." He checked to be sure Tati was still safely inside his car as another vehicle approached.

"Need any help?" a man in the other car called out.

"Not unless you can pull this out." Michael already knew the little import he was driving would be no help.

"Sorry. Haven't got enough power."

"Thanks anyway."

As the other car drove off he heard door locks click. A moment later Ashley opened her door. In the light of her car Michael thought he saw tears on her pale cheeks.

"Are you hurt? Anything broken?" he asked, checking her face, her clothes. But aside from the tear tracks, Ashley Adams looked as immaculate as she always did.

"I'm fine. It was a soft landing." She stood staring up at him, her big gray eyes filled with shadows, her voice trembling. "I'm so glad you came."

"So am I." He took her arm, helped her over the crust of snow and onto the road. "Go get in my car. I'll lock up here. Do you have your keys?"

Confusion filled her face. "I don't know."

Something was obviously wrong, but he wasn't going to question her now. Michael bent, glanced at the ignition.

"They're here. I'll bring them. Can you make it to the car or do you need help in those boots?"

"I'll wait for you," she said, so softly he barely heard.

She sounded terrified. Utterly unlike Ashley.

Frowning, Michael removed the keys, locked the doors, then turned to grasp her elbow. "Okay, let's go. Tati must be wondering what's taking so long."

"Tati. Yes." She hurried along beside him, glancing over one shoulder, then the other as if expecting something to jump out of the bush.

He helped her inside his car and closed the door. A shot of surprise filled him when she quickly locked it. Something was definitely wrong. Michael unlocked his door, climbed inside, glad for once of Tatiana's chatty voice.

"Did you get pushed in the snow? Wanda says lots of people will have trouble in this storm. She says people never drive with the proper equ—" She paused. "What's the word, Daddy?"

"Equipment."

"Yes. Equipment. Anyway, that's what Wanda says. Is that what happened to you, Ashley?" Tati leaned forward, tapped her on the shoulder when no immediately answer was forthcoming.

"Uh, yes. I guess it is." Though Ashley managed a smile, her color had still not returned.

"We passed a number of people who'd gone off the road and there are only two tow trucks in Serenity Bay so you'll have a bit of a wait. But you're welcome to stay with us as long as you like," he told her, concentrating on turning the slippery corner. "I'm sure you'll want to phone Piper and let her and Jason know you're okay."

"They're out of town."

"Oh. Well, good thing we came along then."

"Yes, it is. I tried my cell but it wouldn't work." She huddled in the corner as if afraid he'd bite.

"Service is iffy when you get down in the valley here," Michael explained, unable to rid himself of the feeling that something else had happened to shake that reserved manner she usually clung to like a cloak. "We'll be home in a minute. You can call the service station from there."

"Thanks."

Tati chatted about her day the rest of the way home, leaving little space for any other discussion. Michael hit the remote for the garage door, then pulled inside, glad to be off the road.

"We made it." He climbed out, helped Tati down from her seat. By then Ashley was out of the car, standing beside him. "Come on inside."

He unlocked the door for them before rescuing the pan of lasagne his mother had placed in a box in the trunk. After sliding it into the oven and setting the temperature as she'd directed, he shed his coat, helped Ashley out of hers and hung all three on the pegs by the door. Tati's boots took a little longer. By the time he had them off Ashley had slid her feet out of her own smooth calf-leather footwear. Her feet were bare.

Michael grabbed a pair of his socks from the laundry room.

"You'd better put these on or your toes will freeze on these cold floors."

She didn't argue. "Thanks."

"The phone's over here. The number is on the wall above it. At least that's the one I've used. The book is in the drawer if you'd rather try someone else."

"I have an auto club," she told him. She drew her wallet out of her bag, took out the card and dialed the number on the back. She gave the information then turned to him. "I don't know where to tell them I am," she said quietly.

"I'll explain." He took the phone, gave the directions then asked that the truck call them just before arrival so they could meet it. "How long?"

"At least a couple of hours, I'd imagine. We've got a whole list before you. Everyone's working as fast as they can."

"Okay, thanks." He handed the phone back to Ashley who spoke for a moment then hung up. "All right?"

"Yes, thank you. She said to expect a long wait." She looked at him through her lashes, her gray eyes shaded. "I'm sorry to intrude on your evening like this, Michael."

"Don't be silly. My mother sent supper. I'll just get the rest of my stuff from the car and when everything's ready we'll eat. Tati, you show Ashley the living room. Maybe she'd like to watch the news."

"I don't like news. I like to paint. Do you want to see my paintings, Ashley?"

"I'd love to."

At least she'd warmed up to his daughter, Michael mused as he lugged in the groceries he'd stocked up on. His mother had insisted on sending along a full meal. Garlic bread, a Caesar salad, fresh blueberry pie and a bag of lemon coconut cookies for Tati. A perfect dinner and no cooking.

As Michael set the pie at the back of the stove to warm, he glanced into the living room. Ashley was seated on the floor, a crayon in her hand as she followed Tatiana's directions for drawing a butterfly. Whatever had bothered her out there seemed to be gone now.

Tati switched on the lamp and it shone down on their guest's blond head. A burgundy turtleneck hugged her curves. She wore matching wool slacks. When she moved, a faint tinkling at her waist drew his attention to the golden belt cinched around it.

Ashley was every bit as gorgeous as he'd remembered her. Better than that, she was at his home for dinner and couldn't leave even if she wanted to.

Michael smiled at the irony.

But his smile quickly disappeared when she rose, went to the windows and pushed aside the drapes to peer outside into the yard. So she wasn't totally in control. Which meant that she was still afraid. He made up his mind to find out what had caused this reaction.

"Dinner's ready. Wash your hands, Tati."

His daughter grumbled all the way to the bathroom, but she skipped back happily enough, presenting her palms for him to sniff. "I used soap," she told him.

"I can smell it. Good girl. Ashley, have a seat there, if you'd like."

"Thanks."

"We hold hands to say grace. Is that okay?"

Ashley said nothing but when he stretched out his hand, she paused before sliding hers into it. Her skin felt like silk against his work-roughened fingers. He tried not to notice when she grasped Tati's little mitt with no apparent hesitation.

"God is great, God is good. And we thank him for this food. Amen."

The words barely left Tati's mouth before Ashley tugged her hand out of his, her cheeks a bright pink.

"We haven't got any food to eat, Daddy."

Michael gulped, told himself to get a grip. He rose,

slid the lasagne from the oven and set it in the middle of the table.

"If you can reach the salad, Ashley, I'll get the garlic bread."

She placed the salad on the table, then smoothed her napkin in her lap. Michael passed her the bread, then began serving the lasagne.

"How did you go off the road?" he asked to break the silence.

"A truck was behind me. It was following too close so I edged over to let it pass. When it passed me it kicked up snow flurries and I lost sight of the road. By the time I realized I was off-kilter, the damage had already been done. I slid off."

"A big red truck?" he asked. "Wheels high up off the ground?"

She nodded, wide eyes luminous. "How did you know?"

"Tommy Cliburn. He just got his license. For some reason his parents thought that truck would keep him safe." Michael watched her pick at her food, noticed that the color in her cheeks had returned to its usual pale translucence. "You do realize that you can't keep driving that car in the winter?"

"I'll have to get snow tires."

He shook his head. "It's not the tires. The undercarriage isn't built for these kinds of roads. Every drive from Piper's down those switchback roads will be a nightmare—worse if it's icy. You need something safer."

"I'll be fine."

Not wanting to belabor the subject, Michael changed the subject.

"You said you went to boarding school. Why?"

"My mother thought it would be a stabilizing influence." She sipped her water. When she spoke again her voice had lost the quaver. "She hated winter in the Bay, so after Thanksgiving, she stayed with my grandparents in Hawaii. Since I would have had to change schools in the fall and spring, she thought boarding school would be a better option."

"That must have been hard for you."

"Actually it wasn't. There was a very constant routine, I knew exactly what was happening from day to day, what to expect." She shrugged. "I really liked it. Pip and Row were there, too, so that made it even better."

Constant routine? The comment struck him as odd. "I'm afraid I don't remember much about your father."

"No, you wouldn't. He traveled a lot with his job. We were always here for the Christmas holidays, though." She plucked the soft center out of her bread just like his daughter did.

"Where's Hawaii?" Tati asked.

"I'll show you on the map after dinner," he promised.

"What's it like, Ashley?"

"It's an island. It has water all around it and it's lovely to swim in. They never get winter in Hawaii." Ashley smiled as the child's eyes grew. "I used to love playing on the beach."

"I like beaches." Tati reached out for her milk, hit the edge of the glass and knocked it over into Ashley's plate, spattering droplets in an arc across her sweater and pants.

"I'm sorry." Fat tears welled on Tati's cheeks as the milk spread across the table and dripped onto the floor.

Sighing, Michael rose, fetched a damp cloth for Ashley. "Here," he offered. Then he began to mop up the spill.

"I didn't mean to do it," Tati sobbed.

"Don't worry about it, honey. I'm sure Ashley will forgive you."

"Of course I will. It was an accident. Everybody has them. I had one tonight, remember?" Ashley dabbed at the table, made a face at her drenched plate. "I think I'm finished my lasagne."

"Here, I'll take care of that."

This was not exactly romantic. But then who'd said anything about romance? Ashley was simply waiting for a tow truck.

"Do you need another cloth?" he asked, wondering if her clothes were ruined.

"I'm fine." She sat down, giggled at the croutons floating across Tati's plate. "I think she's finished, too."

"Mom sent over some pie, if you're interested."

"Maybe later."

"My hands are icky." Tati held them up for inspection.

"Yes, you may be excused. Go and wash them off."

"Okay." Having been forgiven, she dashed out of the room, banging into a stool as she went, which sent the cat's dish flying.

"I'm seeing a pattern here." Ashley chuckled at his pained glare. "Don't be such a grump. She'll grow out of it soon enough."

"I hope so," he muttered. What had seemed so appetizing before now looked like leftovers. Would a meal ever be just a meal again? Michael began clearing the table. Ashley helped, scraping plates and stacking them in the dishwasher.

He stored the leftover lasagne in the fridge, knowing he'd be glad of it tomorrow. Anything not to have to cook. He wanted every extra minute to work on his carving.

"Okay, that's enough cleaning," he told her when she finished scrubbing the counter. "Let's have some tea."

Ashley checked her watch, glanced out the window. "It's taking quite a while for the tow truck, isn't it?"

"All the more time for the grader to clear your road," he said quietly.

She nodded but the faint line of worry across her brow didn't disappear. "I guess."

"Can we play this?" Tati emerged from her room holding a game she loved that involved hippos and marbles.

"Want to play?" he asked, watching Ashley's face for signs that she was bored.

"I haven't played this for years!" She helped Tati open the game, ran a finger over the hippos' backs. "But I used to be quite good."

It was asking for trouble to let Tatiana play it now when she was tired. He'd probably spend the rest of the night hunting for marbles but Michael figured that would be worth it for the pleasure of watching Ashley relax, even giggle as she tried to beat Tatiana.

"Okay, sweetie," he said when all the marbles were safely stored inside the last hippo. "I want you to get ready for bed."

"I don't want to sleep when Ashley's here!"

Her indignant words made him smile.

"I didn't say you had to go to bed, but I want you in your pajamas. When the tow truck calls we'll take Ashley to her car."

"In my pajamas?" she asked, wide-eyed.

"Uh-huh. Until then you can stay up—as long as you can stay awake."

"Wait till Wanda hears about this!" The little girl dashed from the room.

"I'm sorry I'm keeping her up. I never intended to be here so long." Ashley picked up two stray marbles from the floor and tucked them into the box. "I must be ruining your evening, too."

"Not at all. It's nice to have the company." Normally he was loathe to give up a second of his free evenings once Tati was tucked in, but Ashley being here was different. "Do you like mint tea?"

"Yes."

He carried it through to the living room, poured her a cup and handed it to her. She stood in front of the fireplace, holding her mug, but Michael knew it wasn't because she was cold. Her gaze kept straying to the window.

"What really happened out there today?"

She turned, frowning. "I told you."

"Not all of it." He sat, waiting.

Ashley's gray eyes rested on him for several minutes. Finally she drew a deep breath, nodded. "After I went into the snowbank, a man frightened me," she admitted quietly.

"What man?"

"I don't know his name."

"What did he do?" he asked as a spurt of anger bubbled up inside, right beside the wish to protect her.

"It's not so much what he did today," she said, her voice halting. "He just...scared me."

"I see." But Michael didn't see, not at all. She'd been terrified, had kept looking around during the entire ride home. There was more to it than she'd admitted, but he could see by her expression that she wasn't going to tell him. Not now anyway.

Tati came racing into the room in what she called her ballerina pajamas just as the phone rang. He answered, agreed to meet the tow truck in ten minutes.

"I guess it's time to go." Ashley rose, returned her cup to the kitchen and pulled on her boots. "I'm sorry to make you go out again, Mick."

"It's no problem." He bundled up his daughter, pulled on his own things and waited while Ashley drew on her kid gloves. "Ready?"

"Yes."

They drove back to her car, saying little save for Tatiana's chatter and even that didn't last long. Soon her head drooped against her seat and soft snores emanated from the back.

Michael pulled in behind Ashley's car, parked and left the motor running.

"I know it wasn't the nicest experience for you but I'm glad we could spend some time together."

"You've been very gracious." She tilted her head to peer through the windshield. "It's getting quite cold. I'm glad I didn't have to stay out here for long."

"Ashley?"

"Yes?" She turned her head to stare at him.

"You can tell me the truth you know," he said softly. "I only want to help."

"Thank you." But she said no more.

Behind him Michael could see the tow truck coming, its lights flashing over the snow. He bit back his frustration.

"Stay here. I'll talk to him." He got out, used her keys to unlock the door and set the gearshift into neutral. Then he returned to his car, waited by the hood as the little sports car was winched free.

Ashley joined him as soon as her car broke free of the snow's embrace. Michael didn't miss her quick scan of the area nor the way she hurried toward her vehicle just a shade too fast, as if she couldn't wait to get away. He followed, waited while she climbed inside and started the engine.

"Let it warm up for a couple of minutes. I'll follow you to the end of this road, just to make sure everything's okay," he said as the truck driver removed his chain. "I'd appreciate it if you'd call me when you get home. Otherwise I'll worry that you're stranded somewhere else along the way."

"That's not necessary, really. I'll be fine. And it will take me a while to get there. You have things to do."

There it was again, that quick inspection. As if she thought someone was tailing her.

"I'm sure you'll be fine, but phone me anyway." Michael placed his hand on the door, stopping her from rolling up the window, then bent to look straight into her gaze. "Please, Ashley?"

After a moment she nodded. "Okay. Thank you for everything. Say bye to Tati for me."

"I will. Take care."

There were a lot of other things he wanted to say, but Ashley rolled up the window. As soon as she could see through the windshield she shifted into gear then moved off. Michael could do little more but follow her to the end of the road and watch as her taillights faded into the night.

Michael drove home, put Tati to bed and went to his studio. But he couldn't work. He kept seeing Ashley's face when he'd first confronted her. She'd been white, shaking. Who was this man, what had he done to her?

Michael grabbed the phone on its first ring.

"I'm here. I'm sorry it took so long. Piper phoned just as I got in the door. She was frantic and it took a while to explain."

"Is everything okay?"

"Yes, it's fine. The plow had already been through so I had no trouble."

"Good." He waited, hoping, praying she'd explain.

"Thanks for rescuing me, Mick. It's nice to have a friend." The soft words were barely audible.

But Michael heard every word and a rush of sweet joy filled him at the implication. At least they could be friends.

It was enough. For now.

Chapter Six

"We've invested so much time and effort in planning this winter festival. It's going to seem anticlimactic without the final event."

"I wish I could do something."

"Thanks, Ash. But you're doing enough." Piper folded her legs beneath her as she glared at the fireplace. "I don't understand why it's so difficult to find someone to build those sets, but without them we can't do the play."

"Are you sure?" Ashley felt sorry for her friend. Piper devoted hours of time outside of work to make sure every detail of her various publicity campaigns went off without a hitch. But despite her best efforts, this one just wasn't working out.

"The play needs those backdrops to make it fit the time period and we don't have enough in the budget to pay someone to build them." She sighed, leaned back and closed her eyes. A moment later she'd regained her equanimity. "Guess I'll have to keep praying about it. What are your plans today, Ash?"

"I have the art class at school. And there's a weaver I want to visit—Tracey. Have you met her?"

"Oh, yes." Piper's eyes sparkled. "She does excellent

work. Are you still pursuing the idea of a show for the artists?"

A rush of excitement filled Ashley as she thought about the works she'd seen in the past few weeks.

"I suggested it to the art guild and they decided to sponsor an indoor sale and show during the winter festival. And why not? Their work is fantastic—so much innovation and ingenuity. It's not just the same old thing with these people. They've tons of talent and use them very creatively, but with the Bay being so isolated, they are each locked away in their own little world." She sighed. "I just wish I could get someone from the city to come out here and see what I see."

"Maybe you'll have to organize a showing yourself." Piper swallowed a last mouthful of coffee, rose and stretched before putting her cup in the dishwasher. "I've got to go for a fitting for my dress today. Want to come?"

"Yes!"

They agreed to meet at noon. Piper paused before she left.

"The panic thing—is it any better now, Ash?"

"That night—on the road, it was worse than it's been for a while," she admitted. "In the back of my mind I think I figured I'd feel safer when I got here. It's so isolated that I guess I thought there wouldn't be any surprises in good old Serenity Bay. It's not turning out that way."

"Not all surprises are bad, Ash." Piper hugged her, then held her back, meeting her gaze. "You probably won't like me saying this, but I don't think you came here looking for safety. I think you came because you need answers and because a lot of your questions are tied up with the Bay. Can I give you a piece of advice?"

"You will anyway."

"Yes, I will." Piper smiled. "I think you have to stop

looking around you and begin searching inside. God doesn't let things happen to us randomly. There's always a reason and if we let Him, He will use them to teach us. Maybe you should start asking what He's trying to teach you."

One more hug then Piper hurried off to work. Ashley pondered what she'd said, refilled her coffee and opened her Bible. But she couldn't seem to dig into any of the verses she read. They were just words, some of them she'd even memorized. But nothing spoke to the apprehensive feeling she couldn't quite suppress.

Dissatisfied, she finally closed the leather cover. A small bookmark fell out: Perfect love casts out fear.

"Either I don't have perfect love for You, Lord, or I don't understand this verse." She thought about Michael, his quiet request for her to trust him. But she couldn't. She didn't dare, and she wasn't exactly sure why. He wasn't like Kent and in her head she knew that, but it didn't seem to matter. She had to deal with her recurring dread in her own way.

Ashley prayed for peace, but though she felt better when she'd finished, the angst, the underlying sense of disquiet remained hidden inside her heart and she knew why.

Because no matter how she wanted it to be finished, no matter the ways she'd learned or devised to chase away the fears, pretend they didn't exist, or attribute them to something else—the truth was that the man who'd abducted her all those years ago was still out there.

For years she'd kept that night locked away in her mind, refused to face it. She'd never told Rowena or Piper until recently because her parents had insisted that she'd imagined it all and she wasn't certain they were wrong.

Ashley admitted she'd been upset. Her parents' breakup, teen hormones, her grandmother's sudden death—her emotions had fluctuated wildly that year. Eventually she'd taken a psychologist's advice, which coincided with her parents', and convinced herself she'd let her too-vivid imagination take over back then, that it had all been a horrid dream. That there was no man.

Until she'd returned to the Bay, and the face had reappeared. Twice.

Now, no matter how she denied it, she had known that face, recognized his voice when he'd rapped on her window. And that couldn't have happened if it was her imagination.

So what was she supposed to do about it?

Piper would be shocked if she knew Ashley had spent the last two weeks scanning newspaper files for reports of missing or abducted children. She'd found a couple of incidents, both of which police claimed were parental abductions. But no record of another child being taken.

So was her case a fluke? Had he changed his modus operandi? Moved? Gone farther afield?

So many questions, so few answers.

Thinking about it only added to her tension, so Ashley whispered a soft plea for help, then headed for the weaver's house.

"I feel like I've hit the mother lode," Ashley exclaimed as she stared at the pieces displayed around Tracey's room. "Haven't you ever shown these?"

"I tried once. But the galleries prefer artists who've already had good showings. Except, how do you get a good showing if you can't show?" Tracey made a face.

"Vicious circle."

"It's not just that. It's such an effort to pack everything up, take it in there, then try to display it properly. Then there's the expense of finding a sitter and staying in the city while they evaluate everything." Tracey glanced at her toddler. "It's so much easier to sell them on the Internet. At least while the kids are small."

"I understand, believe me." Ashley watched her cuddle her little boy. "These times are special. You don't want to trade them for the off chance that someone will maybe let you display."

They talked about Tracey's plans for the winter festival show and about her other two preschoolers playing just outside the big picture window.

"It must be nice to allow them the freedom to play in the yard alone." Ashley watched the pair digging holes for a snow cave. No worries there.

"They're always up to something," Tracey giggled. "I have to keep my eyes on them every moment, but I will say I like living here a lot better than living in the city. I feel safer. Here everyone's so friendly. We know all our neighbors and they are only too eager to pitch in whenever I ask."

"Serenity Bay's a great place. I should know. I grew up here."

"And now you're back."

"For a little while. Until Piper's wedding and the winter festival are over. I agreed to stick around that long. Then I need to get back to work."

"But I thought you said you'd lost your job?" Tracey asked, tapping on the window and shaking her head. "See what I mean? Always into something."

"I'll get another job." After the freedom of calling her time her own, Ashley couldn't quite reconcile herself to going back to a stuffy gallery, but by the end of February she'd probably be over trekking through snow and only too ready to go back to mild Vancouver.

"Why don't you stay here? You could open a gallery, hold weekend showings when the skiers come down."

"I don't think that's going to be possible," Ashley told her.

"No, I suppose it takes a lot of money." Tracey grinned. "Can't blame a girl for trying, though. I notice you're driving a new car."

"I rented it. A friend helped me realize my other one just couldn't handle the winter roads around here." She glanced at her watch. "Speaking of roads, I'd better get on one. I'm meeting Piper for lunch. Can I take this piece?" she asked, lifting a beautiful tapestry from the table.

"If you like."

"I know exactly where I want to place it to get some shots. Then I'll contact someone I know. I promise I'll return it in mint condition."

Tracey wrapped the weaving in tissue and set it inside a box.

"Feel free to stop by anytime," she said as Ashley left. "I'm always glad to have someone older than five to talk to."

Ashley tossed a snowball at the kids, then scrambled to get into her SUV before they sent a volley of missiles back. Michael had been right, she admitted as she headed for the seamstress Piper had hired. She did feel safer driving in this bigger vehicle.

She paused at the stop light, glanced to the right. A stray sunbeam drew her attention to a rusty truck parked in front of the post office. The same truck that had stopped the day her car had gone off the road.

The horn behind her roused Ashley into action. She drove around the block for a second look, but by the time she arrived back at the spot, the truck was gone and the church bell was signaling twelve noon.

It wasn't him. She was imagining the similarity. But her hands were clenched around the steering wheel as she pulled in next to Piper's car. She sat for a few moments forcing herself to calm down before she stepped out of her vehicle and went to the door.

"Come on in," someone called.

Ashley opened the door and stepped inside the snug cottage. Emma Dickens loved everything about fabrics. Her home bore the stamp of her passion from soft yellow curtains to plump coordinated cushions to the suedelike cover on her sofa.

"It's just me," Ashley called, doffing her coat on a kitchen chair before she walked into the living room. "Wow!"

Piper stood on a stool, her white velvet dress glistening like ice crystals on snow.

"It's gorgeous, Pip."

"Isn't it?" Piper smoothed a hand over the nap. "Emma's done an amazing job."

"Well I'm glad you both like it but you're going to have to hold still if you want me to get this hem right." Emma peeked around the skirt to wave at Ashley. "Have a seat and talk to her. She's been as nervous as a kitten."

"I don't know why." Contrary to Emma's advice, Ashley moved around Piper, taking in the details. "The high waist fits like a glove, Pip. And that scooped neck is adorable."

"Do you think the sleeves are all right?" The bride-to-be wiggled to get a better look at the long sleeves. "They're not too full?"

"No. They're perfect. So is that bit of train." Ashley sank onto the sofa, thrilled by the glow that lit Piper's face. "You'll be a beautiful bride, Pip."

"Thanks. Emma made something so I'll even be cosy outside. New Year's Eve is never warm around here, and since Jason wants some pictures outdoors—" She grinned. "Show her, Em."

Emma draped a full-length, soft white, fuzzy cape lined with pure white satin and trimmed with silken ribbon around Piper's shoulders, then handed her a faux fur muff.

"Gorgeous!"

"We all have one of these," Piper explained, holding out the muff. "Aren't they cute?"

"But they don't all have one of these." Emma disappeared into a room and returned with a tiny white hat, which she set on Piper's head. A fluff of veiling tacked onto the back was perfect.

"Emma, I commend you." Ashley blinked, stunned by how well everything went together. "It looks as though Piper shopped in Paris."

"I've always wanted to do a winter wedding. Most brides seem to think summer is better, but I've always thought winter was perfectly suited to a wedding."

"I agree."

Piper glanced at her watch, shrieked. "I've got to get back to work. I've got a conference call in fifteen minutes."

"Ashley, help us," Emma commanded as she unzipped her creation.

Moments later Piper was free to dress in her street clothes.

"Now, I'll need a fitting for your dress, Ashley. I don't know what I'm going to do if you keep losing weight. I've already taken out two inches."

"Then I'll look very chic," Ashley demurred.

"You'll look like a scarecrow if you lose much more." Emma was always blunt. "Put this on." She held out a dress in midnight-blue velvet.

The style was patterned after Piper's, long and sleek as it draped around her feet.

"Look at this!" Emma scrunched up fabric at the waist. "Can't you get this girl to eat?" she complained to Piper.

Piper had one arm in her coat, but she stopped to frown at Ashley.

"You've lost more weight? Ash, you're supposed to be getting better, not starving yourself. You'll get sick if you continue like this."

"I never was a big eater."

"You don't eat anything! You spend hours cooking for us and then poke at your own meals. What's wrong?"

"Nothing's wrong. I'll soon be eating you out of house and home, it's just taking a while to get my strength back, that's all. Hadn't you better go?" she asked, tilting her head toward the mantel clock.

"Yes. But I'm not letting you off the hook. I'll be on your case tonight, Ash, and you will eat. You can't miss my wedding."

"I won't. Now go." Ashley stood silent as Emma measured, pinned, tucked and adjusted. Then she waited a little longer while the matching cape with the iridescent white lining was fitted. "It looks wonderful, Emma. Beautiful."

"Well, I'm not unpinning this velvet again so you get some good food into you."

"You have to take the waist in. It's too big!"

"Maybe I'll do one last fit just before Christmas to make sure. Until then, get some meat on your bones, girl!"

"Yes, ma'am." Ashley changed, agreed to eat the remaining half of a chicken sandwich Emma had made for Piper. "Happy now?" she asked Emma, who made a face at her.

"I won't be happy until I get the go-ahead for those costumes for the play Piper's always talking about. It takes time to get period pieces right and if she doesn't soon get that play nailed down, I'm not going to be able to do them."

"Oh, no! But that's what makes the play come alive. We have to have your costumes."

"Then you'd better find someone who can build those sets."

Ashley mulled it over as she drove to the school to give her weekly slide show. If only Michael would do it. He kept claiming he didn't have time, but she'd seen him playing football with Jason the week after the big snowstorm had melted. If he needed help with Tati she could help.

Maybe it was time to confront him again. Maybe if he knew the play was about to be cancelled.

The boisterous but interested art class was always a fun hour, but there were so many questions that Ashley ended up entering the staff room to get her coat ten minutes after the last bell of the day had gone. Michael bumped into her on the way out.

"Hi," she said brightly, wondering how to broach the subject of the sets.

"Hey, beautiful. How'd art class go?" He grabbed his coat, thrust his arms into it.

"Don't leave yet, Masters," the principal called. "We have a staff meeting today."

"I've got to pick up Tati. I hope you don't mind if I bring her back here because it's either that or I miss the meeting. I couldn't get a sitter."

The principal frowned, but after a moment she nodded permission. "Get back fast," she ordered. "We've got a full agenda today."

"Right." He matched his step to Ashley's. "She has no idea what she's in for," he mumbled as they walked down the hall.

"What do you mean?"

"Principal Zilk likes lots of debate on everything. Tati's not good at either sitting still or being patient. I can only imagine the disaster that's about to befall Serenity Bay High. Today's skating day and my daughter does not like missing her skating."

"Why don't I take her?" The offer popped out before Ashley could even think about it, but now that it was said, she wasn't sorry. She liked Tatiana.

"You skate?" He raised one eyebrow as if he found the idea utterly impossible.

"I used to. Fairly well, actually." She could see he didn't believe her. "In fact, I started figure skating when I was five and finished at boarding school. I was a soloist for several winter carnivals and played the Sugar Plum Fairy once at Christmas."

"Well, good for you. But Tati—" He stopped, shook his head.

"Look, how hard can it be to get one little girl on the ice, Michael?"

His eyes opened very wide as he came to an abrupt halt in the middle of the hall. Teens flooded around them on either side but Michael seemed oblivious.

"You have no idea," he told her softly.

"Don't be so melodramatic. She's a little girl. I'm an adult. I can do it. You go to your meeting. I'll take care of Tatiana. When you're finished, you can come and pick us up. Around five?"

He looked stunned, but after several seconds he nodded and told her how to find the day care.

"I'll phone the lady in charge of the day care so she knows you're coming," he said.

"Good." She grinned. "You look worried. Don't. I won't let anything happen to Tati."

"Tati will be fine. It's you I'm worried about. You look like dandelion fluff that a good wind could pick up and toss across the bay. And Tati is a lot more than a mere wind."

"Oh, stop it. You're just trying to scare me." She laughed, but noticed he didn't join in. "I'll see you later," Ashley promised before turning to leave.

"Ashley," he called, just loudly enough for her to hear. She glanced over one shoulder. "Try to keep her away from the other kids, will you?"

Hard as she looked, Ashley couldn't see a glimmer of humor in his eyes. She walked out of the school, changed from her high-heeled boots to a pair of lower ones in the car, then drove to the address Michael had given her. Tati was dressed and waiting at the door, her skates zipped inside leather bags slung around her shoulders.

"Are you really taking me skating?" she asked excitedly.

"Sure."

"Are you going to skate, too?"

"I might try. If there are some skates my size."

"They have big girls' skates at the sporting goods store. Wanda's aunt got some. Can we go there first?"

"Why not?"

Half an hour later with the white skates tied on, Ashley lifted her foot to step delicately onto the ice.

"Please don't let me embarrass myself and fall on my behind," she prayed as the blade slid out of her control.

She thought she heard God laugh.

Michael stepped inside the rink to the sound of raised voices. His protective instincts zipped up like mercury on a hot day as he rushed toward the ice. In one glance he assessed the problem.

With her usual penchant for accidents Tati had apparently taken down an entire chain of skaters—and they were not happy about it. Ashley sat on the ice as well, a pained look on her face.

"Oh, boy." He laced up his skates and took off across the ice, rushing in behind Tati to lift her off her feet and out of the path of a boy her age who looked ready to push her down—once he got back on his feet. "Hi, kiddo."

"Daddy!" She smiled and his heart sang. "Ashley and I are skating."

"I can see that." He checked Ashley's face, knew he'd arrived in the nick of time. He offered a hand to pull her up then glanced around. "You guys playing bowling or something? Why's everyone sitting down?"

"Very funny," she muttered as she dusted herself off.

Michael forced himself not to stare at the length of her legs displayed so elegantly in the black jeans. He turned instead to survey the group. "Let's try Crack the Whip. Anyone interested?"

It was a favorite because even the little ones could cling on to someone else as they formed a long chain that circled round and round the ice. Loud agreement greeted his suggestion. He set Tati down, grabbed Ashley's gloved hand and placed it into his daughter's.

"Hang on," he advised as he started the circle. More and more children grabbed on until they were turning in a giant pinwheel. Fifteen minutes later the group had completely forgotten about Tati's misadventure and he judged it safe to leave the ice.

"That was fun, Daddy."

"It was, wasn't it?" He scooped her off the ice onto

a bench and began unfastening her skates until he noticed that Ashley hadn't moved an inch after sitting down. "What's wrong?"

"Nothing yet." She shifted positions gingerly on the hard bench and winced. "But I have a hunch there will be by tomorrow. Contrary to my earlier boast, I'm not quite ready for the Olympics. Ow." She closed her eyes, groaned.

As soon as Tati's feet were tucked inside her boots, she wandered over to watch the other skaters. Michael set to work on Ashley's skates, unlacing them, then easing them off her feet. A soft sigh slipped from her lips as he massaged her toes.

"Don't think this will wipe the slate clean," she told him softly, that diamond glint back in her gray eyes. "You still owe me. Big-time. You realize I probably won't be able to walk tomorrow?"

He chuckled, slid her other foot free. "Which part of you hurts the most?"

"Never mind." She drew her foot away, bent to put on her boots. "Being in a car accident doesn't even begin to compare to this."

"Are you comparing my daughter to an accident?" he joked as he put his own shoes back on.

"I refuse to answer that for fear of self-incrimination." She glanced at Tati, kept her voice low. "You might get a call tonight. A woman was here teaching her daughter to skate. Tatiana apparently knows them. She kept trying to help but—" Ashley chuckled "—I don't think it was appreciated."

"I'll handle her." He picked up the skates, slung them over his shoulder. "I can't thank you enough, Ashley. It was a boring meeting. Tati would have driven them crazy.

How about if I buy you supper as a down payment on my massive debt?"

He thought she'd refuse. But after staring at him for a moment, Ashley finally nodded.

"Dinner would be nice—if they have very soft chairs."

A rush of satisfaction filled him, until she continued.

"It's about time Piper and Jason spent an evening alone together, without me playing third wheel."

Slightly deflated, he collected Tati and walked outside beside her, not realizing until they stopped that they would have too many vehicles. Ashley clicked a button and the locks on a big SUV opened.

Michael gulped.

"Boy, when you take advice, you really take advice," he said, studying the latest features on her brand-new model.

She grinned, a quick flash of humor that did amazing things to her beautiful face. "I'm a quick study," she told him. "One dump in a snowbank is enough for me."

"Can we go in Ashley's new car?" Tati asked, dragging on his hand.

Michael couldn't have said it better himself.

"Do you mind? According to the rental agreement I have tons of mileage available and I probably won't make a dent in it." Ashley started the motor and the heater. "I could drive you back here after dinner."

He nodded. "I'll get Tati's car seat."

"Don't bother. There's a child's jump seat in the back. It's good enough to go to the restaurant and back, isn't it?" Ashley blinked. "After all, she rode over here in it."

Good point.

He nodded. "Okay. In you go, honey." He boosted her up, made sure the belt was securely fastened, then pulled open his door. "It's a great vehicle," he told Ashley, buckling his own belt.

"Where do you want to eat?"

"Pizza!" Tati chirped from behind them.

"Pizza it is." Ashley pulled out from her parking spot and drove toward the town's favorite pizza spot.

"It's not a bad choice," Michael told her. "They've got a play area for kids. She can burn off her excess energy while we talk."

"Excess energy?" Ashley blinked. "I don't think so."

"Wait. You'll see."

"What do you want to talk about?" A small frown hit her mouth.

He shrugged. "Anything." Everything about you.

They were a bit early for the supper crowd. Michael chose a table where he could see Tati, but where their conversation wouldn't be overheard.

"Is this okay?"

"Perfect." She allowed him to take her coat and hang it up with Tati's, then eased onto the plush seat.

"Soft enough?" he asked, tongue-in-cheek.

She blushed. "Yes, thank you. Doesn't it smell wonderful?"

"Trying to change the subject?"

"Yes."

Tati hurried off to play. An awkward silence fell.

"I really want—"

"You have a wonderful—"

He grinned. "Ladies first."

"I was just going to tell you how much I enjoyed being with Tatiana. She's a lovely child. So inquisitive and open to new experiences. And she just plunges into life, doesn't she?"

A crash emanated from the play area. Michael glanced over, made a face as his daughter's head appeared poking out of the ball pit.

"Like that, you mean?" He loved Ashley's smile, the way it encompassed her whole face.

"I envy her the freedom to be so abandoned."

The softly murmured words surprised him. "Why would you envy her? You're free to plunge into whatever you want, aren't you?"

She stared at him for a long moment. Finally she nodded. But a second later she changed the subject.

"What is your shop class working on now?"

"Finishing up their individual projects. There are those students who get everything done ahead of time, those who meet the deadline and those who leave everything to the last minute. I seem to have a majority from the latter group. Hurry isn't a good thing when you're working with tools so I like to allocate some extra classroom time, just in case."

"What about the ones who are already finished?"

"They can start something new, or work with one of the others." He held her gaze, shook his head. "I do not want to talk about school, Ashley."

"Why not? Don't you like your job?"

He waited until they'd given their order to the server before answering.

"It's okay. For now."

"What would you rather be doing?"

He couldn't very well explain without looking as if he wanted her help, and at this moment in time, Michael wasn't ready to talk about his carvings. He'd read a verse in his devotions this morning about trusting God for the perfect timing. Maybe it was a hint to stop worrying about a showing next summer. He needed time to think about what that would mean to his dream.

"Michael?"

"Sorry. Got sidetracked." He pushed the doubts away. "Let's talk about you instead of me. What did you do today?"

"School. Went with Piper for a dress fitting. Went skating." She sipped her coffee. "Oh, yes, and I went to see a weaver this morning. I'm going to look for a gallery to display her work."

His heart rate quickened but Michael ignored it.

"Do you think they'll agree?"

"No one has so far." She played with her spoon, her face pensive. "I'm finding a certain reluctance among many gallery owners to feature artists who don't have some previous gallery experience, or who don't come from one of the schools that teach textiles, painting, whatever. It's frustrating because the work here is so innovative. It's going to take someone with vision and commitment to see the potential. So far I haven't run into that person."

"Sounds to me like you're her, Ashley."

"Tracey said something like that, too." She leaned forward. "Why did you say it?"

"You obviously have an eye for exceptional work. You have gallery experience, I'm told. And you have an insight into how to market an artist." Michael shrugged. "Maybe you should think about starting your own gallery."

The pizza arrived, followed seconds later by Tati who was red-faced and glowering. "There's a very bad boy over there."

"Well, he can play by himself while we eat. But first you need a wash. Let's go clean up." Michael took her by the hand and headed for the bathroom. When he returned, Ashley gave him a quizzical look he couldn't interpret.

The server refilled their glasses and left extra grated cheese.

"I'm starved."

"So am I."

They finished all but the last piece. Tati begged for another go at the play area now that the miscreant had left. Michael agreed, hoping it would wear her out so sleep would come quickly tonight. He hadn't done anything in his studio for days.

"Today one of the art students showed me drawings she'd done for the sets for the winter festival play," Ashley murmured after sipping her coffee.

Uh-oh.

"She said some of your students thought they could build them with some leadership. From you."

"Ashley, I can't. I explained all this."

"I'd be willing to help you, watch Tatiana if you needed it."

He found himself considering it. Not because he needed help with Tati, though that would be nice. But he wanted the chance to know Ashley better. She intrigued him, made him think life might hold something he hadn't dared dream of again, something he never planned to risk.

He couldn't walk away from her offer.

"While we were skating, Tatiana told me about her mother. I didn't realize she was a famous ballerina."

"Carissa would have liked to hear that," he mused aloud. "Her goal was to be a household name around the world. She hated being ill, not being allowed to dance. It was her reason for getting up in the morning." He clamped his lips together, afraid he'd said too much.

"How long has she been gone?"

"Five months." He studied her, decided it was better to get the truth out now. "Ashley, I never knew I had a daughter until six months ago."

"What?" She looked stunned.

"Carissa and I were married only a few months when she was offered a six-month contract with the Bolshoi Ballet. My dad was ill, I was in the middle of—" he looked for the right word "—studies in New York. I couldn't drop everything and follow her, but Carissa promised she'd be back as soon as the contract was over. Two months after she left, I got a letter telling me she'd made a mistake, that she wanted a divorce, that all she wanted was to dance."

"Oh my." Her eyes grew huge. "She never told you she was pregnant?"

He shook his head.

"I tried to get in touch with her, to phone her. I wrote dozens of letters. They all came back. I learned her contract with the company had been suspended, but that's all I could find out." He pushed a hand through his hair as the memory of those dark days returned. "Dad died and everything else got pushed to the back burner for a while. Then the divorce papers arrived."

"So you signed them?"

"It had been over a year. I couldn't reach her. I had no access, other than through her former lawyer." He swallowed, looked down at the table. "Besides, by then I knew she was right. We'd made a mistake."

"I'm sorry." She reached out, touched his hand.

Surprised by the voluntary contact from such a reticent person, Michael covered her hand with his, and glancing up, found only compassion on her face.

"Thanks." He sighed. "I thought it was over, that the

only people we'd hurt were ourselves. I was living in New York when I happened to read a small newspaper article that said Carissa was there convalescing. I decided to visit her, to make sure she was all right, you know?"

Ashley nodded, removed her hand from his grip.

"I phoned, but her manager said she didn't want to see me. I decided to go anyway. I figured I owed her that." It still rankled. "A friend who worked at her hotel got me up to her room. I knocked on the door and this little sprite answered. It was Tati. I would have known my daughter anywhere."

"Oh, Michael." She sounded as if she understood what he'd missed, the pain that had gutted him at what he'd never been allowed to experience.

"Carissa wasn't going to let me know until after she died. She'd married again. A man she met in Russia. Vlad was nice, rich, adored the ground she walked on, but he couldn't buy her the cure she needed."

"Cure?"

"When I saw her she was in the last stages of lung cancer. It was very aggressive. She wanted Tati with her as long as possible. Vlad was to bring her to me after Carissa died."

"But how did you— I'm sorry. It's none of my business."

"No, it's okay. It's kind of nice to explain instead of watching you imagine all kinds of weird scenarios." He checked to be sure Tati was still busy, that she couldn't overhear. "Carissa kept hoping, right to the end, that she would go into remission, find a cure, something. Vlad got her to come to New York on the pretext of seeing a specialist, but I think it was more because of Tati. He was afraid there would be problems with her custody and he wanted to honor Carissa's wish for me to take care of her."

It galled him to say it even now, months later. He pushed away his coffee cup, stretched his legs and drew several breaths to ease the tension gathering at the back of his neck.

"But why wait so long?"

He smiled but felt no mirth. "We weren't married very long but Carissa knew that if I'd known I had a daughter, I would have insisted on being with her. If she hadn't fallen sick I'm not sure I'd ever have known about my daughter."

"I'm sorry."

"So am I. Fortunately for all of us, Tati is very accepting. She'd always called Vlad by his first name. From the moment Carissa introduced us I was Daddy."

"I'm sorry she got sick, but I don't understand her actions at all. To deny a child her father—it's awful."

"You have to understand Carissa. No one ever said no to her. She'd pushed herself up through the ranks, made herself a household name. It was hard to match wills with her." He stared at the little girl who'd lit up his life so sweetly. "But I'd have done it and more if I'd known."

"Of course you would have." She summoned a smile. "You're very lucky to have Tatiana."

"I think so, too," he said warmly, appreciating her staunch defense. "So now perhaps you'll understand why I was so defensive about being a father that day we were on the boat. I'm trying to forgive Carissa, but the whole thing still rankles a bit whenever I think of what I missed."

"No wonder." She shook her head. "Now I'm doubly sorry I said it. How thoughtless!"

"You couldn't have known." He took a deep breath, decided to risk it. "Maybe knowing our history will make you feel more comfortable. I'm not looking to dash into anything, to make another mistake. I learned that lesson the hard way. But I am looking for a friend. Can we be friends, Ashley?"

She studied him for a moment, eyes large and luminous in her pale face. He held his breath, waiting. Finally she nodded.

"I've made mistakes, too," she said softly. "I've been engaged twice, both times to the wrong man. I don't trust myself not to make another mistake, that's why I said what I did."

Michael could tell it was a big admission for her. Delighted that she'd shared as much with him, he decided to press a little further, especially since Tati was happily involved with another little girl in the ball pit.

"But your mistakes—that's not what has made you so afraid, is it?"

The soft rose flush that had tinted her cheeks a moment ago faded to white. "No."

"Can you tell me about it?" He touched her arm, turned her hand over and slid his fingers between hers. "I'm a good listener."

"It's hard to explain."

"Just start at the beginning," he encouraged.

"Something happened to me a long time ago." She stared at their entwined hands, briefly explained the almost-abduction. "It's not just that. I don't think I've ever really felt secure."

"What does that mean? Is someone after you now?"

"I'm not—"

A loud squeal interrupted. Tati. With an apologetic look, Michael withdrew his hand and went to find out the problem. His sobbing daughter stood in the middle of the ball pit, a bruise forming at one corner of her cheek.

"She fell against the edge," a woman explained. "I'm

sure it won't leave a lasting mark, but according to my son's experience with the same thing last week, it hurts a lot more than it shows."

"Thanks." He picked Tati up, hugged her close after inspecting the damage. "It's only a bruise, sweetie. You're fine. And it's way past your bedtime."

"But I wanted to play some more," she sobbed against his neck.

Recognizing the signs of overtiredness, Michael didn't argue, simply carried her back to the table.

"I'm sorry, Ashley. I think it's time we went home. Can you drive us back to the rink?"

"Sure. Is she okay?"

"Just a bump."

They left quickly, arrived at the rink with little more being said. Once Tati was settled into her own car seat, Ashley leaned in to kiss her goodnight, then closed the door. She tilted her head to one side as she studied Michael.

"I enjoyed this evening," she said quietly. "Thank you."

"No, thank *you*," he said, admiring her ethereal beauty. "I'm sure falling on the ice wasn't part of your plan for today."

"It had its moments."

Michael knew what he was going to say and didn't even try to stop the words.

"Tell Piper that if she really wants, I'll build the sets. I'll make it a project for the kids. Extra marks."

"You will? Really?" At his nod Ashley grinned, reached out and hugged him. "Thank you, Michael! Thank you very much."

"You're welcome." He hugged her back, relishing the touch of her silky cheek against his.

"Oh, sorry." She drew back, her face a soft rich pink.

"Anytime," he told her with a grin. And meant it.

"Maybe you could get copies of those drawings from your art student and bring them to the school shop tomorrow. We'll need to order the wood right away."

"Sure. I'll do that. Thanks, Michael." Her smile flared again. "This is so great."

Then she looked at him and her eyes held a thousand secrets as a tiny smile kicked up the corners of her mouth.

Michael wanted to prolong the moment but he needed to get home, to do some work.

"I'll see you tomorrow, then."

"Yes. See you." She climbed into her vehicle, waited for him to precede her out of the lot.

As he drove home Michael suddenly realized that only once during their time outside the rink had Ashley checked over her shoulder or scanned the lot.

Did that mean she trusted him?

Chapter Seven

"Did you have a happy Thanksgiving, Ashley?" Tati stood in the doorway, surveying her visitor. Orange icing was smeared above one eyebrow.

"Yes, I did. Thank you, honey. How about you?"

"I had two pieces of pumpkin pie."

"Two, huh? You must have been stuffed. I'm surely glad all the snow melted so we could see the pumpkin display at the library. Aren't you?"

"Uh-huh. I liked the scarecrow best."

"I liked the roosters and the sunflowers. Can I come in?"

"Sure."

Ashley followed her into the house, sniffed and wrinkled her nose. "Is something burning?"

"Don't ask," Michael told her sticking his head out of the kitchen. "We're decorating cupcakes for her class. The teacher got sick and missed their Thanksgiving party." He frowned.

"Really?" She couldn't imagine that.

"Really. But these things—" he pointed to a dozen round brown blobs perched on the counter "—aren't nearly as funny as I remember."

"What are they?" she asked, pondering the misshapen lumps.

"I think it's bad if you have to ask."

She grinned. "Sorry."

"They're pumpkins, of course." Tati looked offended. "We're going to decorate them when they cool off."

Michael winked at her. "Want to try one? I'll even ice it for you."

"Thanks, anyway, but I just had lunch."

"Hey! They're not that bad. Even I can bake a cake mix."

"I'm sure they're delicious," she offered reassuringly. "It's just that orange icing does odd things to my taste buds. Especially that particular shade of orange. If you ice them, you'll have to watch how you wrap them."

"Huh?"

"The plastic wrap will stick to the icing."

"At school the teacher uses toothpicks."

Ashley smiled. Tatiana believed she was far too old for day care so she called it school and reprimanded anyone who termed it otherwise.

"Wanda doesn't think I can bring pumpkins but I told her Daddy would do it. He builds lots of stuff."

"He sure does. And he's very good at it, too." Ashley chuckled at Michael's preening. "I was talking about the sets, not your current, er, construction."

"Be nice, Ashley." He winked, held up the spatula and let a blob of orange drop off it into the bowl. "Or I'll make you taste this."

"Eww!" She glanced at Tati who was mucking about in the sink. "Hey, what about our trip?"

"Oh, we're still going. I was just soaking the dishes. Now I'll get my jacket." She raced out of the room.

"Soaking the dishes, her clothes, the floor, the curtains."

"She's a sweetie."

"Yes, she is. And she has such faith in me. It's scary."

"Why? Every little girl thinks her daddy is invincible."

"Yeah, but what happens when she finds out I'm not?" Michael made a face at his creations. "I'm afraid I'm going to disappoint her at this tender age because other than plastering this icing on top, I don't know how to make these things look a bit like pumpkins."

"Hmm. Do you have any chocolate chips?" Ashley accepted the bag he retrieved from the cupboard, arranged a stem on the one he'd iced. "Buy some green gumdrops for leaves and you're done. The kids will probably pick them off but it looks good."

"Yeah. Good idea. Thanks." He grinned at her as if they'd achieved an impossible feat, then covered the icing and stored it in the fridge. He glanced down, grinned. "Ah, new boots for our ride on the quads. I liked your other ones better."

"I thought you said you liked the heels I had on yesterday."

"I did."

"And my sandals that I wore that day on the houseboat?"

"I liked those, too." He deadpanned an innocent look.

"You seem to notice my footwear a lot, Michael. Why *is* that?"

"No comment. Except to say that given a choice, I prefer the heels." He grinned a wolfish smile that did nice things for her ego. "Though I do understand you couldn't wear them today."

"Well, hardly." She shook her head at his teasing and tried to quash the ripple of warning that told her to be careful. Stifling it, she checked to make sure Tati had not yet reappeared. "You have heard about the cougar, haven't you?"

"Sure." He nodded. "There have been lots of stories at school about one coming down from the hills. But we've had cougars in the area before. They seldom attack people."

"Still—" She didn't want to say anymore, not with Tatiana liable to appear at any moment.

"We'll be fine, Ashley. I wouldn't endanger my daughter."

No, that was true, but it didn't help much. When Tati reappeared, Michael sent her to the basement on an errand, then walked around the counter to face Ashley. He pressed his forefinger under her chin, tilting it up so she had to look at him.

"You worry a lot, don't you?"

"I don't know what you mean."

"Really?" It was clear Michael saw right through her pitiful defense. "Your footwear isn't the only thing I notice, Ashley. When we were on the boat that afternoon, you kept checking Tati's life jacket. And your own. Over and over, as if there might be something wrong with them."

"Did I?" She looked away.

"Yes, you did. And the night you went off the road you kept looking around."

"I explained that."

"Uh-huh." He touched her arm. "But there's something you haven't told me, isn't there? That night at the restaurant you said you've never really felt secure. I've been thinking about that. It seems so out of character."

"It does?" She wondered if he'd spoken to his mother, heard her story of crazy Ashley's abduction.

"You're a strong, confident woman who's lived and worked in a big city. You've handled complicated showings, done your job with people coming and going all the time. So I'm guessing your anxiety level went up about the time you came back to Serenity Bay, right?"

"It was already up. But, yes, something like that."

"You're *still* talking?" Tatiana stood in the doorway, hands on her hips as she glared at them. "Are we going or what?"

"We are definitely going. I'll just get us a couple of drinks and some snacks," Michael told her.

"Don't bother. I have some stuff in my backpack." His surprised look made Ashley chuckle. "Seems only fair. You provide the wheels. I take care of the munchies."

"I'm good with that." He grabbed his jacket and a couple of thick wool blankets from a closet.

"What are those for?" she asked, following him outside and watching as he tucked them into the box on the back of his quad.

"You're not the only one who can surprise."

"Oh?" Ashley swallowed. He couldn't know that she wasn't big on surprises. "It might be better to prepare me."

He shook his head. "You'll just have to wait and see."

She could hardly stamp her foot and demand to know. Besides, Michael was clearly delighted with his little secret. A crooked smile tugged at his lips and his eyes glinted with mischief.

Ashley shoved back the apprehension. Michael was one of the nice guys. He didn't pretend to be what he wasn't. His confidence in himself extended to his relationships with other people. He gave and expected honesty. Pretty soon he was going to press her for details and she'd have to explain or push him away.

But just as she hadn't told him the whole truth about her fears, Ashley was beginning to realize there was something he hadn't shared, either. He'd taken the plans for the sets and she knew the kids had begun to work on them, but Michael didn't spend weekends at it, as she'd expected.

Not even when Tati had gone with his mother last weekend to see a puppeteer.

So what had he been doing?

"Ashley?"

"Yes?" She blinked, realized he'd been speaking to her.

"I asked if you'd ridden one of these before."

She glanced at the machine, shook her head.

"It's really quite easy." He demonstrated how the controls worked, then moved so she could take his place. "Go ahead, try a practice run. Just don't accelerate too fast."

Michael took Tati's hand, waiting with her on the side of the yard while Ashley practiced using the levers to start and stop around the yard. She'd assumed turning would be difficult but was able to manipulate the vehicle in sharp angles with little trouble. A silly sense of achievement rushed through her as she pulled to a stop in front of him.

"I did it!"

Michael grinned. "I'm guessing you're ready to go, then?"

"Yes."

"I want to ride with Ashley," Tati squealed, trying to squeeze in behind. Her father grasped her by the waist and set her on the ground.

"No, honey. We'll give Ashley a chance to get used to riding before we put a wiggling bundle of energy behind her. You ride with me. We'll talk about changing later."

For one rebellious moment her chubby face squinched up tightly and she opened her mouth to argue.

"Or I could ask Wanda's mom if you can stay with them while Ashley and I go by ourselves," he added.

Knowing how Tatiana and Wanda competed, Ashley suspected the little girl had been bragging to her friend about the planned outing. Sure enough, Tati climbed onto her father's four-wheeler without another word. Michael winked at Ashley.

"Ready to go?"

"You're sure we have lots of gas?"

He rolled his eyes. "Ashley, Ashley. When will you learn to trust me? There's a spare can on the back of your bike, just in case. Satisfied?"

Feeling chastened, she nodded.

"Try to keep up. You don't have to be right on my tail, but don't get too far behind, either. I'll try to keep an even pace, but sometimes there are rocks or branches I can't go over. Keep your eyes peeled in case I have to stop quickly. Also, watch for branches. They could snap back and catch you."

"Got it."

They set off following a winding path out of the yard, moving at a steady clip. After several miles Ashley pushed her sunglasses to the top of her head. There was no need for them here in the forest where the sun barely skimmed the forest floor, thanks to massive pine and spruce boughs overhead. She inhaled the fresh scent, ordered her brain to relax.

After they'd crossed a particularly rough part, Michael pulled into a glade near a bubbling stream. Ashley drove in beside him, realizing as she climbed off that her legs were a bit stiff from pressing against the center of the seat. "I thought we'd take a break," he explained as he lifted Tati off.

"I want a drink, Daddy."

From her backpack, Ashley removed two thermoses of hot chocolate, a container of cookies and several disposable cups which she set on a huge stone by the water. As a table it worked perfectly. Better yet, it sat in the middle of a warm pool of sunshine.

"Here, Tati," she said as she poured a cup half full. She waited until the little girl was seated on the boulder then handed her the cup. Pulling napkins out of her bag, she laid one on the stone and set the cookies on top.

"Thank you." Tati munched away happily. "It's just like a picnic."

"Yes, it is." Michael accepted his cup and cookies, sat down beside her. "Hot chocolate was a great idea. It's cooler than I realized out here."

"I thought maybe we'd see some animals," Ashley admitted after sipping her own drink. "But I suppose the sound of the motors scares them away."

"We might see something yet." He had that twinkle in his eye again.

"I didn't spill anything," Tati said happily. She held out her cup. "May I please have some more?"

"Sure." Ashley refilled the cup half full. "But spills don't really matter out here, honey." It wasn't the first time she'd wondered about Tati's fretting over accidents. Now that she knew some of her history, she suspected that living in hotel rooms and moving among ballet costumes would have offered an open invitation to accidents for such an active little girl.

"Spills don't matter anywhere," her father championed. "We just clean 'em up and move on. Can you hear that blue jay calling?"

Tati listened, nodded, her brown eyes bright. "And a robin, Daddy. How come they haven't flown away yet?"

"They will pretty soon. It's getting cold at night and robins don't hang around for snow."

"Do they go to Hawaii, like Ashley did?"

Michael laughed. "Not that far."

"Oh."

Silence fell, save for the twittering of birds high above

them and the forest sounds that Ashley couldn't identify. Noticing that Michael had closed his eyes and lain back against the warm stone, she took the opportunity to scour the area for a sign that someone or something had followed them. She saw nothing.

Ashley leaned against a tree and allowed herself to relax just the tiniest bit. With Michael nearby she was safe.

"Mommy didn't like snow, either. She said it's messy. Is there snow in heaven, Daddy?"

The yearning underlying that query touched Ashley's heart so she knew it had to hit Michael hard. To his credit he didn't show anything but love as he lifted Tati off the stone and cradled her in his arms.

"I don't know, sweetheart. But I'm positive Mommy's not cold. Heaven's a beautiful place and God wouldn't let your mommy get too cold or too hot."

"Just right. Like the little bear's porridge, right, Daddy?"

"Exactly right!" He tickled her until she was wiggling with delight, her squeals echoing around them. "Now finish up that cookie because we've got to show Ashley the secret, but don't tell!"

Tatiana shook her head, her eyes huge. She stuffed the rest of the cookie into her mouth as if to keep herself from talking, then held up her hands, palms outward.

"Sticky," was the only part Ashley understood.

"Fortunately for you, Miss Tati, we have the means to fix that." Michael carried her to the stream, held her so she could dip her hands into the water. She dried them against his pants, leaving brown streaks from the chocolate chips.

"Sorry. I should have rethought the cookie choice," Ashley murmured as he helped her gather their things.

"Why? It's a trip into the woods." He glanced down, shrugged. "I can wash my jeans later."

Five minutes later they were back on the trail, penetrating deeper into the forest. The gloom, the shadowy undergrowth, the flick of branches against her legs—all of these things contributed to Ashley's unease. She struggled to concentrate on her driving. Michael was there, she reminded herself over and over. He could be counted on if needed.

Finally they stopped at the edge of a clearing. Michael climbed off his bike, motioned with one finger across his lips for them to be quiet. He took Tati's hand. Ashley followed as he led them to the base of a tree and pulled on something. A rope ladder cascaded down.

He helped Tati up the first rung, waited till she'd climbed all the way, then motioned for Ashley to go next.

They were standing beneath some kind of a platform. Obviously they were going to sit up there. But why? She frowned at him.

"You wanted to see wild animals. If we're very quiet we may see a bear or two today. A friend of mine told me about a big brown mother that's been bringing her cubs here to eat the berries." His words brushed against her ear so softly she doubted Tati heard a thing. "Wait. I'll get your backpack. We can't leave any food down here."

He retrieved the pack and the blankets, passed them up, then swiftly followed Ashley up the ladder. Tati, who'd obviously been there before and knew the rules, stood quietly as she waited for him to prepare their seats. Then she snuggled into her father's lap.

It wasn't just a platform. It was a sort of box with a wide window that offered a perfect view of the clearing. The roof extended to give protection from the elements, the plywood sides kept out the wind. They could sit up here and observe without being observed.

"Look!"

Ashley followed his pointing finger, saw a big brown

bear ambling out of the woods beyond. Twigs and branches snapped under her massive paws but she paid them no mind. Her attention was on a bush loaded with dark purple berries.

"Babies!" Tati's gasp burst out as two chubby cubs twice her size followed their mother.

Mama Bear paused a moment, glanced around as if to check on their safety, then went back to eating the berries, joined seconds later by her greedy children.

The animals were fascinating to Ashley who'd never experienced them in a setting like this, perched up high with no fear for her safety. It wasn't until the cubs moved away and began tumbling on the ground that she noticed a gray shadow lurking behind the trees.

Without thinking she grabbed Michael's arm, pointed.

"Yes, I've been watching him," he murmured. "He's checking out the cubs. He's downwind, so that Mama can't smell him yet."

The cougar remained crouched, frozen in position. Ashley's nerves stretched tautly as she waited for something to happen. A memory flickered, her father's quiet voice. *She was only eight, no contest for a hungry cougar.*

A child had been attacked on the outskirts of Serenity Bay one year, causing an uproar in town. Search parties had combed the hills trying to find the cat and put it down before it claimed another victim. But Ashley couldn't recall whether or not the cougar had been found.

Suddenly the cat moved—just slightly, but it was enough to alert the cubs' mother. She swung around, tilted back on her hind legs and let out a yowl of anger. Her giant paws, claws extended, swiped through the air as the cubs darted behind her.

Tatiana's eyes grew huge as she watched the drama before them. For her sake Ashley hoped the cat would leave.

It didn't. Not immediately. But after prowling the edge of the glade, the cougar finally slunk away. Shortly after that the bears left, too.

Silence fell.

"Not a bad afternoon's entertainment," Mick murmured in her ear some time later. "You can let go now, if you want. Or do you need a hug?" His eyes twinkled with teasing.

Ashley blushed, realizing that had she gripped his arm at some point during the melée and was still clinging to him as if he were her life preserver.

"Sorry." She released him and moved back.

"Don't be. About the hug—"

She shook her head, reprimanding him visually. "I'm fine, Michael. But thank you for offering."

"Not a problem."

His gaze held hers, transmitting an unspoken message that only emphasized the zap of connection she always felt humming between them. The knowledge that he'd read her so easily brought back her blush.

Tati scrambled upright. "Are we going home now, Daddy?"

"I think it's time. It will be dark in a couple of hours." He gathered up his blankets and Ashley's backpack, climbed down the ladder then waited for them to follow.

Once they were all on the ground, he returned the ladder to its hidden position and walked beside Ashley to the quads with Tati skipping ahead.

"Amazing, isn't it? God's creatures cohabiting with one another, working out the parameters of their relationships. It always makes me wonder why we humans, who are supposed to be the brains on this earth, can't find a better way to live together."

"Maybe it's because we don't all go by the same rules,"

she murmured as she scanned their surroundings. Shadows, movements, branches swaying—she felt as if a thousand hidden eyes were watching.

"Ashley?" His hand on her arm made her jump.

"Sorry." She faked a smile. "Guess I'm a little nervous."

"There's no need to be. We're perfectly safe. The cougar is gone. I doubt he'd attack a group of three anyway."

"There were three bears," she pointed out.

"Yes, but he didn't attack and even if he had, he would have waited till he'd isolated one of the cubs from its mother, not taken on all three."

She frowned as he stored his blankets in the box of his four-wheeler. "You sound very knowledgeable."

"My father liked to hunt. He taught me to shoot, but after a while he tired of the killing and preferred to take pictures. He'd take me with him to spend a day snapping shots of animals that he sold for postcards. I learned a lot about animal habits, reactions and interactions from those trips with him."

"I would have been terrified to be there with only a camera for defense."

"Animals sense fear, Ashley. If you ever come face-to-face with a bear, don't turn your back or run."

"If my legs would work that'd be my first instinct."

"No." He grasped her shoulders. "You stand your ground, face them and yell at them to go away. If challenged, most of the time an animal will back down unless it's hurt or starving. But if you turn away or run they know you're afraid and they'll attack because they sense a weakness."

"Sounds like some people I've met," she muttered darkly, easing out of his grasp.

"In a way, I think it is a reflection of life. You can't get anywhere if you're afraid to take a risk." Michael's attention seemed focused on some distant feature. "My dad taught me a lot about life during those hours together. Remembering is what helped me after he died."

"I know what you mean. I have some good memories of when my father taught me to swim. No way he was going to live beside a lake with a kid who couldn't keep herself afloat for at least a little while." Ashley smiled, but couldn't shake the sense that someone, or something, was watching them.

Michael touched her arm, waited till her gaze met his. "What is it?"

"I'm not sure I can explain it."

He nodded. "You need to figure out what's causing this fear and try to get past it."

"You don't think I've tried?" She gave him a half smile that was less than heartfelt. "Don't fuss about me, Michael. It's just a silly case of nerves, probably a result of living in the noisy city. I'll get over it. Or I'll leave here and return to my habitat and it won't matter."

She could tell he didn't buy it, but he said no more except to call Tati from her exploration of the denuded berry bushes. The ride home seemed shorter to Ashley. With every mile she lost a little of her jitteriness and relaxed.

By the time they reached his house, Tatiana was noticeably weary. Michael had left meat stewing in a slow cooker and he insisted Ashley share it. Tati fell asleep at the table, her head drooping onto the side of her plate. A pang of sadness echoed inside Ashley at the soft little whisper of "Mommy" when Michael picked her up.

"I'll just be a minute tucking her in," he said. "Don't rush away."

Ashley cleared the table, put the dishes in the dishwasher and stored the remaining food, noting that none of them had seemed very hungry even though they'd been out in the fresh air all day.

After setting the kettle to boil, she wandered into the living room to peer at the row of snapshots he'd lined up on a coffee table. They were all unposed shots of Tati. Mick had caught her happy little smile as she carved a pumpkin, the way the tip of her tongue stuck out when she concentrated on skating, her saucy stance, hands clamped on her hips as she glared at another little girl who looked equally determined. Ashley guessed that was Wanda.

"What do you think?"

"I think that if you want to give up teaching you could probably make a good living doing portraits of kids. These are perfect."

"Easy subject," he said, moving to stand beside her.

"Yes, she is." She turned, but his hand on her arm stopped her. "I should get home." She glanced at him, meeting his stare.

"Ashley, you know there's something there between us. Every time I talk to you, every time I get within a hundred feet of you, it's as if I can feel you pulling me toward you. And we both know it's more than friendship." He reached up, drew a strand of hair from her eyes. His voice dropped to a husky drawl.

"When I'm supposed to be teaching, I'm thinking about you. When I'm reading Tati a story about one of her fairy princesses, I think of you, how your cheek curves, how your hair looks with the light sparkling on it." He leaned closer, touched her lips with his thumb. "You have to feel it, too."

"I do feel it." The whisper slipped out in spite of her determination to remain silent. "I don't want to, but I do."

"You don't want to? Why not?" Understanding dawned;

he frowned. "It's because I was married. Because I have Tati?"

"It's because you're dangerous," she corrected, wishing she'd never made that stupid comment to Piper.

"Dangerous—me?" He blinked. A quirky smile tugged at his mouth. "Don't you like to play with fire?"

He was teasing but Ashley was deadly serious.

"No." She shook her head. "I don't do danger, Michael. In fact, I run as far the other way as I can."

"Why?" His fingers moved to brush against her cheek and into her hair.

"Because I'm afraid."

"Of what?" he asked on a whisper. "I'm not going to hurt you."

"No, you're not," she agreed softly, stepping back so his hands dropped away. "Because I won't let you. I c-can't."

Moments stretched between them as he struggled to decipher her meaning. Finally he motioned to the armchair.

"Will you explain that to me, please?"

Ashley perched on the edge of the cushion, wishing she'd gone straight home. But she was as bad as he was—she dreamed about Michael, thought about Michael, imagined Michael.

It would have to stop.

"You're a kind, generous man who deserves to have love and happiness in his life, but I can't be more than your friend, Michael."

He studied her, brow furrowed. "Okay. Can you tell me why?"

"I don't know." It was so hard to put into words. "I'm not…normal."

"Agreed." He smiled at her glare. "Go on."

"I've been engaged twice."

"Ashley, I don't care about your past."

"But you have to. Because it's made me who I am now. It's the reason—" she stopped, regrouped. "I was engaged to a man who was a good friend. I'd known him a long time. I wanted that marriage, wanted it badly. I'd planned my life around being married to him. Then I found out he was in love with someone else, that he was afraid to tell me about her."

"That sounds cowardly."

"It wasn't." She smiled. "It was decent and honorable and very kind of him to believe he had to honor his commitment to me. But it was wrong and I knew it. I broke our engagement off immediately, told him I wanted him to marry the woman he loved, that I intended to be there for his wedding. And I was."

"That took guts." He kept watching her. "Then you were engaged a second time?"

"Yes." She sighed. "Not such a decent and honorable choice this time. I think I knew I'd made a mistake almost immediately but the accident forced me to accept that marriage between us would not work."

He waited and when she said no more, he hunkered down in front of her, clasped her hands in his. "Why did you tell me that, Ashley?"

"So you'd understand."

"Understand that you'd been hurt? That you'd made mistakes. That's part of life."

"That's not what I meant." She stared into his clear brown eyes and prayed for help.

"What *did* you mean?"

"I'm a coward, Michael. I'm afraid of life. I hung on to Parker even though I knew he didn't love me because I was afraid that if I didn't marry him, I'd be left alone. With him I was protected. I didn't have to fear."

"But you figured out it was wrong. You corrected your mistake."

"No, I didn't." She sighed, wishing—but it had to be said. "I latched on to Kent, ignored all the warning signs and told myself somebody was better than nobody. I lent him money, I covered for him, I even lied for him." She hung her head in shame.

"Because you loved him."

She raised her head, met his gaze. "No. Because I *needed* him. As long as I was with him, I wasn't alone. It took a car accident to force me to realize that Kent didn't want *me*. He wanted what he thought he could get from me and he was willing to do anything to get it—even put me in danger."

"What he could get from you?" He looked confused.

"My grandfather left me money. A lot of money. Kent wanted it."

"So you dumped him. Good." He grimaced. "I've made mistakes, too."

"I'm not talking about mistakes." She rose, stepped away from him. "I came to Serenity Bay to heal. Well, in order to really heal what's inside, I'm realizing that I have to learn how to face life without fear."

"You're afraid a relationship between us will turn you into that needy person again, is that it?"

"That's part of it," she admitted softly. "The other part is that you have to be here for your daughter. She needs stability and that comes first. I understand that, I admire that about you and there's no way I would ask or even want you to change that. Tatiana belongs with you."

"Yes, she does. But that doesn't mean—"

"Yes, it does. Because first and foremost you are her father and she needs you." She stepped in front of him, cupped his cheek in her hand. "You have a big heart. You want to help everyone and you think you can make me better, scare all the bogeymen away for me. I love you for thinking that, but you can't do it."

"Why?"

"Because I have to figure out my life on my terms." She leaned her head against his chest and let him hold her, just for a moment. The words poured out of their own accord. "The truth is, I've lived in the shadow of fear for years."

"But how—"

"I managed it. In Vancouver I had my life mapped out, every step of my day was thought out in deliberate detail to cover every eventuality. I thought I was safe, but now I realize I missed really living. And I want to."

"Tell me what you want from me."

She leaned back, stared into his eyes.

"I want a friend." She pressed a finger against his lips, shook her head. "I know you want more, but for now that's what I need most. And that's all I can give."

"Then that's what you've got." He bent his head and pressed his lips against hers in a kiss so soft and gentle it made her want to weep. Then he let his arms fall away and took a step back.

Ashley watched him, aching to be held, to be protected, yet knowing it wasn't enough.

"I'm here whenever you need me, Ashley. I'll gladly come if you call, I'll do whatever you ask. But most of all I'll pray for you."

Pray? She hadn't expected that.

"I think you coming home to Serenity Bay is part of God's plan. I don't think it's an accident that God brought us both here to begin again. I don't know what He's got planned, but I do know He wants you to be able to trust Him completely, that your life will only be complete when you stop worrying and start depending on Him. That's what I'm going to pray for. I think we should start right now."

And before she could protest he closed his eyes and began to ask God to show her His love and care. When he was finished Ashley knew she had a lot of thinking to do.

"Thank you," she whispered.

Michael simply smiled, helped her into her coat, handed over her gloves, then waited while she pulled on her boots.

"I'm glad you told me," he said quietly before she opened the door. "Maybe that's the first step to facing whatever you have to face."

"Maybe. Goodnight, Michael. And thanks."

As she drove to Piper's, Ashley automatically slipped into planning mode. Where should she live, what should she do? How could she get past the fear that a future full of unknowns held?

As quickly as the questions came and the worry rose up to choke her, she shoved them away.

"God has not given us a spirit of fear," she quoted out loud.

She said it over and over, all the way home, and she tried to believe it.

Chapter Eight

"You have to be crazy to have let yourself be talked into this, Masters."

Michael glared at the jagged edges of poorly sawn plywood that were supposed to represent the northern lights. Somebody wasn't very good with a jigsaw. He'd have to fix it. Grumbling to himself, he let it fall against the floor with a loud clap.

"Obviously I'm as looney as they come."

"I think that's a bad sign."

He jerked around, grimaced at Ashley's laughing face.

"Answering yourself, I mean. Talking to yourself is perfectly normal."

"Really?" He was content to stand there and stare his fill.

"Maybe you need to think about a holiday, Michael."

"You tell me where and when and I'll be there," he muttered, embarrassed that she'd overheard him complaining.

"Christmas isn't that far away."

"Now you sound like Tati." He moved the pieces so they were lined up in sequence. "Does this look right to you?"

"No." She stepped nearer, pulled a paper out of the file

she was carrying. "You're missing a section." She held out the paper for him to see.

"That's Marc. I figured his project would take longer than anyone else's. He's not exactly organized. What are you doing here?" He dusted off his hands while his eyes feasted on the woman who hadn't been out of his thoughts for more than half an hour, even though he hadn't seen her in two weeks.

According to Jason, Ashley had taken a trip to Toronto to try to drum up gallery interest in her artists. He couldn't help but wonder how she'd done.

"Checking on your progress. The kids have already started rehearsals. The drama teacher is delighted with the script. He's got a mixture of local talent helping him." She frowned, touched her finger to the end of his nose, showed him the sawdust. "A new fashion statement?"

"Nothing close to yours." He admired the jade-green suit she wore and the high black boots that did great things for her legs. "What's the occasion? My art teacher never dressed like you."

"No class today. I'm working on something else. Something I came to ask your help with."

Michael heard the hesitation and ignored it. "Shoot."

"I need you to look at a house."

"A house?" He raised one eyebrow. "Why?"

"Because I'm thinking about buying it."

"Wow! What brought this on?" She was going to live here permanently? His heart swelled.

"I struck out in Toronto, Montreal, Vancouver and New York. And it makes me furious."

She looked steamed. Her silver-gilt hair danced over her shoulders shooting out sparks where the light hit it.

"They wouldn't agree to a full-scale show," he guessed.

"Not for the weavings, the paintings, the stained glass.

Not even all together. Nobody will do more than take a couple of pieces on a trial basis." She flopped down on an upturned crate, her gray eyes steely. "Not a visionary among them. Philistines!"

"I see." Been there, done that. Which made thoughts of his own showing next summer seem an impossibility. "And buying a house will help you because—?"

"I'm going to turn it into a gallery," Ashley said. Her chin jutted out as if she expected an argument. "At least I think I am. If you'll tell me whether the thing is stable and worth renovating. Will you?"

The excitement of her project radiated from her, lighting her face from within. She'd obviously come to a decision and was now plunging full speed ahead. But Michael couldn't help wondering if she was running into something, or away from something.

"Ashley, I'm not an architect or an engineer," he warned. "You should have the structure checked by a professional."

"I will, after I hear your opinion." Her big gray eyes studied him. "Will you do it? If you'd rather not be involved, just say so."

"Sure, I can look. No problem. I'm just not sure my opinion is worth anything." He dusted off his clothes.

"It is to me," she said quietly.

Michael froze. There it was—an almost-admission that she wanted him in her life—as more than a friend?

"Just look at it, listen to my ideas, and then tell me if you think I'm nuts. That's all I'm asking. P-please?"

The tone of her voice, that soft wobbly note that told him she was having second thoughts, that's what did him in.

"When?"

"Whenever you want."

There was no way he could turn her down, not when she

wore that look—the same one Tati got when she begged for another bedtime story.

"We could go now. School's almost out and I don't have a class this period."

"That would be great." Her eyes shone with anticipation. "I'll drive."

"Okay." He had to go back to the staff room to retrieve his coat so he met her in the parking lot. "You're excited about this, aren't you?"

"Yes. For the first time in a long time I feel like I'm being proactive instead of reacting."

"That's good." He noted where they were going, frowning when she turned down a familiar lane. "Isn't this—" Michael paused when she stopped in front of her childhood home.

"I have a kind of love-hate relationship with this house," Ashley explained as she switched off the motor. "When I wasn't here, I wanted to be, and when I got here in the summer, it didn't feel like I thought it should. After a while it became oppressive, the source of bad memories. When my father died, I was glad to sell it."

"But now you want it back?"

"I want to start changing the bad memories, make them into something good."

Michael got out of her vehicle, followed her up the path. He did a quick appraisal of the area as she unlocked the door.

"It's a residential neighborhood. The town council might have something to say about rezoning it for your purposes."

"I've already asked Jason about that. I thought that as mayor he'd know the ins and outs."

"You've thought this through, I see."

"A bit." She grinned. "Since it's a cul de sac, Jason thinks the council probably won't kick up much of a fuss, especially since I intend to buy the lots on either side for parking."

"Big parking lot," he mused.

"I have some other ideas but I'll tell you about them another time." She grasped his arm, drew him into the house. "Imagine this as a big open space. Those walls will come down, of course."

She went on, pointing out changes she'd make, indicating special spots she'd dedicate to sit and look at specific works. Michael followed, trying to visualize through her eyes.

"The kitchen will stay, altered of course, but I want to make it an area where different artists could come and demonstrate, hold a workshop or speak to those interested while others come and go through the rest of the place. If there's a reception or something for a showing it will be handy."

"Good idea."

Ashley walked forward, pushed open a door and waved a hand.

"I'm going to extend this toward the water, screen part of it in." She went on and on, describing a variety of activities that could all be held within the confines of the house.

As they moved through it, Michael checked for repairs that would be needed.

"I could have kids' classes down here," she said, stepping downstairs.

The basement seemed solid, no foundation problems. The second floor seemed equally solid though the roof in one room gave him pause.

"I think you might need new shingles," he murmured, running one hand over the yellow stained plaster. "And someone to fix this."

"Yes, I saw that the other day. I think the bathrooms will have to be redone, too, especially if I intend to stay."

"You'll live here?" he asked, amazed that she'd even consider it.

"I have to live somewhere. I don't want to be at Piper's after she's married. Besides, there's plenty of room here."

"Yes, there is." He studied her, noted the way her fingers gripped the doorknob. She was putting up a brave front, but it was obvious the thought terrified her. "I think it would probably take a while to do the work here. I'm sure Piper and Jason wouldn't mind you staying."

"*I'd* mind. Newlyweds need privacy."

"True." He followed her to the room at the back. She waved a hand.

"This is my room."

"From when you were a child?"

She nodded. "I used to sit in this window seat and dream. Or paint. I've drawn those hills a hundred times."

"They are beautiful," he agreed.

Michael studied the view with her, finally touching her arm. He waited until she faced him.

"This is a really big commitment, Ashley." The sunlight flooding the room turned her hair into a cloud of silver-gold. "Not just of money but of time. Are you sure you want to do it?"

"I have to." Her voice cracked, but she cleared her throat, kept going. "I realize now that I can't go back to the city. Not until I'm free."

That shocked him. "Free of what?"

"Well, I'm still figuring that out." A funny crooked smile touched her lips.

Michael leaned forward, pressed his lips against her forehead, tapped her chin with his fist.

"Good for you." He stepped back. "As far as I can tell

the house looks solid, but I'd have someone check it thoroughly before you sign anything. You'll probably want assurances on the rezoning first, too."

She nodded.

"Probably. But I *am* going to buy this house, Michael. If the gallery doesn't work out, I'll move in, live here, make it my home. For a while anyway."

"Why is this house so important to you, Ashley?"

Her shoulders went back, her face tightened. Those big gray eyes, usually so troubled, now seemed to clear.

"I think because this is where it started. It's the first link in the chain, Michael. It's one of the things I've attached negatives to."

"How?" Maybe talking about it would help.

"I thought I was secure here. Then one day everything changed." She sank down on the window seat. "My parents' divorce came as a great shock to me. I knew we didn't live the same as everyone else, but somehow I never twigged on to just how different my family's lives were. Since I've come back to the Bay, I've begun to realize that I never really dealt with my own feelings about their split."

"Because?"

"Good question. Maybe because I was too busy worrying about them." She frowned. "My father seemed like the victim to me. He had nobody else, no other family. He traveled too much to have many close friends. He used to say Serenity Bay was the only place he'd ever retire. It's sad he didn't get to do that."

"You felt guilty because you left him here alone."

"Yes." She blinked quickly to clear the tears that glazed her eyes. "I know I couldn't live here by myself when he was gone. And I really did enjoy school. Rowena and Piper made it fun. Then summer would come."

"They came back here with you, though." He had a

hunch he knew what was going on beneath the flawless makeup but Michael probed anyway in hopes of helping her clarify her thoughts.

"We all came back. And we had wonderful times. But for me it was a kind of game, a way to erase the pain of my broken family. I used to pretend I was like Rowena, coming home to my dad."

"But it wasn't the same?"

"No." She stared out the window, pensive. "Rowena's father went away every winter to work in the oil fields. She didn't have a mother. I did."

"So when you were with him you felt guilty?"

She nodded.

"And when I wasn't here I felt guilty. He took the summers off. For two months I was the center of his life, he was here whenever I needed him."

"And you didn't like that?"

"Oh, I loved it, because for a little while I could pretend everything was okay." A tremulous smile lifted her lips. "I adored feeling protected, wanted. More than that, I loved seeing him relax. His face would lose its lines and he'd start to laugh—until the day I had to leave and the sadness returned. Every time I said goodbye I felt like I was abandoning him."

"Ashley, I'm sure your father didn't think that."

"I know. But I did and that's the problem." Ashley traced an invisible line on the window, her voice so quiet he had to lean in to hear.

"Piper's grandparents would take us to school. I'd stand in the living room, in his arms, holding on as long as I could. Then he'd kiss me goodbye and I'd walk out the door and reality would smack me in the face. I was alone again. On my own."

"But you didn't let it hold you back. You went to school, finished your training."

She nodded. "Yes. I *managed* very well. Maybe too well. I'm still managing."

He didn't know what to say, how to help her. So Michael kept up a silent vigil of prayer while he waited for her to continue.

After a while Ashley sighed, offered him an apologetic smile.

"I'm sorry. This must all sound rather silly to you."

"Silly? No. It sounds like a child who did what she had to do to get through her life." He knelt in front of her, took her hands. "There's no shame in that, Ashley. The thing you have to focus on is moving ahead. Getting past whatever has held you back."

She nodded.

"I'm trying. And that's why I want this house." She grasped his hands with hers. "Listen. I was painting this morning and I had the television on. There was a woman speaking. Something she said clicked with me."

This mattered, he could see it in the flash of inner fire that altered her eyes from gray to silver.

"She quoted a Bible verse about walking by faith. And then she said that when we walk in faith we take one step, then another step, then a third. It's a progression, facing each thing and believing God will get us through that, then facing the next one."

"That's true."

"She said faith isn't a big enlightenment we get that lifts us up like a magic-carpet ride and takes us to better things. It's staying in the program, even when it gets rough, believing God will make it better and pressing on."

The clarity of that intrigued him, made him consider his own situation.

"She ended with that verse that says without faith it is impossible to please God. That got me thinking about my faith." Ashley drew her hands from his, motioned around the room. "This house was full of pain because I endowed it with those feelings."

"How does that tie in with faith?" He didn't get where she was going.

"When I get up in the morning questions run through my mind—what if this happens? What if that comes about? That's fear. They're little threats I've been feeding myself for years. If I'm not careful about this, something bad will happen. If my parents divorce, my life will be ruined. If I leave, my dad will suffer."

Her face glowed with newfound knowledge. Michael could see confidence growing in the way her body stance changed. She was beautiful.

"I taught myself to believe the worst would happen and then the panic started. Even when I should have moved on from the divorce I couldn't because I let the fear remain and it kept growing."

He'd never thought of it that way, but now Michael began to apply her ideas to his own life. Is that what he was doing—letting doubt make it impossible to reach his own goal by suspecting God's will for him?

"The fear came because my thinking was wrong, not because what I felt was true." Her eyes widened, she stared at him.

"So what you're saying is—"

"I've let myself believe lies. I told myself lies and I believed them because I was afraid of what might happen. And I think I know why."

"You want to share?"

"Yes, though it might sound jumbled."

"Don't worry about that. Just talk."

In her excitement, Ashley rose, paced across the room and back.

"When I was eight my grandmother came to visit one summer. It was the only time. My parents must have been having problems even then because I recall my mother weeping a lot whenever Dad was gone."

"Go on."

"One night I couldn't sleep. We were having a heat wave that summer. I don't remember where Dad was, but he wasn't home. I could hear voices. Mom and my gran were on the back deck talking—my window was open. I sat on the window seat and listened to them." She jerked to a stop. Her whole body went still.

"Are you okay?"

"Yes. No." She peered at him through the waning light. "Gran was talking."

"About what?"

She looked at him, her face pale. "I don't know. I only remember she said, 'It will ruin Ashley's life, tear apart her world. She'll never recover.' I was so scared. I got back into bed and lay there awake for a long time."

She paused, stared at him.

"I kept expecting something bad to happen. Maybe my parents were sick or I was. But nothing happened. Not all summer. I left for school dreading leaving here."

"And that's when the fear first began?"

"I think so." She stared into the distance, remembering. "I wrote tons of letters that winter. Everything seemed okay. Time went by. Nothing changed—nothing I noticed."

"Maybe you didn't want to."

"Maybe. Anyway, I remember I came home for Easter. I was thirteen that year. That's when they told me." Her face lost all color. "It was the same day that a man grabbed me, t-tried to abduct me."

"It's okay. You're safe." He wrapped his arms around her, held her shaking body until she finally went still. "That's when the fear really grabbed hold, isn't it?"

"Yes," she whispered. She lifted her tear-stained face, met his gaze. "My mother insisted that I'd made the whole thing up. I was a bit of a drama queen back then."

He brushed the tears from her cheek, stung by her sad little smile.

"She said I'd make them a laughingstock if I told people. She insisted I forget about it. So when the police couldn't find anyone who looked like the man I saw, I finally decided I must have dreamed it." She gulped. "I pushed the memories down, but I still had the nightmares."

"What did she say about the nightmares?"

Ashley shook her head. "I never told her or Dad. I thought that if I didn't make waves, if I was perfect, that somehow I could fix whatever was wrong between them. Because I knew. By then I knew my world was falling apart."

Michael waited until she'd regained her composure, had drawn away from him. Then he asked the question uppermost in his mind.

"So did it really happen, Ashley? Or did you imagine it?"

She kept her head bent, never flinched, never moved a muscle. Her voice emerged whisper-soft, begging him for an answer.

"I've got a better question. If it never happened, how come I keep seeing that same face, seventeen years later? How come I've only ever seen it here, in Serenity Bay?"

Chapter Nine

"I'm sorry. I don't seem to have shed the drama-queen image yet."

Ashley drew a tissue from her pocket, dabbed at her face, embarrassed that she'd dumped her woes all over him.

"Don't."

She forced herself to look at Michael, saw only tenderness in his eyes. A trickle of relief flickered through her. He seemed to understand.

"Tell me how faith figures into this."

"Well," she drew a deep breath. "If I believe God is there, helping me, then I have to believe that He will send what I need. The Bible says He's a rewarder of those who seek Him. That I'm to walk in faith, that I should ask in faith."

"Agreed."

"Asking means I expect God to do something. I might not see it yet, but I believe it will happen. That's faith." She waited for his nod. "But the thing is, when I let myself worry, when I see how wrong things are, I focus on fear. And that's what prevents my progress on this path of faith."

Michael leaned against the wall, frowning.

"So buying this house, changing it into something good is…what?"

"It's my way of saying I believe God has something wonderful in store for me. That I may have been stuck on what-ifs but I'm changing that to what-could-be. I'm going to start living in this moment, here and now, and stop worrying about what might happen."

"Good for you."

"I don't know if I'll ever see that man again. If I do, I'll deal with it. With God's help. But today I'm moving on."

Michael pushed away from the wall, walked toward her. He stopped when he was just a few inches away. Though he never touched her, his voice reached out to wrap her in a gentle hug of support.

"Do you know how strong you are, Ashley? It takes a lot of nerve to face your fears, to put your ideas into actions. I admire your courage."

"I haven't succeeded yet, so don't congratulate me too soon. The pit of my stomach is still fluttering with nerves. But I think this place—" she waved a hand around "—might be my first turning point. Thanks for coming with me."

"I'm glad you chose me." He glanced at his watch. "Can I take you out for dinner to celebrate?"

The idea held instant appeal. Ashley nodded, then paused. "What about Tati?"

"It's Friday. My mother picks her up from day care and the two are together until tomorrow morning. I think it's facials this week." He wrinkled his nose as if the idea of plastering goop on his cheeks was abhorrent. "And maybe pedicures, too. I didn't pay a lot of attention."

"Hmm, maybe I should join them," she teased. "I haven't had a pedicure in ages."

"Aw, come on! What if I throw in a movie. That new chick flick is in town."

"I saw it with Piper last week."

"Oh."

He looked so disappointed, Ashley had to laugh. "I'd love to have dinner with you, Michael."

"Me, too." His smile hit her squarely in the chest. "Let's go, Ms. New Property Owner."

"I have to make a stop first," she said when they were in her car. "My landlord shipped my skis and I have to pick them up at the freight office."

"You're going skiing?"

She frowned. "Uh-huh. I was going to ask you if I could teach Tatiana."

"You're kidding, right?"

"No. Of course not. Why?"

"Ashley. Dear, sweet Ashley." Michael's knowing smirk made her frown. "I love my daughter very much but she's about as inept as a kid can be. Whatever genes Carissa passed down, grace wasn't one of them. Put Tati on a ski slope and I can't guarantee you won't be wearing crutches with your bridesmaid's dress."

"She's not inept. She's just—" How to put it delicately? "A bit awkward."

"A *bit?*" He hooted with laughter. "There is none so blind as she who will not see."

"Well, I'd still like to teach her to ski." She pulled up beside his mother's café. "And I don't know where we're going to dinner so I'm stopping here."

"Not here," he begged, after one quick look inside. "Please?"

After a glance at his face, she moved farther down the street. "Is this all right?"

"Better." He took a quick look behind them. "My

mother has this cook. Her skill as an interrogator exceeds her skill as a chef, which is very good. Better I don't give her anything to grill me about."

"Oh, good pun." Ashley chuckled at his pained look. "Where shall we go then?"

"How about the steak house just outside of town? You could drop me at the school on the way and I'll pick up my car."

"Okay. Do you mind if I stop at the depot first?"

He shrugged so Ashley parked in front of the delivery building.

"I'll just be a couple of minutes."

Michael got out, and walked beside her. "I'll carry them."

"Thanks." Once the skis were safely stored on her roof rack, Ashley headed for the school. "I'm probably not supposed to say this, but I hope it snows soon."

"Weren't you the one who went off the road not too long ago?" he asked, tongue-in-cheek.

"Yes, but I wasn't prepared. Besides, it was too early for us to have snow then."

"In my opinion, it still is. Thanksgiving is barely past."

"How did the pumpkin cakes go over, by the way?"

"Wanda said they didn't look exactly like pumpkins but they tasted all right," he repeated in a squeaky imitation of his daughter.

"Faint praise indeed." Ashley chuckled. "I'd like to meet this discerner of pumpkins."

"Hang around with Tati for long and you probably will. By the way, you should know that Wanda can ski like a trouper."

"Ah. What about you?" He ducked his head, avoided her glance. "Michael? What did I say wrong?"

"Nothing, but I, uh— My daughter comes by her clumsiness naturally, I'm afraid." He sighed when she didn't give up. "I'm a klutz on the ski hill, okay?"

Ashley giggled at his embarrassment. She was still enjoying his discomfiture when she stopped beside his car.

"No problem. I'll teach you both," she offered. "I used to instruct years ago. I've taught all kinds of klutzes."

"That's very kind but—we'll see." He scrambled out of her car a little too quickly. "I'll follow you to the restaurant, okay?"

"Okay." His rush to leave made her smile for the rest of the drive.

Since they were a bit early, they had their choice of tables to choose from. Michael chose one beside the fireplace, a table for two tucked into a little alcove. Once they'd ordered, Ashley posed the question uppermost in her mind.

"What do you do with your spare time? If you have any, I mean. Do you have a hobby?" She fiddled with the napkin, wishing that hadn't come out sounding quite so nosy.

"Truthfully?" Michael smiled. "There isn't a lot of time to spare when you're a single parent."

"I don't imagine so. But you have tonight and tomorrow. You must have something you want to do. And your evenings, when Tati's asleep. Surely you don't spend all of them checking school work?"

"Not all, no."

It was obvious that he didn't want to tell her. He avoided looking at her, kept his focus on the table.

"Okay, then. Maybe I should change the subject." His snub hurt, especially after she'd shared so much with him. "Your mother told me you lived in New York. You said you studied there. Did you like it?"

He nodded and his face brightened.

"I liked the convenience of having everything accessible

without the long drives to Toronto that we have here. The galleries, the plays, the energy—it seems to spark something creative inside, you know?"

"Some cities have a way of doing that."

"After a while it wore a bit thin, though. I guess I'm a country boy at heart. And then with Tati—well, I needed a job and I figured having Mom nearby couldn't hurt. The Bay just seemed like the perfect place."

"Tati's adjusted well. She seems to have accepted you and Serenity Bay as her home."

"For the most part. She still asks the odd question about her mother, but mostly she's busy and happy." He met her steady gaze. "I'm sorry if I seem rude, Ashley. It's just that I don't have a very interesting life. Let's talk about the wedding. You do know I'm Jason's groomsman?"

He was putting her off and Ashley didn't understand why. Did he think she was getting too familiar? Asking too much? But he was the one who'd suggested dinner.

"I know. I think it's going to be a lovely wedding. Jason's taking her to the Caribbean on a honeymoon cruise for two weeks, but don't tell Piper. He had to tell me so I can pack a suitcase for her. She thinks they're going to Toronto."

"Good for Jason."

"I want to plan a shower, a couples' shower. But I'm not really sure how to arrange it."

"Why not ask someone at the church to help? They're both well known there, the fellowship hall would work and you could make it an open invitation."

"But I barely know anyone there. Besides, I want to surprise them."

"You can still do that. Why don't you talk to my mother? She's good at arranging stuff like this. You give me the date and time and I'll make sure the happy couple are both there."

"I appreciate your help, but if you're too busy—"

"I want to help, Ashley. They're my friends, too."

"Okay. Thank you." She pulled a calendar out of her purse. "I thought it should be before Christmas, maybe even before the party season really gets underway. Everyone gets booked up fast at Christmas."

They chose a date, discussed decorations, games and a way to contact everyone without the couple knowing.

When the meal was over, Ashley was delighted to have her plans solidified, even more delighted when thick fluffy snowflakes began to tumble to earth as they left the restaurant.

"If this keeps up, skiing lessons will be sooner than you think." She clapped her hands together. "Just think, father and daughter, sharing a new healthy experience."

His one look said a thousand words.

"It'll be fun."

"Sure it will." His face brightened. "If I'm to share this fun, I think you should share some new experiences, too. Do you know how to snowshoe, Ashley?"

"No. It's never been a priority living in Vancouver." She stared at him. "Why?"

"Two students of mine have challenged me to race them in the winter festival. Snowshoe racing. I need a partner." He clapped a hand on his hip, his smirk daring her to refuse. "Well?"

"I'd love to learn," she told him, then raised one eyebrow. "If you have time?"

"Touché." He tapped the end of her nose with his finger. "Thanks for sharing my dinner. I enjoyed it."

"I did, too. And thanks again for going through the house with me." Ashley paused at the side of her car. "I appreciate you listening to me. It helped."

"It helped me, too."

"Oh?"

"I'm going to push ahead and practice a little more faith in my own life."

What did that mean?

He moved forward, pressed his lips against hers in a gentle kiss that could have meant so many things. "Good night, Ashley."

"Good night." Half bemused, she climbed into her car, waited while he got into his. He followed her back to town, then they separated.

Ashley was halfway to Piper's when she noticed the letter. She pulled over, picked it off the floor of her SUV and read his name. Michael must have dropped it. Maybe it was important. Or maybe she just wanted an excuse. She turned around, drove toward his home.

Michael's car wasn't visible when she arrived but car tracks in the dusting of snow led to the garage and the house lights were on so she assumed he was inside.

Leaving the motor running, Ashley collected the letter and walked toward the door. It hadn't completely closed. She stretched out her hand to knock but his voice stopped her.

"No, I haven't told Ashley, Mom, and I'm not going to." He sounded angry, frustrated.

Ashley wanted to turn and run away, but her feet seemed frozen to the stairs. He was speaking again.

"I know you mean well, but if I can't make it on my own, my carvings don't mean anything. Ashley's got money, Mom. She's at home in the art world. Sure, she could be a great help, but she might also hate my work and not want to tell me the truth. I don't want her involved. If I do this showing, I'll do it on my own. Without her interference."

Ashley stepped back as if she'd been struck. She glanced

around, saw the mailbox at the edge of the drive. Without a second thought she climbed into her vehicle, drove up beside it and tucked the letter inside. Then she drove away, blocking out all feeling as she rode back to Piper's.

She made small talk with her friend for a few minutes, watched a comedy they both loved and then excused herself for bed. But once she was in her room, the questions wouldn't stop.

Michael hadn't told her about his "hobby" because he didn't trust her. She wondered for a moment what he did, then pushed that away as the pain hit. She was falling for a man who thought she'd interfere.

Once again she'd chosen the wrong man to give her heart to. Michael Masters didn't want her *interference* in the part of his life that mattered so much he kept it a secret.

No one at school had mentioned his carving, she'd seen no sign of it around town. No one in the artists' guild had said anything. Why was it such a secret—especially when she'd shared hers with him? If he couldn't tell her about something he loved, what else was he hiding?

Ashley sank onto the big plushy bed in Piper's home and wondered how long it would take for this hurt to go away. Her gaze fell on the Bible she'd left beside her bed, to the section where she'd left off reading in Corinthians: *For we walk by faith, not by sight...*

"This, too, God?" she asked.

Faith.

Bowing her head, Ashley prayed for the courage and faith to rest in God's promise to keep her safe.

The couples' shower was everything Ashley had hoped it would be.

At least that's what Michael thought. He stood in a corner, watching her lead a game that soon had the room erupting in laughter. He could feel the distance between them even though she'd barely glanced his way.

She'd been cool, standoffish, busy for weeks now. Piper explained it away by saying she'd once again seen the man she was so afraid of. That she'd attempted to follow him this time made his blood run cold. He knew she wanted answers, but to go it alone—

What do you expect? She's not exactly leaning on you for support.

No, she wasn't. In fact, she'd been extraordinarily missing from his life lately. The purchase of the house, the rezoning, the renovations—he knew it all consumed her time.

But she'd made it a point to visit Tati, even tried her on skis. Just not when he was at his mother's.

"You keep staring at her like that, you'll have people talking, buddy," Jason murmured in his ear. He grinned at Michael's jerk of surprise.

"How does a great hulk like you creep up on people?"

"Most of them aren't in a daze. Want to talk about it?"

Jason had become his best friend since he'd moved back here. But Michael wasn't sure he wanted to ask him the questions he needed answers to.

"Aren't you supposed to be in there with your fiancée?"

"Ashley kicked me out for some game they're playing. So talk and make it quick before I have to go back."

"She looks thinner."

"Piper said Emma will have to take Ashley's dress in again." Jason drew him out of the hall into the adjoining cloakroom. "She's been running herself ragged with that house and her plans to make it a gallery."

"I heard." His mother was a regular fountain of information about Ashley Adams.

"How come you haven't been around there?"

"She didn't ask. I invited her to go for a snowmobile ride after we got all that new snow last week, but—" he shrugged "—she said she's too busy right now."

"And the next time you asked?" Jason quirked one eyebrow upward. "Don't tell me you just gave up? Not Mr. Persistence?"

"I've been a little busy building sets for your fiancée's play, Nosy."

"That's an excuse not to call Ashley?" Jason shook his head. "You're nowhere near as bright as I figured."

"She's going through stuff, Jay. Things get a little too personal when we're together."

"And this is a problem because?"

"I was divorced. I have a child."

"Yes, I know. She knows, too. I believe you belonged to both those categories before she met you?"

Michael moved back into the doorway so he could watch her, wishing that smile she lavished on everyone else would flash at him. "That's not the point."

"You gonna tell me what is?"

"No."

"Okay." Jason opened a tin someone had left on a table, picked out a piece of fudge. "Mmm, this is great. Maybe we shouldn't add it to the rest of the stuff in the kitchen. I'll just sneak it out and take it home."

"She's got money, Jason."

"A ton of it. I know." He blinked at Michael's glare. "So?"

"You don't see a problem there?"

"Doesn't matter what I see. I doubt if Ashley cares much about her grandfather's inheritance except that it makes people look at her differently." He raised his eyebrows. "Like you're thinking right now."

"She's opening a gallery in Serenity Bay, Jason. What

am I supposed to say? 'Oh, by the way, I just happen to have some pieces I've been working on. I wonder if you'd show them for me.'"

"Sounds good to me. Honest, forthright. Ow! What?" he asked when Michael thunked him on the shoulder.

"It sounds like I was wangling to get an in with her." He refused the fudge Jason offered. "She'll feel obliged to take them and I'll never know if I could have made it on my own."

"Ah." Jason grinned, his eyes dancing. "Now I get it. We're talking about pride."

"Yes. That and the fact that she doesn't want to get involved while she's still sorting out this fear thing."

"Involved. Oh, my. I didn't realize you were involved." Jason mocked his embarrassment. "Look, man. You're obviously not as experienced as me in matters of the heart so let me give you some advice."

"*You're* giving *me* advice?" Michael wanted to hoot with laughter, but Ashley was in the next room and he didn't want to draw attention to himself so he controlled the urge. "This is going to be good. Go ahead. Share your wisdom, groom."

"Thanks, I will." Jason drew him farther back into the cloakroom where they wouldn't be overheard. "Did you ever think Ashley's fear problems are tied up with her parents' problems?"

"Sure." Michael narrowed his gaze. "Hey! How do you know this?"

"Piper told me. And if you say a word…" he warned, glaring.

"I might have pushed a little too hard," Michael admitted. "She told me she had some issues to work through, that she only wanted to be friends, for now."

"See? That's a good place to start. But friends keep in

touch, they don't just disappear because things get busy.
Ask her out again. You're my best man, she's a bridesmaid—you can talk about us!"

"Oh, goody." Michael frowned. "It's gone quiet in there.
Shouldn't you be back in there with your bride-to-be?"

"Nope."

"Why not?"

"Because I told him not to come back until I said so."
Ashley appeared in the doorway, glancing from one to the
other. "Hello, Michael."

"Hi, yourself. Sorry I was late."

"No problem." She turned her focus back to Jason,
brushed a finger against the dark crumbs on his cheek.
Her gaze narrowed. "You've been into that fudge I brought,
haven't you? How much is left?"

Since Michael had just watched Jason slip the last piece
into his mouth, he knew his friend couldn't speak.

"It's all gone," he said, enjoying his friend's discomfort.

"Jason Franklin, you know very well I was going to
use that as a prize!"

"I'm sorry, Ashley but I'm starved. I didn't get any dinner and then I had to rush over here. It was too tempting."

"Ooh!"

"Don't kill him yet, Ashley," Michael advised softly,
stifling his laughter. "We've got to get them married first.
Then it's Piper's job to make him behave."

"Good luck to her. Well, you're going to be the one who
provides this prize, Jason. So get thinking about it. Maybe
all the sugar will help." She grabbed his arm, drew him
forward. "Come on. It's time to face the music and the advice of our panel."

"He can use it," Michael told her, gazing into her eyes.
"He has the strangest ideas about love."

"Really." She didn't look away until someone in the audience cleared her throat. Then she launched back into her role of hostess as if it had never been interrupted.

Michael admired her aplomb. He had none. Whenever Ashley looked at him like that, the world stopped. He felt as if he'd been kicked in the stomach. There was a chair against the wall and he sank into it, his knees suddenly too weak to hold him upright.

But as the evening progressed, as the group finally broke for refreshments, his eyes never left Ashley.

Maybe that's why he noticed the exact moment when she almost dropped the tray she was carrying. He got to her as fast as he could, handed the tray to someone else and helped her sit down.

"Breathe, in and out."

She obeyed, but her hands clamped around his like vises. She stared at him and he could see the fear taking control.

"What's wrong?"

"I saw him. He thrust his head around the corner, looked at me, then disappeared. But I saw him!"

"The same man?" he asked knowing exactly who she was referring to.

"Yes. It was him, Michael. He was here. Maybe he followed me."

"Stay here. I'll go check." He eased in and out of the crowd, working his way across the room until he finally got to the door. He stepped outside, raced down the steps and surveyed the church parking lot.

All he saw was a host of cars and trucks, none of them with their lights on or leaving the grounds.

Michael waited several minutes, finally he went back inside.

"Did you find him?" Ashley whispered from just inside the door.

He shook his head.

"He's gone now," he whispered.

She sagged against him, her fingers spread against his chest. Her eyes closed.

"Oh, God," she whispered in a prayer of desperation. "Please help me."

"He will, Ashley. Just keep hanging on to your faith."

But as he stood holding her in the cloakroom, a tiny doubt flickered through his own mind.

There had been no one outside. Which begged the questions—was this man real?

Or was Ashley imagining it all?

Chapter Ten

"Seven days till Christmas, folks. If you haven't done your shopping yet, you'd better get to it."

Ashley didn't need the radio deejay's reminder. A square silver box tied with bright red ribbon lying under Piper's tree was a constant reminder that she'd be leaving shortly to spend Christmas with her mother and she needed to make a delivery first. Two of them actually.

She'd spent days stewing over how and when to give Tatiana and Michael the Christmas gifts she'd chosen especially for them. Since she was driving to Toronto tomorrow, procrastination was no longer possible.

Outside, Jason and Piper were supposedly putting up Christmas decorations but the peals of laughter made them sound more like kids who'd just been released from school. Ashley tugged on her coat, snatched up the two gifts and hurried outside before she could change her mind.

"I don't know when I'll be back," she called. "Don't wait up."

Piper waved. Jason threw a snowball that smashed against her windshield.

"You're going to get coal for Christmas," she warned.

"Doesn't matter," he called. "I'm already getting everything I want for New Year's."

Ashley climbed inside the car before he could bombard her with another from the stack of snowballs he had piled beside him. She smiled as Piper caught him off guard, the snow splattering across his face in a wet sopping mess. He retaliated six for her one. When he ran out, he kissed her nose then urged her onto the old sled they'd found. As she whizzed down the hill, Piper squealed with delight, the sound echoing back from the surrounding hills over and over.

Ashley had never seen her friend happier. Their love was as solid and firm as Cathcart House, Piper's grandparents' home. They'd disagree, argue, maybe even hold grudges. But that house would be filled with love.

As it always had been.

"Stop moping about the past, woman. You've made a new beginning. Get on with it."

She drove the roads easily, trying not to check every nook and cranny. She was getting better at trusting. If only she hadn't seen his face at the shower. Everything else was going so well, but she couldn't work her brain past the fear that still clutched her whenever she saw him.

The radio was playing Christmas songs and Ashley sang along as she drove, joy bubbling inside. She loved Christmas, always had. Not being able to open the gallery in time for the season stung, but she'd prayed for the courage to wait.

Wait. That's all she seemed to do lately. Wait for understanding, wait for the gallery work to be finished, wait, wait, wait. Michael had phoned several times, asking her to dinner, hinting that he was ready for his skiing lesson, but Ashley had put him off every time.

She couldn't get past what she'd overheard, and she

didn't want to embarrass herself by letting him see that Ashley Adams was infatuated with him—again.

Only it was more than that, and she knew it.

She pulled into his yard, then blinked. There were no tracks. Maybe he wasn't even home.

"I'll just have to leave the gifts, then," she muttered, gathering them up and climbing out of the car. She walked up the steps, struggling not to recall the last time she'd been here.

Tati, still wearing her fuzzy pink nightgown, had the door open before she got to it.

"Ashley, hi! Are those presents?" Her saucer-wide eyes glittered with excitement.

"They sure are. One for you, one for your dad. Can you put them under your tree?"

"We don't have one yet." Tatiana checked the name tags, noted that her present was the largest. Then she pushed them both onto the counter. "Daddy said maybe today. After we bake cookies."

"I said nothing about making cookies, Tati. Oh, hi, Ashley." Michael closed the door behind her. "How are you?"

"I'm fine." He looked tired and a little grumpy. Ashley decided to make it quick. "If you're baking I don't want to intrude. It's just that I'm leaving for Hawaii tomorrow and I wanted to drop these off first. Merry Christmas."

"Thank you. Tati has something for you, too. At least stay long enough for tea. And just so it's very clear, I'm not baking anything. I never said I would. Tati's just trying to talk me into it." He took her coat, hung it up.

"And you're not persuaded?"

"Daddy says he does breakfast, dinner and supper and sometimes pumpkins, but that's it. But he could make cookies. Wanda says her dad helps her mom lots of times."

Exasperation appeared on Michael's face, but he kept his voice gentle.

"I told you that if you could play quietly with your doll for a little while, then after lunch we'd go hunt for a tree. So far you haven't helped me much."

"I will." Tati sat herself at the table. "After I have tea with Ashley."

"Well then, thank you. I'd love to stay for tea. Though I don't usually have it in the morning."

"We slept in a little later today."

"I see." Ashley turned to listen as the little girl described her wish list. "You want quite a lot, don't you?"

"Yeah. I'll get it, too."

"Presents aren't everything, Tati. It's the—"

"Spirit of the season," Tati finished as if she'd heard her father a hundred times before. "I remember." She sighed. "I wish you could have come to my Christmas concert at school, Ashley."

"I did, honey. I was a bit late, but I watched you." Ashley pretended not to see Michael's start of surprise. "I stayed in the back so I wouldn't disturb anyone, but I was so proud of you."

"I didn't forget one word." Tatiana's chest puffed out with pride. "Daddy bought me ice cream to celebrate."

"Good for Daddy." She risked a glance at him, found his gaze on her. "I really liked your angel dress. It was so sparkly."

"Wanda and I both had matching ones. I wish I could have had my special dress to wear."

"Your special one?" Ashley wondered if she should change the subject. Certainly Michael didn't look encouraging.

"Yes. The one I want for Christmas. I'll show you." She clambered down from her seat and dashed out of the room.

"Bad subject?" Ashley whispered.

Michael shook his head. "I've got it covered. Not exactly as shown, though."

She admired the picture of the princess dress, as Tati termed it.

"It reminds me of Piper's wedding dress," Ashley told her. "Wait till you see it." She grabbed a piece of paper and sketched out the lines of the dress. "It floats around her feet just like your princess dress."

"Do all ladies get to wear a dress like that when they have weddings?"

"Not all. Different ladies have different ideas about how they want to get married. Some don't like fancy weddings. When you're a lady you'll be able to choose whatever you want."

Ashley tried to explain about weddings to Tati, but her attention was still fixed on Michael. He kept glancing at his watch, as if she was holding him up.

"I'm sure you're busy," she said, rising as soon as she'd sipped the last of her tea. "I'll let you and Tatiana get on with your day."

"But you could stay and help us bake cookies. Couldn't she, Daddy?" Tati's beseeching voice touched a soft spot in Ashley's heart.

"She's welcome to stay and bake whatever she wants," he said quietly, meeting her glance. "In fact, I'd really appreciate it if you could stay, Ashley. Unless you're too busy?"

"But this is a time for you and Tati—"

"Daddy said he has to work for two hours," Tatiana complained. "But we could make cookies while he's working. Then we could all go get our Christmas tree. Couldn't we, Daddy?"

Ashley saw the truth as if it was written across his face.

No wonder he wasn't planning on baking cookies, he was trying to prepare something for his daughter's first Christmas with him.

"You need a break?"

"I do have some things to do," he admitted. "It's not fair to assume you'll babysit on a moment's notice, though."

"But…?"

He assumed an innocence she knew was a mask.

"But if you did happen to have some time to spare and wanted to help Tati make cookies, I wouldn't try to talk you out of it."

"While you work, I assume." She glared at him, shook her head. "Is it too hard to say, 'Ashley, can you help us out?'"

"Ashley, could you please help us out?" he repeated quietly.

"Of course. Go. Do whatever you need to do. Take all day if you want. We could even go for the tree after supper if that works for you." She stopped when he shook his head adamantly.

"After lunch would be better." Michael asked Tati to get dressed. When she'd left the room he spoke again, his voice lowered so as not to be overheard. "Our neighbor's dog was attacked by a cougar yesterday evening. I don't want to go into the woods after dark unless it's absolutely necessary."

"I see." A shiver of fear whisked across her nerve endings. Ashley shuddered. "How awful."

"Yes, it is. There's a lot of talk about hunting it down before it attacks a human. There have been reports from neighboring counties about adults being chased. One woman even had to fight it off with a stick. Fortunately for her, a deer came by and the cougar found it easier prey."

"I hope they find it before the winter festival. That

would really ruin the tourist trade. Many of the events are scheduled after dark."

He nodded but said no more as Tati returned.

"Well, Miss T.," Ashley said, hiding a smile at Tati's lace top, dirty jeans and black patent shoes. "What kind of cookies did you have in mind?"

"Gingerbread men."

Michael mouthed "thank you," then left the room. Ashley assumed he had an office or something at the other end of the house. Not that it mattered.

Thanks to her little helper they were both soon dusted in flour. They made gingerbread boys, chocolate chip mounds, pecan drops and a host of shortbread cutouts. While Tati was engaged in decorating them, Ashley mixed up some gooey chocolate squares, a batch of fudge and a chocolate cake. A withered group of apples huddled at the back of the fridge so she decided to make an apple betty. She managed to almost finish cleaning up before Tati tired of decorating the cookies.

"I'm hungry."

"So am I. Shall we make your dad some lunch?"

"Okay." Tatiana's eyes sparkled. "What should we make?"

"Vegetable soup?" She could use up what was in the fridge and he could stock up on fresh food for the holidays.

"It won't have beets in it, will it? I don't like beets."

"No beets," Ashley promised. She gave the child a peeler and set her to work on the carrots. Soon they had a pot of vegetable soup bubbling on the stove, filling the house with a delicious aroma.

But Michael did not reappear.

When the biscuits were ready, Ashley checked the clock. If they didn't eat soon, there wouldn't be time to go for a tree.

"Your daddy seems to be lost. I wonder if we should find him and tell him lunch is ready."

Tati carefully placed the last spoon on the table. "He always forgets when he goes in the workshop."

The place of his carving? "Let's go tell him, then."

With Tati leading the way, Ashley followed, until they came to a side door. Tatiana opened it.

"It's lunchtime, Daddy. Me and Ashley made soup."

Ashley didn't hear his response, she was too busy ogling the room. There were faces everywhere. A series of cunning faces arranged on the far wall were particularly fanciful, chiseled out of oddly shaped driftwood. There were larger, chunkier pieces carved out of tree trunks and logs. Thin slices of mahogany, oak and birch lay along a workbench like masks, each expression different from the next.

Entranced by the detail she saw, Ashley moved forward to inspect them more closely.

"*This* is what you do in your spare time." She turned to face him. "They're fantastic!"

"Thank you." He remained still, the chisel motionless in his hand as he watched her.

She could sense his reserve. "Why didn't you tell me?"

Michael shrugged. "I guess it hasn't really come up."

She fixed him with a look. "Hasn't it?"

"I'm hungry. Can't we eat the soup now?" Tati begged.

"We sure can, honey." Michael rose, placed his chisel on his counter, laid his leather work apron on top. But he didn't look at her.

That bothered Ashley more than the fact that he'd kept silent about his art.

She followed Tatiana out of the room, served the soup and biscuits, accepted their praise. But she couldn't get the questions out of her mind. Michael knew she was collecting works for her gallery. Why hadn't he offered some of his? Did he think Serenity Bay was too small-town to show in? Or was it her gallery he thought too small?

"Maybe you and Tatiana should go get your tree by yourselves," she offered quietly when Tati left to wash her hands and get her snow clothes ready. "It's something you should share together, not with me."

"But we'd like you to go with us." Michael shook his head. "I know what you're thinking, Ashley, and it isn't true. But I can't talk now. Wait until later. Please? I promise, there's a good reason why I didn't explain."

Sure there was. He didn't want to hurt her feelings.

She thought about it as they cleared the table together. Then she remembered the cougar.

"I suppose it would be smarter to go together," she agreed. "That way I can keep an eye on Tatiana while you cut down the tree."

"That isn't why I was asking you."

"Isn't it?" Ashley didn't know what to make of Michael's secret. But she did want to hear his explanation. "I've got my ski suit in the car. I'll go get it."

He nodded, but it was what Michael didn't say that mattered.

Chapter Eleven

Michael closed the door to Tati's room with a sigh of relief. Finally he'd get a few minutes alone with Ashley. He prayed for the right words to explain and realized there wasn't a good way to say it.

"The tree looks good, don't you think?" She looked at him with her big silver eyes and his heart started doing somersaults. "Tatiana did a great job with the popcorn strings and her star is very pretty."

"Ashley, I—"

"It's getting late. I should probably get moving." She rose, sidestepped him and headed for the door.

"Wait!"

From the way she came to a stop he knew he'd surprised her but he had to tell her—now.

"Will you let me explain about the carving?"

"You don't owe me any explanations, Michael. Your private life is your own business."

The tinge of hurt frosting the edges of those words hit him hard and he wished he'd handled this before. But regrets did no one any good.

"Please?"

She studied him for several moments, finally nodded.

He motioned to the sofa and she sat, but on the edge, as if she couldn't wait to leave.

"I've been trying to carve for ages," he began. "I earned my teaching degree, used it for a few years, but I wanted to carve. So I spent two years in New York working with Hans Leder. Have you heard of him?"

Dumb question.

"Who hasn't?" She tipped her head to one side. "He doesn't usually take students. You must have impressed him. After seeing your work I can understand why."

"I didn't carve faces then. I was more into sculpture. I even had a showing." He swallowed. "It didn't go well."

"First showings often don't." She leaned back in the chair. "Go on."

"Actually it went very badly. Hans tried. He talked to several galleries, even arranged for some of my pieces to be shown along with his. That was a mistake. The reviews were less than kind. I went back to teaching."

"But you didn't quit carving."

"I couldn't. Somehow the wood just kept calling." He laughed at himself. "That sounds stupid, but it's how I felt."

"It's not an unusual feeling for a creative person."

"I guess. Anyway, I was teaching math then. A girl came into my class midterm. Her name was Maria. She was fourteen and she had brain cancer. Inoperable."

"Oh, no."

"Yes. Maria knew she didn't have much longer, but she wanted to spend as long as she could being what she called 'normal.'" He closed his eyes, tipped his head back and remembered. "I don't think I've ever met a person who touched my spirit so deeply. Her face would wrinkle, she'd get this determined look in her eye and push for an explanation until the concept was clear to her. She was a delight to teach."

He opened his eyes to see if she understood. Ashley sat watching him, her face expressionless, except for those expressive eyes. They shone with unshed tears.

"Maria wasn't pretty but she was beautiful. Do you know what I mean?" Michael saw her nod. "From the inside, radiating out. You'd start out feeling so badly when you saw her return day after day, thinner, paler, wasting away. But Maria would have you laughing in a minute and then she'd join in."

"I wish I'd known her."

"I do, too. Anyway, I became intrigued by her personality and one evening I was fooling with a piece of wood. I could see her face in it and I began to carve her as I'd first seen her. When I was finished that, I carved another and then another, trying to catch a certain look, a glint, a spark in the likeness. She died two days after school dismissed for the summer."

"The cancer finally took over. That's sad."

"It was. Her death prodded me back into carving in a new way. I began to look at the world through Maria's eyes and because of her I saw things in people's faces, things others ignored."

"Your pieces do have fantastic insight. It's like they ask you to look behind what everyone else sees." Her gaze never left his face. "I understand wanting the time and space to create, Michael, but that doesn't explain why you couldn't tell me. Or why you had to keep it a secret."

"It wasn't really a secret," he muttered. "Okay, it sort of was."

"Because?"

It was confession time. "That showing I told you about—it did a number on my ego."

"I can imagine."

"But it was more than that." He ran his fingers through

his hair, remembering the depths his soul had plummeted to. "I was so certain that carving was what I was supposed to do, and so I plunged into it, believed I had a future. When I read those reviews I felt abandoned, as if God was mocking me. Like everyone else was."

Ashley said nothing, allowing him to feel his way through.

"Maybe that's why I became infatuated with Carissa. She was a success, doing what she loved, acclaimed all over the world."

"And next to her you felt like a failure."

"I *was* a failure." He swallowed. "At first she reminded me of Maria, always laughing, relishing life. I grabbed and held on. It was only after we were married that I saw beneath the mask."

He paused, recalling that day as clearly as yesterday. Carissa had been sitting in the hotel room, so silent he'd wondered about her mental state. Then a fan had arrived.

"Tell me, Michael." Her soft encouragement drew the words from him.

"Carissa came alive when she danced. She lived for the ballet. Without it she was lost. I realized that she'd left New York, and me, because I asked too much of her. I needed too much and she couldn't give it. No one could. It's something I had to find within myself."

"Except that you have a daughter now."

Michael nodded, wishing there was a way to avoid discussing his ex-wife. He never had before. But Ashley was different. He needed her to understand.

"Yes. But with Tati came the same old feelings—the need to prove that I was good enough, as good as her mother. That I was excellent at one specific thing."

"It sounds like you were in competition with your ex-wife."

Shame washed over his face. "In a way I guess I am."

"Why?"

"Haven't you heard Tati? My mommy this and my mommy that." He felt like a fool saying it, but in another way it was a relief to get it out. "She idolized Carissa. How do I compare to that, Ashley?"

"Why do you have to?" She leaned forward to study him. Her voice dropped. "Carissa is gone. You are Tatiana's father. Every night you get to tuck her into bed, listen to her prayers, kiss her cheek. Isn't that enough?"

"No." He raked a hand through his hair. "I know it sounds stupid, but when she talks about going to the theme park in Paris or spending Christmas in the Alps—I have nothing to compare to that."

"And you want to." She wasn't asking. "You want to hear her brag about you. But she does, Michael."

"Yeah, she talks about the sets we're building or the cupcakes—stuff like that. Stupid little things that—"

"Mean the world to her," she whispered. "You put aside your hopes and dreams, took the teaching job to support you both. When you have a spare moment, you spend it on the wood. There's nothing to be ashamed of in that. You're doing more than a lot of men who have a wife to help them."

She didn't understand. How could she?

"It isn't enough." He was going to come clean and he prayed Ashley would understand. "I had a plan, you see. I figured that if I had enough pieces and a gallery would choose some that I'd risk it again, one last time. I'd hold another showing. If I blew it—well, then I'd know I misread God, that I wasn't good enough, never would be."

"But I could have helped you with that. You know I have connections with a number of galleries. Why didn't you ask?"

He huffed his disgust. "I wasn't going to be another hanger-on, Ashley, like Kent."

"You're nothing like Kent."

He ignored that, begging her to see it through his eyes.

"Since you've come here, how many people have stopped you on the street, asked you to look at what they're doing? How many more since you've started work on the gallery?"

"Lots of them." Her mouth pursed. She shook her head at him. "I'm not going to lie and tell someone their stuff is good if I don't think it is, but at the same time, I want the opportunity to be the first to show artists from Serenity Bay. That's what my gallery is about."

The glint of hurt in her eyes forced him to realize she was on the wrong track. There could be no pretending now. Either he told her the truth and looked a fool or Ashley believed he thought her gallery wasn't good enough.

"I'm scared. Okay?" He kicked his toe against the carpet, hating the words.

"What?" She stared at him as if he'd just asked her to swim in the bay.

"I said I'm scared. I wanted to keep my little secret in the back room, get those carvings done and ship them off to someone who doesn't know me."

"Ah." She actually had the nerve to smile. "I see."

"I don't think it's funny."

"I do. I'm the one who's been confiding her fears and you're telling me you've been keeping your own secret." Ashley wagged a finger at him. "That's not playing fair."

"It's not about fairness. It's about taking the risk, doing what I told myself I'd do and living with the consequences. If what's in there is a lot of garbage, then I'll know and I can forget about my silly dreams."

"It's not garbage, Michael. Far from it."

It was his turn to smile. "Thank you. You're very kind. But you'll forgive me if I don't pin my hopes on that."

"Are you deliberately trying to be offensive?" she demanded. "I've scouted out some of the best pieces for a number of galleries across the country. I think I know what I'm talking about."

"I'm sure you do." He leaned over, brushed his knuckles against her cheek. "But you're not exactly impartial, Ashley."

"Oh. So I'd lie, tell you it was good even if it wasn't? That's insulting."

"I didn't mean it to be. I just meant—" Michael struggled with the appropriate words. "You wouldn't want to hurt my feelings. Believe me, I appreciate that."

"And if I did?" She rose, stood glaring at him. "If I told you that your work is nice, pretty, but it isn't the kind of work a gallery can promote, not the sort of carving anyone will long to collect—if I told you that, what would you do?"

"Stop carving." He didn't even have to think about it.

"Finally some truth." She slapped her hands on her hips, her eyes frosty. "That's why you kept it a secret, Michael. Not because of any of your silly reasons, but because you're afraid you'll have to hand your dream over, put it in someone else's hands. And if they say it isn't great, you're willing to stop doing what you love. That's really sad."

"I just want to get enough done for a show," he tried to explain, rising to follow as she left the room. "Where are you going?"

He didn't need to ask. She was headed for the workroom. His workroom.

"Ashley, I—"

"Hush!" She quelled his protest with one glare. He'd never seen her so angry. She picked up a sculpture of

Tati. "What were you thinking of when you did this? You weren't thinking of a showing then, were you?"

"No," he admitted.

"I can tell. It's a work from your heart." She set that one down, picked up another of his daughter. "This one is for your show, isn't it?" She inclined her head, waited for his nod. "Do you know how I can tell?"

"No." Her intuition amazed him.

"Then I'll tell you. It's not that it isn't good. It is. Very good. But the sparkle is missing. The little whimsical tilt to the eye or the uplift of the nose—I don't know. It's just not there. This piece is more intricate than the first, much more difficult, I'm sure. But it doesn't have the same presence. I can't hear her laughter when I look at it."

"Oh." Michael sat down, feeling as if he'd been sucker-punched and couldn't catch his breath.

Ashley's face softened. She walked over to stand in front of him, put her hand under his chin to force him to meet her gaze.

"I know you want a showing, Michael. You want to prove that you have what it takes, you want to stuff the critics' words in their faces and show the world. You want the satisfaction that a successful show would give, the approval sticker that you interpreted God's plan for your life correctly."

"Yes."

"But most of all I think you want to give Tati something to brag about, to get yourself onto an equal footing with Carissa, maybe even show her up. Why? Because of the way she handled Tati?"

He said nothing, because he couldn't deny it.

"I'm not saying these pieces wouldn't give you acclaim. Any gallery would take them and be happy to sell them." She leaned in, her breath whispering across his cheek. "But is that enough for you? You have so much more to give. A God-given talent to see beyond, inside, to the heart, and to let us see there too, if we're intuitive enough to look."

Her quiet words humbled him.

"Stop thinking about showing your work, Michael. Think about what's hidden in the wood, what you want to reveal. That's when you'll know you've fallen in with God's plan. That's when the sparkle will burst out of your work and draw in people who just want to see it. That's the reason Tati will be proud."

He rose, drew her into his arms, rested his chin on her head.

"You are a very smart woman, Ashley Adams."

"I know art," she shot back. "Plus, I'm very good at telling other people what they should do. Just not so good at following my own advice. But I'm trying." She tipped her head, met his gaze. "I'm really trying."

He wanted to kiss her.

But a rap on the front door drew them apart.

"Can you see who that is?" he asked. "I'm just going to check on Tati, make sure we haven't disturbed her."

"Okay." She walked out of the room, leaving him alone to get himself together.

Michael closed the studio door and was about to enter Tati's room when a sharp cry pieced the silence of the house.

"Go away!"

His walk toward the front door turned into a run as Ashley's terrified voice begged for help.

"Michael! Make him go away."

Oh God, please help.

Ashley backed away from the door, away from the face that, no matter how much she prayed, never left her dreams. She pasted herself against the wall, slid along it until she came to the kitchen. She ducked inside, grabbed a knife from the block as if it could protect her from the monster at the door.

How had he found her? Why had he come here? To take Tati?

"Ashley? What's wrong?"

"Make him go," she whispered. "Make him go away."

She heard Michael speaking, then he said something and the door closed. A moment later he was beside her, his hands easing the knife from her fingers, drawing on her arms, urging her toward the table.

"Come sit down. Come on, Ashley. You're all right. I'm here."

"Is he gone?" Her voice emerged in a croak. She surveyed the room, dared to look into the living room. No one.

"He's gone now. It's okay. You're safe."

She concentrated on breathing deeply, exhaling slowly, forcing a sense of calm onto her body. Eventually she was able to look at Michael.

"You saw him, didn't you? You saw the man at the door."

"Yes." He frowned, clearly surprised by her outburst.

"It was him! That's the man who grabbed me. Now we can call the police." She rose, reached for the phone. Michael's hand on her arm stopped her from dialing. "What's wrong?"

"Wait a minute. Just let me think this through."

She sat again while Michael frowned.

"That's the man who grabbed you when you were a child?"

"Yes. I told you that." He was acting so strangely. Ashley frowned. "Do you know him?"

"Of course. Ned Ainsworth."

"The police can find him from that." She tried to reach for the phone but again he stopped her.

"Wait!" he ordered when she pulled away. "Ashley, you can't go accusing this man of abducting you almost twenty years ago."

"Why? He did."

"Are you sure?"

Ashley froze, felt the rise of panic inside. "You don't believe me?"

"Yes, but—" He tried to take her hand, but she pulled away. "It doesn't make sense. Ned's a carver, like I am."

"Where does he live?"

"I don't know. I only met him once. Somewhere up by Cathcart House, I think. But—"

"By Piper's house?" She stared at him as the faith she'd tried so hard to bolster ebbed away. The hairs on her arm rose. "You mean he's been living near me all along? Where?"

"I don't know. That's what I'm saying. I'm not sure anyone knows anything much about Ned. I don't think he lives here year-round. When he is here, he keeps to himself." Michael flushed at her indignant glare. "I know you don't want to hear this, but I can't believe he'd do something like that, Ashley. I just can't. Tati met him when I did. She was never afraid."

"Those are the kind of people you should fear the most." She turned her back, stared at the wall, willing the tears to subside. Of all people, she'd been so sure Mick believed her. "I'd better go."

"Wait, Ashley." He gripped her shoulders, turned her to face him. "It's not that I don't believe you. It's that I think there has to be some other explanation."

"Like what?"

"I don't know," he admitted, his voice troubled. "If we could find him, you could ask him—"

"I don't ever want to talk to that man again." She struggled to keep a lid on the cauldron of worry that bubbled inside. "Besides, I'm leaving tomorrow."

"Then I'll look while you're gone." He shrugged. "There has to be some explanation. I think he's had a place around here for a long time. I can't imagine he's stayed knowing you could identify him."

"There was never a formal charge."

"No, but he'd have it constantly hanging over his head. If he was some kind of pedophile, wouldn't it have happened again? As far as I know, it hasn't."

"That's true," she admitted quietly. "I checked the newspapers. There haven't been any reports that are similar to what I experienced."

As numbness invaded she pulled on her coat and her boots.

"I'm sorry," he murmured, his face troubled. "You've come so far. And now for this to happen—it's hard."

"Maybe it's the wake-up call I needed," she whispered as she dragged on her gloves.

"What does that mean?"

She looked at him, really looked. He was a man she'd admired, had a crush on, fallen in love with. He had a rare talent for capturing expressions with his carving. He was a wonderful father to a little girl, who reached inside and grabbed her heart with both hands.

But when push came to shove he hadn't trusted her. He didn't believe her.

The sting of knowing that she'd trusted wrongly again bit deeply. Ashley forced down the tears with an iron will. She wondered how he'd react to the picture inside the flat box she'd left on the counter.

"I hope you have a very Merry Christmas, Michael. Just do me one favor, will you?"

"If I can."

"Don't let Tatiana out of your sight. If it happened once it could happen again. And I wouldn't wish what I've gone through on my worst enemy."

"Oh, Ashley." He drew her into his arms, kissed her. When she didn't respond he sighed, drew back. "Tati isn't only my child, she belongs to God, as well. He'll protect her."

She nodded, pulled open the door.

"That's what I thought," she whispered. "But look what happened. My attacker is still free. And I'm still afraid."

She closed the door and slowly walked to her car while scanning the yard for signs of the cat that had terrorized the town or the man who still had the power to terrify her.

As always, fear was her companion on the ride home.

"I wonder what Ashley's doing now," Tati murmured as she waited for Michael to braid her hair. "Do they have Christmas in Hawaii?"

"Of course. I'm sure she's getting ready to have dinner with her family, just like we are." The gift he'd shipped overnight express would have arrived by now. He wondered if she'd understand the significance.

"I think she'll go swimming today. That's what I'd do. Wanda says—"

Tuning out Wanda's sage advice, Michael finished braiding Tati's hair, tied on the pink satin ribbons and helped button the dress he'd scoured online catalogs to find.

"You look very pretty, Tati. Just like a princess."

"Thank you, Daddy." She hugged him tightly, then

pulled away, her face wistful. "Do you think Mommy's having Christmas?"

He caught his breath at the yearning that washed over her face, struggled to stuff down the imp of jealousy that danced inside.

"I'm sure she's singing carols with the angels, Tati. Or maybe dancing a special ballet for God." It was the best he could do on such short notice. "Now you go watch your new video about Baby Jesus while I get ready, okay?" He debated the next words only for a moment. "And don't open the door for anyone."

"I know, Daddy. You told me a bunch of times." She favored him with a frown then skipped out of the room and down the hall, her shoes tapping a rhythm that expressed her happiness.

Michael climbed into the shower with a prayer that the Christmas spirit would wash away all their cares and worries—if only for today. He'd just lathered his hair when Tati burst into the room.

"Ashley phoned, Daddy! I'm going to talk to her now, but you can have a turn after me."

"I'm coming," he said, to the sound of the bathroom door slamming shut.

Grumbling about her timing while his brain gave praise, Michael rinsed off, pulled on his robe and grabbed the phone by his bed.

"Daddy said we could sleep in today but I didn't sleep in. I was too awake. I was thinking about my mommy." A tiny pause. "But I'm glad you called."

"Me, too, Tati."

"Did you go swimming on Christmas?"

"Yes. I just got out of the water. I pretended it was a big snowbank and that you and I were making snow angels."

"I like swimming. And snow angels. Santa brought me a princess dress, Ashley."

"Are you wearing it now?" an amused voice asked.

"Yes. It's so pretty. It's not white. It's pink. I think that's nicer than white. And I have matching tights and—"

"Merry Christmas, Ashley."

"Merry Christmas, Michael."

Silence lasted about three seconds until Tati burst in again, explaining how much she loved the artist's set Ashley had given her.

"I already did two drawings," she said. "Daddy said they're the best he's ever seen."

"And I love the Christmas picture you gave me. You must do another so I can put it up in my gallery when it opens."

So she was coming back. He felt relief, and a bubbling joy that couldn't be quelled. Michael let his daughter babble on while he got a grip on his emotions, then spoke up.

"Give me a chance now, honey, will you?" he asked.

"Okay, Daddy. Bye, Ashley. Merry Christmas. I love you."

"I love you, too, sweetie."

The phone banged down so hard Michael winced.

"Sorry about that."

"She sounds delighted with her dress."

"Yeah. Some things are easy."

"She was talking about Carissa. Did she have a bad dream?"

"No, nothing like that." They kept the repartee of small talk going but all he wanted to ask her was if she'd forgiven him.

"She's adjusting well. I hope all her memories will remain sweet."

"Yeah."

"Are you cooking Christmas dinner?"

"Are you kidding? We're going over to Mom's. The girls are home. It will be bedlam."

"It sounds wonderful."

Another awkward pause.

"I got your gift this morning, Michael. It's beautiful. Thank you."

Disappointment welled up. She hadn't understood the significance of it.

"I called it Faith," he told her quietly.

"Yes, I saw that. It's a beautiful depiction. I don't know how you got the fingers so perfect."

He let that go. "I know I disappointed you, Ashley."

"It doesn't matter."

"Yes, it does. I didn't mean to diminish what you went through but I did and that hurt you. I apologize."

"I didn't make it up, Michael. I'm more certain than ever that it happened."

"I know."

"You believe me?" she asked, her surprise evident. "Really?"

Faith. He'd worked it out while his fingers had smoothed the rough edges of the cypress wood carving of her face. The carving still wasn't quite finished but his decision was made. Either he put his faith in her, wholeheartedly trusted her and moved on from there, or he didn't and Ashley shut him out. He chose the former.

"I believe you, Ashley."

Her silent doubt transmitted clearly across the phone line.

"That's what my carving means. I don't know why Ned did it, what caused his actions. I can't accept that he wanted to harm you, but I do believe that you were abducted by Ned."

"Thank you."

"I also have faith that you're going to get past it." He heard a sniff and his insides melted. "Don't cry," he begged, hurting at the thought of her tears. "This is supposed to be a happy day," he chided, wishing he could hold her.

"It is, isn't it?" The trembling eased out of her voice. "How did you like your gift?"

What gift? He'd seen nothing from her but Tati's present.

"You didn't find it?" she guessed. "But I left it on the counter."

"I'll have another check around. I thought we'd opened everything but the place is such a mess it could be hidden anywhere."

"I hope you like it."

"It's from you, so I know I will." This conversation was too difficult to have over the phone. "When are you coming back?"

"My ticket says the twenty-ninth."

There was that silence again.

"Do you need someone to pick you up at the airport?" he asked, knowing she'd left her car there and was perfectly capable of getting herself back to Serenity Bay.

"I'll be fine, Michael." The lilt was back in her voice. "Send my regards to your mother."

"I will."

"I'd better go. Dinner's ready. Bye."

"Goodbye, Ashley. Take care of yourself."

"You, too."

He hung on to the phone even after she'd hung up, feeling like a schoolboy.

"Aren't we going to Granny's?" Tati asked, standing in the doorway.

"Uh-huh."

"Then you have to get dressed, Daddy. You can't wear that on Christmas."

Michael glanced down, saw the robe. "Two minutes," he promised. "Give me two minutes."

As he pulled up in front of his mother's house, Michael knew exactly how he was going to spend the next few days until Ashley's return.

He was going to find Ned Ainsworth. And when he did, he'd find out the truth.

It was time.

Chapter Twelve

The big grandfather clock chimed twelve times.

"Happy New Year, Michael."

Ashley tilted her punch glass so it tinkled against Michael's and wished this night would never end. After a perfect wedding, Piper and Jason were on their way to a tropical honeymoon. Yet the guests lingered on at Cathcart House, as loathe as she to let the romantic evening end.

"Happy New Year, Ashley."

Michael's eyes glowed as dark as the chocolate fountain dripping behind him. He held her gaze as he sipped from his glass. His regard intensified the tension that always zinged between them, stretching it even more taut as the room faded into oblivion and there were only the two of them.

A moment later he lifted her glass from her hand and set both their glasses down on a nearby table.

"Don't you—"

"Shh...."

The words died in her throat as he touched her lips with the tip of his finger and drew her into his arms. He bent his head and kissed her as if he was starving.

It was a perfect kiss, the kind all teenage girls fantasize

over. Ashley had been dreaming about this moment for a long time. She twined her arms around his neck and kissed him back—until the applause grew too loud to ignore.

She peeked over Michael's shoulder and saw her friend, Rowena, clad in a gown identical to her own, holding her own glass aloft in a salute. The rest of the room watched them.

"Go, Ashley!"

Ashley tossed Rowena a look meant to kill. When that didn't work, she hid her burning cheeks against Michael's gleaming white tuxedo shirt. Michael apparently had no problem with them being the center of attention.

"It's midnight and there's mistletoe all over the place," he chided, his grin flashing. "Don't you folks have anything better to do?"

Amid the laughter he drew Ashley across the room, wrapped her cape around her and pulled on his own jacket.

"Let's go outside."

"Okay." Still half bemused, she hugged the velvet around her neck and stepped through the French doors onto the cleared deck.

"Is it too cold?" His arm found her waist, nestled her against his side.

"It's perfect," she whispered, awed by the glory of a midnight-black sky with stars sprinkled across it like diamonds scattered from a jeweler's pouch.

"You're perfect. You look lovely, Ashley."

"So do you, Mr. Groomsman. We make good wedding attendants." She smiled, but a slight sense of unease gripped her at the blackness of the valley. She twisted a little, so it was out of sight. "It was a beautiful wedding."

"Yes, it was." As if he sensed that she didn't want to talk, Michael fell silent, his gaze flickering across the gilded snow, lit by a full moon.

Ashley studied him. He'd been calling her for days, asking if they could meet, saying they needed to talk. Part of her had longed to go, but the other part fussed and fumed over what he wanted to talk about. So she'd gladly run errands for Piper and used them as an excuse when Michael called again and again.

But tonight there was no escape.

She'd have to tell him. The decisions she'd made at Christmas—to stay in the Bay, open the gallery and let God teach her to keep trusting—that had all changed after a phone call this morning. Now the doubts were tumbling around again. What did God want her to do?

"You're very quiet."

"Sorry. I was thinking about a call I received this morning." She faced him, determined to have truth between them. "I've been offered a job."

"A job? But what about—"

She squeezed his fingers, begging him to wait. Michael clamped his lips together, inclined his head. "Go on."

"It's to manage a gallery. In Paris."

"Paris? As in France?" He swallowed at her nod. "Wow! Big step up."

"Yes."

"Are you going to take it?"

She'd asked herself the same thing a thousand times. "I don't know."

"But you want to."

"Paris is the center of the art world. There is such a vibrant arts culture there. To be part of it—" She let it hang.

He exhaled. His hands dropped from her waist.

"Then you should go."

"Is that what you really think?" she whispered, longing for him to tell her to stay, to point out the negatives about a job in Paris. To tell her she was needed here.

"No."

His admission was so quiet she barely heard it. "Michael, I—"

"I want you to stay, Ashley. I want a chance to go to the winter festival with you, to go sailing in the bay. I want you here when I finally have my showing."

So he was still focused on that. She was glad. Talent like his shouldn't be wasted. Still there was something he wasn't saying. "But?"

"But you have to decide for yourself what you want to do, Ashley. Nobody else can tell you."

"I know that."

"Coming back here, facing the past—that's been very difficult for you. I realize that. Especially since you haven't found the answers you want. I wish I could have helped you there, but I have to admit I've failed."

"What do you mean?" She frowned. Something sad, almost defensive, underlaid his words. "Failed at what?"

"I've been doing some investigating, talking to people. About Ned Ainsworth."

Anger surged up like a geyser. Ashley squeezed her fingers tighter into the soft smooth velvet of her cape but remained silent.

"If you could just talk to him, get his side of the story."

"Do you think anything he said would erase the nightmares I've had?" She met his steady stare, refused to back down. "Do you really imagine some paltry excuse from him would make it better, Michael?" She thrust out her chin. "Not going to happen."

"Sweetheart, what's the alternative? Bury it deep down inside and let it fester a little longer?" He shook his head, his eyes brimming with sympathy, but determination, too. His hands gripped her arms. "This one incident has haunted you for more than half your life, Ashley. You've already said you had bad dreams, that you stayed away from the Bay because of fear. When you did come back, you had to talk yourself into it."

"And you think I should add a little more fear, open myself to the lies and distortions some maniac has to offer?" She jerked out of his grip. "I don't think that's very good advice, *Dr.* Masters."

He stared at her for several moments, the hurt in his eyes visible. But Ashley couldn't back down. The thought of being anywhere near that man—

"Why are you so afraid of the truth?"

She couldn't believe what she'd heard. "You, more than anyone, should know how I've tried to get past my past. How dare you say that to me?"

"I have to say it, Ashley." He cupped her face so she was forced to look at him. "I'm in love with you."

The words, emphatic and clear in the midnight air shocked her. Ashley swallowed, struggled to organize her thoughts. But Michael didn't give her time. He spoke again, his voice earnest.

"I never thought I'd fall in love again, never wanted to even risk the possibility. But I see now that God had something else in mind, that's why He brought both of us here." One finger traced the angle of her jaw. "I fell in love with you in spite of all my plans, Ashley. You walk into the room and my heart takes off like a jet plane. You're here." He patted his chest. "Inside my heart. I couldn't get you out even if I wanted to. And I don't."

"Michael, I—"

She was afraid of this—afraid of hearing him say what they'd danced around for so long.

"I want to begin thinking about the future, what we can build and share together. I thought you'd come to a decision, that opening the gallery meant you were ready to look beyond—" He stopped, let his hands fall away as he regrouped. His face changed, firmed somehow.

She needed to stop him, to stem words that once spoken couldn't be taken back, but Michael kept going.

"Maybe I was expecting too much too soon. That's okay. I can wait, because I think what we could share is worth waiting for. But I hate seeing you stuck in the past."

"I'm not!"

"Aren't you?" His sad, knowing smile reached out and squeezed her heart. "Your hands shake when your mask slips and you can't cover the fear fast enough, Ashley. Even when you came out here tonight, you did a quick check, just in case there was something bad lurking. Didn't you?"

"I can't help my reactions. I'm trying," she protested trying to ignore the persistent hum of anxiety that never quite went away.

"Are you really trying?"

"Of course."

"Then what is this talk about a new job?" He grasped her hands to stop her from turning away. His dark gaze met hers. His voice dropped to a whisper. "Why now, when you've got the gallery almost ready, would you even consider leaving?"

"It's a great opportunity." Ashley could tell from the look on his face that he wasn't buying that. She scrambled to justify herself. "It's not every day someone dangles a job in Paris in front of my nose. It's something I've wanted to do for a long time."

"Is it?" He didn't look convinced. "I think you're running away."

"Why do you say that? Can't I change my mind?" But there was more to it than that and pretending otherwise was childish.

"What about us, Ashley?"

"I don't know." She frowned, trying to sort it out.

"You told me once before that you had to get the fear sorted out before you could talk about a relationship. I could see the damage the past was doing to you and I agreed. Now I wish I hadn't."

"What damage?" she whispered.

Michael just looked at her. "You know."

She did.

"Maybe it's for the best." He sighed. "If you're this unsure about your future, if you think running to Paris will make you feel safe, then I guess I have my answer."

"I never said I was going...yet. I said I have to think about it. But we can still be friends," she hurried to assure him. "That won't change."

"It already has." His dark eyes brimmed with hurt and anger and a yearning that reached out to touch her soul. "Don't you understand? I want more than just friendship, Ashley. I want to start thinking about a future with you. I want to marry you."

She gasped, shocked to hear him admit it out loud. He smiled.

"I'm not saying we have to get married tomorrow or next week. But I thought—hoped—we could start looking toward the future. I see now that you aren't able to do that."

So soft, so quiet the words. She could hear how much it cost him to admit that.

"I'm sorry, Michael. I really am." She pressed her palm against his chest to emphasize her point. "You know I care for you. More than I've ever cared for anyone. But I'm just not ready to commit to anything more than what we have now."

"And what is it that we have, Ashley?" The chill in his voice worried her. "What exactly is it? A few stolen kisses here and there, you playing house with Tati?"

He sounded angry, bitter. She drew back, hid her hands inside her cape. "I'm sorry if that isn't enough."

"No, it's not enough," he snapped. "You're creating some kind of fairy-tale world so you'll feel safe. It's not fair to any of us."

"Fairy tale? I don't know what you mean." Ashley began to wonder if she knew him as well as she thought. Those melting eyes hardened into chips of black ice, his face tightened to chiseled marble. She stepped back, shocked by the anger in his next words.

"Do you think I don't hear you with her? You organize each detail, plan and strategize everything. There's no spontaneity because you have to think about all the what-ifs and take precautions in case this monster of fear attacks you." He shoved his hands in his pockets, glared at her. "I've heard you warning her over and over to be careful, to watch out, to check, to make sure."

"There's a cougar out there, in case you've forgotten."

"Yes, there is." He nodded. "And there are rough boys in her day care who could beat her up. Tati might get cut when she goes skating. I might get an incurable disease and not be there for her. They're all possibilities."

"So?" She frowned. This sourness, this wasn't like him.

"Can't you see it, Ashley?"

"See what?"

"How this one thing from your past is impacting everything in your life? Not just how you manage. You cope in your own way, I know that, and maybe that's enough for you. But it's gone beyond just you now. Your fear affects how you deal with everyone else."

The wind picked up. He stepped closer as if to shield her, pushed the hair from her eyes.

"Do you think Tati hasn't picked up on your attitude? She has, Ashley, and it's changed her. She doesn't rush into life the way she once did. Lately she's nervous, fusses if I'm late. At night she asks what-if questions."

"I'm sorry, but I don't think it's a bad thing to be aware." Ashley swallowed her denial when Michael shook his head, his frustration evident.

"I'm not talking about awareness and you know it." He stopped, waited as someone else checked the patio then went back inside. When he spoke again his voice was softer, calmer. "Before Christmas, before you left, you said you were going to try to trust God."

"I am trying. Every day."

"Are you? Really?" Michael's eyes met hers and there was no hiding. "Then why can't you trust God to learn the truth and then to get you through whatever really happened?"

The words hit her like a ton of bricks, each one breaking through to her subconscious. Like a snake uncoiling, the fear rose inside her, seeping through her body until every nerve was taut.

"I *know* what happened! That's what you don't seem to understand. I was there, Michael. I lived it."

He didn't flinch.

"Then why haven't you gone to the police, Ashley? Filed a report, asked them to investigate Ned—done everything you could to stop him from hurting someone else? If you're so sure his intention was to hurt you, why haven't you done something?"

"It's too long ago—"

"I know all the reasons you'll quote, Ashley." Michael smiled, ticked them off on his fingers. "It happened too long ago, your parents didn't believe you, there's no evidence, my mother didn't see anyone. Everyone thought you imagined it. Even you thought that for a while."

"Why are you doing this?" she whispered as the tears welled. "Why do you keep pushing me?"

"Because I love you and I don't want to see you hurting any more." He didn't touch her physically, but she felt imprisoned by the steady knowing light in his eyes. His breath brushed over her like a caress. "You're afraid to live, Ashley. You've already wasted years letting fear eat away at your life, taking control of who you are, of what you can and can't do."

He held his hands palms up, as if offering her something.

"Aren't you tired of it? Don't you want to be free?"

She shook her head slowly as the truth flared in her brain. "I'll never be free of what happened to me. It's part of who I am."

Michael stepped back as if she'd physically pushed him away. His face whitened, but he remained still. After several moments he spoke, but pain echoed through his low throaty voice.

"It's part of who you *were,* sweetheart. It doesn't have to be part of who you are now. Not unless you let it."

"Michael, I—"

"No, don't say anything else. Let it go." He closed his eyes, shook his head, sighed. "I've been a fool. It doesn't matter what I say, the only way you're going to break free of this snowbank of fear that's got you imprisoned is to face it down. I realize now that you're not ready to do that. I'll pray God will help you, Ashley. I don't think anyone else can."

He looked at her for several moments, as if storing up a mental picture of her. Then he walked toward the door.

"Wait, Michael. What—"

He didn't turn around.

"If you need me, if you decide to stay, if you want to

meet with Ned—" His breath whooshed out. "I'm here, Ashley. I love you, and more than anything in the world I want you to be whole. But I can't live looking over one shoulder at the past. When you're ready to look at the future with me, all you have to do is call me. I'll be here."

Then he opened the door, slipped through and closed it quietly behind him. The silence was deafening.

"Daddy?"

"Yes, sweetie?"

"Why doesn't Ashley come to visit me anymore? Did I do something wrong?"

Michael closed his eyes and prayed for the wisdom to be the parent Tatiana needed.

"You didn't do anything wrong, Tati. Ashley's been very busy with her new gallery. And she's helping Piper with the winter festival. She's very busy."

"She said that yesterday."

"You saw her? When?"

"When we went to the library. All the kids get to go on Thursdays, you know that."

Yes, he did. He also knew how many times he'd longed to drive up to the house on the hill and bang on the door, demanding Ashley tell him whether or not she was leaving. But he'd heard nothing from her for weeks.

Maybe it was better that way.

"Tomorrow her gallery is opening. Can we go?"

"Tati, I'm not sure Ashley would want us—"

"She wants me to come. She said I should bring my picture so she can hang it up. Can we go, Daddy? Please?"

Those big eyes reached into his soul and Michael knew he couldn't deny her. "Okay, we'll go tomorrow afternoon. Grannie's going to take you to the play in the evening while

I work backstage. Then we're going to Piper's house for a party. How does that sound?"

"Good!" Tati wrapped her arms around his neck and squeezed as hard as she could. "Thank you, Daddy. I love you this much."

"I love you, too, sweetie. Now it's time to sleep."

"Are you going to work in your shop?" she asked, clouds filling her wise eyes.

"For a while. But I'll have the monitor. If you call, I'll hear you."

"Okay." But she didn't lie back. Instead she scanned the room. "It couldn't get in the window, could it, Daddy? Wanda says cougars can break into a house if they're really hungry."

"Wanda's not right about that," he said, wishing Wanda would keep her thoughts about that marauding cougar to herself. "The glass is too heavy. Anyway, the blinds are closed so he wouldn't be able to tell you're in here. You're safe here with me, sweetheart. And if you start to worry, you know what to do."

She nodded. "Pray."

"That's right. God will always hear you." He tucked her in, gave her a butterfly kiss and waited for the giggle that completed their ritual. "Sleep tight," he whispered as he switched off the light.

Michael waited a few minutes until he was sure Tati was settled, then he entered his workroom, setting the monitor on a table. A cursory glance around the room drew a frown of worry. Were they good enough? Would anyone want to display his work?

Would he ever make it as an artist?

The phone broke through his self-doubts.

"Hi, honey. Are you working?"

"Hi, Mom. Just got Tati to bed. What's up?"

"I've just had word that a friend of mine is going in for major surgery tomorrow afternoon and I'd like to be there for her. But I promised to take care of Tati while you're working the sets for the play. I was wondering if you'd mind if I took her with me. I might stay over."

"Mom, you don't want Tatiana in a hospital."

"Well, you can't keep her backstage, either."

"No." He stifled the sigh. Despite his original protests Michael had come to enjoy the play and the actors, even agreed to be set manager. He couldn't very well quit the day of the final rehearsal. "I'll find someone to watch her, Mom. You go, be with your friend."

"You're sure? I could ask Ashley—"

"I'll handle it. Thanks."

"What happened, son? I thought you cared about her."

"I do. But Ashley doesn't feel the same way."

"Oh. I'm so sorry."

"Yeah. Me, too," he said with heartfelt sadness.

"Keep trusting God, Michael. He'll see you through it."

"Thanks."

"Don't bother looking after the house while I'm gone. Ida Cranbrook will stop over. She and Harold overheard me on the phone at the coffee shop."

"Okay. Have a good trip."

After he'd hung up, he stared at the snapshot he'd pinned to the wall before Christmas—Ashley laughing as she chucked a snowball at him. His heart squeezed at the emptiness of life without her.

Why bring her here if not to heal her fear? Why can't I push her out of my heart if she's not Your choice?

The questions never changed and answers weren't forthcoming. For the first night in a very long time Michael gave up on any idea of carving, switched off the lights, and, after a quick check on Tati, returned to the living room. He lit a fire then sank down beside it with his Bible in hand. It fell open to Ecclesiastes.

"Everything is meaningless," says the Teacher, "utterly meaningless! What do people get for all their hard work? Generations come and go, but nothing really changes."

"That's depressing," Michael mumbled, but he kept reading, hoping for some ray of light that would explain his current predicament. He pressed on through twelve chapters, his heart searching. In the final verse of the final chapter Michael read,

Here is my final conclusion; Fear God and obey His commands, for this is the duty of every person. God will judge us for everything we do, including every secret thing, whether good or bad.

Every secret thing. Every secret thing.
Why did that stick in his mind?
He glanced at the opposite wall where Ashley's Christmas gift, a charcoal drawing of Tati, hung. She'd captured his daughter's every nuance from her tip-tilted nose to her dusty cheeks and mud-spattered overalls, half in, half out of her boots.
Carissa would never have allowed such a picture to hang on her wall. Carissa had been all about perfection. In her dancing, in her costumes, in her life. She'd risen to the top of her field because she gave nothing less than her best. And people applauded that.
Michael froze, caught the thought and held it.
People's applause. Did it really mean so much?
How many times had his daughter raved about her

mother and the hordes of fans who asked for her autograph after a performance, the people who flocked to the side doors just to catch a glimpse of her? Carissa, whom adoring fans mourned, whom newspapers applauded, whom his own mother had revered—was he envious of her fame, of her ability to make people notice her?

Michael set aside his Bible, walked back to his workroom and studied the pieces he'd selected to show. Shutting out all emotion he assessed them clinically.

Except for a few, they were showy pieces, larger-than-life faces that didn't require analysis to discern their meaning. The majority were crowd pleasers, faces that would draw a laugh or two.

Yet there, in the middle of them all, sat Maria, staring at him.

The contrast in his work bowled him over. He sank down on his carving stool, stunned by the differences between the pieces. Why? How had he managed to create something totally unique in some and settled for "good enough" in the others?

Ashley's words echoed with haunting clarity.

Stop thinking about showing your work. Think about what's hidden in the wood, what you want to reveal. That's when you'll know you've fallen in with God's plan.

Suddenly he understood why that first showing had been a disaster. He hadn't found the glory because he hadn't given his customers anything to think about. The question was, would another show follow the same path?

Michael turned a piece of mahogany over and over, but no picture sprang to mind. For once his mind was too busy assimilating the truth he'd kept hidden inside for so long.

He couldn't compete with Carissa. He couldn't give his daughter a fine home, fancy clothes, a rich and famous lifestyle. And even if he could, what good would it do to diminish his daughter's mother by trying to outdo her? Tati loved Carissa. She had only memories to cling to. It was his job, as her father, to help her keep those intact.

The truth was, it wasn't just Tati he'd been trying to impress.

What he really wanted was to prove to Ashley Adams that his work—that *he*—was as good as anyone she'd ever find, including whatever was in Paris.

Chapter Thirteen

The Adams Gallery.

Smooth brass letters pressed against the stacked stone wall were classically cool and elegant. Totally Ashley. Michael stepped through the front door and swallowed.

She'd created a home for beauty.

He held tightly to Tatiana's chubby fingers as they stepped out of the foyer into the main rooms. Simple plain walls stood stark and bare save for the pieces Ashley had displayed in a wash of natural and artificial light.

"Daddy, look!"

Tati's tug on his sleeve drew his attention to a long narrow window on the right, in what was once the dining room. Framed by the window stood—Faith?

He couldn't believe it. He moved nearer to get a better look. The sculpture he'd given her for Christmas perched atop a white cube, catching the light from outside and reflecting it back.

Michael stared at the polished black walnut, his fingers curling as he remembered how he'd felt releasing the image. A hand reached upward, into the light, pressing through a heavy covering of black so that each fingertip, each knuckle, each flexing muscle was revealed.

"It's beautiful, isn't it?" a woman said. "I've looked at it from many different angles and I see something new each time." She pointed to the palm of the hand cupping the little bit of paper he'd enclosed at the last minute, naming his gift. "It's called Faith. I wonder who the artist is."

"My daddy—"

Michael shushed Tati before she could say anything. The woman smiled then moved away to examine a brilliant blue weaving. Only then did Michael notice the small plaque on the clear plastic case covering Faith. Not for sale.

"Hi Ashley." Tati's cheerful voice drew his attention.

Michael turned, saw the woman who inhabited his dreams standing across the room, speaking to someone. He was about to hush his daughter again when Ashley grinned, waved and after murmuring something to her guest, hurried toward them.

"Hello, sweetie," she said, hugging Tati. "Michael." Her gaze never quite met his. "Did you bring your picture, Tatiana?"

"Yes." Tati waved the sheet she'd created.

"Good. Let's you and I go hang it up while your daddy has a look around." She glanced at him. "It's okay, isn't it?"

"If you have time." He watched them leave, his heart thumping madly as he noted the hollows in her cheeks and the narrowness of her waist. Clearly she hadn't yet resolved her problems. But at least Ashley was still here and not in Paris.

"Excuse me." The man Ashley had been speaking to touched his arm. "I understand you're Faith's creator."

Michael smiled. "I think that distinction belongs to God. But if you mean the sculpture, yes, it's mine. Or rather Ashley's. I gave it to her."

"Nice gift." He thrust out a hand. "Ferris Strang."

"Michael Masters. You're visiting Serenity Bay for the winter festival?"

"Mostly to see Ashley's gallery. I was half hoping it would be horrible and she'd have to come back and work for me. I should have known better."

"She's certainly talented." Michael moved from one exhibit to the next, amazed by the details she'd thought to include. Nothing had been left to chance.

Strang followed him through the building, pointing out things Michael wouldn't have noticed.

"Clever to hide the lights in here," he said when they moved down the hall. "The natural light is great but on a cloudy day the pieces need a boost. The ordinary person wouldn't notice the subtleties but Ashley has a way of honing in on these things. I've never met anyone more adept at display."

By the time they arrived in the sunroom where Ashley was just emerging from the kitchen, Michael had to agree.

"It's perfect," he told her quietly. "You've done a fantastic job."

"Thank you." She motioned toward the kitchen. "I've just put on a pot of coffee. Are you two interested?"

"I'm more interested in what else your friend has done," Ferris hinted.

"Of course. Michael, why don't you—"

"Actually, I don't have anything I want to show at the moment," he interrupted, ignoring Ashley's surprised look. "I'm in the middle of revising my approach."

"From the looks of that piece out there, I don't think you should. It's an amazing work. I interpret it as an inner struggle, to break free of the doubts and believe. Am I close?"

"Exactly." Michael nodded. He accepted the coffee from Ashley, sat where she indicated. Tati was busy at the table creating a new picture, her tongue peeking out from be-tween her lips.

"Ashley mentioned you're a teacher."

"Yes, I teach a shop class at the high school. We built the sets for the play that's starting tonight."

"I see." His nose turned up just the tiniest bit. "Will you send me some pieces when you're ready? I'd be interested in seeing them."

Michael couldn't look away from Ashley, though she barely looked at him.

"That's a good idea, Michael. You have some great pieces and Ferris puts on wonderful shows. I know that's what you were working toward…"

The words flowed past, but he barely heard them. His mind was too busy realizing that she was distancing her-self. He faced the truth. She would leave, move on as best she could, still carrying that daunting fear, never quite free. Managing.

He couldn't bear to think of all she'd miss.

In that instant Michael made up his mind to do the only thing he could for a woman he would always hold in his heart.

"Tell you what, Ashley. I'll give the Adams Gallery first dibs if I decide to sell. If you think any would suit Ferris, you go ahead. Minus your commission, of course."

"But I wouldn't dream of—" A customer interrupted and Ashley left to deal with her inquiry, but only after frowning at him.

Michael ignored her glower, rose, set his cup in the sink and picked up his daughter's jacket. "Come on, Tati. I've got to go to the school and get the sets organized for the play tonight."

"But I'm not finished with my picture." Her cupid's mouth set in the stubborn line that spelled trouble.

Michael wasn't in the mood to bargain.

"You can finish it there. The art kit Ashley gave you for Christmas is in the car. Okay? Now let's go." He zipped up her jacket, pulled on her mittens and buttoned his own coat. "Nice to meet you, Ferris. I hope we see you at the party tonight."

"Well, I don't know—"

"Good. See you." Michael didn't stick around to hear the rest of it. An idea flickered at the back of his mind. He needed to get out of here, needed time and space to think things through.

Ashley frowned, fluttered a hand when Tati called goodbye, though she didn't move from her patron. That was okay with Michael. He just wanted to escape.

He drove toward the school with thoughts circling his brain like bees near honey. The dress rehearsal plodded on with a thousand flaws. He listened to each request the director made, adjusted the sets as best he could, all the while watching Tati busily drawing her picture.

When everything was set, every last detail in place, he gathered up his daughter and packed her and her art supplies into the car.

"This isn't the way home. Where are we going, Daddy?"

"We're going on a little errand. It shouldn't take long."

He pulled up in front of the town office, his mother's voice echoing. Ida Cranbrook. Why hadn't he thought of her before? Ida made it her business to know everything that had anything to do with Serenity Bay. As town clerk she certainly ought to be able to tell him where to find Ned Ainsworth.

It took Ida four phone calls to adjacent counties and a talk with one of the oldest members of Serenity Bay, but by the time Michael left he had a piece of paper with a name and a phone number.

"Please let it be enough," he prayed as he headed for the fast-food joint that would fulfil Tati's demand for supper. While they were there they met Wanda and her mother.

God must have approved Mick's plan because his daughter was invited for a sleepover at her best friend's home, leaving him free to carry out his idea.

Cathcart House teemed with people. Piper and Jason had invited everyone who'd assisted in any way with the winter festival, and it seemed that no one had declined.

Ashley refilled coffee carafes, stacked canapes on platters and generally assisted as best she could until Piper caught her and insisted Rowena do something to get their friend to mingle among the guests.

"This is a night to celebrate. Don't you dare let her hide out in the kitchen, Row."

"Yes, ma'am!" Rowena slipped her hand through Ashley's arm and drew her among the milling crowd. "It's quite a tribute to our Pip, isn't it?"

"She deserves it. She's put in hours on this project. Jason, too." Ashley sipped her fruit punch, trying to pretend a nonchalance she didn't feel.

"He's over in the corner, watching you."

"Who?"

Rowena shook her head. "Oh, Ash. Don't you know you can't fool me? I know you." She tugged on her arm. "Come on, you can reintroduce me to Michael. I must say he's improved a lot over the past ten or so years."

"No!" Ashley jerked to a halt, grimaced at the sticky sweetness that spilled over onto her fingers from the punch glass. "Stop teasing, Row. It's not funny."

"No, I can see that." Rowena met her glare, warm sympathy lurking in the depths of her eyes. "I'm sorry, sweetie. I know you care about him."

"I don't want to talk about it." She motioned to the left. "Did you meet the man who plays the lead in the play? He's right over here." Ashley drew her friend toward the burly bearded fellow who'd brought the stage to life.

"We'll talk later," Row whispered before she was drawn into another conversation.

Ashley ignored that, kept herself busy moving from group to group, accepting compliments on the gallery, speaking to the friends she'd made. But her eyes disobeyed and kept returning to Michael.

He finally approached her when the crowd had thinned out and only a few people were left.

"Ashley, I need to talk to you. It's important."

She wore a white mohair sweater and matching wool slacks that were fully lined but still she felt a cold shiver of apprehension crawl up her nerves.

"You didn't bring Tatiana?"

"No, she's staying with Wanda. A sleepover." He frowned. "Can we talk? In the den?"

"I thought we'd said it all last time," she murmured, praying her friends would be too busy to notice them.

"Not quite." He had her arm and was leading her toward the study.

Ashley followed, wondering what more there was to add. He'd basically told her goodbye on New Year's Eve.

He drew her into the room, closed the door and stood in front of it. She frowned, wondering at the odd look on his face. She followed his glance, gasped and reached for the doorknob as panic filled her body.

"Get him out!" she panted. "Get him out of here."

"Wait a minute. Just hear me out. Ned didn't kidnap you, Ashley. I asked him and he said—"

"What does it take to get through to you?" she snapped, shoving her shaking hands into her pockets as she gauged the distance between herself and her nemesis. She glared at Mick. "I do not want to talk to this man. Ever. I do not care what he has to say. I do not care what you have to say."

"But if you'd only listen."

"*You* listen, Michael Masters." She moved until she was only inches from him. "You know how I feel." She didn't care that her voice sounded raw, only that her heart was breaking. "You of all people know. The fact that you could bring him here, into this house where I'm living—" She shook her head, fought for a measure of control.

"Ashley, listen."

She pushed past him, gripped the doorknob and pulled open the door as she drew a calming breath.

"I trusted you, Michael. How could you do this?"

"I wish you would trust me, Ashley. But more than that, I wish you'd trust God."

"Get out. And don't come back. Either of you."

She pulled the door closed behind her, turned into the hall and climbed the stairs. Once inside her room she locked the door. A long time later Piper knocked and asked if she was all right.

"I'm fine, Pip. It was a lovely party. I'm going to sleep."

"Okay."

Silence. Then Rowena scrabbled at the door.

"I won't go away until you open it."

She'd expected that. Ashley rose, calmly walked across the room and opened the door.

"I'm fine, Rowena. Really. Just a little tired. I'll see you in the morning, okay?"

"You're sure? Michael said—"

"I'll *see* you in the morning." She quietly closed the door, twisted the lock. Then she prepared for bed, but before she climbed into the big four-poster she checked the window lock and rechecked the door.

He knew where she was. He'd actually been here. That was bad enough.

But the deep twisting hurt of knowing that Michael had led him straight to her burned more deeply than she could have dreamed.

She curled up into a ball under the downy quilt and pretended to sleep.

Tomorrow she'd leave for Paris.

Chapter Fourteen

"Ashley! Ashley, wake up. Please wake up."

The panic in Piper's voice drew her back from the edge of the nightmare. She flicked on the lamp, hurried to open the door.

"What's wrong?"

"It's Tati. She and Wanda are missing."

"Missing?" She tried to comprehend what Piper was saying.

"The girls were having a sleepover at Wanda's. Wanda's mom said they went outside to play on the new swing set. When she went to check they were gone. With a storm blowing in and all those cougar reports, everybody's worried. A search party has been formed. They're going out to look. I thought you might like to help."

"Yes." Ashley scrambled for clothes.

"Jason and I are supposed to coordinate things so we're leaving immediately. Once you're ready, you and Rowena can check in and see where you'd be needed most. She's making coffee."

"Okay. Thanks."

"Pray, Ash. They're just little girls and they've already been gone for over an hour." Piper didn't say all the things that could go wrong. She didn't have to. Her face tele-graphed her worry.

Ashley knew the dangers of being lost in these woods as well as she. The nights were frigid. Hypothermia was only a matter of time. And then there was that cougar. There had been reports of stalking, animals ravaged. If they didn't find the girls soon...

A new thought rushed in, supplanting all the others. Ashley grabbed her socks, rushed downstairs.

"Piper," she called as her friend was about to close the front door. "Where is Wanda's home?"

"If you didn't take the turn at the top of the hill that leads here but kept going across the hills you'd come to it. There." She pointed.

"Okay. Just one more thing."

Piper frowned, but waited.

"Do you know where Ned Ainsworth lives?"

"That's funny. I'd never heard of him until Ida was talking about him yesterday," Piper mused. "Why do you want to know?"

"Just tell me," she begged, unwilling to get into it now.

"I can't. I don't know. Hang on." She pulled out her cell phone, dialed. "Ida, can you tell me where Ned Ainsworth lives? You were talking about him yesterday. Michael did? Oh. Okay. Thanks." She flipped the phone closed. "He's on an acreage past Prime Vista Road."

"Where's that? I've never heard of it."

"It's only recently been opened to public traffic. Past Lookout Point somewhere."

"Piper?" Jason stuck his head in the door. "We have to go, honey."

"I'm coming." She hugged Ashley. "You and Row take your cell phones. The coordinating center is my number at the town office. If you find anything, call there. Be careful, okay?"

"You, too."

The door closed behind her. Ashley bent to pull on her thick socks, dragged on ski pants, then a pair of warm hiking boots she'd purchased a few weeks ago. She turned to find Rowena capping a couple of thermoses.

"How long till you're ready?"

"Just have to put on my coat." She pushed cups, thermoses, some cookies and a couple of wrapped sandwiches into a backpack. "In case we find them and they're hungry."

"Good thinking. I'll get my car. Meet you out there."

Thankfully, Ashley remembered she had a full tank of gas. Rowena had barely closed the car door before they were heading out of the yard and down the road Piper had indicated.

"Um, do you know where we're going?" Row asked as she buckled her seat belt.

"I have a hunch I want to check out." Even the thought of it kept her fingers clenched around the steering wheel, but though the old clammy fear threatened to swamp her, Ashley refused to back down. Not now. If he'd taken the girls she was going to know, and then she was going to stop him.

For good.

Rowena said nothing more as they bumped and slid down the rutted hill, perhaps because she was too busy hanging onto the armrest. When they finally came to a small narrow track, Ashley shifted into four-wheel drive.

"Ash, are you sure this is where you want to go?"

"I'm sure." Then, because she couldn't bottle it inside anymore she told the whole story, how she'd seen Ned several times, how the fear had overtaken her life, driven a wedge between her and Michael. "It's probably a stupid idea and one I'll regret, but I'm going to face down Ned Ainsworth, Row. If it is him, if he's taken the girls, I'm going to get them back. And then I'll make sure he never does it again."

"And if it isn't him? What if you're wrong?"

Ashley didn't have an answer to that. She pulled into the yard, turned off the engine.

"I have to do this, Row. For Tati, for Michael, but most of all for me. I should have done it long ago."

"Your hands are shaking."

"Everything I own is shaking. I'm scared stiff and I can't catch my breath, but I'm not leaving here until I know." She glanced at her friend. "Will you come with me to the door?"

"Try and stop me."

They walked through the drifting snow that blew off the roof and covered the path. Ashley rapped on the door, then stepped back, praying as she never had before.

"Nobody seems to be home. But there's a truck in the shed." Rowena tried the door handle of the house. "It's open." She pushed inside, glanced around. "There's a fire going. I'd guess he's around here somewhere."

Ashley remained glued to the doorstep. Suddenly she heard a noise. She wheeled around. Across the yard at the edge of a cliff, a hand appeared. Ned. Grabbing onto the saplings he pulled himself up. A child lay across his shoulders.

"Rowena!"

Ashley raced across the snow, falling several times in the swirling drifts, but each time picking herself up until she was within three feet. Then fear took over and she froze.

"Help her," he gasped.

"What have you done? Oh, what have you done?" She lifted the child from his arms, pushed back the hood. It wasn't Tatiana.

"Take her to the house, Ash. I'll help him," Rowena ordered.

Ashley didn't understand why he needed help, but she did understand the splint on the little girl's arm. She pushed inside the house, laid the child on a sofa.

"Are you okay, sweetheart?" she whispered as the eyelashes fluttered. "What's your name?"

"Wanda. You have to help Tati. She hurt her head when we fell into the water."

"Water?" Ashley's blood ran cold. The falls were near here, weren't they? Tons of rushing water—enough to sweep away a little girl if someone didn't stop her.

"We didn't mean to go out of the yard," Wanda sobbed. "We only wanted to get one of the big sticks from the tree—for the snowman's arms. I slid down the hill and Tati had to rescue me. But we couldn't stop. She went in the water and then I couldn't see her for a while. When she got out she had a big cut on her head. She said her tummy hurt."

Ashley shared a worried look with Row, who was helping Ned sit. How badly? she wanted to ask.

"They must have fallen down a ridge," Ned's gruff voice explained. "I found tracks to a cave. I'm pretty sure the other child is in there." He rose, wavered a little, grabbed a chair to support himself. "It's rough terrain. I slipped myself."

That's when Ashley saw his blood-soaked leg and the gash that needed stitches.

"I can't get her alone. One of you will have to help me."

"I'll do it." Rowena found the first aid kit he pointed out and began wrapping his leg.

Ashley took a deep breath. "No, I'll go. She doesn't know you, Row."

"Whichever of you is going, we have to hurry. I saw cougar tracks following hers." Ned reached for his rifle but grabbed the mantel instead, then collapsed in a chair. "You'd better call for help," he whispered just before his head lolled back.

"He's out," Rowena muttered. She made sure his leg was elevated then began removing Wanda's coat. "Let's have a look at you, sweetie."

Ashley heard and saw everything as if through a fog. Her gaze rested on the man who'd filled her dreams for years. That coat—she knew that coat. It was older, more ragged now, but it was the same horrid shade of green.

She gasped at the sight of the faded, shabby crest on the right arm, thought back to that April day. It was as if she was young again. She felt those arms close around her, relived the terror of being shoved in that car.

"Ash, what's wrong with you? Call Piper. Get us some help up here."

Ashley dialed automatically, explained.

"Ned Ainsworth's. We have Wanda. Her arm, I think. We need Michael, some rescue people and some medical help. I'm going after Tati," she whispered, staring at Ned's unconscious body.

"No. Stay where you are."

"I can't. Ned says he saw cougar tracks. I have to get Tati. I have to, Piper." She hung up, slipped the phone into her pocket and pulled on her gloves.

"Ashley, you can't go down there by yourself," Rowena protested. "You have to wait for help."

"I can't leave her alone, not with that cat out there. I'll use the rope he used to climb down."

"Take the rifle."

"I don't know how to use it, Row. And even if I did, I can't climb with it. I'll figure out something else to keep her safe. Just get some help down there as fast as you can." She saw a box of matches and a flashlight on the mantel. They went into her pocket. She zipped it closed, saw Wanda's dry coat and tucked it into a bag that she slung over one shoulder. "To keep her warm. Okay. I'm going."

Rowena hugged her. "I'll be praying, Ash. You know that. God will be there with you. Just call on Him."

"I have been since we left Piper's." She glanced around once more, then let herself out.

The snow fell harder now. The wind swirled it around, almost obliterating Ned's bloody tracks. She gulped down her fear, kept her focus on the point where she'd watched him climb over the ridge. Once there, Ashley dug the rope out of the snow and began her climb down.

"Our relationship wasn't a total write-off, Kent. At least you taught me the basics of rock-climbing," she muttered as she lowered herself over the precipice and began feeling with her boot for something to use as a toehold.

Slowly, carefully, she crept down, thankful for the security of the rope to support her. Her arms ached like fire. Finally she was at the bottom. She whispered a breath of thanks. It was darker here, somehow colder, though the wind wasn't nearly as sharp. Ashley eased away from the wall, took her bearings then sought for something to show her where to go.

A cave, he'd said. She glanced around, thought about calling, then decided that might draw the cat's attention, if it wasn't already nearby.

"Lord, I don't know where to go. Please help me find Tati. And bring Michael soon."

She stepped forward, saw drops of blood and decided she was on the right track. The rocks were slippery, the loud rush of water blocking out most sounds. It was getting more and more difficult to see, too. The forest above shielded out so much light. She moved quietly, praying constantly for help.

When she found nothing Ashley's hope began to flicker. Where was Tati?

Out of the corner of her eye she caught movement. The cougar? She couldn't tell right away, not until it snarled a warning.

"Where is she, God? Please help."

Fear, the nemesis she'd never been able to shake, crept upon her, more cunning than the cougar. She could hardly breathe, her throat began to close as her fingers clenched inside her gloves. Every nerve tautened until she wanted to run.

But that would draw the cougar.

I am holding you by your right hand—I the Lord your God—and I say to you, Don't be afraid; I am here to help you.

The words she'd read last night returned with crystal clarity.

"Don't be afraid," she whispered, forcing her eyes to peer straight ahead. "Don't be afraid. God is here."

Like a beam of sunshine, peace crept into her heart and swelled as she repeated the words over and over.

And then she heard it, softer, quieter than usual, but that sweet lilting voice was Tati's.

"And God if you could s-send Ashley, too, I'd really like it. She knows about being scared and I'm really s-scared right now."

"Tati?" Ashley crept forward, into the opening of a cave so small she had to bend to get inside. "Honey, are you in here?"

"Yes."

"Why don't you crawl over here so I can see you?"

Silence, then a little sob.

"I don't want to. It hurts too bad."

"Okay, you stay put." She crawled on hands and knees toward the voice. "Tell me where it hurts, sweetie."

"My head. And my side. I fell into the water. I'm c-cold."

"I know. Wanda told us. I brought her jacket. Do you think we can take yours off so you can wear hers?" Finally she reached the little girl who was lying on the ground. "Hi." She grinned, so relieved to see that precious face.

She removed Wanda's coat from the bag and with the utmost care helped Tati remove her damp sweater and jacket. She zipped up the dry one, pulled the hood over her head.

"Now you just wait there. I've got some matches and I"m going to try to light a fire to keep us warm. Okay?"

"I want my daddy."

"Oh, he's coming. He didn't know you were here so he was looking for you somewhere else, but I phoned Piper and told her and she said he'd come right away."

"W-Wanda doesn't like o-other kids to wear her stuff."

"She won't mind this time." Was her voice quieter? Ashley wished she'd thought to tuck Row's snack into this bag. "I have to get some bark to start the fire. I'll be just outside the cave so if you need me, you yell and I'll come. Okay?"

"Uh-huh. But I won't be afraid now that you're here."

"Good."

Ashley crawled back out of the cave, gathered a few branches and some twigs and carried them back. Twice she thought she saw the cat sneaking through the woods nearby, twice she repeated the words that had comforted her and broken the grip on the fear that had obsessed her.

Something else glimmered in the back of her mind,

some memory that hadn't quite cleared. There was no time now to think about it, but later...

"Ashley?"

She hurried back to the cave, found Tati weeping.

"Sweetheart, what's wrong?"

"An animal, it was looking at me."

The cougar was getting braver. She had to get a fire going.

Cold seeped through her clothes. Her fingers were growing numb but still Ashley kept foraging, searching for bits of anything she could burn. Finally she had a small pile of debris gathered in the bag she'd brought. It was time to snap down some larger dead branches to feed the fire, keep it going long enough to warm them both until help came.

She backed into the cave, sensing the animal following her, feeling its feral study of every move she made. It was waiting, she knew that. Biding its time until it could strike.

"Oh, God, protect us. Keep Tati safe," she whispered.

"Is it still there?" Tati's voice, weaker now, came from the back of the cave.

"Yes. It's still here." Fear clawed its way through her body as Ashley caught the glint of eyes studying them, the snap of teeth that could tear apart a deer. She shuddered, fought to remain calm as she prayed without speaking.

And suddenly she realized that the fear she'd lived with for so long was like that cougar. It had already robbed her of so much. If left to prowl her mind it would devour everything, her security, peace, joy. All the things she as a Christian was supposed to have had been diminished because of fear. Even the love she'd found in Serenity Bay would be gone because she hadn't dealt with the root that grew its tentacles around her spirit.

Now she understood why Michael had pushed so hard,

why he'd insisted she talk to Ned. With a clarity she'd never found before, Ashley realized that the only way to live, to fully engage in life, was to challenge the fear, to meet it head-on. Freedom from fear lay in facing the worst and dealing with whatever happened next.

She'd been told that before, of course. But until this moment she'd never quite understood how important taking a stance and holding her ground would be.

Ashley made up her mind. She would do it. The moment she got out of here she would face Ned and ask for an explanation. A wisp of uncertainty trembled on the edge of her mind, but she pushed it away. She would know the truth. And perhaps it would set her free.

But that would come later.

Right now she had to find a way to hold off the cat.

She huddled down on the ground, assembled her pitiful stash of materials. But she kept one eye on the opening. Removing the box of matches, she opened it carefully, lifted out one, struck it against the side of the box. It flared. She quickly set it against the bed of pine needles and bark she'd placed in a tiny heap, but a whisper of wind blew out the yellow-orange flame before it could take.

"It didn't work," Tati rasped.

"Not this time. I'll try again." She did, striking match after match but with no success. "Paper. I need some paper."

Ashley rifled through the pockets of her ski pants, found a tissue. She tucked it under the needles, lit another match. The tissue caught, flamed, then went out as quickly, barely skimming the needles.

"Light," she begged. "Please light."

But either the material was too wet or she wasn't doing it right because one by one the matches lit up the dark-

ness for a second, maybe two, then went out. Soon she
had only three left.

"Ashley?"

Tati's hushed whisper drew her attention to the cave
opening. The big cat stealthily approached, his ominous
growl sending shivers over her body.

"Get out of here! Go!" She grabbed a big branch and
waved it wildly, jabbing forward in thrusts aimed at him
as she yelled. The cougar backed down, turned and moved
back. But it didn't leave.

Ashley knelt, tried another match. But her fingers were
shaking too badly and the match went out. The others fell
to the damp ground as the big cat edged stealthily closer.

Forget the fire. She had to fight him with what she had.

Ashley grabbed a thick straight stick and jabbed at the
glow of eyes. She hit something. The cat growled, backed
away, but soon slunk forward again. She jabbed harder
and kept at it, even though she had to crawl on hands and
knees.

And she prayed.

Finally she'd backed it up to the cave opening. Just a few
more feet, then she could stand, use the fallen willow as a
weapon. She swung once, twice, then slipped on the rock.

In slow motion she felt herself go down, down, until
she hit rock and the stick flew out of her hand. She felt
the swipe of a paw against her arm, felt the fabric of her
jacket tear.

In that second she thought to bury her head, protect her
face. But Michael's words rang clearly through her mind.

Don't ever show your fear. Face it head-on.

She lifted her head, glared at the cat as she scrabbled
behind her for something to strike with. She felt a small
stick, grabbed hold and swung with all her might, striking the animal so it backed off long enough for her to rise.

"Get out of here," she hollered as loudly as she could. "Go!"

But the cougar knew his advantage. He moved forward, closer, closer.

"I tried, Michael," she whispered as the cougar prepared to pounce. "I really tried."

In a flash of fur the animal jumped toward her.

Now!

Michael inhaled, took his shot and pressed the trigger.

The big cat fell directly on top of Ashley and for a moment he thought he'd missed. He tore through the bushes and brambles, uncaring of the scratches they left. He had to get to her.

She lay almost covered by the cougar's thick fur coat. One check ensured he'd caught his prey squarely between the eyes, then he dragged it off her, lifted her head.

"Ashley? Come on, sweetheart. Talk to me."

"Tati," she whispered. "Inside the cave. She's hurt."

Michael's blood ran cold at the scratch on her cheek that could have been so much worse. He grabbed his radio and asked for two stretchers.

"Not for me," she husked, dragging herself into a sitting position. "But Tati needs one. I think she hurt her ribs." She pushed him toward the mouth of the cave. "In there."

"Stay here," he whispered, brushing his lips across her forehead. "Someone will help in a minute."

She nodded, twisted to touch her arm. Blood.

"You're hurt."

"I'm fine, Michael. Now go get Tati."

Because her voice was so strong he did as she asked, hunkered down and eased inside the cave.

"Tati? It's Daddy. Where are you, brave girl?"

"Here." Her voice was faint, her face so pale his throat clogged in terror. "I hurt, Daddy."

"I know you do, sweetie. Just lie still while I check." His measly first aid course wasn't much help but he guessed ribs, too. "I'll put my coat over you so you'll warm up." He stripped it off, laid it over her. "There. Pretty soon some men will bring a little bed and we'll get you out of here."

"Why can't you carry me, Daddy? Did it hurt you?"

"No. I'm fine." He brushed the hair back off her face. "I just want to make sure you don't have some broken bones before we go up the hill. Wanda hurt her arm. She went to the hospital but she said to tell you she's not mad that you wore her coat."

"Where's Ashley?" Tati tried to sit, moaned and put her head back down.

"Ashley's waiting for you just outside. She stopped the cougar from coming in. It scratched her, but she's going to be okay."

"Are you sure?"

"Positive." He heard a noise. "I'm going to go tell the men we're hiding in here. Will you be okay by yourself for a minute?"

"Yes. I prayed, Daddy. I prayed really hard for you to come. I was scared."

"I know, baby. But you're safe now." He went outside, used his radio and waited until he saw someone heading toward them. Then after a shared look with Ashley he slipped back inside the cave to wait by Tati's side.

"We didn't mean to disobey, Daddy. We fell down the hill."

"I know. It's all right. Here's the doctor." He moved aside, pointed to his ribs to indicate the injury. The paramedic, a young man obviously at ease with children, soon had Tati cared for and fastened to a stretcher. Michael slid his coat back on while the others moved her out slowly, careful not to jar her. Ashley sat outside with another man who held a thick pad of gauze against her arm as he taped it.

"How bad?" he asked the medic.

"Several stitches and a tetanus shot. She was very lucky."

"Luck had nothing to do with it." Ashley might be hurting but she'd lost none of her spunk. "I had a whole lot of help from the Man upstairs. And from this guy right here." She grinned at him.

"If you knew how long it's been since I shot a gun—" Michael shook his head, helped her stand. "We are going to need a second stretcher," he said. "There's no way Ashley can climb with that arm."

"You always have to be right," she complained as she accepted his help to get across the rocks. "You okay, Tati?" she asked, leaning over the bundled little form.

"Yes." But she looked terrified.

Ashley kissed her forehead. "You're going to get a ride up this big hill now," she explained.

"I'm scared," she whispered as they began to fasten the ropes that would help carry her to the top.

"That's okay. We all get scared sometimes. You just close your eyes and pretend you're sitting in your dad's lap and he's rocking you to sleep."

"Is that what you did when you got scared? Really?"

Ashley nodded. "Really."

"Okay." Tati closed her eyes. A tiny smile curved her blue-white lips. "See you at the top, Daddy."

"Yes, you will, baby. I love you."

He stood back, let the rescuers do what they were trained to do. Then he helped fasten Ashley into another harness.

"When did you start dreaming of rocking in your father's arms?" he asked, prolonging the moment before they took her away.

"Fairly recently." She grinned. "About two seconds before you shot that rifle, when I thought heaven was pretty close. Thanks for being there."

He shook his head. "You saved my daughter." His eyes sought hers. "I'll talk to you later," he promised before kissing her.

"Count on it." And for the first time Ashley kissed him back without restraint.

The search-and-rescue guys snickered as they elbowed him out of the way. "Can you folks maybe pick this up later?"

"Absolutely."

While they pulled Ashley topside, Michael grabbed a free line and began climbing up. Only when he'd reached the top did he remember.

"I left Ned's rifle at the bottom," he told Bud Neely, the police chief.

"I'll see that it's put back in his cabin. They took him to the hospital. His leg's bad." He looked grim. "I'm glad you got that creature. Now you'd better go with your little girl."

"Yes." Tati lay in the ambulance. He climbed in beside her, looked around for Ashley.

"Her friends said they'd take her," the paramedic told him. "She said you needed time with your little girl."

"Thanks." He and Tati did need time. But that didn't mean he would let Ashley leave, not without begging her, one last time, to stay where she belonged—with him.

Chapter Fifteen

Ashley eased into the room, trying not to make a sound.

The man she'd feared for so long lay on the narrow white bed covered by a thin sheet and a pale blanket.

She stared at his face, went over each detail in her mind. As it had with the cougar, fear crept forward, tried to take over. She didn't fight it. She invited it, let herself imagine all the things it promised.

And when none of them came to pass, it quietly died.

"Hello." Ned peered at her through the gloom. "Is the little girl okay?"

"She's fine. Bruised ribs, a cut on her forehead and very cold, but otherwise she's fine."

A smile flickered across his face. "I'm glad."

"Me, too." She didn't know where to start. "How are you?"

"Tougher than old boots. They had to do some work on my leg but it will heal. Word is the girl's father shot the cat."

"Yes."

"I'm glad. Every so often you get one like that. Gets a taste of humans and won't quit until it's stopped." His face changed, saddened. "One of them attacked my grand-daughter once. Killed her."

"Oh, I'm so sorry." A wave of empathy filled her.

"She was a beautiful child. Happy, easy to be with. And boy, did she ask questions. I'd let her come with me to my cabin for a few days every summer. That child loved the woods as much as me." He fell silent, reminiscing.

"Did she fall down that ravine? Is that how you knew where to look for Wanda and Tatiana?"

"No. She was playing in a sandbox I'd made her, waiting for me to pack some sandwiches so we could go to the brook and fish." He gulped, paused, then continued, his voice broken. "I heard her scream. Couldn't think what was the matter. Raced outside and there it was, tearing at her poor little body."

Oh, God, forgive me for causing this man any pain. The silent prayer burst from Ashley's heart.

"I got her to the hospital as fast as I could. She lived for three days but she'd lost too much blood. I was too late."

"I'm so sorry, Ned."

"Yeah. I went to Toronto for her funeral. Then I came back here and I hunted for that monster." His face blanched, his teeth clenched. "I looked all over the place, spent weeks searching, but I couldn't find the thing. Not one sign. I'd given up, was leaving town the day I saw you."

"By the apple blossom tree," she whispered, closing her fingers around the hard steel of the bed frame as her throat tightened and her knees melted.

"Yes. You were crying. I was going to drive past until I saw it."

"A cougar?"

He nodded. "Crouched behind you about fifty feet, deciding whether he could get you or not. It was the same animal. I recognized the marks on his left hind."

"I didn't know," she whispered, aghast at the thought of what could have happened. "I didn't hear a thing."

"You wouldn't. They're good hunters." His finger played with the coverlet. "My rifle was in the trunk, I didn't have time to get help. All I could think of was to get you out of there."

"So you grabbed me, shoved me in your car." Suddenly she remembered the way he'd kept looking in his rearview mirror. "When I got out at the coffee shop, why didn't you come in, explain?"

"I had to get that cat. I couldn't risk letting it take another child. I tracked it and I shot it. I thought I'd feel better." He shook his head. "But it didn't bring my granddaughter back. I knew I had to get out of there if I was ever going to put it behind me. I never came back. Then last summer I got a letter. Someone wanted to buy the old cabin."

"You decided to sell?"

"I was going to. But I had to come back one more time." He shook his head. "I'm retired now. No job I have to get to, my time's my own."

Ashley said nothing. It was enough to absorb each word, fit them together and see the truth.

"A lot of time has gone past. When I got back last June, the first thing I saw were the wildflowers. Lara always called them bluebells. Then I found the sundial we'd made. I listened to the waterfall and I thought I could hear her laughter."

"It was your healing place," she whispered.

Ned nodded. "I used to carve things. I thought I'd try that again. Not to sell, just for something to do. Summer passed, fall went and winter came and I decided I didn't want to leave. I liked feeling close to God, talking to Him, listening to the ways He talked back to me. I decided to stay through the winter."

"I'm so glad you did."

He blinked, studied her.

"I never meant to hurt you. If I'd known what you thought—I never realized you'd be so scared or I'd have come back, explained. But I thought you'd know. I'm very sorry."

"Don't be sorry. You saved my life. I would never have known that if I hadn't come back to Serenity Bay, stayed here and faced my fear."

"And I couldn't have found peace about Lara if I hadn't come back," he whispered.

Awe filled Ashley at the wonder of God's ways.

"Thank you," she whispered when she'd finally absorbed it all. "Thank you so much."

"I second that, Ned. I don't know what we'd have done if you hadn't been there." Michael stood behind her.

"God would have found another way. His plans for us are good and right. He always follows through on His promises."

"Yes."

The nurse hurried in and asked them to leave so the patient could rest. After assuring Ned that they'd be back, Ashley followed Mick out of the room, to a waiting area.

"Tati?" she asked quietly.

"Is asleep. I'm going to hang around here tonight."

"Of course you are. That's what loving parents do." She reached up, touched his cheek.

"I do love her. More than anything." His face glowed. "I'd do anything for her, Ashley. I'd die for her if she needed that."

"She doesn't. Tati needs you to live, to love her, to be

there for her. She doesn't care whether you're famous or not, whether you've had the most successful showing in North America. All any little girl really wants is to know that her daddy will be there for her."

"I know. And I will be," he promised. "What about you, Ashley Adams? What do you need?"

She took her time before answering. "Not a job in Paris."

"Oh?"

"Nope. Too far. And I don't need a sports car or a big strong he-man like Kent to protect me, either." She smiled, let him see her joy. "I've got God. I'm free, Michael. Free. I faced the monster—and it was me."

He didn't ask questions, didn't need an explanation. He simply smiled, opened his arms and said, "I'm glad."

She relaxed into the warmth of his hold, tucked her head under his chin and told her daddy in heaven how much she loved this man.

"You didn't answer my question. What do *you* need, Ashley?"

She picked up the challenge without a qualm, leaning back in his arms to study his dear face.

"I'll tell you what I need, Michael Masters. I need love. Real love, not the pretend stuff that wears off during the tough times. I need a man who isn't afraid to tell me the truth, to push me until I figure out the hard parts. I need a man who won't let me get away with skating by on life, a guy who will insist I dig in and live every moment."

"I think I might know someone like that," he murmured, his eyes dark and melting.

"So do I." She drew him close. "I love you. When I was fifteen I had a crush on you. Who would have guessed it would last all this time and then blossom into love?"

"I always thought you were a very discerning fifteen-year-old when you were hiding behind my mother's ficus plant."

"Say it," she begged.

"I love you, Ashley Adams." He bent his head, covered her lips with his as he told her how much he cared. And he never used a single word.

By the time she drew away Ashley was breathless—and happier than she'd ever thought she could be.

"When are you going to marry me?"

She stared at him as the events of the past months fluttered through her mind. What an amazing God they served.

"Ashley? You are going to marry me?"

"Of course I am. In the spring, under the apple blossom tree. And I'm going to ask Ned to give me away. Fitting, don't you think?"

"Perfect," he said.

"You do realize I have to okay all the wedding plans with Tati first?" Ashley grinned.

He didn't say anything for a moment, which was unusual for Michael. Then he touched her cheek. "Thank you," he whispered.

"Excuse me, Mr. Masters?"

"Yes?"

The nurse beckoned. "Your daughter would like to speak to you."

"Ashley's coming, too. We're getting married."

"Congratulations."

They broke the news to Tati who was so excited she couldn't get back to sleep. Finally Ashley leaned down to whisper something in her ear.

"But you have to keep it a secret and you have to go to sleep now so you can get better. Promise?"

Tati's eyes closed immediately.

Epilogue

April in cottage country could be iffy. Sudden snow squalls, frosts, high winds. Anything could happen.

But on April twenty-sixth the weather turned out to be better than any fairy tale could have promised. Fresh spring flowers bloomed all around Serenity Bay, but especially in front of the old church by the brook, next to the radiantly blooming apple tree.

The wedding took place outdoors with white chairs dotting the church lawn, balloons tied to the streetlamp and big pots of tulips and daffodils blooming all over. Folks said the bride's best friend had hauled them all the way from Toronto.

At precisely two-thirty in the afternoon, a small electric organ sounded the "Wedding March." All the guests rose as the very handsome groom took his place beside the minister. Next, two beautiful women emerged from the church. The first they knew as their own economic development officer, Piper Franklin. Her husband, the mayor, stood beside the groom.

Following her, a slim redhead moved gracefully down the aisle clad in a sleeveless gown of the palest pink imaginable. Each woman carried a small round bouquet of baby's breath and tiny pink rosebuds.

Once they'd taken their places a hush descended on the group as a small girl stepped out of the church. Her dark curls gleamed in the sunlight, a perfect foil for the tiny seed pearls sprinkled among the curls. She stepped down the aisle in a frilly white organza dress nipped in at the waist by wide satin ribbons. Her full rustling skirt burst out like a flower in full bloom all the way to her shiny white shoes. She carried a small white wicker basket and from it she chose tiny pink rosebuds to drop all the way down the aisle. Then she took her place beside her father who just happened to be the handsome groom.

"Aren't I pretty, Daddy? Wanda said I couldn't do it, but I did!" At which point she dropped her basket.

Her daddy only smiled, lifted her into his arms and kissed her cheek. Then they all waited.

Finally the bride emerged from the church, tall and slim. She walked very slowly, perhaps because of the very high heels she wore. Rumor had it the groom had chosen the shoes.

Everyone in Serenity Bay knew that the bride could have shopped in Paris but had instead asked their very own Emma to make her dress. And what a dress! Gossamer silk, as delicate as butterfly wings, swathed around Ashley's creamy shoulders framing her beautiful face. Then it tucked in, caressed her model-thin figure in a smooth elegant flow of pearly iridescence that tumbled down to skim the tips of her white sandals.

The bride didn't wear a veil but had instead tucked a few white rosebuds into her upswept silver-blond hair. She carried a single long-stemmed pink rose in one hand. The other clung to the arm of a tall man wearing a plain black suit. Friends claimed the pearl earrings she wore were a gift from Ned Ainsworth.

He walked with her down the aisle then passed her hand from his to her betrothed when the minister asked, "Who gives this woman to be married?"

He turned and took a seat beside the bride's mother in the front row while the groom set down the flower girl and nodded at his mother to watch her.

"Dearly beloved, we are gathered here—"

Tears welled in many eyes as the ceremony that joined a man and a woman neared the exchanging of rings.

"Is it time now, Daddy?" the little girl asked loudly.

He nodded and she dug in her basket, found what she wanted and handed it to him. The groom slipped a perfect wooden circlet onto the bride's ring finger. Those in the know said he'd painstakingly carved it from a piece of the old oak tree that had once stood in the backyard of her childhood home.

"I now pronounce you husband and wife. You may kiss your bride."

A torrent of "oohs" filled the little glade as the couple sealed their pledges in an age-old fashion. Then a torrent of rice filled the air as Ashley and Michael Masters walked down the aisle, Tatiana skipping happily behind them.

Folks from the Bay said the afternoon was a delight of funny stories, good food and love. Around five the bride prepared to throw her bouquet until the flower girl, who'd been having the time of her life, suddenly yelled, "Wait!"

She rushed up to the bride, pulled at her skirt until Ashley leaned down to hear her whisper. The bride nodded once, kissed her rosy cheek and brushed away a smudge of dirt.

Tatiana ordered everyone into a circle, and when they had complied she gave the bride a signal. The single pink rose was held up high as the bride turned her back and tossed it way up into the air.

The little girl followed its progress down as she darted here and there among the guests. At the last moment she bumped against one of them, knocking her out of the way so the rose landed in the hands of bridesmaid Rowena Davis.

Tatiana and the bride share a grin of fulfillment before the groom kissed his daughter goodbye.

"You do what Uncle Ned and your grannies tell you to do. No disobeying. Right?"

"Yes, Daddy. I will." She waited, then hugged Ashley and whispered something in her ear.

"You're welcome, sweetheart. I think you look exactly like Snow White."

"Me, too," Wanda said in utter amazement.

Tati glowed.

"Daddy and I are going to send you a card and a present so be sure you check the mail every day."

"Goodbye!"

"Goodbye!"

The groom held the door while the bride climbed into the sports car. They drove down the road, empty cans rattling behind them. After a moment they paused, looked back and saw Tatiana and Wanda picking icing roses off what was left of the wedding cake.

The groom turned his attention to Ashley.

"Welcome to my world, Mrs. Masters."

"Welcome to mine, Mr. Masters."

He kissed his new wife, cast one last frown at his icing-covered daughter, then shrugged.

"Is marriage anything like you expected?" she asked.

"It's getting better by the moment." He lifted his arm

so she could snuggle against his side. "Let's keep it that way for the next sixty years or so."

"Piece of cake," she told him.

Their laughter carried into the hills and the valleys of Serenity Bay, and bounced right up to the Father who had arranged it all.

* * * * *

Dear Reader,

Welcome back to Serenity Bay. Don't you just love getting away for a while, escaping the phones and duties and just relaxing, enjoying life? Serenity Bay is that kind of place. Small town, lake, lots of beach. But for Ashley, it also held dark places, trepidation and fears she could never quite escape.

Our lives mirror Ashley's in many ways. Each of us has dreads and terrors we choose to live with, adapt to and work around. Instead of facing them we often choose to deny their existence. And our lives are poorer because we refuse to live fully, in the moment. We miss out on some of God's richest blessings.

As you search your own heart and pull out the weeds of fear, I pray you'll find hope and comfort in knowing that nothing is ever hidden from God. That He sees, He knows and He loves you anyway. I wish you renewed faith, everlasting hope and a love that spreads through your life and brings you true serenity.

Lois
Richer

Love Inspired®
CLASSICS

Four sweet, heartfelt stories from fan-favorite
Love Inspired® authors!

HIS BUNDLE OF LOVE and
THE COLOR OF COURAGE
by Patricia Davids

HIS WINTER ROSE and
APPLE BLOSSOM BRIDE
by Lois Richer

Get two happily-ever-afters for the price of one!

Available in April 2013 wherever books are sold.

www.LoveInspiredBooks.com

LIC65159

REQUEST YOUR FREE BOOKS!

2 FREE INSPIRATIONAL NOVELS

PLUS 2 FREE MYSTERY GIFTS

Love Inspired™

YES! Please send me 2 FREE Love Inspired® novels and my 2 FREE mystery gifts (gifts are worth about $10). After receiving them, if I don't wish to receive any more books, I can return the shipping statement marked "cancel." If I don't cancel, I will receive 6 brand-new novels every month and be billed just $4.49 per book in the U.S. or $4.99 per book in Canada. That's a saving of at least 22% off the cover price. It's quite a bargain! Shipping and handling is just 50¢ per book in the U.S. and 75¢ per book in Canada.* I understand that accepting the 2 free books and gifts places me under no obligation to buy anything. I can always return a shipment and cancel at any time. Even if I never buy another book, the two free books and gifts are mine to keep forever.

105/305 IDN FVV7

Name _____ (PLEASE PRINT)

Address _____ Apt. #

City _____ State/Prov. _____ Zip/Postal Code

Signature (if under 18, a parent or guardian must sign)

Mail to the Harlequin® Reader Service:
IN U.S.A.: P.O. Box 1867, Buffalo, NY 14240-1867
IN CANADA: P.O. Box 609, Fort Erie, Ontario L2A 5X3

**Are you a subscriber to Love Inspired books
and want to receive the larger-print edition?
Call 1-800-873-8635 or visit www.ReaderService.com.**

* Terms and prices subject to change without notice. Prices do not include applicable taxes. Sales tax applicable in N.Y. Canadian residents will be charged applicable taxes. Offer not valid in Quebec. This offer is limited to one order per household. Not valid for current subscribers to Love Inspired books. All orders subject to credit approval. Credit or debit balances in a customer's account(s) may be offset by any other outstanding balance owed by or to the customer. Please allow 4 to 6 weeks for delivery. Offer available while quantities last.

Your Privacy—The Harlequin® Reader Service is committed to protecting your privacy. Our Privacy Policy is available online at www.ReaderService.com or upon request from the Harlequin Reader Service.

We make a portion of our mailing list available to reputable third parties that offer products we believe may interest you. If you prefer that we not exchange your name with third parties, or if you wish to clarify or modify your communication preferences, please visit us at www.ReaderService.com/consumerschoice or write to us at Harlequin Reader Service Preference Service, P.O. Box 9062, Buffalo, NY 14269. Include your complete name and address.

LI13

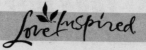
Jolie followed Morgan outside. There was a large gnarled oak tree still bent over as it had been all those years ago. She didn't stop until she reached it, turning his way only after they were beneath the wide expanse of limbs.

Morgan crossed his arms and studied the tree. "I remember having to climb up this tree and talk you down after you scrambled up to the top and froze."

She hadn't expected him to bring up old memories—it caught her a little off guard. "I remember how mad you were at having to rescue the silly little new girl."

A hint of a smile teased his lips, fraying Jolie's nerves at the edges. It had been a long time since she'd seen that smile.

"I got used to it, though," he said, his voice warming.

Electricity hummed between them as they stared at each other. Jolie sucked in a wobbly breath. Then the hardness in Morgan's tone matched the accusation in his eyes.

"What are you doing here, Jolie? Why aren't you taming rapids in some far-off place?"

"I...I'm—" She stumbled over her words. "I'm taking a leave from competition for a little while. I had a bad run in Virginia." She couldn't bring herself to say that she'd almost died. "Your dad offered me this teaching opportunity."

"I heard about the accident and I'm real sorry about that, Jolie," Morgan said. "But why come here after all this time?"

"This is my *home*."

Jolie saw anger in Morgan's eyes. Well, he had a right to it, and more than a right to point it straight at her.

But she'd thought she'd prepared for it.

She was wrong.

"Morgan," Jolie said, almost as a whisper. "I'd hoped we could forget the past and move forward."

Heart pounding, she reached across the space between them and placed her hand on his arm. It was just a touch, but the feeling of connecting with Morgan McDermott again after so much time rocked her straight to her core, and suddenly she wasn't so sure coming home had been the right thing to do after all.

Will Morgan ever allow Jolie back into his life—and his heart?

Pick up HER UNFORGETTABLE COWBOY from Love Inspired Books.

SPECIAL EXCERPT FROM

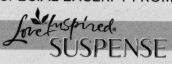
Love Inspired.
SUSPENSE

*The Texas K-9 Unit is on the trail of a crime ring,
and a fellow officer faces scrutiny.*

*Read on for a preview of
SCENT OF DANGER by Terri Reed.*

Detective Melody Zachary halted abruptly at the sight of her office door of the Sagebrush Youth Center cracked open. Unease slithered down her spine. She'd locked the door last night when she left the center.

Pushing back her suit jacket, she withdrew her weapon. She pushed the door wide with the toe of her boot. Stepping inside the room, she reached for the overhead light switch and froze.

A shadow moved.

Not a shadow. A man.

Dressed from head to toe in black. Black gloves, black ski mask....

Palming her piece in both hands, she aimed her weapon. "Halt! Police!"

The intruder dove straight at her. She didn't have time to react, before he slammed into her chest, knocking her backward against the wall. Her head smacked hard, sending pain slicing through her brain.

The man bolted through the open doorway and disappeared.

Melody pushed away from the wall. For a moment her off-balance equilibrium sent the world spinning.

The exit door at the end of the hall banged shut. He was escaping.

Melody chased after the intruder. Out on the sidewalk, she searched for the trespasser. Sagebrush Boulevard was empty.

Holstering her piece and pulling her jacket closed, she retraced her steps and entered Sagebrush Youth Center's single-story brick building.

She stopped in her office doorway. The place had been ransacked. The filing cabinet had been emptied, the files strewn all over. The pictures of her family had been knocked off the desk.

A sense of violation cramped her chest. She was used to investigating this sort of vandalism, not being the victim herself.

Yanking her cell phone out of her purse, she dialed the Sagebrush police dispatch and reported the crime.

For the past several years, a crime wave had terrorized the citizens of Sagebrush. The mastermind behind the crime syndicate was a faceless, nameless entity that even the thugs who worked for "The Boss" feared.

A short time later, the center's front door opened. A small dog with his black nose pressed to the ground entered. Melody recognized the beagle as Sherlock, part of the K-9 unit. A harness attached to a leash led to the handsome man at the other end. Melody blinked.

What were narcotics detective Parker Adams and his K-9 partner doing here?

To find out, pick up SCENT OF DANGER
wherever Love Inspired Suspense books are sold.
Available May 2013

Love Inspired

Will You Marry Me?

Bold widow Johanna Yoder stuns Roland Byler when she asks him to be her husband. To Johanna, it seems very sensible that they marry. She has two children, he has a son. Why shouldn't their families become one? But the widower has never forgotten his long-ago love for her; it was his foolish mistake that split them apart. This could be a fresh start for both of them—until she reveals she wants a marriage of convenience only. It's up to Roland to woo the stubborn Johanna and convince her to accept him as her groom in her home and in her heart.

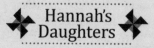

Hannah's
Daughters

Johanna's Bridegroom

by

Emma Miller

Available May 2013

www.LoveInspiredBooks.com

LI8781